HUNTING PARTY

SAMUEL THOMAS FRASER

sam.t.fraser@gmail.com.

First Amazon edition published in 2025.
First paperback edition published in 2025.

Cover design by Shaun Stevens
Cover typeset in Rumble Brave (Alit Suarnegara) and Grenze (Omnibus-Type)
Text set in Book Antiqua and Arial Unicode MS

ISBN: 978-1-7771190-4-1

To learn more about the author, visit:

https://samuelthomasfraser.com/
https://www.facebook.com/STFupperlip
https://twitter.com/STFupperlip
https://www.instagram.com/samuelthomasfraser/

PROLOGUE: AUGUST

IT'S NOT what you've done. It's what Abigail Henderson has done."

Those were the words the man in sunglasses used to get himself in the front door. He'd told Sergeant Mona Brady that his name was Jones, that he worked for the Canadian Department of Advanced Research and Special Defence, and that he'd come here to ask her some questions about a potential national security concern. Two of those statements were true.

When he received the okay to come in, Jones picked up the black leather briefcase he'd left sitting on the front step, out of view of the peephole through which Sgt. Brady had made him introduce himself. He came into the front hall, briefcase in hand, and tucked his sunglasses into the breast pocket of his white linen shirt. He smiled to put the sergeant at ease. Since the start of the cleanup operation thirty-six hours ago, the Department had put together a full psychological brief of Sgt. Mona Brady. Based on a careful scrape of her social media profiles and her employment records, Jones knew Mona was a smart woman and an honest cop. Never distinguished, but thoroughly reliable. Protective as all hell of her son William (ten years old, father deceased). Jones knew how he must have looked to an overprotective single mother, working in law enforcement and currently recovering from a very recent traumatic experience. He wanted her to feel at ease. That would make the next part go faster.

"Nice place you have here," he said in an easy, affable tone.

"It's not mine," she replied. "A… friend is putting us up for a bit. Our place is unusable right now." She didn't say why. Jones didn't ask. He already knew it was connected with the extraplanar incursion he'd been sent here to investigate. He'd have all the details by the time he left.

She showed him through into the living room. The son was there on the couch, laughing at something on the TV. Jones glanced at the screen, saw Bugs Bunny and Elmer Fudd arguing over something. Daffy Duck was holding his smoking beak in one hand and being uncharacteristically quiet.

Mona made the introductions. "Will? This is Mr. Jones—"

"Agent Jones," he corrected.

"Sorry. This is Agent Jones. He's here to ask me a few questions, okay? I was just going to take him through to the kitchen. Do you want anything while I'm in there?"

Jones was impressed. The sergeant was making sure he knew she wasn't alone in the house. Establishing witnesses and a timeline in case anything happened to her. Good head on her shoulders, this one. He threw another look back at the TV, allowed himself a laugh. Best to make sure the kid knew he was on the level, too. "I think I've seen this one," he said.

Will Brady paused the TV and cocked his head to one side, looking at Jones warily. With hair that colour, he reminded Jones of an Irish setter looking at a piece of cheese. "Is this about the Harcourt House?" he asked.

"Actually," Jones replied, "it is a little bit." Turning to Mona: "I wonder if we could all go into the kitchen, Sergeant? I think your boy here could help me answer some of these annoying questions I have."

Involving the kid so quickly turned out to be a mistake. So did letting it slip that he knew something about the Harcourt House. Mona was immediately on the defensive. "Before we answer any questions, Agent Jones, I'd like to know exactly what this is about. You said at the door that

Abby Henderson was involved. What do she and the Harcourt House have to do with national security?"

Will looked between Jones and his mother with worry in his eyes. "What about Abby? Mom, is Abby in trouble?"

Jones smiled them his easiest smile. "Nobody's in trouble here, Will. I'm just trying to establish some facts."

"What facts exactly?" asked Mona.

Jones let out a breath. Obviously, this wasn't going to be a short visit. "There's no easy way to say this, so I'll just say it. I represent an organization that investigates... well, disturbances in the ordinary fabric of reality. Events and entities that don't conform to established scientific norms."

Will gasped. "Like the Federal Bureau of Control!"

Jones looked at him, bemused. "I'm sorry?"

"The Federal Bureau of Control," Will repeated. "It's from a video game. Mom won't let me play it, but my cousin Walt's showed me clips. Walt does a lot of livestreaming. The Federal Bureau of Control are this super-secret spy agency that investigate all kinds of supernatural phenomena, like envelopes that teleport and a room that's just full of clocks that come out of nowhere and a phone that connects to this weird talking pyramid thing. There's one scene where a fridge eats a guy!"

Jones smiled. When he joined the Department twenty years ago, everyone's point of reference had been *The X-Files.* Times certainly were changing. "Well, I don't know about fridges that eat people, but if one ever showed up, I'm sure the Department would look into it. It's our job to explain the unexplainable and ensure that no harm comes to Her Majesty's Government of Canada or the Canadian public."

He could see Mona relax. He wasn't a threat, just a brother in law enforcement. He pressed his advantage. "I want to ask you two some questions about what's happened the last few days here in Delapore. Feel free to tell me the truth, as completely as you remember it. Believe me, I won't think you're crazy."

"You said you wanted to know about Abby Henderson," Mona reminded him. "Why?"

"I just need to know where she fits into all this. There was an incident in Vancouver last autumn, and we've heard conflicting reports about the degree of her involvement. Now we have evidence she was involved in this Harcourt House business, but we don't know how."

"It sounds like you're building a profile on her," said Mona.

Jones shrugged. "You're in law enforcement, Sergeant. You know how it is when the same person of interest keeps popping up."

"I suppose I do," she admitted at last. "Okay. We'll talk in the kitchen."

"I'd like that."

The three of them talked for twenty minutes. More specifically, Mona and Will talked for twenty minutes. Jones listened. He asked a few questions, mostly for clarification. The whole story was captured on the mini tape recorder which Jones pulled from his briefcase and placed in the middle of the table. When Mona Brady first saw it, she smiled for the first time since Jones had come into the house. "Very retro," she said. Then, "Diane: 11:30AM, February 24th. Entering the town of Twin Peaks." Jones smiled back and shrugged. It was a decent joke, and it put her at ease.

Eventually, he had a complete picture. The Dead Room. The ghosts of Josiah, Isaac, and Hector Harcourt. The possession of Constable Linus Foley by an extraplanar entity, and the eventual destruction of the Harcourt House in the interplanar space that Abby Henderson and her friends referred to as "the Elsewhere." He thanked Will and Mona sincerely for the help they'd given him and put his tape recorder back in his briefcase. Then Mona asked him what would happen next.

"For you? Nothing happens, Sergeant Brady. You can go back to the lives you had before. The Department deals with phenomena like this every day. We'll worry about the clean-up. You just worry about getting a good night's sleep."

"What about my job? What about counselling? I'm suspended pending an investigation by the IIO. They think I shot Linus Foley, but he wasn't Linus Foley anymore. Not really. If I tried to explain any of this to a psych eval panel… " She shook her head. "They'd never let me wear a badge again. I wouldn't blame them."

"We'll make some calls on our end," Jones reassured her, "see if we can't get that smoothed out for you. We have protocols for this sort of thing."

"Do you have protocols to stop me from screaming in my sleep?"

"Believe it or not," said Jones, "there is a procedure."

He put on his sunglasses. Then he pulled a pair of surgical gloves from his back pocket. Put those on. From the bottom of the briefcase, he slowly, carefully took out a thin black box, lined all around the inside with one-sixteenth-inch-thick lead foil. When he opened the box, a rich blue light from within caught Mona and Will Brady's eyes.

One gloved hand extracted the Lethe crystal from the box and set it in the center of the table. The Bradys stared at it, rapt. The crystal was a six-sided prism, about seven inches long, half that around the middle, and tapered to a point at both ends. It was the richest, most perfect blue Jones had ever seen in his life, and he'd never dared to look at it without protective eyewear.

"Lethe crystal" wasn't the scientific name, nor any kind of folkloric designation. It was just what the Department called them. A field team had discovered them at the bottom of the Pingualuit Crater in the late 1970s, and forty years of testing had yielded no clues about where they came from or exactly how they worked. They were as hard as diamonds at a fraction of the density, and they emitted a constant, high-frequency telepathic field that made the average person more suggestible than any other known form of hypnosis.

In the new digital age, the Lethe crystal was the Department's last line of defence against information leaks. People, as a general rule, got panicky and stupid if you confronted them with things they didn't understand, and very few people understood the supernatural. Worse than the panic was the opportunism. Some folks over the years had got the idea in their heads that magic could solve all their problems for them. When those folks jumped in with both feet without knowing what they were doing, it usually didn't end well for them. History was full of examples of what happened when someone stupid or opportunistic enough bit off more than they could chew with supernatural forces: the Roanoke colony, Tunguska, Jack Parsons, and so on.

Better to take the gun out of the child's hands before they accidentally fired it off. Better still, according to over seven decades' worth of government policy, to not even tell the child that there was a gun in the first place. The Department couldn't stop people from seeing things. But they could stop them from repeating the story. Contain the uncomfortable truth, and guide witnesses to a place where they weren't troubled by the memories of what they'd seen. The name "Lethe" hadn't been chosen randomly.

"Listen to me, both of you," said Jones. The pair did not answer. They sat, slack-jawed, totally entranced by the telepathic force emitted by the crystal. "You've given me some very valuable information today. But now I want you to forget that information. Mona: what happened to Linus Foley was not your fault. He had kidnapped your son with the intent to kill him, and you acted in self-defence. But Linus Foley was working alone. He did not receive guidance from the ghosts of Josiah or Isaac Harcourt. There were no ghosts in the Harcourt House. You did not enter an interplanar space at any point. This was a dream you had. The Harcourt House was destroyed by a fire on the hill. Will: the things you saw were just dreams as well. You had a dream about a woman named Abby Normal, but you did not meet her, or anyone who claimed to be associated with her. You have never seen a ghost. You have never met a telepath or a sorcerer."

As Jones spoke, the crystal glowed brilliantly. It vibrated slightly on the table. He put two fingers on it to keep it still. Will and Mona Brady's eyes clouded over with a blue haze. Jones didn't know what messages exactly the crystal was communicating to them, what false memories it was concocting to paper over the real ones. He never liked to ask questions about this bit. The Bradys stared at the crystal in silence for several long minutes. At one point, Mona's nose started to bleed. Jones pulled a tissue from his pocket, reached across the table, and wiped Mona's nose for her. This was nothing he hadn't seen before.

Eventually, the crystal ceased its vibrations. The glow faded. Will and Mona's eyes cleared. "I'm going to put this away now," said Jones. "After I do, we'll just sit here for a bit and catch our breath. Then I'll snap my fingers and you will wake up." He did as he'd promised. He disposed of the bloody tissue in the garbage under the kitchen sink. When the Lethe crystal was back in its box, and the box back in the briefcase, Jones took off his sunglasses and his gloves and snapped his fingers.

Mona Brady blinked and slowly came back to herself. Will followed her a few seconds later. "What… I'm sorry," Mona said. "What happened just now? What were we talking about?"

"You were telling me about Abigail Henderson," Jones said.

"Who?" Will asked. "Mom, who's Abigail Henderson?"

Mona scowled. "She was one of those damn ghost-chasers who were in town a few days ago. She was convinced there was something supernatural happening in the Harcourt House. So convinced that we almost slapped her with a B&E charge."

"You mean she broke into the Harcourt House?"

"Pembroke hit the roof when that nut got processed," Mona said. "I think she's skipped town now. Good riddance, I say." To Jones: "I don't know what your department wants with that girl, but you can have her, as far as I'm concerned. She's more trouble than I need right now."

"We certainly intend to have a long talk with her, when we get the chance," said Jones. He stood. Collected up his things. "You've been a great help, both of you. If there's anything else we need, you'll hear from us. We know how to get in touch. Have a good rest of your Sunday, folks."

With hardly another word, Jones walked back out into the hot summer sun and made for the car. He put his briefcase in the trunk, cranked the air-conditioning to maximum, wiped the sweat from his forehead, and turned on the radio. The station was classic rock. The band was Chilliwack. The song was "My Girl."

Jones checked the list of names sitting on the passenger seat. *Margot Pembroke. Ben Rickards. Phil Campbell.* A few others. Last known addresses and phone numbers were provided for each of them. For Phil Campbell, there was a room number at Kelowna General Hospital. Jones adjusted the rearview mirror and backed out of the driveway. He had a few more stops to make today. A few more stories to straighten out.

BOOK ONE:
POUND OF FLESH

Up the airy mountain,
Down the rushy glen,
We daren't go a-hunting
For fear of little men

*

"The Fairies"
William Allingham

EIGHT WEEKS LATER

CHAPTER 1

CASH ON DELIVERY

PAIN. ALL he could think about was the pain.

Pain in his wrists, where the nylon ropes rubbed his skin raw. Pain in his knees, where the joints were stretched to their limit. Pain in the base of his skull, where some ugly bastard had beaned him with a crescent wrench.

Pain in his nose, as the car stopped with a jerk and his face connected with the inside of the trunk.

"Mother*fucker*!" hissed Robin Whittaker, son of Goodfellow. Well, he tried to hiss. The tube sock stuffed in his mouth didn't do much for conversation.

The engine stopped. He heard the front door open, then footsteps. Sounded like the driver was stepping over hard concrete. Okay, that was good to know. The first hour of the drive had been over mostly dirt and gravel. But concrete was good. Concrete most likely meant the city. Whittaker knew the city. If he could talk his way away from whoever had cold-cocked him and stuffed him in this car, he could disappear into the rain and get himself somewhere safe before morning came. And he was pretty sure he could talk himself to safety, once he got rid of this damn sock.

To be fair, it wasn't like he hadn't been expecting this. Actually, it was kind of nice to finally get it over with. He'd been looking over his shoulder for almost a year now, just waiting for someone to jump out of the shadows and drag him off the street. *Never get involved with demons*, he said to himself.

Bad for business and bad for your heath. Same goes for zombies, psychics, and fuckin' wizards.

This time last year, the imp called R.G. Whittaker had been one of the high rollers of the Vancouver underworld. He had a stake in just about every mortal and supernatural racket in the city, and not a single shady deal went down that he didn't know about. All it had taken was for one deal to go south, and before you knew it, the price on his head was higher than the GDP of some small countries.

The trunk opened suddenly and a hand on Whittaker's shoulder rolled him over. He groaned behind the tube sock and shut his eyes at the sudden burst of light. "Wake up, smart mouth," growled the driver.

Two hands seized the lapels of his Savile Row suit and pulled him out of the car. The sock muffled a yowl of pain as he landed hard on the pavement and choked him as he tried to take in a breath. Then the driver yanked the sock out of his mouth and thumped him on the back.

"Easy. Don't want you going belly-up before I get you to the buyer."

Whittaker sucked in a grateful breath and blinked. As his eyes adjusted to the light, he saw that they were in an underground parkade. No clue where. If you'd seen one underground parkade in Metro Vancouver, you'd seen 'em all. He recognized the driver, though. Shaved head, twice-broken nose, and a mud-spattered Canadian tuxedo stretched over a stocky wall of muscle. It could only be—

"Ted!" Whittaker exclaimed. "Ted Purdy! Oh man, are you a sight for sore eyes!" He flashed his best used-car-salesman smile and tried to pull himself up to look at his captor—not easy, with his hands and feet tied into a tight ball at the small of his back. "Been a while, hasn't it? Don't think I've seen you since they nailed you for that B&E in Coal Harbour! What have you been up to, pal? Still working security for Sai—"

Ted Purdy drove one muddy steel-toed boot into the imp's stomach and hissed, "Shut it."

Whittaker coughed and threw up a little on the concrete. "Jesus, Ted," he croaked. "A kick like that, you should've played for the fuckin' Whitecaps."

Purdy smirked. "That wouldn't pay half as well as this." He hoisted all of Whittaker's rail-thin four feet and eleven inches up over his shoulder and carried the imp like a sack of potatoes across the parkade. It was hard to keep track of the time what with the whole "being stuffed in a trunk" thing, but by Whittaker's mental math, it was probably going on two or three in the morning. The lot was mostly empty, and Purdy didn't say a word as he hauled Whittaker over to a dark back corner of the parkade, where a full-sized black delivery van was parked almost six inches over the line. Purdy set Whittaker down, thumped three times on the van's back door, and gave a sharp whistle.

The door opened and the van groaned on its axles as a massive creature with stone-grey skin, a flat nose, and no neck seemed to melt out of the black shadows within, looming over Whittaker like a refrigerator with bad breath. A Pacific mountain troll. That was good. That was real good. Mountain trolls were some of the dumbest motherfuckers out there. If Purdy was going to leave him with Mr. Big and Tall here, then Whittaker could probably weasel out of this mess inside an hour.

Two more figures emerged from the van's dark interior and flanked Mr. Big and Tall. Short, withered creatures with pot bellies, wide mouths, and large hands that ended in long, black-taloned fingers. One of the creatures wore a bright red Che Guevara beret, while the other sported a baseball hat with an American political slogan on it. Redcaps. That was less good. Redcaps were a lot smarter than trolls, hostile to just about everyone they met, and resilient as all get out. It would be a lot harder for Whittaker to talk his way out of a redcap's bony clutches. But still, he'd dealt with worse.

Mr. Big and Tall retrieved a large, weather-beaten briefcase from the back of the van and handed it off to Ted

Purdy. Purdy opened it, extracted a thick gold coin the size of an eyeglass lens, and gave a satisfied nod.

"As we agreed," hissed the redcap in the beret. "Half your share now, and half when the bounty is paid."

Mr. Big and Tall undid the short length of rope connecting Whittaker's wrists and ankles. The imp unfolded with a little whimper of relief, and then his brain kicked into overdrive. There had to be something he could say to get himself out of this.

"Give you any trouble?" the other redcap asked in a croaking, reedy voice.

Ted Purdy shook his head and set the closed briefcase at his feet. "Little asshole never even saw me. I got up behind him in a blind alley and then it was goodnight, Irene."

"Kind of a punk way for R.G. Whittaker to go out," hissed the redcap in the MAGA hat. "How do you know he's not going to pull something?"

Purdy smiled. Among the races collectively referred to as the Fair Folk, imps were particularly adept at the magic of teleportation and illusion. It was a useful defence mechanism when your adult males maxed out at five foot zilch. The only catch was, the Fair Folk couldn't work their magic in the presence of iron. It stopped them cold, as surely as kryptonite did the big guy in the red underoos. A pair of solid iron manacles clamped to Whittaker's wrists just below the ropes meant he wasn't going anywhere. "It was a custom job," Purdy bragged. "But when I told the smith who it was for, he gave me a fuckin' 20% discount!"

The troll barked out a laugh. "No shit!" He tapped Whittaker with one toe and growled, "Guess ya ain't got many friends left on either side of the Elsewhere, do ya, Whittaker?"

"Guess not," Whittaker chuckled, doing his best to play along. "Obviously plenty of enemies, though. I can't remember the last time I had this warm a welcome. And what a collection of personalities! Half-breed, troll, redcap:

this is like a 'walks into a bar' joke waiting to happen! I'm flattered, boys, I really am. I mean, three natural enemies burying the hatchet just for the sake of little ol' me? Almost brings a tear to my eye."

The Che Guevara redcap's eyes nearly rolled out of their sockets. "Do me a favour and shut him up," he growled at Purdy.

As Purdy rolled up the sock and aimed it at Whittaker's mouth, the imp raised his voice. "So, is this your racket? Deliver me to the big muckamuck in Vael Ardenne, split the bounty, and then yuk it up while I get my head stuck on a pole? That seems pretty small-time for a crew like this. Come on: what are you boys really after? 'Cause it sure ain't the money! If it were—and this is just from me to you, Ted—if it were just the money, you wouldn't have settled for just half up front! Not with a couple of redcaps in the mix!"

The MAGAt redcap gave Whittaker a kick and snapped, "Cork him! Now!"

Whittaker sucked in a breath and groaned, "Come on, Ted. You know the stories. You know what redcaps are like with cash. Trust me, if you don't get payment in full right this second, you are never seeing the rest of your cut!"

The MAGAt kicked him again and pointed an angry finger at Purdy. "I told you to shut him up, you stupid skunk!"

Purdy dropped the sock and made a fist. "What the fuck did you just say to me?"

"You heard me."

Whittaker looked between them for a second and grinned. "Oh, I get it. Yeah, this is a respect thing, isn't it, Teddy? That's why you need these yahoos! Auberon's retainers would make hamburger out of your mortal ass if you tried to collect the bounty yourself. But who knows? If you let the Gruesome Threesome make the handoff in the Otherlands, then maybe word gets out that you 'helped' with the operation. Maybe you can finally sit at the big boys' table instead of being spat at by every dwarf, sprite, and hobgoblin who passes you by on the street!" He gave a short, sharp laugh. "Good fuckin' luck with that if you're dealing with these assholes! I'll bet you dollars to donuts they've already worked out the quickest way for you to have a fatal accident tonight."

Purdy glared suspiciously at the redcaps. The creatures bared their teeth and flexed their long, groping fingers. The mountain troll cracked his knuckles.

"Don't listen to him," said Che Guevara.

"Don't do anything stupid," said the MAGAt.

"You know… the little asshole might have a point," Purdy muttered. "Do any of you realize how hard it is to pin down an imp? I had to track this bastard's movements for four days before I could get in close enough to take him out. I got a discount on the restraints, but they still cost a fair chunk of change. And I had to drive across two bridges to get him from there to here. That's a hell of a lot of gas money. Maybe I do deserve a little more for my trouble."

"Watch yourself, Purdy," said Che Guevara. "You don't want to make this harder than it has to be. We made a deal. You'll get the rest of your money."

"Lotta ways out of a deal like that," murmured Whittaker. "They promised you'd get your money, Ted, but did they promise your brakes would still be working when you drove outta here?"

The MAGAt bent down and grabbed Whittaker by his lapels. "That's it! If you won't shut him up, I will! Give it here!" He held out his hand for the tube sock. When Purdy hesitated, the redcap snapped, "Are you deaf, skunk? I said give it to me!"

Purdy kept his voice low, but Whittaker could hear the rage bubbling to the surface. "I already told you, I do not like that word."

"That's what you are, isn't it?" hissed the MAGAt. "That's all you'll ever be. A low-rent thug for hire and an oath-breaking, good-for-nothing, half-blood skunk."

Purdy drew a pistol from the waistband of his jeans. "Say that to my face," he hissed. "Say that word to me one more fucking time."

The MAGAt dropped Whittaker roughly and bared his teeth. As Che Guevara tried to calm his counterpart down and Mr. Big and Tall reached for the gun, Whittaker started to wriggle away like an inchworm, all but forgotten, and put all his attention toward his manacles.

He worked himself into a sitting position and stretched until he could get his wrists beneath his legs and, eventually, out in front of him. He had just got them to his knees when something landed on top of the van with a hollow metallic thud. The roof buckled and the parkade went silent as everyone looked to the source of the noise.

A long, low black shape on four legs was perched on the roof, staring down at Ted Purdy and the Gruesome Threesome. Its features were hazy and indistinct, concealed beneath a layer of what appeared to be living shadow. In the middle of what must have been its face, two cold blue points of light glowed like stars. Its lips peeled back to reveal rows of snow-white teeth, nothing at all like the crowded, carrion-chewing needles of the redcaps. These were the ripping daggers of an alpha predator. At the end of each leg, Whittaker saw three claws of similar proportion exuding a vapour like dry ice.

The shape howled, and sparks burst from under the hood of the van. The ceiling lights exploded in a shower of glass and Ted Purdy aimed his gun into the falling darkness. The shape lunged at him. There was a spray of arterial blood, a scream, and a thud. Purdy's piece and shooting arm hung from the shape's mouth, and after a few seconds of noisy chewing, they disappeared completely.

The redcaps tripped over each other to be the first one back into the safety of the van. Mr. Big and Tall grabbed the shape around the middle and hauled it off the pile of meat that used to be Ted Purdy. The shape growled and slithered out of Mr. Big and Tall's grip, fixed its cold blue eyes on him, and sank its icy claws into the soft meat of his belly. The redcaps screamed and locked themselves in the van as the shape unspooled Mr. Big and Tall's intestines like a string of sausages.

Only Whittaker held his tongue. While the shape chowed down on Mr. Big and Tall, Whittaker got his hands in front of him as quietly as he could and reached for his tie. He wasn't an idiot. He'd been handcuffed like this before. That was why every single tie pin he owned was hand-cut into a lockpick. He worried the heavy iron manacles against the length of silk at his neck and worked it up out of his waistcoat. As the shape raked its claws against the van's back doors, Whittaker bit down on the head of his tie pin and drew it out with his teeth, then jammed it into the lock on the right cuff. He nearly swallowed it as the shape bashed the door in with its head, leaped into the van, and ate the redcaps alive. His shirt was damp with sweat, his mouth dry and filled with the silvery tang of his tie pin. He worked it around until the lock went click and the iron manacle fell heavily from his hand. Then he set to work on the other side. As the shape finished with the redcaps and jumped back out of the van, its sleek black body now flecked all over with red, the second manacle gave way. Whittaker scooted out of the iron's effective range, keeping one eye on the shape. His ankles were still tied, but he could deal with that later.

As the shape came sprinting toward him, its teeth shining in the darkness, Whittaker snapped his fingers. The air made a whip-crack noise as he disappeared from the shape's path, leaving only his tie pin and his fetters behind. A second *crack* followed a second later, as he appeared over Ted Purdy's body and picked up the briefcase full of coins. One more *crack* echoed off the cold concrete, and the imp made good his escape.

SHE STEPS into the rain, blinks to adjust her eyes to the lights over her head, and takes in a deep breath. Cold power rushes through her body from tip to tail. Taut muscles tense in her core. Frozen claws sharp on four sturdy legs. Teeth like ripping daggers fixed to jaws that can crush bone. It is old magic that powers her, that drives her forward on The Hunt.

Some part of her knows that this is not The Hunt. There is hunting, and there is The Hunt. Hunting satisfies a hunger. The Hunt is primeval. It is sovereign. All nature trembles on a night of The Hunt.

She had been on The Hunt, before the monsters came. She calls them monsters, because her language has no words severe enough for the crime they have committed. They made her sleep. They brought her away from her home. They put bars in front of her and denied her food and reduced her to mere hunting. She hears them now, calling her back to them. She does not want to go, but she knows she must, or they will hurt her.

The hunger still gnaws at her. She has hunted for them, she has fed, but it is not enough. It will never be enough, and when she returns to them, she knows they will put the bars in front of her again and take away her food. She will starve, until the next time they send her out to hunt.

She is ashamed of what she does next. She pauses. Sniffs the air again. In the shadows of the great grey stone that stretches across the sky, there is something warm. Something living. Despite the call from the monsters, she pads away in that direction. The scent grows stronger. Sweat and stale urine mixed with cheap alcohol and… and… wet fur, she thinks.

Too many lights out here. Lights racing across the great stone. Lights on street corners, elevated on long metal stalks. Lights shining out from towers of glass and steel. Her eyes are better in the shadows. If she concentrated, she might be able to send out a pulse of magic that would extinguish the lights around her. But that would draw attention. She hears wheels rumbling on the great stone above her. This world is still so strange to her, but she knows that the wheels and the lights are often connected. Powered by the same magic. Destroy the lights, and she will stop the wheels. People will notice that.

It's darker under the stone than on the street. As she lopes into the long shadows, she sees more clearly. She can see the man in the shabby clothes sleeping against a great pillar, beneath a lean-to made of a blue material and strange green cords. Old bottles and papers line the ground around and under him like a nest. Lying at the man's feet, atop a large sheet of thicker paper that reads "4K OLED," is a shaggy, too-skinny hound. She does not know what "4K OLED" means. Is that what this creature's master calls it?

4Koled's ears prick up as she comes near. It doesn't stand or open its eyes, but a low rumble emerges from its throat.

The man stirs and raises one foot. He scratches the dog's belly with his toes and whispers, "S'okay, Jake. S'okay. Ain't nothin' out there." Ah, then 4Koled is not a name.

She takes one more step forward, and the dog called Jake springs to life, barking like mad and bunching his shoulders in a defensive gesture. Animals are always the first ones to know, aren't they?

She springs forward. As Jake the dog leaps to meet her, she jinks around him and catches his neck in her jaws. She is sorry to do this, but she must sate the hunger, for she knows the monsters will not. One flick of her head, and SNAP go the vertebrae. The man stirs at his companion's dying yelps, but before he can scream, she spits out the wet furry carcass and jumps at him. Her front paws cave in his ribs, her claws pierce his skin, and she keeps the pressure up until she's punctured his heart and lungs. Then she sinks in her teeth, tears his carotid artery in half, and shivers at the simple joy of warm blood on her tongue.

CHAPTER 2

NIGHT TERRORS

FOR ONCE, Abby Henderson managed to wake up without screaming. She just held her breath, sank her teeth into her tongue, and counted backwards from thirty until the urge to panic had passed. Already, the afterimage of the dream was eroding to vague impressions in her mind. Memories of sensations rather than events. Hunger, excitement, pride. And anger. Anger at what, Abby couldn't say, but she knew it was there. It was as real as the taste of blood on her tongue.

Without turning on the light, Abby slipped out of bed, tiptoed toward her dresser, opened the bottom drawer, and then slinked toward the bathroom. Her head was already hurting as a burning needle of pain inserted itself between her eyes, and she tilted her head back to stop her nose from bleeding even before it started.

She shut the bathroom door behind her and fiddled with the dimmer switch until her eyes could take the light. Then she filled the glass she always kept by the sink, pulled the bottle of industrial-strength aspirin from the medicine cabinet, and popped two into her mouth. She always got headaches after dreams like this. It was her body's typical unconscious reaction to sudden psychic phenomena.

Nearly a year ago, Abby had discovered that she was descended from an ancient lineage of psychics and telepaths called the Gospels, so named because of their ability to foretell and relay the *gōd spell*—the good news. But good news had been scarce since she had learned about her abilities: she had been tortured by a vicious cult who wanted to use her power for their own ends, she'd lost people she loved, and more than one supernatural psycho had tried to kill her. It seemed that as soon as the magical world—the Nocturn, as it was known by those within it—learned that you had power, it would throw all kinds of horrors your way to test your mettle.

Unless she'd missed her guess, the Nocturn was in a mettle-testing mood again. She didn't know whose eyes she'd been looking through when that homeless man was torn apart, but her gut told her that wasn't going to be the end of it. She looked at the black-and-purple Vokarion crystal she'd grabbed from the bottom drawer of her dresser, shut her eyes, and concentrated. The crystal began to glow as it picked up her thoughts, sorted them into a coherent telepathic message, and transmitted that message into the aether.

Natalie, said the little voice in Abby's head. *If you're there, pick up. Something's happened. I had a dream.*

There were a few seconds of silence before her Vokarion crystal picked up the signal from another, and she heard the telepathic response of a deep female voice with a thick Haitian accent. *Talk to me, Abby,* said the voice. *What's going on?*

Straight to business, as usual. There were only a small handful of people who had consistently stood with Abby whenever the Nocturn threw a fresh terror her way, and of those few, Natalie Arnaud was the strongest advocate of the direct approach. The sapient zombie preferred to solve problems with two fists, a machete, and her regenerative healing factor rather than her words. It was always best to give Natalie the short version, so that's what Abby did as she recounted what she'd seen in the dream.

I don't think this was the first kill of the night, either, she added. *The creature had already fed on… something before it went after this guy under the Viaduct.*

Do you remember what 'something' was?

Sorry, no. That part of the dream's really fuzzy. All I remember was a parkade… a… a van… and I think… I think Whittaker might have been there…

Whittaker? Are you sure?

Yeah. Unless there's another imp in Vancouver with a taste for $5000 suits.

That does sound like our Whittaker, Natalie admitted. *Okay, I'll check this out. I'll start at the Viaduct and work my way back. Do you know exactly where this went down?*

Wasn't far from BC Place. You know where Cirque du Soleil set up the last time they were in town? Around there. I remember a blue tarp and a bunch of newspaper and cardboard under one of the concrete supports.

I'll probably recognize it when I see it. If Simon's awake, I'll let him know what's up, and then I'll go and have the look at the scene. I might be able to get some info on what this thing is. Don't you want some backup?

Negative. I doubt it will have stuck around after it ate, and even if it did, I wouldn't confront it right away. If it did as much damage in one night as you say it did, we don't want to make a lot of noise before we know what it is.

You're almost starting to sound like Simon.

Ugh. I hope not. She harrumphed and went into a surprisingly accurate impression of Simon Lockhart's posh accent. "Don't be hasty, Natalie. We need to start slow: observe the creature's tactics and behaviour so we know what we're dealing with before we run in mob-handed and get our faces bitten off." I'll see what I can find at the scene. Keep your crystal near on the off chance I do need you. We'll convene tomorrow. For now, try and get some sleep.

Okay. Good luck out there.

Here's hoping I don't need it. Is there anything else I should know about?

There was the briefest hesitation before Abby replied, *No. No, that's everything.*

Alright then, said Natalie, and Abby thought she could hear a faint trace of doubt in her friend's voice. I guess we'll talk tomorrow.

Yeah. I guess we will.

The glow from the crystal faded as the telepathic connection broke. Abby felt another stab of pain between her eyes, and this time it was answered by a twinge in her side, just above her left kidney. She lifted her pyjama top, laid a hand over the knotty web of scar tissue that covered the skin there, and remembered with a shiver the cold black claws that had ripped through her flesh, forever marking her as the property of the Cult of the Following.

She hung her head, closed her eyes, and popped a third aspirin in her mouth to soothe the pain. As she knocked back the rest of her water, another voice circled around her head. "'That's everything'?" it asked. "Are you sure you're not forgetting anything? Any*one*?"

Abby set down the glass and stared into the mirror. The dead woman on the other side stared back at her and crossed her arms. "Only, I can't help but notice," said Karen Henderson, "that you still haven't told anyone about me."

*****

Abby's mother had not been perfect. Karen Rose Henderson (née McAllister) was born into a family of veteran demon-hunters and monster-slayers, who had trained her in their ways almost from the moment she could walk. But with that training came a certain arrogance, and Karen started biting off more than she could chew. Then one day, she had choked.

The Deacon, an ancient demon with a vendetta against the McAllister family, had come into Karen's crosshairs. As a honeymoon gift to herself, Karen and her new husband Don had devised a plan to destroy the Deacon and his cult of demonic acolytes and rid the world of a scourge that had taken countless lives. But the Deacon and his Following had been ready. They broke Karen and Don Henderson down to nothing, and then the Deacon offered Karen a deal: twenty-five years of peace between the Hendersons and the Following, all for the low, low price of a child's soul. Karen had been only eight weeks pregnant when the Deacon broke her, and in panic and desperation, she had bequeathed her future to a monster. That was how Abby had ended up in the bowels of the abandoned Applegate Asylum last November, stripped naked and screaming as the Deacon's claws tore through her. And yet… she did not hate her mother for what had happened. She couldn't. What Karen had done, she had done out of love. She had given Abby a chance at life that wouldn't have been available to her otherwise. The Deacon had wanted Abby's power one way or another. If Karen hadn't taken the deal, the Deacon probably would have thrown her in a padded cell deep in the asylum and then claimed Abby for himself the minute she was born. And when the Following had come to collect, Karen had done what she could to protect her daughter and force a way out of the deal. She had sacrificed her life to buy Abby some time. How could Abby dream of hating her after that?

Abby had wanted to say all of this and more to her mother for most of a year now. She had tried so many times to reach out through the Bridge—the mystical trance that allowed a Gospel to make contact with the spirits of the dead—but Karen had never answered Abby's summons. And that only made what happened next hurt all the worse.

Around the start of September, Karen had just… appeared. For the first week or so, she'd been a glimmer in the mirror or a shape in the corner of her daughter's eye, but she'd been there. Just standing there, watching. She retreated whenever Abby turned to face her, like water receding from the thirsty Tantalus. As fall came, Karen moved closer to the centre of Abby's gaze. She started talking to her. But she never answered when Abby tried to talk back, about all the things they needed to talk about. Karen's words were empty of wisdom or mirth, or any of the good things that Abby remembered about her mother. They just reminded Abby of what had been missing for the last year. With that hurt in her heart newly roused from its hibernation, Abby turned away from the face in the mirror, switched off the bathroom light, and returned to bed. It was several long hours before she fell asleep again, and for all that time, Karen stood silently over her.

CHAPTER 3

HAIR OF THE DOG

WHEN ABBY awoke in the morning, her mother was still there, standing by the window and saying nothing. She stood at Abby's shoulder while her daughter ate breakfast, hovered in the doorway as Abby kissed her partner goodbye, and took the empty seat beside her when Abby boarded the bus to work. When Abby arrived at MacReady's Social House and took her regular position at the hostess stand, Karen seated herself in the waiting area at the front of the restaurant.

Right here in this restaurant was where all of Abby's worst nightmares had come home to roost last October, when the Deacon sent his most zealous acolyte to collect the debt that was owed him. The restaurant had been extensively remodeled since Varr'rak the Shadow-walker had ransacked it in his pursuit of Abby, but she could still recall exactly where she'd been standing and what she'd been thinking when everything went to shit. Every detail—from the tinny chorus of "Old-Time Religion" to the sensation of crawling over hot glass from the exploded light bulbs—was etched into her memory, and as the day dragged on and the clouds outside grew thick with rain, it all came flooding back with a vengeance. Truthfully, she remembered it all afresh every day when she walked into work, but it seemed more poignant today. Maybe it was because the wheel of the seasons was finally turning back toward that rainy autumnal greyness, or maybe it was because the vision of her mother was still sitting ten feet away.

Or maybe it was because of the tall Black woman and the skinny white Englishman now walking toward the hostess stand.

Abby tried to hide her shock as Natalie Arnaud—all six-and-a-half undead feet of her—deposited her massive black umbrella in the basket at the front door reserved for that purpose. Her tongue twisted itself into an unsolvable knot as Simon Lockhart, leaning on a cane and grimacing uncomfortably, requested a table for two. And she felt like crying when she realized that the other hostess had rapidly made herself scarce and it was now down to Abby herself to make the pair feel welcome. While her mother watched silently, Abby produced two menus and led Simon and Natalie to a quiet booth in the darkest, farthest corner of the restaurant. She made sure they were sitting comfortably, told them their server would be along in a minute, then leaned in close and hissed, "What the *hell* are you two doing here?"

"Well, that's a fine how-do-you-do!" Simon huffed. "We're just here for lunch, Abigail, honestly. I've been cooped up in the Letterbox so long that I needed some fresh air." He studied the menu for a moment and then said, "Hmm. The striploin sounds rather appetizing, doesn't it, Natalie?"

She agreed that it did, adding, "But they better make mine nice and rare."

Abby took a breath and counted backward from ten. "Look, I'm sorry if I seem a little testy, you guys, but, uh, the way I remember it, you two kind of destroyed the place the last time you were here."

"Now, Abby, you *know* most of that was Varr'rak's work," Simon sniffed.

"Well, you certainly didn't help."

Simon turned to his companion and said, a little haughtily, "Remind me, Natalie, whose life did we come to save the last time we were in this fine establishment?"

Natalie looked Abby dead in the eye and screwed up her face in a simulation of deep concentration. "You know, it's right on the tip of my tongue, but... no, it's not coming to me."

Abby surrendered. "Okay, I'm sorry. I might have been out of line there. Didn't get a lot of sleep last night."

"Neither did I, to tell the truth," Simon said. "I'm sorry if I'm a little punchy myself today. These curse wounds, you know?"

Abby nodded. During a magical duel in the summer, a psychotic warlock had hit Simon with a curse that left him in need of eighteen stitches. The wounds were still healing, and he'd complained about the pain on countless occasions since August. It was a poignant reminder to Abby that, despite his youthful face and his strength as a sorcerer, Simon was one of the oldest and most mortal people she had ever met.

"Speaking of sleep," Natalie interjected, "that's the other reason we're here. I checked into that dream you had. Simon's up to speed, and I'll fill you in later. When can you get away?"

"An hour, maybe? Hour and a half? That's when I take my break, usually."

"We'll be out back," Simon promised. "Now you should probably get back to work."

Abby nodded. "I should. *Please* don't trash the place this time."

Natalie smirked. "No promises."

*****

At the start of her break, Abby ducked out the back door of the restaurant, crossed the parking lot as stealthily as she could, and climbed into the back seat of a battered, antique

Thunderbird. She had to shove a pile of dirty towels, blankets, and other detritus out of her way before she sat, and when she was semi-comfortable, she pulled a granola bar out her purse and checked her watch. "Let's do this quickly," she said between bites. "I only have half an hour."

Natalie and Simon had been waiting for her in the driver's seat and the front passenger seat, respectively, and as she chewed, they turned to face her with their patented Very Serious, We've-Got-a-Problem faces. "Here," said Natalie, reaching into the pocket of her great trench coat and passing over a stack of Polaroid photos, "these are from the scene of your dream."

Abby finished her granola bar, wiped her crumby hands on her skirt, and looked over the photos. The underpass from her dream looked more like an abattoir now: blood painted the concrete in long, agitated streaks and made a soggy mush of the victim's cardboard bedding; the bungee cords and blue tarp had been sliced clean through and lay among a clotted mess of fur, denim, and animal shit; splinters of white bone poked through small globules of offal and rotting red meat. Whatever had done this had eaten the lion's share of the kill with tremendous zeal. Everything that remained of man and dog likely could have fit into a single garbage bag.

"What the hell did this?" She struggled to get the words out without regurgitating her granola bar.

"We were rather hoping you could answer that," Simon said. "You saw it happen."

"Yeah, but I didn't see *it*. It was more like… like I was looking through its eyes as it fed."

"Is there nothing you can tell us about this creature?"

Abby shrugged. "Big, fast, angry, and strong. That's about all I got. What we should do is try and get in touch with Whittaker. He saw this thing in action. Maybe he can give us a clue."

"I did think to ask him, but you know what Whittaker's like."

There was a sudden snap of fingers, and the pile of crap on the sea beside her transformed into an unhappy imp in a rumpled Savile Row suit. "Hey! Don't talk about me like I'm not here!"

"Jesus Christ!" Abby gasped and slapped a hand over her heart. Goddamn imps and their goddamn illusions. You never knew when they were going to turn up. "Have you been there this whole time?"

"Unfortunately," Natalie grumbled. "He showed up at the Letterbox about half an hour after I got back from recon last night. When we told him we were going out, he insisted on coming."

"Doing his best impersonation of some laundry, apparently," said Abby, still trying to coax her pulse back into a normal rhythm.

"Safest place for me is with these two," Whittaker replied. "Much as I hate to say it. No way I'm going it alone with that thing on the loose!"

"You did see it then?" said Abby. "Any idea what the hell it was?"

"I know as much as you do, chickadee. Big, fast, angry, strong. I'll also throw hungry into the mix. Before it chowed down under the Viaduct, it helped itself to two redcaps, a mountain troll, and one of my ex-business associates. If you put a gun to my head, I'd have said it was some kind of dog. I mean, I think it was. It was all kind of… hazy. Like smoke, you know?"

Abby gulped, remembering the pack of shadowy hellhounds that carried the gestalt consciousness of Varr'rak the Shadow-walker. "Whittaker… " she said nervously, "I have to ask: how many… heads did this dog have?"

Whittaker looked at her like she was out of her mind. "If you're asking me whether this thing crawled out of the pits of Hades: no, I don't think it did. It only had the one head, far as I could see."

Abby exhaled in relief. Varr'rak's hellhounds had all been blessed with three heads apiece. But as quickly as that notion vanished, another one sprang to mind. "Wait, was it a full moon last night?"

Natalie shook her head. "That was three nights ago. Besides, there hasn't been a werewolf attack in the Lower Mainland for nearly twenty years."

"Yeah, and we ought to know," Whittaker added with a smirk.

Simon cleared his throat sharply, glaring at the two as if they'd already said more than enough. Clearly, there was some secret there that they didn't have the time to go into right now. "Okay," Abby said, changing the subject, "we need to know what the fuck we're dealing with and we need to know yesterday. I want to see the scene of the first attack for myself. Maybe my Gospel senses can pick up something."

"It's a place to start, at least," said Simon. "Unfortunately, we don't know precisely where the first attack was."

"I tried to trace the creature's route back to where it started," said Natalie. "But I lost the trail. Got the feeling it was using some kind of teleportation magic."

"That wouldn't surprise me," Whittaker replied. "Damn thing just dropped in out of nowhere. Like from the sky."

Abby smiled and clapped Whittaker on the shoulder. "Good thing we have a living witness. I'm sure you could find your way back there if you really tried. Then I can do my thing."

Whittaker's eyes nearly popped out of his head. "Are you fucking *loopy*? My arm still smarts after the last scrape you idiots pulled me into! There's no way I'm going back to that slaughterhouse again!"

Simon's voice was low and dangerous. "Whittaker, are you perhaps forgetting our arrangement?"

The imp snorted. "Oh, what are you going to do, Ætheriċ? Call down the king of the faeries on me if I don't walk back into that arterial Jackson Pollock?"

"No, but I may decide that providing you with sanctuary is not the most sensible use of the Letterbox's resources. You outsmarted this creature once before; I'm sure you could do so again."

Whittaker ground his teeth together in impotent fury. "You sure you don't have a bit of Fair Folk blood in you, Ætheriċ? Cuz you drive a real hard bargain."

"Since it's the only language you seem to understand, it's rather in my best interest to speak it fluently."

"Alright, *fine*! If it's that important, then yeah, I can probably try and find my way back to where that thing almost chowed down on me."

"Excellent. If you lead Abby to the spot, then she can take the lay of the land with her second sight. Hopefully, she'll be able to turn up some useful information on this creature and we can devise a way to stop it before it does any more harm."

The imp jabbed a finger at Simon. "If this bites me in the ass like last time, you and I are going to have words, bucko."

Abby left the boys to their dick-measuring and walked back to the restaurant. Her mother followed her the whole way. So focused was Abby on the apparition that she never saw the low-slung black Cadillac parked by the dumpsters. She didn't see the muscular man with the military haircut and the dark suit seated behind the wheel. And she certainly didn't see the expensive camera and telephoto lens he had pointed right at her.

CHAPTER 4

MEN IN BLACK

WHEN HER shift ended, Abby stepped out into the rain and tapped on the window of a little blue VW Golf parked curbside. The passenger window rolled down, and Abby stuck her head in and gave the driver an inviting smile. "Hey, stranger," she said with a wink, "going my way?"

The woman behind the wheel was short, blonde, and round, with thick Buddy Holly glasses. With a smile and a shake of her head, she said, "Sorry, I don't have time to pick up floozies off the street. I'm looking for my girlfriend. You haven't seen her, have you? Skinny, lots of tattoos, short purple hair? Never stops talking?"

"Hey! I'm not that much of a blabbermouth!"

"Abby, have you seen you and Simon together?"

"He gets me wound up," she said defensively. "I can't help it."

Leanne Waller smiled and reached across the passenger seat to open the door. "Get in, Henderson."

Abby got in, kissed her partner, then laid her head back and closed her eyes. She'd made the mistake of looking in the rear-view mirror as she fastened her seatbelt and had noticed her mother sliding into the back seat, her eyes somehow both mournful and accusatory.

"Are you okay?" Leanne asked, laying her hand on Abby's.

"I'm fine," Abby replied, eyes still firmly closed. "Just… really long day."

"Couldn't get back to sleep, huh?" Besides Simon and Natalie, Leanne was the last of the small cohort who always had Abby's back when things got spooky. She'd been there when the Cult of the Following burned and when a mad ghost tried to steal Will Brady's life force. She knew what sleepless nights meant for Abby, and over breakfast Abby had given her the skinny on her latest dream.

Abby stifled a yawn. "Simon and Natalie came by earlier. I think it's time to throw down again."

Leanne nodded. "They stopped by the Shoppe too. I expect you heard the same spiel I did."

"Probably. We made plans to head out to the scene of the first attack at eleven tonight. You good to lend a helping hand?"

"If I'm needed." Suddenly, Leanne's face soured. "You know they brought *Whittaker* to the Shoppe? Whittaker! Of all the nasty little… things!"

"Of all the gin joints in all the towns in all the world… yeah, Whittaker was here too. But I don't think there's much incentive for him to misbehave right now. Whatever did this, he saw it, and I think it really scared the shit out of him."

"I know you want to give him the benefit of the doubt after how he helped us in Delapore, but… he's a little *snake*, Abby! We can't forget what he did to Kelly!"

"No, we can't. And he still deserves every punishment in the world for that mess at Avalon. But if he's a material witness to last night's attack, we'd be smart to keep him in our good graces. At least until he stops being useful."

"You've gotten ruthless over the last year. Did you know that?"

Abby finally worked up the nerve to look in the rear-view mirror. Her mother's staring eyes seemed to fill the glass. "Well… I've had a lot of growing up to do… "

As Leanne pulled out into the evening traffic, the driver of the low-slung black Cadillac kept a close eye on her from his spot by the dumpsters. When she had built up a respectable lead, he put the car into first gear and rolled out of the lot.

*****

A jet-black 1969 Cadillac Coupe DeVille will stick out on just about any road it travels. Luckily, the guy tailing Abby and Leanne had fifteen years of training in how not to stick out, even when he was sat behind the wheel of a boat like this. He kept to half a kilometre under the speed limit the whole way, obeyed every traffic light and road sign to a T, and always made sure he was at least four cars back from Leanne's little blue Golf. In this way, he kept them in sight until they turned into the underground parking lot of their apartment building. Following them in would have been too much of a giveaway, so instead he parked the Caddy in front of a little mom-and-pop jeweller's across the street and made the rest of the journey on foot. He crossed at the crosswalk, checked his watch, and murmured, "They're on their way up. They haven't seen me."

"Copy that," said his watch.

*****

When Abby walked into her apartment and saw the tall man in the dark suit seated at her kitchen table, she wasn't sure at first if he was actually there. It wasn't until Leanne came in behind her and yelped, "Who are you?" that Abby was fully convinced.

The man was well-built, square-jawed, and clean-shaven, with blond hair in a high-and-tight military cut. By way of an answer, he reached into the inner pocket of his blazer and produced an ID card in a black leather case. "Miss

Henderson. Miss Waller. My name is David Jones, Special Agent Fourteen of the Canadian Department of Advanced Research and Special Defence."

"Never heard of them," Abby said sharply. "Do you mind explaining how the fuck you got into our apartment?"

"You haven't heard of us, but we've sure heard of you. Please, ladies. Sit down. We need to talk."

"We need to talk about how the fuck you got in here," Abby repeated. "So answer the damn question, or I'm calling the cops."

"That won't be necessary."

Abby snarled. "Fine. We can play it that way if that's how you want it. Leanne, get the Webley."

"*That* won't be necessary either." He lifted one black-gloved hand and laid an antique Webley revolver on the table in front of him. Half a second later, the driver of the '69 Cadillac materialized in the doorway behind Abby and Leanne and ushered them into the apartment, shutting and locking the door behind him with his own gloved hands. The newcomer was cut from the same cloth as Jones (or Agent Fourteen or whatever he wanted to call himself), with that athlete's frame, square jaw, and blond high-and-tight. As he herded Abby and Leanne toward the table, Abby noticed the dark bulge of a holster beneath his suit jacket. The newcomer made no attempt to hide the gun, and she quickly realized that Agent Fourteen was currently stretching in such a way as to make his own holster conspicuous.

"My colleague," explained Agent Fourteen, as the newcomer helped Abby and Leanne into their chairs. "John Smith, Special Agent Six."

As she sat, Abby's eyes drifted away from Fourteen's and locked onto the luminous aura surrounding him. Simon had once described auras to her as being like an afterimage of the reaction that occurred when a soul was touched by the primordial energies of the universe. In a person's aura, a Gospel could read the truth of who they were and sense how in touch they were with the forces of the True Magic. When she checked out Fourteen's aura, Abby was relieved to learn that he was, undoubtedly, a human being with no particular magical talent. He did work for the organization he said he worked for and his name was David Jones—or at least he firmly believed it was. She couldn't rule out the possibility that his mind had been tampered with by some external force she couldn't yet detect. But she remained perturbed by the fact that these two gorillas had laid a trap for her in her own home and she had no clue what the Canadian Department of Advanced Thingummy actually was.

The newcomer—Smith, Six, whatever—circled around the table and took a seat beside his colleague. Sitting together, they looked like clones or reflections of each other. She tried to imagine the job listing these two must have answered: "VAGUELY MENACING ARYAN SUPERMEN WANTED TO HARASS NEIGHBOURHOOD PSYCHIC. MILITARY EXPERIENCE AND HAIRCUTS PREFERRED. MUST SUPPLY OWN DARK SUIT AND TIGHT-ASS DEMEANOR."

"I'll come right to it," said Agent Fourteen. "In the past year, the pair of you have been involved in two high-profile Category Five EPIs."

"Extraplanar incursions," Agent Six provided, not waiting for Abby to ask. "Encounters with creatures or phenomena from beyond the material plane of existence."

"Our organization deals with EPIs every day. A lot of what you've seen, we've seen. But the difference is that we're trained to deal with these things. We know how not to be observed when we do. And then you two come along: civilians with no military or intelligence experience to speak of, working side-by-side with two walking EPIs, and with apparently no concern about who knows where you go and what you see."

"Is this about... my blog?" Abby asked incredulously.

"This is about assessing a potential threat to the security of Her Majesty's Government," Agent Six replied. "Frankly speaking, Miss Henderson, we're not convinced that your efforts to... assist with the neutralization of these EPIs have been to this country's benefit."

"Well, I haven't made things worse, if that's what you're implying!"

"Since August of this year, a video of you and your friends at the public library in Delapore, BC, has attracted more than 300 000 views on social media. A blog post describing the events leading up to the fire at the George and Elizabeth Applegate Home for the Mentally Unstable has been copied and reposted to Reddit and Tumblr so often that it has received nearly a million likes and shares. Rumours are starting to circulate about... bizarre, otherworldly entities running amok in this province."

Abby swallowed. "It has? They are?"

"You don't read your own press, do you, Miss Henderson? Your escapades are beginning to cause a lot of speculation. They're encouraging people to ask questions that don't have easy answers."

"And that puts our organization in a very difficult position," said Fourteen. "For the last seven decades, we've worked hard to keep the Canadian public safe from EPIs like the ones you've encountered. And that doesn't always mean running in guns blazing, shooting anything with too many eyes or teeth, and then publishing the results online."

"Sometimes, it's in humankind's own interest if they don't know what's hiding in the shadows. Nations have gone to war in the name of magical superiority. Civilizations have been wiped out completely."

Abby blinked. Were these two referring to the War of the Ancients? The millennium-long, interdimensional war between the old gods and the demons was the subject of many a horror story for magic-users, but she had always assumed that it had passed out of mortal memory.

"You have to understand, Miss Henderson," said Agent Six, "there are beings out there that don't appreciate the attention you're giving them. We're talking entire supernatural races that we've brokered peace agreements with, on the condition that we do what we can to keep Joe Sixpack ignorant of their existence. When you tell people to take a closer look at these things after we have promised to preserve their anonymity, the situation can become... untenable."

"Nobody wants another war between the demons and the humans. Nobody wants to go back to the days of witch-trials and public executions."

"Nobody wants another Josiah Harcourt or John Leland to discover the truth one day and make somebody suffer for it."

When they dropped those names on her, Abby tried not to squirm in her seat. Surely her little blog couldn't create another monster like Leland, could it? Her intent was only to advise caution, to make people that much safer by sharing her insider knowledge. But people were people, and people, historically, had done hideous things in the pursuit of knowledge. Statistically speaking, when you told the world a dirty little secret, there would always be a few who'd try to figure out how it could benefit *them*.

"We're saying this for your own benefit, Miss Henderson," Fourteen said. "It's time to turn off your laptop, get offline, and call it a day. You've had your fun playing Scooby-Doo, but that fun ends now. This is not a request. As of today, Abby Normal is officially retired."

Abby was still trying not to squirm. She imagined herself as an ant on a hot sidewalk, trapped beneath a little boy's magnifying glass. Except that the little boy was the Prime Minister and the magnifying glass was... God knew what. Waterboarding? Solitary confinement? But then she felt a pressure at the end of her arm. Leanne was squeezing her hand, and out the corner of her eye Abby saw her partner give a small but firm shake of the head. *No,* Leanne mouthed silently. As in, *no, we're not giving up. No, we're not going to let these goons push us around.*

Abby looked back to Six and Fourteen. "Sorry, boys. That's not how this is going to happen. Maybe I don't have your training or your federal budget, but I do have a gift. It's my responsibility to use these powers to help people, however I can. And it's not like I go looking for this stuff, right? It comes to me. That gets me thinking that somebody way above your pay grade wants me out there, fighting the good fight. If you don't like that, then like you said, I have two walking EPIs on speed dial who I'm sure would just love to knock some sense into you."

Fourteen looked at Six. Six looked at Fourteen. "Satisfied?" Fourteen asked.

Six shrugged. "All I said was let's try good cop. Didn't say it would work."

Fourteen pulled an 8x10 photo from his inner pocket and set it on the table before Abby. "Do you know what this is, Miss Henderson?"

Abby looked at the photo. It showed a prismatic crystal, deep blue and pointed at both ends. "That," said Agent Fourteen, "is a Lethe crystal. Do you know why it's called that?"

She opened her mouth. Before she could form the word no, Fourteen answered his own question again. "The Lethe crystal is a psionically empowered artifact, possibly extraplanar in origin, possibly extraterrestrial. Applied correctly, it can remove unhelpful or unwanted memories from the mind of a human subject. Very useful for stemming rumours about supernatural phenomena."

"That's assuming an average level of psychic attunement," Six clarified. "Frankly, we have no idea what it would do to a Gospel. And we didn't receive clearance to find out today."

"The crystals are a last resort for the Department, you understand," said Fourteen. "But their success rate is near one hundred percent. There is a very good chance that if you looked at the real thing right now, Miss Henderson, it would erase everything. Every encounter you've ever had with extraplanar phenomena. The names and faces of everyone who's ever been in the same room with you during an EPI. Worst-case scenario, Abby Henderson could cease to exist." As one, he and Six stood and buttoned their jackets. "This is the only warning you get. Shut Abby Normal down, or the next time we speak, you won't be looking at a photo."

Abby curled her hands into fists on the table. "Big, strong soldier boys. If your bosses thought they could get away with wiping my memory, they would have sent you out here with more than a photo."

Fourteen smirked. "You know, we have a file on your mother, Abigail. I've read it. Look where the tough-guy act got her."

"Get out of my home," Abby hissed. "Don't say another word. Just get the fuck out."

"If you want to play it that way, that's your call," Fourteen said, "but you will be hearing from us very shortly." Agent Six deposited the Webley in an inner pocket of his dark jacket. Then the two of them left as quietly as they'd arrived.

CHAPTER 5

THREE GENTLEMEN OF CARCOSA

IT WAS a grimacing and shirtless Simon who greeted Abby and Leanne when they arrived at the Letterbox, the semi-sentient pocket dimension that he and Natalie called home. He was in the front room, perched on a three-legged stool as a stout, elderly Black woman in a long blue gown and burgundy stole rubbed a pungent ointment on the dull green scars running up and down his chest. These were the remaining marks of the Cutting Curse he'd suffered at the Harcourt House.

"Do you want us to come back?" Leanne asked.

"No, no, I'll only be a moment," Simon replied. "Just getting a routine checkup. Actually, I'm rather glad you all finally have a chance to meet. Abby, Leanne, this is Mother Hyld, of the Order of Wulfredda. Mother Hyld, these are the young ladies I was telling you about. Miss Munro's friends."

The old woman did not look up from her work, but she raised one hand in a small wave of greeting. A few silent moments passed before she straightened up, nodded, and said to Simon, "It goes well with you, O Ætheriċ, son of Wulfrecg. Your convalescence progresses swiftly. If you continue to have your rest and abstain from the power of the True Magic, you shall regain your full strength by Hallowmas."

"No magic until Halloween? Blimey. Cure's always worse than the disease with you lot." Against one wall of the lounge there stood a tall, wooden armoire of unguessable age, inside of which hung a round silver dish polished to a mirror shine. Simon's collared shirt and waistcoat hung in front of the silver dish, and as he got up and put them on, he inspected himself in its reflective surface.

"If you run blindly into a lion's den, do not be surprised to find teeth in your thigh," said Mother Hyld. She spoke with a Caribbean accent, her voice surprisingly deep for a woman who was not much taller than Leanne. The woman turned and reached for a six-foot-long staff of pine wood that rested against the other armchair. She used this as a walking aid as she approached Abby and Leanne and offered them a hand to shake. "But I forget my manners. It is good to meet you, O friends of Kelly."

Mother Hyld barely had the words out before Abby rushed forward to shake her hand. She had heard a lot about the Order of Wulfredda—the Faroe Islands-based folk healers whose magic was adapted from the practices of Simon's own race, the Vanguard—but she had never met one in person. She found herself unexpectedly thrilled at the opportunity and started firing off questions like rounds from a machine gun. Many of these questions concerned Kelly, who had been crippled by the Deacon back at Applegate Asylum and had spent most of the last year in the Order's care.

With a grandmotherly smile, Mother Hyld let Abby babble for a moment and then patted Abby's hand with her free one. "There will be time for all this presently, O Last of the Gospels. When we have a moment of leisure, I shall answer any question you wish about your friend. But now is not a moment of leisure, is it?" She adopted a knowing expression that passed from Abby to Leanne and then to Simon.

"Unfortunately, it's not," Simon agreed. "We have a fair bit of work ahead of us. Come on. Natalie and Whittaker are waiting in the library."

The amount of space inside the Letterbox was several orders of magnitude higher than what one might have guessed from looking at the abandoned post office that served as its streetside façade. Despite this, only a few rooms were ever used to their full advantage, and the main library was definitely one of these. Rows of bookshelves forty feet high snaked throughout a room with a high domed ceiling and a red velvet carpet. Reading tables and chairs were set up between every fourth shelf, while lecterns and display cases at the ends of the aisles displayed some of the real gems of the Letterbox's collection. All the shelves were jam-packed with books from every era and in every language, and if you went browsing, it was always a question of whether you would stumble across a tome of medieval Scottish demonology or a dog-eared Nicholas Sparks paperback first.

Natalie and Whittaker were at one of the aforementioned reading tables, looking over a large map of Metro Vancouver and trying to retrace the path back to where the creature had eaten Ted Purdy and the Gruesome Threesome. The current working theory placed the attack somewhere in Burquitlam.

"If you're going out that far," Simon said, "there's something I'd like you to field-test for me. I've been doing some tinkering during my long convalescence." He rummaged around in the pocket of his waistcoat and withdrew a handful of black-and-purple beads, each about the size of an aspirin. "Given my current state, I think it's best if I remain here tonight. But I'd still like to know what all you're seeing when you see it."

Falling into one of the long-winded, overly technical explanations that were his trademark, Simon explained how he'd been experimenting with the Vokarion crystals to see if they could be used to pick up and transmit not only the words that might run through someone's head, but the images as well. He thought he'd found a way to establish a link between the crystals and the optic nerve, so that the former could understand the signals running along the latter and transmit those stimuli through the aether in the same way that—

"So basically you've turned the Vokarion crystals into body cams," Abby interrupted.

"Well, that's the short version. If my maths are correct, these beads, when affixed to one's person, should be able to interact with the visual centres of the brain and send information from said visual centres to another bead in the network. That way, one person can see what another person sees in real time, and vice versa. Tap the bead once to activate, twice to deactivate." He pressed one of the beads to his right temple and tapped it with his finger. Then he handed one to Abby and told her to do the same. She felt a slight pinch in the corner of her brow as she affixed the bead, but it was gone in a matter of seconds. She tapped the crystal bead as Simon had done, and a transparent overlay of her own face appeared in the corner of her right eye. She winked, and the overlay did the same. She stuck out her tongue. The overlay did as well. Then Simon shut his eyes and the overlay disappeared.

"Huh. So I guess you want to see if this works at a distance?" she asked.

"Quite." Simon opened his eyes again. "I haven't been able to determine how reliable the signal is compared to your standard Vokarion crystal, nor whether there's an upper limit on the time and distance at which these beads will function. But if you keep this on, it will be like I'm right there with you."

"I just can't get rid of you, can I?" Abby tried to smile, but realized halfway through that her heart wasn't in it. Not after the day she'd had.

"Is everything alright, Abigail?"

"I'm not sure it is, Simon." Her shoulders dropped as she explained about the earlier visit from the men in black.

"Oh, shit," grumbled Whittaker. "That's just all anybody needs right now: The goddamn Ministry of Uncommon Knowledge."

"For once in his life, Whittaker's absolutely right," Natalie added. "You picked a hell of a time to go and get injured, Simon."

"I guess you've all dealt with these guys before?" Leanne asked.

"Afraid so," Simon said. "It's been quite some years since we had any trouble from the Department—or the Ministry of Uncommon Knowledge, if you prefer the colloquial approach. But I suppose with everyone that's happened this last year, they decided it was time to reinvigorate their Vancouver operation. I'm afraid your first impressions of them are rather representative of the whole."

"When they do come back," said Natalie, "you come to me. I'll sort those pigs out."

"You would have the same offer from me were I at my full strength," said Simon. "However, my ability to intervene directly is somewhat limited in my present condition. But I will offer what support I can."

Abby relaxed a bit. "Thanks, guys. I'm not going to lie, those two really put the fear of God into me for a minute."

"A favourite strategy of theirs," Simon sighed. "Worst part is they believe their intentions are noble, after a fashion. And that's always a dangerous combination."

Natalie snorted. "You know what they say about the road to Hell, after all… "

*****

By the time they set out to look over the scene, the rain was coming down like one solid sheet of water. It seemed like everyone with a roof over their head was hiding under it right now, and everyone without had already high-tailed it to the nearest shelter, tent, or doorway. Abby counted less than a dozen other cars on the road between the Letterbox and the site of the massacre, plus a few half-empty night buses along the main transit routes.

Leanne had volunteered to hang back at the Letterbox and give Simon an extra pair of hands, so it was just Abby, Natalie, and Whittaker braving the elements that night. None of them were surprised to find the parking garage empty, but they did wonder that it was so goddamn clean. The wreck of the redcaps' van had been towed away, and a lingering odor of industrial-strength solvents and cleaning agents hung in the air. Gone were the blood and entrails, plus a layer of gravel, dust, and even Whittaker's errant tie pin. Only a few torn scraps of yellow crime-scene tape suggested that anything nasty had happened here in the last while.

Abby stepped out of the Thunderbird, pressed one of the Vokarion beads to the side of her head, and blinked a couple times. "Alright, we're here. You getting any visual, Simon?"

The larger sister crystal glowed around her neck as Simon's voice echoed in her head. *Hang on a tick. I've almost... just need to adjust this a bit... Ah, yes! There we go! I've got you now!*

"Great. Somebody's definitely cleaned this place up, haven't they?"

Rather, he agreed. *I expect our friends from the Ministry have already collected the evidence they need and started the hushing-up process.*

"Hopefully they haven't cleaned up every trace."

Yes, quite. Talking of which, you had best get to work, young Henderson. I don't pay you to stand around and chit-chat.

She smiled. "You don't pay me at all, dummy. And that's something else we should talk about soon."

Eh? Say again, Abigail, say again? You seem to have broken up there for a second.

She rolled her eyes and raised one middle finger dead in the centre of her field of vision. "You see everything I see, right? Well, what do you see now?"

He had no comeback ready, so she lowered her finger and told Natalie and Whittaker to give her some space and watch for trouble. Then she closed her eyes and put out her psychic feelers.

Sixth sense, third eye, the Force... it didn't matter what she called it (and in all truth, she'd always been too lazy to think up a name). The witchy, Gospel-y part of her woke up, a sensation which she recognized as a low-grade electric tingling all through her body, and she opened her eyes once more to find a world in sharper focus and higher contrast, as if she'd spent her life looking at images on a ten-inch CRT TV and had suddenly upgraded to a 60-inch 4K model. She was aware of the slow beating of her and Whittaker's hearts, as well as the conspicuous lack of any beat from Natalie's. She also noticed a cold sensation on the back of her neck that hadn't been there before.

There was no question that this had been a week for warm jackets, but the cold on her neck went way beyond that. It was the kind of cold that got right under your skin, that cracked your hands and your lips and made your eyes freeze in their sockets. She turned to face the cold and felt the redness come into her cheeks, her nose, her ears. The hairs on her neck prickled and she noticed a white vapour trail drifting down from the ceiling. She moved closer. Squinted. Saw a misshapen ring of ice crystals and small growing things extruding from the concrete. Mushrooms, she realized. Abby raised her hand toward the ring and immediately felt the nip of the cold on her fingertips. "Hey, Simon? Are you seeing this?"

There was a pause and a few seconds of concerned muttering before Simon came back with, *Well... I wasn't expecting that...*

"You know what it is?"

That is a faerie ring. Also called a rond de sorcières *or a* Hexenring. *It's residue left behind by a sudden burst of powerful faerie magic. The spell burns an afterimage of itself into the landscape, and if conditions are right, it will form a ring like that.*

"So we've got faeries in the city."

Yes, I dare say we do. And old ones at that. I've never seen a faerie ring this deep into an urban landscape before. You normally see them in woodlands, swamps, very damp and secluded regions.

There was some note of uncertainty in his voice that put Abby on edge. "What's the problem?" she asked.

Look at the pattern of the ice, the growth of the fungus. Look how it's worn down the concrete around it, as if it's been there for years. The amount of power it would take to accomplish this somewhere so far removed from any kind of foliage… well, I must admit, it's a little frightening. Plus… the fungus itself…

"What about the fungus?"

Unless I miss my guess, that is auricula judae, or Judas's Ear. And I think I see a few velvet shanks in there as well. Both species are very capable of surviving the winter. Put it all together, and we must suspect the involvement of the Court-Among-the-Holly.

"You mean the faeries of winter?"

Precisely. Winter, frost, death, and all that's lovely about the dark half of the year. The evidence is all here. Now I think about it, I wouldn't be surprised if the beast that you and Whittaker saw was a refugee from Holly's blasted heaths.

"And that would be bad for us, wouldn't it?"

Playing with the Court-Among-the-Holly requires an entirely different set of rules. If this road leads where I think it does, we have to be extremely careful.

By now, Whittaker and Natalie had joined Abby by the faerie ring, and they jumped quickly to the same conclusion. Natalie went very still, while Whittaker cursed a blue streak and reached for his cigarettes. "Jumpin' screamin' Jesus H. fucking *Christ*! That's what I get, isn't it? That's just what I fucking get for hanging out with you yahoos! Goddammit, talk about out of the frying pan!"

The glow from Abby's crystal grew more intense as Simon's thoughts became audible to the entire trio. "Everybody, just calm down for a moment. I need a chance to think and reassess the situation. Abby, Natalie, do you suppose the two of you could give me a closer look at the *Hexenring* up there?"

"No problem," said Natalie. She crouched and clasped her large hands together in front of her to make a foothold for Abby. Abby assumed the position, put her hands on Natalie's shoulders, and then felt the chill from the ring sharpen against her face as Natalie lifted her up to get a better look.

From where she was now, she could see that some of the ice crystals around the outer edge of the ring formed a distinct, repeating pattern, invisible to someone on the ground. It was writing, she realized, in an alphabet she recognised as native to the Otherlands.

"What do you have up there?" Natalie grunted.

Realizing she would never have this chance again, Abby called down: "It's some form of Elvish! I can't read it."

"I think what Abigail means to say," Simon announced to all gathered, "is that there's writing up here in High West Elvish. Whittaker, you're the only one of us who speaks that ancient and elegant tongue, so I hope I may trouble you for a translation?"

After the imp had worked through the customary moaning and grumbling of, "What did your last slave die of?", Natalie let Abby down and gave him a boost up so he could read the icy inscription. There was a moment of silence as he worked through the translation in his head, but this was ultimately broken by a croaking gasp and a sharp intake of breath through tightly clenched teeth.

"Whittaker?" said Abby. "Are you okay up there?"

"Ho-ly *shit,*" he whispered. Before anyone could ask for clarification, the imp was already scrambling back down to the ground like a monkey fleeing a tree fire. Without pausing for breath, he pointed to the Thunderbird and said, "We gotta go! We gotta get in the car, get the fuck out of here, and forget we ever saw any of this!" He jumped at some imagined noise in the distance and his eyes darted nervously around the parking garage. "What am I talking about? Not the car! They'll track the car! Everybody grab hold, and I'll snap us back to the Letterbox!" He grabbed one of Abby's hands and told Natalie to take the other one, raising his own free hand so that he might snap his fingers.

"Whittaker, for God's sake, just take a breath!" Abby commanded. "What's the emergency?"

"Yes," said Simon over the crystal relay, "I'm afraid you even have me at a disadvantage here, Whittaker. What do you know that I don't?"

"No time to explain!" Whittaker snapped back. "I'll tell ya when we're clear, but right now we gotta get clear! Now quit yakking and let me do—"

From somewhere in the darkness, they heard a dull whoosh. Whittaker's shoulders tensed up and he slapped a hand over his forearm like he'd just been stung. He let go of Abby's hand, fell to his knees, and as a white froth began to collect at the corners of his mouth, he hissed, "God… dammit… "

Abby reached instinctively for Grandma Meg's Webley, remembering too late that those Ministry creeps had taken it. Suddenly, she knew who had fired that shot from the shadows, and her initial surprise turned to cold fury.

"We told you once already, Miss Henderson!" Agent Six stepped out of the darkness, pocketing what looked like a silver tranquilizer gun. Agent Fourteen followed one step behind. "No more of this Scooby-Doo act. This is where your investigation ends."

Abby caught Whittaker as he fell onto his side, then brushed his hand away from his bicep to see a two-inch metal dart poking out of the fabric of his suit. When she pulled it out, the needle-thin tip and the pinprick wound it had made were both glowing white. "What did you do to him?" For emphasis, she hurled the dart at Six's feet and snapped, "What the *fuck* did you just do to him?"

"Those darts are tipped with five hundred milligrams of pure iron," Six said flatly. "That's enough to put a faerie of that size on its ass for up to an hour in less than five seconds. The imp's not going anywhere, ladies. And neither are you."

Natalie squared her shoulders and stalked toward the agents with a homicidal look in her eye. "We're not, are we?"

"This area is the site of a Category Five extraplanar incursion," Agent Fourteen announced. "Your presence here is a violation of federal law. You've used your one warning, Henderson." He and Agent Six drew the semiautomatic pistols they'd made so obvious during their first visit. Natalie took another step forward.

"Try it, little men. You've got a file on me, right? So you already know those little pop guns won't keep me down long."

"No, they won't," admitted Agent Fourteen. He stepped clear of Natalie and took aim at Abby. "Please, Miss Arnaud, by all means, resist arrest. I've seen footage of you in action. There's no denying that you're fast. But you are not faster than this little pop gun."

Six raised his gun and barked, "Hands above your head, both of you. Now."

"Don't!" Whittaker hissed, throwing a stiff, sluggish hand onto Abby's thigh. "Don't… listen to 'em, chickadee… " His eyes rolled up in their sockets to meet hers. His words were flecked with spittle and came out through gritted teeth. "Gotta go. *Now*."

"You'll be going too, Mr. Whittaker," said Agent Six. "All of you are coming with us."

"No!" Whittaker croaked. "Far away! Gotta get… you don't know what's coming… all of us… in danger… long as we're here… "

"What's coming, Whittaker?" Abby asked. "Why do we have to go?"

"This is ridiculous," growled Agent Fourteen. "I'll say it one more time, Miss Henderson. Stand up and put your hands above your head now."

"Message... in the ice... " His breath was ragged and heavy, his whole chest heaving with every cycle. "It's him... it's his seal... "

"Whose seal?" said Abby.

Whittaker's eyelids fluttered. *"Long... is the winter... "* he croaked, reciting an ancient hymn that he had learned centuries ago. *"And long... is... is The Hunt... "* His eyes closed and he took a deep, desperate breath. *"And long is the night... in... Carcosaaa... "* With that, he passed into unconsciousness.

Abby looked at Natalie. "What's Carcosa?"

Natalie's dark skin was somehow ashy with fear. "He's right. We need to get out of here right now, every one of us." She scooped the imp up in a fireman's carry and pulled Abby to her feet, ignoring the shouted orders from the Ministry men as they re-trained their guns on her.

Agent Fourteen fired a warning shot into the ceiling as Natalie started toward the Thunderbird. Abby cringed and hid herself behind her friend. "Natalie," she said more urgently, "what the hell is Carcosa?"

In the darkness, a whinny. Hoofbeats. Natalie squeezed Abby's hand so hard that Abby thought her fingers might break. "*That,*" Natalie whispered, "is Carcosa."

The stallion hurled itself out of the shadows at a full gallop, jet-black of mane, red of eye, and ejecting flames from its nostrils with every breath. Upon its silver-trimmed saddle sat a pale figure in dark riding leathers and a flowing cloak, with dozens of pointed teeth exposed in an inhumanly wide grin.

"Bloody hell!" yelped Simon. "Dullahan! Everybody, shut your eyes *now*!"

Abby knew she should. She knew that the wild cavalry of the Court-Among-the-Holly could kill with a glance, if anyone was stupid enough to look straight at them when they stopped riding. But knowing and doing weren't the same thing, and the sight of that faerie stallion tramping toward her had put the second one right out of reach for the moment. She stared mindlessly as Agent Fourteen's training kicked in and he emptied his sidearm into the charging horse and rider. Both of them shrugged off the bullets like mosquito bites, and with a shrill hiss of anger, the faerie knight drew a long silver sword and swung the blade clean through Fourteen's neck without slowing down.

It was the dull *plop* of the Ministry man's head the concrete that finally jump-started Abby's brain. She screamed, shut her eyes, and allowed Natalie to drag her toward the Thunderbird even as she heard a second whinny, a second thunderclap of hooves, a second burst of gunfire, from somewhere behind her. She could sense the change in the magical energies around them, and she didn't need to look to know that the second Dullahan had just teleported into the parking garage less than ten feet away.

"Code Black! Code Black!" Agent Six screamed into his comms unit. "We have a Category Five EPI in progress, and an officer is down! Repeat: Category Five EPI, non-civilian casualty! I need backup at my locat—"

The *twang* of a bowstring cut him short, and Abby opened one eye just long enough to see Six fall back with the black shaft of an arrow sticking out from under his collarbone. He shut his eyes and bolted while he still had the chance, firing his sidearm blindly behind him with one hand.

Natalie wrenched open the doors of the Thunderbird and hurled Abby and Whittaker into the back seat half a second before another black arrow pulverized her window. She jumped behind the wheel, cranked the car into reverse, and shouted, "Hang the hell on!"

As the old jalopy rabbited out of the parking garage, Abby stretched out flat across the seat and squeezed the leather with a white-knuckled grip. "Can somebody please… " she panted, "for the everlasting, glory-be, motherfucking *love of God* tell me what's happening here?"

"I'm afraid 'god' is exactly right," said Simon. "Small 'g,' but older than the Old Testament and just as wrothful."

"Carcosa is the capital city of the Court-Among-the-Holly!" Natalie said. "That message in the faerie ring is an ancient motto of Carcosa—"

"And its presence here means the beast we're tracking is sacred to the King-Among-the-Holly," said Simon. "The King's sacred beasts are never supposed to leave the Otherlands unless he does, so if one of them is here—"

"Then either he is too, or he's going to be very soon!" Natalie returned.

"If the former, then we're poking our noses into Holly's affairs, which is not something they take kindly to on the best of days. If the latter, then something's gone dreadfully wrong in the Court-Among-the-Holly, and the entire army of Carcosa is going to be out tracking the creature!"

"Which means that if Holly thinks we might know anything about why the creature left Carcosa without the King's go-ahead, then we are in very—"

"Very—"

"*Very* deep shit."

"Why would they think we're involved?" Abby demanded.

"Sod's law, isn't it?" said Simon. "Humans, zombies, and an imp whose allegiance is to the Court-Among-the-Oak? Those are Holly's prime suspects when anything goes wrong."

There was a flash of white, a blast of frozen air that sent a spider web of frost up the windshield, and another black steed jumped out of the aether and reared up before the Thunderbird, its rider cracking a long whip formed from segments of bleached human bone. Natalie cranked the wheel hard, and Abby barely avoided breaking her nose on the back of the seat in front of her.

"Goddammit!" Natalie screamed as she steered around the third ghastly horseman. "Simon, do me a favour and tell me there's a way out of here!" Three titanic horses and their ghastly riders whinnied and whooped in the dark behind her.

"I'm looking, I'm looking!" They could hear him shouting to Leanne to find him a map of the area, and her shouting back that she was working on it, but he really did need to fix his filing system pronto.

"Goddammit, goddammit!" Natalie pounded the steering wheel with her fist as the Thunderbird tore the wooden arm off the hinge at the security gate. "Any day now, you two!" She took a hard left and the Thunderbird fishtailed onto the sidewalk, flattening a newspaper box and sending inserts from the *Georgia Strait* flying into the air.

While Simon and Natalie continued to scream at each other in blind panic, another voice cut through the Vokarion relay, all cold and calculating and professional. "Arnaud," it said, "you need to listen to me. Just stay calm and follow the directions I give you. I can get you out of this. I can get us all out of this."

"Agent Six?" Abby yelped.

Natalie snarled. "How the hell did you get on this frequency, you fascist creep?"

"Your imp friend dropped his crystal when you hauled ass away from the scene. Not the first time I've used one of these to tap into someone else's party line."

"Oh, you just think you're so clever, don't you, you—"

"Look, cut the bullshit and *listen* to me for two seconds! We don't have many options here." The black Caddy was two car lengths behind the Thunderbird, with the Dullahan riders hot on its tail. "You were right the first time," Agent Six admitted. "If Holly has come to Vancouver, we're all in danger. So let's stop fighting and try to find some common ground against these things, okay? That's what our organization does!"

"Fine!" Natalie spat. "What are your orders, O wise and powerful G-man?"

"Take a right at the next light. Then continue straight on until you hit Broadway. You want to get onto Gaglardi Way, past the university, and then onto Hastings Street."

"Gaglardi—? That's nowhere near the Letterbox!"

"You're not going to the Letterbox. The Department has a field office along the waterfront. You can get there via Hastings Street."

"But—"

"Look, if my organization can track you people so easily, do you think three angry Dullahan will have any trouble? If you head for home, they can lay a trap! If you give them the runaround, you might just make it!"

The air cracked with a sound like thunder as one of the Dullahan snapped his bone-whip above his head. Glass shattered as two more black arrows took out the Thunderbird's taillights, and Natalie gritted her teeth and stifled a howl of rage as she made the turn that Six had suggested.

There was a flash of light to Natalie's immediate left and a rush of frostbitten air flooded through the broken window. One of the Dullahan was upon them, raising his sword and making ready to split Natalie's head in two, so she hauled the wheel to the left and battered the steed with four thousand pounds of chrome. The beast stumbled, gave a frightened whinny, and staggered toward a sheer brick wall at full speed. Another flash, and the Dullahan disappeared back into the aether before it could do any real damage to itself.

Abby looked over the back seat and saw the black mass of Agent Six's Cadillac rushing up behind them. The other two Dullahan had boxed him in on either side and were battering him left and right. Six tried to give back as good as he got, but with the broken shaft of an arrow still stuck in his chest, he was obviously having more trouble. When he slammed on the brakes and left the monsters nothing to batter but each other, Abby couldn't help but cheer him on. She shut her eyes as the whinnying horses collided and sent their riders flying, unsure if watching that would count towards the Dullahan's "drop dead" enchantment.

"Gaglardi!" Natalie announced when at last she made the turn. The momentum sent Abby and the unconscious Whittaker tumbling to the floor, and she realized for the first time that her Gospel senses were still running in the background. She could hear the thunder of hooves on the pavement, the roar of the Thunderbird's and Cadillac's respective V8 engines, and the raindrops slamming against the car's body as clearly as if they were all happening an inch from her head. The noise made her head hurt and blood pool in her nostrils, but there was also something… calculated about it. Like a message in Morse code, being sounded out by the physical world around her. All those noises were words in a language that she had never bothered to study, but as she concentrated on them, she thought that it was a language she could understand nonetheless. It was a language of nature, of rivers freezing over in winter and snow falling from bare tree branches. It was the language in which the seasons would speak to each other, to tell each other that it was time to change.

It was the language of magic.

Long is the storm… Abby heard the magic say. *And long is the slumber…*

Another vengeful whinny broke her concentration. She used the front passenger's seat to pull herself up and looked in the rear-view mirror to see the first of the three Dullahan come bounding out of a frosty white portal less than eight feet behind the Thunderbird. The horse reared up on its hind legs, whinnying and snorting fire, and the rider laughed as it wound one hand through its own tangled mess of black hair, tugged, and lifted its pale, grinning head clear of its shoulders. Suddenly, Abby thought of Ichabod and Mr. Toad.

The Dullahan's eyes flashed red as the creature lobbed its head at the back of the Thunderbird. Its mouth stretched wide, unfurling a long red tentacle of a tongue that flapped in the wind. The laughing head exploded through the rear window and hit Natalie, who hit the steering wheel and sent the car skidding on the rain-washed street. Abby shrieked when the Dullahan's head rolled toward her, then she kicked open the back door and hurled the grinning thing out into the middle of the other lane. She grabbed the wheel with both hands and tried to right the Thunderbird's course, but the tires had no purchase. The big old car fishtailed, the back tires jumped up onto the wet grass, and one of the tailfins went crunch against a streetlight. A volley of black arrows found the front tire, the driver's side mirror, and the engine block, and the rusty Thunderbird died with a pathetic cough.

Looking out the back window, Abby could see the headless Dullahan approaching the Thunderbird in a slow trot, assured in his victory as he slung his bow over his shoulders. The rain turned to hail, beating down on the road like pennies from Heaven, and a thick white mist settled over the empty road. The other two Dullahan and Agent Six's black Cadillac might as well have disappeared into thin air, for all Abby knew.

"Shit," she breathed, as the Dullahan stooped in the saddle and plucked his head from the road. "What do we do now?"

Natalie groaned, wiped the blood from the long cut in her forehead, and squared her shoulders. "Only thing we can do." She looked at Abby with genuine remorse and whispered, "I'm sorry. I am so *goddamn* sorry for what I'm about to do, but we're out of options. I promise, I will explain everything when I get the chance. If I get the chance."

Reaching under her seat, she extracted a machete in a battered leather sheath, a small pistol-grip crossbow, and enough spare bolts to fell a family of deer. "Whatever you do, don't follow me." Then she stepped out of the car and called out, "Hey! Gruesome! If you and your pals want a target, why don't you pick on me, huh? I've been ducking calls from your boss for a lot of years now!" Before the Dullahan could respond, Natalie raised and fired the little crossbow. When the bolt hit the faerie's sternum, its iron head exploded in white fire, and the creature uttered a hiss of pain. Natalie sprinted across the road, leaped into the trees along the shoulder, and began shouting derogatory comments about the Dullahan's mother. The faerie gritted its teeth, dug in its spurs, and raced after her before disappearing in a flash of white light.

Abby bent low and smacked Whittaker on the cheek, pleading with him to wake up. She could hear Natalie raving like a crazy woman as she tried to get herself lost in the woods, could hear the hail pelting the car, could hear the thunder of hooves as the other two Dullahan approached the dead vehicle. Her nose was bleeding freely by now, her ears were ringing and stinging from the cold, and the world around her was screaming at her in the language of the seasons and the rivers and the snow.

Long is the winter, it said. *And long is the Hunt. And long is the night in Carcosa.*

"Come on, Whittaker! Come on, come on!" She sniffed blood down into the back of her throat, winced as a needle of pain worked its way in between her eyes, and tried to shut out the magic.

Long is the storm, said the magic. *And long is the slumber. But longer still is the wrath of…*

CHAPTER 6

GWYN

THE HARVESTER. The Pale Rider. The First Lord of The Hunt. The King-Among-the-Holly had many names, and over the long years of her subsequent acquaintance with him, Abby would come to know them all. Eventually, she would even devise some new ones herself. But in those few anxious moments that she spent kneeling in a dead car on a hail-beaten stretch of Gaglardi Way, there was only one name running through her mind.

Gwyn. Gwyn. Gwyn.

It was in the sound of the hailstones upon the roof of the car. It was in the hoofbeats of the Dullahan's mounts upon the blacktop. It was in the angry, ineffective smack of her palm against Whittaker's unconscious cheek. *Gwyn* was the word on nature's lips in that moment, and as her mind shouted that word in time with the beat of her heart, she could feel a pair of cold blue eyes staring down at her. As she tried not to collapse beneath the weight of that invisible, sub-zero gaze, the hoofbeats outside the Thunderbird slowed to a leisurely trot, and then to nothing at all. Abby shut her eyes tightly and lowered her head as the back door opened and two groping, spidery hands seized her by the shoulders and dragged her out onto the road. She felt the burlap sack being lowered over her head and the short length of bone-whip that the faeries used to bind her hands behind her back.

She was vaguely aware that Simon was saying something to her over the Vokarion relay, trying to give her some advice about how best to stay calm and talk to the Fair Folk when they were this pissed off, but he was cut off when one of the Dullahan pulled the crystal off from around her neck. But she wouldn't have heard him anyway. The only noise that got through to her above the ringing in her ears was *Gwyn. Gwyn. Gwyn.*

They threw her over the back of one of the horses as if she were a saddle blanket. Then the Dullahan snapped the reins and shouted a command in its own language, and the stallion broke into a swift gallop. With a gun to her head, Abby would not have been able to say whether the ride lasted for ten seconds or ten hours. All she knew was that, at some point during the journey, the wind picked up again and the hail turned to flurries of wet and stinging snow. The sound of the horses' hooves, first upon the bare concrete and then crunching through the deepening snow, was *Gwyn, Gwyn, Gwyn* the whole way up. And Abby felt instinctively that up was the right word, as the air around her seemed to be getting marginally thinner and much colder.

They came to a stop at the top of the mountain, smack in the middle of the Simon Fraser University campus. With the burlap sack still covering her head, Abby was pulled off the back of the horse and dropped roughly on her knees upon solid concrete covered with an inch-thick cushion of snow. When one of the faeries removed the sack, the first thing that she noticed was Agent Six kneeling on her right side, sporting a split lip, a livid bruise over one eye, and a large bloodstain where the Dullahan's arrow had struck him. On her left was Whittaker, now fully conscious and with a look in his eyes like he was two seconds away from shitting himself. Their wrists, like hers, were bound behind them, and Abby risked a look at the being whose party this now undoubtedly was.

The King-Among-the-Holly was wrapped in a cloak as black as the night, over top the blood-stained leathers of a master hunter. He held a scythe taller than he was, with an ebony handle and a blade of pure silver. A blast of wind whipped lank black hair across his bone-white face, giving Abby the impression of the moon emerging from behind a patch of storm clouds. He glided down the steps like a rolling mist, neither breathing nor blinking, and making no more sound than a bobcat slinking through a snowdrift. As he drew near, Abby was transfixed by his eyes: they were like two burning neutron stars plucked from the black void of the cosmos and placed in a haunting death mask of a face.

Gwyn ab Nethe, the King-Among-the-Holly, set his neutron-star gaze upon the taller of the two Dullahan, who flanked the prisoners with their broadswords drawn. "EXPLAIN." His voice announced a journey's end, perhaps *every* journey's end. The clouds, the wind, and the snow all seemed to react to it, and the Dullahan bowed their heads in reverence. So did Whittaker. Abby caught Six's eye and silently signalled to him that it would be a really good idea if they did the same.

Head still bowed, the knight to whom the King had spoken offered this explanation: "This woman and her companions were at the scene of the *Ci*'s last hunt, O Great Gwyn. This fugitive," and here he paused to let his blade kiss Whittaker's neck, "was among them. There was also... a grave-walker." He spat out the last word like it was the foulest epithet he could think of. Something in Gwyn ab Nethe's face twitched, and the subsequent thunderclap rattled Abby's teeth.

"When we attempted to interrogate them, they attacked us," the Dullahan continued. "They ran like hares. The grave-walker fled, and Owain ab Gwylem hunts it even now."

The King-Among-the-Holly considered this intelligence for a moment and then looked down at the prisoners kneeling before him. "DOES TARACH AB TELG SPEAK TRUTHFULLY?" he asked. "DID YOU ATTACK MY CAVALRY IN THE COURSE OF THEIR DUTY?" Abby and Agent Six exchanged a few uncertain glances but said nothing. It could be deadly to say as much as one wrong word to a faerie that was in a bad mood. Whittaker, for his part, could make no sound beyond a few wet hiccups, and Abby didn't think his infamous fast talk would be any help here.

"WILL NONE OF YOU SPEAK?" asked the King. "ARE YOUR TONGUES FALLEN FROM YOUR HEADS?" The snow swirling around him suddenly cohered into six long-fingered hands that seized the three captives by their hair and forced their jaws apart. The King, satisfied that they had not been rendered mute by a blade, bared his pointed teeth in what might have been a smile. "NO, INDEED. SO: WHICH OF YOU WILL ANSWER THESE CHARGES? WHO WILL SPEAK FOR THE ACCUSED?"

As the hands groping her face dissolved back into flurries, Abby looked up at the Father of Winter. "I will answer, O King. And I will tell you that this is a misunderstanding. We never meant to attack the Dullahan. We never meant to run from them. But they set upon us so fast that we didn't have a choice. We were scared. We still are. And part of that is… well… frankly, we don't have a goddamn clue what's going on here."

"We misunderstand nothing!" snapped the shorter Dullahan. "Humans! Grave-walkers! Men of Oak! Conspiring at the scene of the crime! Your Majesty, these people know what happened to the *Ci*, and with your blessing, I will force the information from them!"

The King raised his hand for silence. "YOU FORGET YOUR PLACE, PADRAIC AB GALLETH. DO NOT PRESUME TO SPEAK FOR YOUR KING. IF THERE IS A CONSPIRACY HERE, I SHALL FIND IT."

"I—I apologize, Your Majesty. I did not mean to offend."

The King nodded, mollified by this. He looked down at Abby and asked, "BY WHAT NAMES ARE YOU CALLED, GIRL? WHAT IS YOUR LINEAGE? BY WHAT DEEDS MAY WE KNOW YOU?"

Those were the magic words. Abby squared her shoulders, looked the King in his neutron stars, and announced herself in the manner typical of the ancients. "I am Abigail Margaret Henderson, daughter of Donald and Karen. On Steam, I am called WestVanWitch. On Discord, I am OracleInTheAM. I have faced the Cult of the Following and survived. I have walked in spaces where the laws of Earthly physics meant less than nothing, and I have come out the other side. I have survived attacks by mad sorcerers, necromancing ghosts, and one very pissed-off old Southerner. Oh, and my blog has been liked and shared almost a million times. I am Abby Normal, and my lineage is that of the Gospels."

That sent a stir through the courtiers from Carcosa. The Dullahan hissed and their fingers twitched on the hilts of their swords. The King tilted his head to one side, as if appraising Abby anew. "YOU SPEAK WITH CONVICTION FOR ONE SO YOUNG. AND WE HAVE HEARD TELL IN MY LANDS OF A GOSPEL-CHILD WHO STOOD AGAINST THE CULT OF THE FOLLOWING. WHO HALTED AN ENLIGHTENING RITUAL AND AVERTED A NEW WAR WITH THE UNDERLANDS."

"Then you have heard tell of me," Abby said bluntly.

"WE HAVE ALSO HEARD TELL," the King continued, and here his tone became more threatening, "OF A GOSPEL-CHILD WHO ALLIES HERSELF WITH A VANGUARD OATH-BREAKER! A GRAVE-WALKER WHOSE CONSCIOUSNESS IS FUELLED BY DARK MAGICKS THAT DEFY OUR VERY WILL! A COURTIER OF OAK WHO KNOWS NO OATH AND DEFIES ANY WILL AS IT SUITS HIM!" He glided closer and hooked the scythe's blade around the back of Abby's neck. "YOUR LINEAGE DOES YOU CREDIT, ABIGAIL CULT-BREAKER, BUT YOUR CHOICE OF ALLIES IS POOR. YOU HAVE WALKED IN OUR LANDS. YOU WILL KNOW THAT ROBYN AB GODFELWE IS A FUGITIVE FROM OUR JUSTICE. TO CONCEAL AN

ENEMY OF HOLLY AS YOU HAVE DONE IS A CRIME WITH ONLY ONE PUNISHMENT."

Lightning framed Gwyn ab Nethe's dark form as he raised his free hand to the sky. Behind her, Abby heard the hissing breath of the two Dullahan as their silver blades rasped against the concrete and came to rest one apiece against each side of Whittaker's neck. The imp hiccupped and gasped and coughed in wordless panic, and then he screamed, in a perfect imitation of Abby's own voice, "Karen Henderson wasn't perfect!"

Dead silence. The King-Among-the-Holly raised an eyebrow and motioned for the Dullahan to lower their blades. Whittaker's lips were still moving, and the voice that emerged from his mouth was still, somehow, Abby's.

"My mom made some mistakes," said Whittaker in Abby's voice. "If I'm being honest, some of them were pretty big mistakes. I'm still unpacking some of them, and I think I will be for a while. But she always tried to do the right thing."

"What are these words?" hissed the Dullahan called Padraic ab Galleth. "Explain what this means!"

"They're… my words," Abby realized. In the shock of hearing her own voice parroted back at her from another mouth, it had taken her some time to fully process what Whittaker was actually saying. He was repeating the opening lines of the eulogy that Abby had written for her mother's funeral.

When Kelly Munro had been Whittaker's prisoner the previous year, Abby had been ready to give up anything to free her. Ultimately, Whittaker had claimed the eulogy that Abby had written for her mother as his only payment. But to a faerie like him, that was an invaluable prize. The words that he now spoke were words that originally came from Abby's heart, that revealed her innermost self. There was magic in such heartfelt words, and the Fair Folk had known for thousands of years how to take the magic of a heart's words and use it against the heart that spoke them. But so far, Whittaker had never pulled that trigger. Until tonight, he had hardly so much as mentioned it. And now she knew why. Robin Whittaker, son of Goodfellow, was a small fish in a big ocean as far as the Fair Folk went. And if he wanted to avoid getting eaten, well, there was no better bargaining chip than the heart's words of the Last of the Gospels.

The imp cleared his throat. In his own voice, he said, "The Cult-Breaker has given me her heart's words, O Great Gwyn. I have used that power over her to barter for protection from the justice of the Courts. That's why she has concealed me from your sight for so long."

"He lies!" hissed Padraic ab Galleth. "Surely he does, my liege! The word of this creature cannot be trusted!"

"Right breast pocket," said Whittaker. "Her heart's words, next to my own heart."

Once more, the swirling snow coalesced into those spidery hands. They unbuttoned Whittaker's suit jacket for him and went searching in the inner pocket. A crack of thunder was the soundtrack to the scramble of emotions—surprise, excitement, and perhaps even respect for Whittaker's cunning—that danced across Gwyn ab Nethe's face as they found what they were after.

The King-Among-the-Holly extended one hand to the snow. The wintry fingers deposited the little stack of index cards, bound with a single green paper clip, in the King's open palm. A cold, sharp smile played at the corners of his face.

"YOU INTRIGUE ME, ROBIN, SON OF GOODFELLOW. IT IS RARE GUILE THAT CAN WIN SO GRAND A PRIZE FROM A GOSPEL."

Whittaker's eyes darted from Gwyn to Abby to Gwyn again. Then, in a display of the kind of humility that she had never seen from him, he lowered his head and said, "It is a prize of which I am unworthy, O Great Gwyn. I know its worth to be beyond the hoards of all the Dragon-Lords of Ardenne, and that is a weight upon my heart, for I am low in the Courts' esteem. I would that this prize went to one who can match its grandeur." He looked up at the King-Among-the-Holly with eyes full of the most pitiable, fawning obeisance.

The King's smile widened. "YOU WOULD THAT THIS PRIZE WENT TO ME. AND WHAT, I WONDER, WOULD YOU ASK IN RETURN?"

"Only my life, and the life of Abigail Cult-Breaker. You can do what you want with Chuckles over there." He looked across Abby to shoot a nasty look at Agent Six.

Abby didn't know whether she wanted to kiss Whittaker or strangle him. If this worked, then the imp would have just saved her life. Probably Simon's as well, since it was actually him who'd been keeping Whittaker safe in exchange for a few favours. In order to keep Holly's attention off Abby and Simon, the imp was taking on more blame than he deserved. But he'd be saving her by trading the devil she knew for the devil she didn't. This was the Dead Man's Pledge all over again.

"YOU WOULD THAT I SPARED THIS CHILD BESIDES YOURSELF? DO YOU HAVE... AFFECTION FOR THIS GIRL?"

"Is she not more useful alive than dead? I mean, if we're talking heart's words and all. Kill her, and her ghost goes to the Halls of the Dead in Carcosa. But leave her alive, and now you have an agent in the human world. Someone who can cross the barriers between the Nocturn, the Elsewhere, and the mundane spaces of the Mid-lands. Dead, the Cult-Breaker shall be just another bygone soul riding in the ranks of The Hunt. Alive, she'll be influence. Information. The hand of God in the mortal realm."

Thunder rolled across the sky as Gwyn ab Nethe closed his fingers around the index cards. "YOUR FLATTERING WORDS DO NOT BECOME YOU, O ROBIN, GOODFELLOW'S SON. THE MOST HONEYED WORDS THAT ENTER A KING'S EAR OFT BELIE THE FALSEST OF TONGUES. BUT THE GRAVITY OF THIS PRIZE CANNOT BE OVERLOOKED. IT IS A JUST PRICE FOR YOUR LIVES." A flurry of snow blew up around the King. The index cards crushed in his fist became delicate ice crystals that were carried away on the northern wind. But whatever relief Abby felt quickly withered and died, as the scythe inched forward again and the back of her neck stung with the sensation of splitting epidermis.

"BUT THIS IS RECOMPENSE FOR ONE CRIME ONLY," said the King. "THE CULT-BBREAKER STILL HAS MUCH ELSE TO ANSWER FOR. ATTACKING MY CAVALRY. CONSPIRING WITH A GRAVE-WALKER. LEARNING AT THE FEET OF THE VANGUARD *WÆRLOGA*. IF YOU STAND WITH THE ENEMIES OF HOLLY, ABIGAIL, DONALD'S DAUGHTER, THEN IT IS HOLLY OF WHOM YOU MAKE AN ENEMY."

Abby tried her damnedest not to move her head or neck. Through chattering teeth, she forced out the words, "What would you have me do then, O King? How may I convince you that I am not your enemy?"

The King smiled. "IF IT IS MERCY THAT YOU SEEK, THEN YOU WILL TELL ME YOUR STORY. YOU WILL TELL ME WHY YOU WERE TRACKING MY *CI*. YOU WILL TELL ME WHY YOU ATTACKED AND THEN RAN FROM MY DULLAHAN. AND IF I SUSPECT ANY FALSEHOOD IN YOUR NARRATIVE, THEN YOU SHALL KNOW THE WRATH OF CARCOSA AS FEW MORTALS HAVE DONE SINCE THE LAST GREAT WAR. I SHALL NOT DESTROY SUCH A VALUABLE PRIZE AS ROBIN, SON OF GOODFELLOW, HAS OFFERED ME, BUT IF YOU SPEAK FALSELY TO ME, YOU SHALL WISH I HAD."

So, Abby told him. She started from the dream she'd had the previous night and worked her way forward. As a means of both setting the record straight and rubbing salt in the Ministry of Uncommon Knowledge's wounds, she made it very, very clear that Agent Fourteen had been the first one to fire on the Dullahan. "And these men are no allies of mine. They did not take action in accordance with anything I said or did, and I will not be held responsible for them."

The King dug his scythe in a little harder, and Abby felt the first trickle of blood snake down the back of her neck. "HAVE CARE HOW YOU PROCEED, CULT-BREAKER. I WILL DECIDE

WHO BEARS WHAT RESPONSIBILITY. DO NOT PRESUME TO TELL ME OTHERWISE."

"Of course," Abby said in a smaller, more backpedal-y voice. "I apologize, O King. I misspoke. I did not mean to question your most noble judgement."

The King nodded. "SO: YOU RECEIVED A VISION OF MY *CI* ON THE HUNT. AND YOU ELECTED TO TRACK IT. WHY?"

"Before I answer, may I ask for clarification? I'm afraid I don't understand what you mean by *Ci*. I guess that is your word for the creature, but I'm not a hundred percent."

"IN YOUR LANGUAGE, YOU MIGHT SAY 'HOUND.' A VULGAR MIND WOULD CHOOSE THE WORD 'DOG.' *CI* SIGNIFIES ONE OF THE SACRED HOUNDS OF CARCOSA, WHO RUN AT THE SIDE OF THE ROYAL COURT WHEN WE RIDE OUT UPON THE HUNT."

"I chose to track your *Ci*," she said slowly, "because I needed to understand." She had to choose her words carefully here, but she was becoming ever more aware of the bite of the scythe on her neck, the numbing cold at her fingertips, the sensation of her bladder filling as her anxiety spiked. "I saw it hurting people in my city. From what I could tell, some of them were innocent people. I needed to know why this was happening, and if there was something I could do about it. I never want to see magic hurting anyone in my city. I am sorry if we have stuck our noses into something that we should not have. But we had no way of knowing about Holly's interest in this. We were merely trying to protect innocent lives."

It was a long moment before Gwyn spoke again. By the end of it, Abby had lost all feeling in her fingers and she had to pee worse than ever before in her life. Her teeth wanted to chatter and she was clenching her jaw tight so that the motion would not draw her neck any closer to the blade of the scythe. But at last, the King nodded and moved the scythe away from her flesh by half a centimetre. To Abby's frozen, anxiety-racked brain, it seemed as good as a hug and a toast to her health.

"YOUR WORDS... HAVE THE RING OF TRUTH. IT WAS NOT MALICE THAT SET YOU AGAINST MY DULLAHAN THIS NIGHT BUT IGNORANCE OF HOLLY AND ITS WAYS. YET IGNORANCE OF SIN CANNOT ABSOLVE THE SIN ITSELF. YOU HAVE CONSPIRED WITH HOLLY'S ENEMIES. YOU HAVE TAKEN HOSTILE ACTION AGAINST MY KNIGHTS WHILE THEY RODE ON MY ORDERS. WE HAVE BEEN SHOWN DISHONOUR. FOR THIS, THERE MUST BE RECOMPENSE."

"We shall take the grave-walker!" cried Padraic ab Galleth. "She is hunted even now! When Owain ab Gwylem finds her, we shall strip the flesh from her bones and seal her skull in the blackest catacombs of Carcosa! If this woman calls that foul beast a friend, then it shall be a just price for her to watch the creature's destruction!"

Again, the King raised a hand for silence. "THAT BEAST HAS ESCAPED MY GAZE FOR MANY A LONG WINTER. HER DESTRUCTION WOULD BE JUST, BUT IT MUST BE WEIGHED AGAINST THE FULL EXTENT OF HER OWN CRIMES AGAINST HOLLY. TO REDUCE HER TO A MERE PAYMENT FOR THE ACTIONS OF THE GOSPEL-CHILD WOULD LEAVE THE ACCOUNTS UNBALANCED."

"What more would you ask of me, O King?" said Abby. "You have my heart's words from Robyn ab Godfelwe. There is no greater payment I can offer Your Majesty."

The King-Among-the-Holly considered his response for a long moment. Then he said, "*ANOETHAU*."

Behind her, the two Dullahan laughed in high, icy tones that brought her out in goosebumps all over. "*Anoethau*! *Anoethau*!" they jeered. "Let the Cult-Breaker find the *Ci*!"

Abby gulped. "I—I'm sorry, O King... I think you've lost me again. I don't understand what you want."

"YOU SAY YOU WISH TO KNOW WHY MY *CI* ATTACKED THE INNOCENTS OF YOUR CITY. DO YOU STAND BEHIND THIS CLAIM, ABIGAIL CULT-BREAKER?"

She gulped again. Perhaps it was against her better judgement, but she did. And she said so.

"THE CAUSE OF YOUR VISIONS IS TREACHERY!" roared Gwyn ab Nethe. "MY *CI*—ONE OF MY SACRED HOUNDS—IS STOLEN

FROM ME! STOLEN BY HUMANS AND SET AGAINST THOSE WHO HAVE OFFERED HOLLY NO INSULT, WHO HAVE NO VALUE AS PREY! I HAVE SENSED IT, YET I DO NOT KNOW HOW IT HAS HAPPENED." The wind roared around him as he spoke and the snow blew into her eyes.

"And, uh, I'm guessing that's not how that's supposed to work?" she stammered.

"THE *CŴN ANNWN* ARE NOT WILD BEASTS. THEY TAKE PREY ONLY WHEN I COMMAND IT. BUT SOMEONE HAS USURPED MY CONTROL." Thunder cracked. The ground shook. The night itself gave voice to the King's fury. "BY DOING THIS, SOMEONE HAS COMMITTED THE GRAVEST SACRILEGE. AN OFFENCE SO DIRE, A CRIME SO FOUL, THAT IT HAS NO NAME IN MY LANGUAGE OR YOURS."

"A-and you th-think it was… humans who did this?" Abby squeaked.

"THE STINK OF HUMAN FESTERS IN MY NOSTRILS EVERY TIME I TURN MY SIGHT TOWARD THIS SACRILEGE. HUMANS HAVE DONE THIS. HUMANS IN 'YOUR CITY.' OF THIS, I AM CERTAIN."

Abby understood now. Simon had once told her that in centuries past, it had been the custom of the Fair Folk—ever proud and quick to anger—to force human beings who offended them to complete *anoethau*: elaborate and damn near impossible tests of strength or skill. Completing anoethau would get a person off the hook for whatever crime they were perceived as having committed against the faeries. Failing, on the other hand…

"MY KNIGHTS HAVE SEARCHED THIS CITY FROM ONE END TO THE OTHER," said Gwyn ab Nethe, "AND THEY HAVE FOUND NOTHING. YOU KNOW THIS CITY, CULT-BREAKER. YOU KNOW BETTER THAN WE HOW THE TREACHEROUS HUMAN MIND THINKS. YOU SEE THAT WHICH OTHERS DO NOT. YOU SHALL FIND MY *CI* AND BRING TO ME THE CRIMINALS WHO STOLE IT. IF YOU DO THIS, THEN NEITHER YOU NOR YOUR CITY SHALL ANSWER TO HOLLY'S JUSTICE."

Abby's blood ran cold. "Wait, waitwaitwait. What was that last part?"

"MY *CI* IS HERE, AND SO IS THE THIEF. SO LONG AS THIS CITY HIDES THE WAGES OF SIN FROM ME, THEN IT IS THIS CITY THAT HAS SINNED AGAINST ME." Using the flat of the scythe blade, he tilted Abby's chin up until their eyes met. As those neutron stars burned into her, her brain screamed at her to look away. Her nose bled and bile burned the back of her throat.

"THIS IS AN ACT OF WAR AGAINST THE HEART OF HOLLY ITSELF. WERE WE STILL IN THE AGE OF THE OLD KINGS, MY ARMIES WOULD BE RIDING UPON THIS CITY EVEN NOW. WE WOULD PUT EVERY MAN, WOMAN, AND CHILD TO THE BLADE UNTIL MY *CI* WAS RECOVERED, AND WE WOULD BURY THIS LAND IN A WINTER THAT WOULD LAST A THOUSAND YEARS."

"But—there's—there's two million people in Vancouver! You can't destroy two million innocent lives to punish one guilty one!"

"CAN'T? CHILD, YOU KNOW NOT TO WHOM YOU SPEAK." A distant flash of lightning illuminated the stark concrete at the edges of the quad. In the booming thunder that followed, there was an oath.

"I AM HE WHO WAITS IN THE NAMELESS CITY," whispered the wind.

"I AM HE WHO REAPS THE HARVEST IN BITTEREST WIND AND DEEPEST FREEZE," hissed the snows.

"I AM THE BRINGER OF FROST, THE FATHER OF SNOW AND SLEET," bellowed the thunderclouds.

"I AM DEATH," growled Gwyn ab Nethe. "AND THIS IS MY JUDGEMENT. THE HUNT SHALL NOT COME TOGETHER AGAIN UNTIL *NOS GALAN GAEAF*. WHAT YOU WOULD CALL ALL HALLOWS' EVE. BUT I SHALL NOT RIDE WITHOUT THE FULL CONTINGENT OF MY *CŴN ANNWN*. YOU, ABIGAIL CULT-BREAKER, SHALL RETURN TO ME WHAT HAS BEEN STOLEN. YOU SHALL BRING ME THE GUILTY PARTIES, THAT I MAY DISPENSE A KING'S JUSTICE. DO ALL THIS BEFORE THE SETTING OF THE SUN ON *NOS GALAN GAEAF*, AND YOUR PAST SINS WILL BE FORGOTTEN.

FAIL IN THIS TASK, AND THE FIRST SIGHT YOU SEE WITH THE DAWN SHALL BE MY ARMY CRESTING THE HORIZON, TO BRING A THOUSAND YEARS OF THE BLEAKEST CARCOSAN WINTER UPON 'YOUR CITY.' THAT SHALL BALANCE THE ACCOUNTS."

Abby looked helplessly around the quad, first to Six, then to Whittaker, then to the Vokarion crystal—her one link to Simon, the man with all the answers—dangling from the cold hand of Padraic ab Galleth. Whatever choice she made now, it would be the wrong choice. And she was the only one who *could* make it. She found herself thinking of her mother, kneeling at the feet of the Deacon twenty-six autumns past. Was this all that it took to consign one's fate to the mad gods of old?

The King-Among-the-Holly leaned upon his scythe. "Do you accept these terms, Cult-Breaker?"

She lowered her head, shut her eyes, and whispered, "I do."

CHAPTER 7

... AND INTO THE FIRE

IT HAD all happened so fast after that. The Dullahan had cut Abby's bonds, she had shaken the King's icy hand, and a chill like nothing she could ever describe had surged up from the tips of her numb toes up to her stinging, watering eyeballs. Her hand burned, her head screamed, and when the King finally allowed her to break the handshake, she felt ice crystals burrowing beneath her skin, etching the image of a sprig of holly into her bare palm. Now, two hours later, as Mother Hyld applied all her craft back in the safety of the Letterbox, those ice crystals still would not melt. Abby knew that they'd be there until she either found the King's hound or watched as her home disappeared beneath the snow.

"It is an ill wind that blows this night," murmured Mother Hyld as she completed her inspection. "These wounds will heal, but we shall all feel their ache for many a long winter."

Whittaker rolled his eyes and massaged his sore forearm. "Thanks, lady. I could have told you that for free two hours ago. You see, folks, this is why, when you're standing in the middle of a faerie ring, and a faerie tells you to run for the hills, you *run for the fucking hills*. You don't stand around with one thumb shoved up your ass, trying to shoot the messenger full of cold iron!" He fired a venomous look at Agent Six, whose face revealed nothing.

It had surprised everyone when Gwyn ab Nethe consented to let Six walk free, but the King seemed to understand that the Ministry of Uncommon Knowledge answered to the Crown. According to Gwyn's logic, that made Six a knight of equal standing with the Dullahan. He judged that Agent Six had not fired the first shots, but had watched his partner die and had responded as a soldier would have. In his own way, Six had been trying to bring Holly's enemies to justice, and for that reason Holly had no quarrel with him. "LET NO MAN SAY YOU ACTED WITH DISHONOUR, O KNIGHT OF THE REALM," Gwyn had said to six. "YOU HAVE PAID YOUR DUE IN BLOOD, AS A WARRIOR MUST."

Leanne, press-ganged into service as an extra set of hands for Mother Hyld, was distributing mugs of hot herbal tea and keeping her nose well out of something she knew she could only understand a fraction of. But when Whittaker started in on the others, she set his mug down harder than she needed to and said, "I know we're all scared right now, Whittaker. God knows we have the right to be. But lashing out at people who are just trying to help isn't going to solve anything."

"Oh, isn't it?" the imp said in a wide-eyed tone of mock-surprise. "Is it not going to solve anything? I'll tell you what won't solve anything, Glasses." He jabbed a finger at Abby and snapped, "Little Miss 'I Love a Mystery' over here shoving her nose in the Goddamn King-Among-the-Goddamn-Holly's dirty laundry! It was bad enough when we were *just* running straight at a living weapon. Now, we're running straight at a living weapon *and* we've got Holly waiting for us to screw up so they have an excuse to get the knives out."

Leanne squeezed the imp's outstretched finger and turned it back on him. "First of all," she hissed, "my name is Leanne. Second of all, don't raise your voice at me. Thirdly, I was watching Simon's Vokarion-cam the whole time. Let's not forget who it was that traded my girlfriend's soul to the Court-Among-the-Holly to save his own rotten skin, okay?"

"You think I liked doing that? That was the biggest gamble I ever took in my life! And if I hadn't done what I did, you wouldn't even *have* a girlfriend right now. Or a Vanguard, or a Whittaker! So a little appreciation wouldn't be too much to ask."

"What, now you want a medal? Do you even realize how big a target you just put on her back?"

"If we'd run when I said we should run, I wouldn't have had to put that target on her back! And the only reason we didn't run when we should have is because some idiot with a badge went and shot me!" The imp broke free of Leanne's grasp, straightened his tie, and looked at Abby. "This is what happens when you play the hero, chickadee. You can talk all you want about protecting people and doing what's right, but if you try to protect everyone from every single nasty in the shadows, eventually you're going to mess with something that you shouldn't have messed with." He paused for a breath, and some of the anger left his voice. "I've known your family for a lot of years, Normal. I've seen them go down this road before. Don't make the same mistake your mom did."

Abby choked on her tea and slammed her mug down on the table. "What do you want from me, Whittaker? I'm the Last of the Gospels, for Christ's sake. The Gospels were worth their magical weight in gold even back when there were thousands of them, and now there's only this dumb bitch left!" She was on her feet, stomping toward him. She didn't remember deciding to do either. "Sure, maybe I play the hero sometimes. But only because I actually have the fucking capacity to understand that other people's lives matter! And if I can't try to help them when shit goes down, then what the fuck am I supposed to do? What's the point of these stupid powers? Is it to do what the Following wanted? To be the match on the fire that burns reality to a cinder? Because I need my life to mean more than that! After all the shit I've been through, I need this all to mean something!"

"*Enough,*" said Simon. "Leanne's right: we won't get anywhere by shouting at each other. The fact of the matter is that we have accomplished what we set out to do tonight. The *anoeth* notwithstanding, Abby's meeting with the King-Among-the-Holly has provided us with more information about the creature responsible for last night's attacks. If we use our time wisely, we may yet be able to find it before it kills again. All Hallows' Eve is nearly a month away, but there's no better time than now to start planning our next move." He turned to Agent Six. "The Ministry of Uncommon Knowledge seem quite keen to sew this up. What's your perspective on the death of Ted Purdy, if you don't mind my asking?"

Six shook his head. "I'm not at liberty to reveal that. Need-to-know basis."

"Oh, I'm afraid we're well past 'need-to-know basis,' Agent Six. I heard you on the Vokarion relay. If all that talk about finding common ground ever meant anything, then I will kindly ask you to—what was it you said? Cut the bullshit. Tell us what we *need to know*."

It was a long moment before Six spoke again. "To be clear: what I'm about to say does not leave this room. We never had this conversation, and I was never even here. Do you understand?"

Everyone nodded their agreement. Six nodded back and then said, "Are any of you familiar with the name Jack Kang?"

"He was a city councillor," said Leanne. "Used to be a big deal in the provincial NDP, then switched to local politics about five years ago. Did a lot of work in the Downtown Eastside. Wasn't he killed a few months ago?"

"You've done your homework, Miss Waller. I respect that."

Leanne shrugged. "I like to think of myself as an informed citizen."

"Your information is good. This past May, Jack Kang was found dead of blunt force trauma to the head, not far from Oppenheimer Park. The VPD never made any arrests, and officially the case is still open."

"And what does this have to do with the Ministry of Uncommon Knowledge?" asked Simon. "It all sounds quite mundane to me."

"Jack Kang had been a person of interest to us for some time before his death. He had multiple contacts in the local Nocturn—some of them not exactly model citizens. The Department thought it prudent to keep tabs on him."

Abby scoffed. "You mean like how the FBI 'kept tabs' on MLK?"

Six ignored the barb. "Shortly after Mr. Kang's death, our agents took a look at his bank records. For the better part of two years, he'd been making regular payments to one Edward Alan Purdy, a small-time hood with multiple connections in the magical and mundane underworlds."

"Human?" Simon asked.

"In and out of the foster system for most of his youth," Six replied, "but human so far as we could tell, and definitely in the know. We spent months trying to determine what the exact nature of Mr. Kang's and Mr. Purdy's relationship was, and we were getting close."

"Until Ted Purdy got his throat ripped out last night," Whittaker surmised. "And I'm guessing you don't think that's a coincidence."

"No. The Department's official stance is that there is—was—a connection between Jack Kang and Ted Purdy, the exact nature of which we have yet to determine. Gwyn ab Nethe said that his hounds don't kill at random. That means somebody stole one of them from Carcosa and deliberately sicced it on Ted Purdy. And *that* makes two murders of two men who were known to each other and each had connections in the local Nocturn in less than five months."

"Well, that's a pretty good starting point, isn't it?" said Leanne. "If we find out what Jack Kang had to do with Ted Purdy, then maybe we find out if they had any enemies in common. Maybe we find out who threw Ted Purdy to the wolves. Uh, so to speak."

"It's an angle worth exploring," Simon replied. "But there are others we can look into at the same time. The King blames humans for this theft, which raises several questions in itself. To my knowledge, no living human has entered Carcosa for at least three centuries. And if any human incursions have gone unreported, then the perpetrators certainly wouldn't have made it back from there. The security is far too tight."

"Maybe there was an inside man," Abby suggested. "Or an inside faerie or whatever. Someone on that side could have let humans into the city to do the actual deed, cause a literal stink, and put the Court on a false trail."

"Such was my thinking." He turned to Whittaker and said, "I want you to pursue that angle."

Whittaker shook his head and backed toward the door. "Oh, no, no, no. I'm not wading any deeper into this shit-heap. You're going to have to find yourself another chump, because I'm drawing the line this time."

"Whittaker, we can't simply ask for another audience with the King or walk into Carcosa to view the crime scene for ourselves. The Court would never allow it, and frankly most of them are so xenophobic that I doubt they'd even consider it possible for one of their own to work with humans against the King. You have connections in Oak, Holly, and the mortal world, so if actors from multiple realms did in fact cooperate to commit this theft, then you more than anyone should be able to tease out the truth. And don't forget: you've bought mercy from one Court, but that still leaves half of Faerie that wants you dead. If you are unwilling to cooperate, then I will be more than happy to serve you up to them. Or I could simply turn you out on the street and let you try your luck against the *Ci Annwn*."

Whittaker flinched and ground his teeth together. "I'll see what I can do."

"Thank you." He turned back to Agent Six. "As for you… it seems the Ministry's information may also be useful in this matter. Can we rely on your support, Agent Six?"

"Officially, I cannot agree to that in *any* capacity," said Six. Then he dropped the façade a little. "Unofficially… my partner just had his head cut off, we still don't know where your zombie is, and a pagan god of winter has delivered an ultimatum against the entire Metro region. I can't make any promises, but if you need my support in this, I will do what I can to supply you with the information you'll need, and I'll try to keep my colleagues from interfering. But I'll also need something from you, Miss Henderson."

She crossed her arms. "Like what?"

"I need to know that this investigation will be kept quiet. That means not a word about the Court-Among-the-Holly or the *Cŵn Annwn* goes on your blog."

"We have to warn people this thing is—"

"My orders were to shut your operation down completely. I'm doing you a favour by letting you carry on at all. But you have to be careful, or the Department's going to figure out that I disobeyed orders, and then they won't think twice about wiping both our memories and shipping our asses to a black site in northern Saskatchewan. You find this hound, but you do it quietly, and you check in with me every forty-eight hours to debrief."

"Forget it! I'm not your puppet, Six."

"I'm not asking you to be. I'm asking to be kept abreast of your activities so I can protect you and your friends from my colleagues. I have to make a report on what happened tonight. When the Department learns that Fourteen was killed by the Court, they'll send in reinforcements. That's standard procedure after a Category Five. The only way I can keep you out of their path is if you cooperate with me."

Dammit. This was just her night for deals with the Devil, wasn't it? "Fine. But I'm going to go where the trail takes me, not where you tell me to go. You got a problem with how I work, you take it up with the King-Among-the-Holly. Oh, and I want the Webley back. Family heirloom, you know?"

"The gun's already logged as evidence, but I will see what I can do."

"Good." She sipped her tea and let it burn for a second before swallowing. "Now go make your damn report. We need some time to think here."

CHAPTER 8

MONSTERS IN THE CLOSET

BY MIDNIGHT, Natalie had still not returned to the Letterbox, and things were starting to get tense. Agent Six had returned to the field office; Whittaker had gone off to sulk somewhere so far into the dark depths of the Letterbox that no one could find him; Simon and Leanne were hunkered down in the library and studying every text they could find on the Court-Among-the-Holly and the *Cŵn Annwn*; and Abby was curled up on one of the threadbare armchairs in the octagonal front lounge, conversing with the spectre of her late mother.

"Did I do the right thing?" she asked.

"I don't know," said Karen. "Did you?"

"I'm serious, Mom. I… I feel like I just put a target on all our backs, you know? I mean, Whittaker's a little shit, but… maybe he has a point. The Court-Among-the-Holly is bad news, and now I've got us working for them. And if we can't do what the King asked, then that's it. No more rainy-day walks in Stanley Park. No more Shakespeare festivals at English Bay. It all just disappears under the King's second Ice Age."

"Wasn't it going to do that anyway?"

"I guess. If we hadn't got mixed up in this, Gwyn's entire army would probably be running all over the city by now. And if they couldn't find the *Ci*, he would have buried us all beneath 'Holly's justice' anyway."

"Damned if you do," said the woman who wasn't there.

"This is you and the Deacon all over again, isn't it? The rock, the hard place, and the pagan deity laughing at you from a distance."

"'All women become like their mothers. That is their tragedy.'"

Abby's laugh became a sob, and she found herself blinking away tears. Oscar Wilde. The vision before her quoted Oscar Wilde. When Karen was alive, Wilde had been one of her favourites, and she would often bust out a quote or two when something amused her. But there had always been a sparkle in her eyes when she did. She would always press her tongue into her cheek and purse her lips in an effort to keep herself from laughing before she could get through the line in its entirety. In fact, that was always how Abby knew that such a quote was coming.

But the apparition did none of that. Its eyes were blank, its voice hollow, its face an expressionless mask. It went through Karen's motions, but not the emotions. It didn't even bother to complete the line.

Abby's voice cracked as she whispered, "'No man does. That's his.'"

For several long moments, she sat there silently, avoiding her dead mother's eyes but feeling them drill into her all the same. Then, the four torches on the wall of the lounge gave a mighty roar and jumped to twice their normal height. The *whir* and *clank* of massive, invisible machines echoed through the whole Letterbox, and the front wall rippled like a choppy sea as something stepped, or rather stumbled, through the Anointed Gate that separated the dark streets of Vancouver from Simon's little pocket dimension.

One dark-skinned hand came through first, its dirty and broken nails clawing at the empty air. Then a leg, clad in torn and blood-soaked denim and one steel-toed boot. Then the face appeared. Natalie's eyes bulged, a milky white film hiding pupil and iris. Her face was smeared with blood, her mouth a grimace of racking pain. She pulled herself through the Anointed Gate and fell to all fours on the cold stone of the Letterbox, her clothes soaked through with mud, blood, and rainwater. The broken shafts of five Dullahan arrows protruded from her flesh. She held one hand tightly over her stomach, where Abby could see the livid edges of a wicked sword-stroke. She ran to help her friend, but stopped dead when Natalie looked up at her with those milky eyes and growled, "Don't! Stay back!"

Natalie crawled forward slowly and painfully, leaving a trail of her own gore as she proceeded. "Get... Simon... " she hissed through gritted teeth. "I need... ah!" She doubled over as violent tremors racked her whole body. "I need... salt!"

Simon was already there. So was Leanne. The back wall of the room suddenly opened onto a corridor that had not been there five seconds previous, and when Simon saw the state that Natalie was in—shaking and twitching and gnashing her teeth, with her white eyes bulging from her skull—he told Leanne to summon Mother Hyld on the double. "When you've done that, go to the ice-box and fetch the raw steaks I've been saving, and as much salt as you can find in the pantry! Now!"

As soon as Leanne turned down the corridor, Natalie was on her feet. All that Abby and Simon saw was teeth, nails, and blank white eyes as their friend lunged at them and wrapped one huge hand around each of their throats, forcing them both to the ground.

"What the hell are you doing?" Abby demanded. "It's us!" She had both hands up under Natalie's chin, trying to keep her friend's gnashing teeth as far away from her own face as possible. Simon was trying to free himself from Natalie's monster grip and simultaneously cough out an explanation that would somehow solve everything.

"It's not her!" he gasped. "It's the beast inside her!"

Natalie howled and aimed her jaws at his jugular vein. He was apologizing to her even as he made a fist and punched her in the nose.

"You mean... this is the zombie?" Abby croaked.

A flash of green light and a shouted word in an ancient language answered Abby's question for her. Natalie's grip loosened and she went flying clear across the lounge, not stopping until she slammed into the other of the tatty armchairs. Abby and Simon sat up and gasped. Mother Hyld had her staff aimed at Natalie, who writhed and kicked on the floor beneath a dome of hard green light.

Simon massaged his sore larynx and gasped, "We need to lock her up now. Then I'll explain."

*****

From the other side of the barred windows, Abby and Leanne watched in stunned silence as Natalie squatted in the middle of the Letterbox's holding cell and devoured the pile of raw, salted meat before her like it was the first thing she'd eaten since she walked out of a grave in Haiti almost two hundred and fifty years ago.

"This can't be real," Leanne whispered. "That can't be our Natalie."

"Your eyes do not deceive you," Mother Hyld said gravely. "That is the true face of all who rise from the grave after their time."

"It is *not,*" Simon said. "It is not her true face."

"Are you kidding?" Abby spluttered. "Simon, she strangled us half to death! Look at her now and tell me that's not some *Resident Evil* shit right there."

"What you see now is Natalie in the worst of circumstances, Abigail. Look what the Dullahan did to her. Even the hardiest mortal might have died from any one of those wounds. I'm sure her healing factor could only have done so much to keep up with them. Her… baser instincts would have to have taken over eventually."

"Baser instincts?"

"The flesh of a revenant cannot repair itself indefinitely," said Mother Hyld. "When the magic that keeps the body intact can do no more to heal the injuries the body has received, then the creature will turn to a diet of flesh to supplement the repairs."

"So, when she runs out of healing energy, she has to *eat people*," said Abby.

"In extreme cases, a revenant can weave new tissue for itself to repair an old injury," Mother Hyld responded. "But that tissue must come from somewhere. It cannot be created autonomously."

"It must be… converted from raw matter," said Simon.

"So, again, she has to *eat people*!" Abby repeated.

Simon exhaled slowly. "Abigail, do you suppose for a moment that I would have allied myself with her for all these years if it were half so simple as that? Natalie's will is stronger than any undead I have ever met. For centuries, she has sustained herself solely on meat sourced ethically and humanely, and only when absolutely necessary. What happened tonight was a freak accident caused by the extreme circumstances of our engagement with the Court-Among-the-Holly."

"How could you keep this from me? A year now we've been working together, and this is the first time I'm learning about this. Don't you think it would have been good for me and Leanne to know about her appetite in advance of 'extreme circumstances'?"

"The choice was not entirely mine. It's one of a very small number of subjects that could be described as delicate for Natalie. I do not speak of it out of respect for her."

"That's fair enough," said Leanne, "but this is a matter of personal safety. What do we do if something like this happens out in the field someday?"

"I have devised several contingencies for that," Simon admitted. "None of them are particularly pleasant."

Natalie looked up. Her eyes had returned to their normal colour and new skin was weaving itself together over her wounds. "Hey, guys? I know this is a lot to take in, but please don't talk about me like I'm not here."

Simon looked at her through the bars. "How do you feel, Natalie?"

She sat back on the stone floor and tore off another chunk of meat. "Better. I think I'll stay here for the night. Just in case. Is Abby there?"

"I'm here, Natalie."

"Like I said on the mountain: I'm so goddamn sorry for all of that. When I led the Dullahan away, I had a feeling it might get to this point. But I thought I could control it. I didn't think you'd be right in the danger zone."

"It's okay." She wasn't sure if she meant it.

"Do you need anything?" Simon asked. "A book, perhaps? More salt?"

"I think I just want to be alone right now. I need some time to, uh, lick my wounds."

"Of course."

*****

Abby and Leanne spent that night in one of the Letterbox's many spare bedrooms, and Natalie spent it in the holding cell. She didn't want to risk losing control again. Shame and guilt were not like the Natalie they knew, so the last thing Abby and Leanne did before they left for the day was take a detour down to the cell to check on their friend. Leanne brought a mug of something hot and steaming that smelled like black coffee mixed with raw eggs, and until Natalie took a drink, Abby wasn't totally sure if it was meant to be a peace offering or a lethal poison.

"You two shouldn't be in here," Natalie said. "At least stand on the other side of the doors."

Leanne shook her head. "Uh-uh. We wanted to check on our friend, not inspect the prisoners. Right, Abby?"

Abby, still spooked by what had happened the previous night, felt Leanne's elbow poking her in the ribs. "Uh, yeah. Just checking up."

Natalie sipped her witch's brew and sat on the bare army cot that was the cell's only bed. "I get you're scared. I don't blame you. I was out of control last night."

"Last year," Abby said, "after that first time I saw you… get back up from something people don't get up from, Simon told me that he deliberately kept you and me apart when I was growing up because it would have freaked me out too much. He didn't make that decision by himself, did he?"

Natalie shook her head. "I had to talk him down from trying to get us together when you were younger. As soon as he started with the whole Mr. Lockhart charade and all that secret teaching, he wanted me to sit in on some of your lessons, so you'd get used to me. I told him no way, because I couldn't be sure you wouldn't just see… that thing. The thing that I try my hardest not to be. But after everything with Varr'rak, us getting to know each other was kind of unavoidable." She raised her mug. "And here we are now. Once again: I'm sorry things went the way they did."

Abby finally believed her, and she joined Natalie on the cot. The two of them moved over to make room for Leanne, and then they just sat for a moment in silence, letting bygones be bygones.

"This is delicious, by the way," Natalie said, taking another sip. "What is it?"

"That's Eleanor of Grimsby's Tonic to Restore a Mangled Limb," Leanne said brightly. "Simon had the recipe kicking around in the library and I just followed the instructions. Well, mostly. I made a couple tweaks 'cause I wasn't sure how it would interact with undead flesh. I don't think it's meant to in the first place. Mother Hyld did the spell-work to actually make it… " She waved her hands in a spooky way. "… you know, restore, but the rest was all me."

"Good first effort. Needs a bit more salt though."

Leanne fished a pair of restaurant salt packets from the pocket of her sweater. "Got you covered!"

Natalie thanked her, took both packets, and poured the entire contents into her mug. Then she stirred the concoction with her finger and drained the mug in one swallow. "Oh, yeah. That's the way you do it."

"What's all the salt for?" Abby asked.

"Do you know what it is that keeps a zombie going?" Natalie asked. "What the actual specifics of the magic are?"

"I think it's pretty obvious that I don't."

"To reanimate a corpse the way I was reanimated, you need a body, obviously, with no soul inside it. But you also need a soul with no body to dwell in. A feral ghost with no mind of its own and no memory of who it was, but plenty of anger at the living world. The ghost is like a zombie's battery and repair kit all in one."

"I see," said Leanne. "When you came back to the Letterbox last night, it wasn't you that attacked Abby and Simon. It was the ghost that powers your body. It was acting according to its instincts, trying to repair its shell."

"Exactly. You both know I've still got my original soul. The soul of the woman whose body this used to be. That's not supposed to happen. When a necromancer raises a zombie, the ghost that they pour into the body is supposed to be the only life force in there. But I'm here. I've always been here. So has… the other chick. And I use salt to keep her down most of the time. Just enough to make sure she doesn't wake up."

"Until you get your ass handed to you by a headless horseman," said Abby.

"Yeah." The word landed with a heavy thud, full of fear and apprehension and spite. "When I get hurt, the ghost gets stronger. It wants to repair the damage and keep its host body safe. And if there's too much damage and not enough salt in my system, it takes over. And it gets hungry."

"Okay. So if something like that happens again, we know that we should club you to the ground with a salt lick."

Natalie smiled a little. "You know, I don't think anyone's tried that. Might work." Another brief silence passed, and then she stood. "Thanks for checking on me, you two. I think I… really needed it. More than I thought I did." She smiled in such a way that all the ever-present traces of death disappeared from her face, and for a moment she was just a person again.

"Hey, no problem," said Leanne. "You're our friend, Natalie."

Abby nodded. "Yeah. If you say that wasn't you last night, then it wasn't. It took me a while to believe it, but I do now." Looking into those large eyes, which sparked with a thousand thoughts and emotions, and comparing them to the blank and soulless whites that had attacked her, Abby wondered how she *ever* could have thought they were the same eyes.

Abby and Leanne stood together, and they left the holding cell with Natalie between them.

*****

At noon that day, Simon finally found Whittaker.

The imp had made himself comfortable in a cheerful little smoking room three flights of stairs up from Simon's own bedchamber. It was a room that Simon himself hadn't visited since he'd quit smoking in the early '80s—not because it had any ill effects on his Vanguard constitution, but because the cleanup simply wasn't worth it. Frankly, he was a little surprised to learn the room was still here: as a self-aware location, the Letterbox entertained itself primarily through what Simon called "autonomous redecoration." Wallpaper and furniture would change colour or be replaced with newer patterns; corridors and rooms would move from one place to another; and sometimes disused rooms would disappear altogether, cast into a void of who-knew-what and who-knew-where by a *genius loci* that had grown bored of them. He would have expected the smoking room to have been purged years ago, but here was Whittaker, with his shoes off and his feet resting on an expensive burgundy ottoman, enjoying an excellent glass of fifty-year-old scotch from the bar in the back of the room.

"Nice setup you got here, Ætheriċ," the imp said by way of greeting. "I might just set up shop in here and ride out the storm like this until All Hallows' Eve!"

He was wearing a forest-green smoking jacket and matching cap—Simon was fairly certainly they were real garments rather than faerie illusions, though where Whittaker had got them, he hadn't a clue—and he'd evidently burned through the last of his cigarettes. Now, he had a fat Cuban cigar in his hand. Simon was unamused. He winced as he lowered himself into the empty chair opposite Whittaker. Then he stared at the imp for a long moment. "You crossed a line last night."

Whittaker blew a disinterested smoke ring. "Okay. Maybe I did. But what the hell else could I do? The eulogy was my only bargaining chip. If I hadn't played that card, the kid wouldn't be here. You wouldn't be here, if Holly figured out you'd been hiding me. Come Halloween, this city probably wouldn't be here."

"You believe Abby can find the hound in time?"

"It sounds crazy, I know. But look at what she's done already. She killed the Deacon, Ætheriċ. She cracked the Harcourt thing. I'm willing to bet she has a better chance at finding this hound than the Dullahan."

"You don't get to gamble with people's lives like that, Whittaker. Especially not with Abby's. You abused her trust when you made that deal at Avalon. You took advantage of her when she was not thinking clearly. You had no right to hold Kelly Munro hostage as you did, you had no right to ask of Abby the price she paid for her friend, and you certainly had no right to offer her as a trophy to the King-Among-the-Holly."

"I'm Fair Folk, Ætheriċ. It's in my blood."

"Listen to me, because this is the only warning I will give you. You have transgressed in a way that cannot be forgiven. Unfortunately, you still have value to us at the moment, and this is the only reason that you are currently alive. But understand something, Robin, son of Goodfellow: the moment that Gwyn ab Nethe's *Ci* is returned to him, I shall consider your obligation to me paid in full. You will be as disposable as any one of the dozen cigarette butts with which you have choked my ashtray, and I will see you destroyed if you give me the least excuse. You are an active threat to someone I love, and it is the way of the Vanguard to kill those who threaten our loved ones."

Whittaker scoffed. "Is that little speech supposed to scare me?"

Simon smiled. "No. It is supposed to distract you long enough that you don't notice Mother Hyld's teleportation spell."

The imp's eyebrows shot skyward. "Mother Hyld's what?"

The air behind his chair shimmered like a fading mirage in the desert. Natalie and Mother Hyld emerged from nothingness, and before Whittaker could snap his way out of trouble, one massive undead hand wrapped around the imp's throat and the other compressed his fingers together like a misshapen link of yellow sausage. Natalie hoisted Whittaker up over her head and squeezed his fingers like she was trying to force the last of the toothpaste out of the tube. She was smiling when she asked Simon, "How many of them do you want me to break?"

"Do you know, I hadn't decided," Simon said with a placid smile. "That was rather foolish of me, wasn't it, Whittaker?"

The imp spluttered and hissed something that was probably meant to be a curse or an insult about Simon's sexual organs. But with Natalie's hand at his throat, it was rather lost in translation.

"I heard about that shit with the eulogy," Natalie growled. "You're goddamn lucky I wasn't around for that, you little bastard."

Whittaker kicked pathetically in the air. His free hand slapped against Natalie's forearm and he gasped, "Ungha! Ungha! Gahdam! Ungha!"

"What did he say?" Natalie asked, playing the innocent.

Simon paused for dramatic effect. "Hmm… you know, I could swear it sounded like 'uncle.' Is that it then, Whittaker? Would you like her to put you down?"

The imp did his best to nod, and Natalie dropped him unceremoniously to the floor. He stood shakily, gripping the back of his chair for dear life, and sucked in a desperate breath. "Okay," he rasped, "okay, you made your point. I'm *sorry*. Is that what you want to hear? I'm sorry about the fucking eulogy. I'm sorry how I played things with the King. I'm sorry I left you twisting in the wind when Avalon burned up. I'm. Fucking. *Sorry*."

"Well," Simon said brightly, "as long as you're sorry, perhaps you would care to make yourself useful around here." Natalie helped him out of the chair, and the two of them and Mother Hyld walked to the door. "Library, ten minutes. Please don't be tardy."

CHAPTER 9

T.G.W.

THE OFFICES of The Green World Initiative dominated the fifteenth floor of Two Bentall Centre, in Vancouver's downtown core. The spotless white tiles on the floor of the reception area, the marble-topped coffee station, and the framed Group of Seven prints on the walls all proudly announced the organization's financial standing, while the exposed wood beams and the Indigenous carvings opposite the Group of Seven prints beat their chests for the Pacific Northwest.

Agent Six tipped Abby off about The Green World the day after their run-in with the Dullahan and the King-Among-the-Holly, and on the following Monday Abby went to check it out. It was a not-for-profit that provided shelter, food, and jobs training to the underprivileged on the Pacific Coast, finding housing for the unhoused and restoring those parts of the city most ravaged by urban decay. All the newest shelters, parks, and safe injection centres in the city of Vancouver had been built thanks to T.G.W., and the organization was currently consulting on a spirited campaign to secure funding for improvements to mental-health resources at St. Paul's Hospital. The Ministry's deep dive had turned up close ties between Jack Kang and T.G.W., and he'd apparently been a long-time personal friend of its founder and CEO before he died. If the team wanted to know more about Kang and his associates, this was the place to start.

So here Abby was, with last month's Maclean's open on her lap and a paper cup—her second already—of some of the most delicious tea she had ever tasted, waiting for an audience with the woman who, according to Agent Six's intelligence, had known Jack Kang better than anyone.

An electronic bell chimed above the door as Leanne returned from the ladies' room and took her seat beside Abby once again. "Have you been in there?" she asked, rubbing her hands together. "God, the hand soap smells *amazing*." Then she picked up her own paper cup and took a sip. "And this tea! I've never tasted anything like this! We have to get some of this stuff for home."

"If we do, are you going to let me drink any of it? That's your fourth cup in like an hour."

"I can't help it. It's just *soooo* good!" She took another deeply satisfied swallow.

"Okay, well, slow down. I don't want to have to press pause when we're talking to Dr. Swann so you can run off to the bathroom again. And again, and again."

Leanne saluted and took another sip. "Roger that. Last cup, I promise."

They waited another five minutes before the woman they had come to see finally appeared from the tight corridor that separated the reception area from the rest of the floor. She was willowy and platinum-blonde, with full lips, alabaster skin, and eyes as green as jade. Her navy-blue business suit fit her perfectly, and she did not walk so much as glide toward Abby and Leanne in her three-inch stilettos. In one hand, she carried a smartphone with some sort of rectangular yellow crystal stuck in the middle of its casing, around which someone had etched a circular pattern of runic symbols inlaid with gold. The kid at the front desk had the same sort of thing on the back of his computer. So did the light fixtures overhead.

As the woman approached, all smiles and apologies that Abby and Leanne had waited so long, Abby noticed that she projected no aura. That little tidbit confirmed her first suspicion about the woman's true nature beyond a doubt, though for the moment she said nothing.

It wouldn't technically be inaccurate to say that the Fair Folk came from an alternate universe. Their home realm of the Otherlands was not composed of any kind of matter remotely like that which made up the mortal world or the spirit plane of the Elsewhere, and neither were its inhabitants. Magic interacted with faerie bodies differently than it did with just about anything else in existence, and they weren't beholden to the same laws of physics or metaphysics. One curious side-effect of this was that pure-blooded faeries projected absolutely no auras. None. Zilch.

"Dr. Jacqueline Swann," the faerie woman said with a smile. "But you can call me Jacquie." She shook Abby's hand and then Leanne's. Abby had foreseen this eventuality, and had donned a pair of fingerless black gloves in order to hide the pattern of ice crystals that still scarred her right palm.

"Again, I am so sorry for the wait," Jacquie Swann continued, "but we are some busy bees down here." She glanced at the front desk, where the young man working reception was presently juggling two different phone calls at once. A few bodies crossed at the other end of the corridor and snatches of conversation drifted across the long space. Abby didn't catch many specifics, but the tones of voice were matter-of-fact and the bodies moved like they had somewhere important to be.

"It's no problem," said Abby. "We did kind of spring this on you."

"Don't apologize, please. If this has to do with Jack, then you have my full attention." She looked over to the front desk and waved. "Chris, my love! Hold all my calls until I'm finished with these young ladies, will you?" The receptionist gave her a thumbs-up, and she blew him a kiss. "You're a peach, Christopher!" She led Abby and Leanne down the way she had come and through a spacious open-plan office packed with dozens of bodies. All of them were concentrating on their tasks, but not so hard that they did not notice when the boss walked past. A few raised their heads to smile, wave, or give Swann a kind greeting, and she returned every single one. Abby was staggered by the mosaic of mundane and supernatural energies that jumped out at her from the workers' auras. Humans, magicians, half-breeds… with so much magical flying around, it was a wonder they could even keep the lights from blowing out in this place, let alone run all the computers, smartphones, and other electronics. But as they walked, she noticed more of the same crystal-and-rune workings on each and every device. Obviously, the Fair Folk had worked out some means of getting magic to mix with electricity without frying the circuits. Abby thought she would have to ask about that before she left; she couldn't so much as turn her phone on in the Letterbox without bricking the whole thing.

Leanne must have had the same thought, and as they walked, she turned to Jacquie for an explanation. The faerie was happy to oblige, and pointed out the gold-and-crystal inlay on the back of every gizmo in the office. "That's the mark of the Shattergrip clan: dwarven artificers from the Five Mothers. That's our name for the mountain range that separates Oak and Holly's territories. The Shattergrip are one of the last guild-families still working the craft in the old way in their traditional territory, but some of the younger generation crossed over to Earth in the '70s and '80s. They've been trying to crack the magic vs. electricity problem for most of that time. I invested in their work a couple years ago and… well…" She smiled and shrugged.

"They cracked it." Leanne sounded impressed.

"They're still working on bringing the technology to market, but they were happy to make a deal because I gave them that last boost. We've been running on their systems for about six months now."

Abby missed the rest of the conversation thanks to the ever-louder ringing in her ears. By the time they reached Jacquie's office, she was leaning on Leanne for support. Without question, T.G.W. bore the highest concentration of magic in the smallest space that Abby had experienced since the night she met Whittaker, and just as had happened then, the chaotic hodgepodge of energies made her dizzy. Just to keep herself from falling over, she had to shut her eyes and grip her partner's arm, and she didn't let go until they were in the office with the door shut behind them.

The office of T.G.W.'s founder was much the same as the reception area: spotless floors, wall art that spoke of a deep love for the outdoors, and windows that stretched from the floor to the ceiling. A solid oak credenza stood against one wall, topped with a fully stocked tea and coffee station. Water for the kettle came from the executive washroom a few metres further along the same wall, which lay beyond a door also made of oak. The desk was, guess what, the same wood again, with a green baize cover, and lined with so many photos that there was hardly room for Jacqueline Swann's computer or pencil mug. Abby caught a glimpse of some of them as she and Leanne came in, and in each one Jacquie was out in the wild with someone, doing something to work up a sweat—kayaking, skiing, archery, it didn't seem to matter as long as she was getting a workout. More personal photos lined the walls, and here the story was the same. A few faces recurred, Jack Kang's most prominently, but there were also several shots featuring a pale, narrow-jawed man with the same platinum shade of hair as Jacquie. All the pictures of them together seemed somehow more recent than the rest. She wondered what the deal was there. A period of estrangement and then a reconciliation, perhaps?

Jacquie invited Abby and Leanne to sit and gave Abby a chance to collect herself. "Sorry about that. I should have figured this place might be a little overwhelming for… someone like you."

Abby blinked and rubbed her temples as the room stopped spinning and the spots disappeared from her eyes. "Someone like me."

Jacquie leaned forward, her elbows on the desk and her hands clasped together. "I don't want to waste your time or try to pretend we don't all know what's going on here. I think you're both too smart for that. I've heard stories about what happened to the Following and I know what you are, Abby Henderson—or I can call you Abby Normal if you like. And by now you must know exactly what I am."

Abby gave her head one last shake. A couple deep breaths later, and she felt like her feet were on solid ground once again. "You're Fair Folk. You don't project any kind of aura, which means you weren't born in this reality or on the spirit plane, and neither were any of your ancestors. I don't want to stereotype, but… elegance, beauty, lots of wood furniture and a thing for the outdoors? I'm going to put my money on elf."

Jacquie pulled her hair back, revealing for the first time the long points at the tops of her ears. With a shrug and a smile, she said, "You got me. I don't hide myself from humans as much as most of my people do, but even then, I think you would be at an advantage, O Last of the Gospels."

Abby shrugged back. "You got me."

Jacquie let her hair fall back into place and looked at Leanne. "I confess that your name does not come into the tales I have heard, Leanne Waller, but I do not think you would be here now if the Last of the Gospels did not trust you implicitly."

"My deeds don't stack up next to hers," Leanne admitted, "but I stand by her when it counts. I think I've earned her trust, and I hope that's enough of a character reference for you."

Jacquie smiled. "If the woman who killed the Deacon puts her faith in you, that is more than good enough." She leaned back in her chair. "But you didn't come here to compare great deeds."

"No, we didn't," said Abby. "Let's start with you, Jacquie Swann. In a word: what's a girl like you doing in a place like this?"

Jacquie laughed. "You mean why does an elf care so much for a human city like this one? Why have I put so much effort into T.G.W. when this isn't even my world to try and save?" Her smile, when she cast her eyes to the ceiling, was nostalgic and melancholy. "That probably comes from my parents. They came out of the Otherlands at the start of the last century, looking for a change. They settled here and they tried to be as human as they could. They got human jobs, paid a human mortgage, gave me and my brother human names—yes, Jacquie Swann is the name I was born with—and they raised us to think the same way." She shrugged. "I didn't have to go to a human university. I didn't have to spend ten years practicing as a cardiac surgeon at a human hospital. But I did. I like being among humans. You've got a… a spirit. A drive. Humanity sets a lot of obstacles for itself, but you always overcome. I like working with your kind, and I've brought that forward into T.G.W. This place isn't just about creating a healthier and safer world; it's about creating a more unified one."

"Humans and the supernatural coming together as one," said Abby. "The Green World."

"Do either of you know what that term really means?"

"It was Northrop Frye's idea, wasn't it?" Leanne said. "A place where literary heroes overcome obstacles and achieve their greatest desires."

"According to Frye, the green world is a key motif in Shakespeare's comedies," Abby added. "It's a secondary world where normal people can experience supernatural interventions that transform them in some way or put them on the right track in life."

Leanne smiled. "Did we mention we both have English degrees?"

Jacquie laughed. "I might have guessed! Well, you both clearly paid attention in class. Frye's ideas of the green world are very important to me not just as a literary motif, but as a way of living. I'm not kidding when I say that humans have overcome a lot in their time. But think of how much *more* they could overcome if they had a little magic behind them. T.G.W. is about bringing the magic and the mundane together, healing a world that I've chosen to live on for nearly 100 years, and sewing up the wounds left over by the War of the Ancients."

A world where people and magic co-existed… was such a thing even possible? Abby tried to picture it. Transportation could be made much easier if teleportation magic were applied on a grand scale. That would mean fewer vehicles clogging the roads and choking the skies. People wouldn't have to fight for land or resources if they could just will more into existence. A post-scarcity society might actually be achievable. But then she remembered what the Ministry men had said to her the other day. In the wrong hands, magic could lead to catastrophe. The Last Great War of the Ancients was a case study in that. Was Jacquie Swann an optimist, or was she just naïve?

Jacquie leaned back, tenting her fingers together, and studied Abby with those big jade eyes. "But that's enough about me," she said. "Why do you two want to know about Jack Kang?"

"I've recently been, um, contracted," Abby began, "to recover some missing property for a third party who shall have to remain nameless. It's… a weapon, of sorts, and it was recently used on somebody that we think Jack Kang had ties with."

"But we don't know exactly what those ties were," Leanne added. "If we can figure that out, we might be able to learn who fired the weapon and get it back to its rightful owner."

"Why come to me?" Jacquie asked. "Gospels speak to the dead, don't they? Surely you could contact the spirit of whoever this 'weapon' was used on and ask them directly."

"It's on the agenda. But the problem is that time gets messy when I do that. I could plan to spend fifteen minutes in a Bridge and wake up to find that I've lost five hours. For now, this is more convenient. From what we understand, nobody alive knew Jack Kang better than you."

Jacquie smiled again, but her eyes were filled with grief. "As far as I know, nobody did. When I founded T.G.W., Jack was still involved in provincial politics. We're talking almost ten years ago now. Back then, I had no clout in your mortal government. I couldn't get a meeting with anyone I needed to get a meeting with, so I couldn't get any projects off the ground. Jack went to bat for me from day one. With all his heart, he believed in T.G.W. as much as I do. I don't think we'd be where we are without him."

"That's why we're here," said Abby. "If anyone alive knows what links Jack Kang had with Ted Purdy—he's the one the 'weapon' was fired at—it must be you. There's a possibility that his death and Jack Kang's are connected, so if you can tell us anything, Jacquie, you might be helping us get justice for them both." *And,* she thought to herself, *you might be helping us track down a four-legged killing machine and quiet the wrath of an insane pagan god.*

Jacquie pursed her lips and took a moment to think. "I'm afraid 'Purdy' doesn't ring a bell... but I assume Ted would be short for Edward?"

Abby nodded.

"I think I do remember hearing something... about a month before he died, Jack and I had dinner at a place over on Broadway. I'm afraid I don't remember the name. I went outside to take a phone call at one point, and when I came back, Jack was on his own phone at the table. It sounded like a conversation he didn't want to be having. He addressed the caller as Edward."

"Do you know what they talked about?"

"Not really. I only caught a few bits and pieces. But Jack said it had to stop and this was the last time he'd do this."

"Do what?"

"If I knew, I'd tell you."

"Was Jack in any kind of financial trouble?"

"Not that I know of. Why?"

Abby told her about the payments that Jack Kang had made to Ted Purdy for almost two years. Jacquie seemed genuinely surprised to learn about this, and Abby figured it must be a pretty big secret if not even Jack Kang's closest friend knew of it. Which raised the question: what sort of dirt did Ted Purdy have on Jack Kang, and what did Kang think the consequences would be if he stopped paying?

"Auberon king..." whispered Jacquie. She managed to put the same inflection on the words that a human might put on the phrase *Jesus Christ*. "Do you think this man was blackmailing Jack?"

Abby was still turning the question over in her mind, so Leanne answered for her. "It seems pretty likely right now."

"With what?" Jacquie gasped. "Jack didn't have any enemies! He didn't have any scandals or secrets."

"It sounds like he had one," said Leanne.

"No!" Now she was getting defensive. "No, I would have known. I knew everything about Jack! He and I, we—"

"Were a lot closer than you're admitting," Abby said, snapping suddenly out of her reverie. She didn't need to peek into Jacquie's nonexistent aura to make that leap. The hurt, the betrayal, the sadness were all written plainly on the woman's face.

Jacquie stopped. "My word. You are good, Abby Henderson." She took a deep breath and calmed herself. "Yes. There's no use lying to you. Jack and I were... a lot more than just friends." Her voice caught and her jade eyes blurred with tears as she picked up a photo on her desk. "We had been for a while." She turned the photo outward so Abby and Leanne could see it. A grinning, jade-eyed elf with her hair tied back in a ponytail stood on a forest path, arm-in-arm with a bald, athletic Chinese-Canadian man. Jack Kang had his arm around Jacquie's shoulder and his lips pressed firmly to her cheek. Her face was scrunched up in a laugh, and she had one hand raised to the camera to show off an expensive diamond ring.

"We took that picture ten days before… before…" She broke off, wiping tears from her eyes and cursing to herself. She set the picture down, reached under her collar, and drew out a length of gold chain, at the end of which sat the same diamond ring. "I haven't worn it properly since he died," she said. "I can't. It's a promise he'll never be able to keep to me now. But I can keep him next to my heart." She closed her eyes and wept. Leanne grabbed a few napkins from the coffee station and passed them to Jacquie, who nodded mute thanks and wiped her eyes.

When Jacquie had composed herself, Abby tried to steer her back to the subject of Jack Kang, but there wasn't any more she could offer that they didn't know already. Eventually, they thanked Jacquie for her time and made their own way back to the reception area. Leanne immediately broke her promise and fixed herself a fifth cup of that amazing tea "for the road." She did, in fact, have to run to the bathroom again while it was steeping, and while Abby was waiting for her to return, the receptionist waved her over.

"Miss Henderson! Someone left a message for you? I don't know how they knew you were here, but…" He held up a folded piece of paper. "Well, here it is."

Abby took the paper. "Thanks, um…"

"Chris."

"Right. Thanks, Chris." Then she looked at the message.

Update me when you're done. Robson Square.
No phone calls. No crystals. My people are listening.
-Vi

"Is this it?" Abby asked.

"That's all," Chris said with a shrug.

"And you're sure it was *Vi* who left the message?" She couldn't help putting a sardonic twist on the name when she said it. There were silly aliases, and then there were *silly* aliases.

"That was the name."

Abby balled the paper up and chucked it at the wastebasket. "Thanks." She hung around until Leanne returned, then relayed the message to her as they walked to the elevator.

"'Vi'?" Leanne said. "We don't know a V— " She paused and thought about it for a moment. "Oh, I get it. Vee-eye. Clever."

"I'm sure he thought so," Abby scoffed. "Well, come on. We don't want to keep Agent Six waiting."

CHAPTER 10

SPEAKER FOR THE DEAD

TWO DAYS after her meeting with Jacquie Swann, Abby interrogated a dead man.

She hadn't been kidding when she said that timing a Bridge was difficult. Barely an hour after her debriefing with Agent Six, she'd had to be at MacReady's to work an afternoon shift. The day after that she'd worked a double, and she'd been so tired when she returned home that she'd fallen asleep within half an hour of eating dinner. She couldn't exactly take a sick day to summon ghosts, either; she'd missed or been late for work more times than she wanted to admit in the last year, and her manager was starting to give her the stink-eye. How the hell did guys like Clark Kent do the whole double life routine?

But today—oh, miracle of miracles—she was not on the schedule. Leanne was working, so Abby had the apartment all to herself. She shut the curtains, dimmed the lights, and lit one of the faintly citrus-scented candles she'd bought back in September, partly to help with her meditations and partly to cover the horrid stink of the potion that helped her induce the actual trance. Then she took a seat on the couch with her legs crossed beneath her, closed her eyes, and slipped into the Bridge.

It was getting easier with practice; last year, she would have needed an entire cup of the soupy potion to get her mind in the right state, but now it only took a couple sips.

That was a blessing, because the stuff tasted as lousy as it smelled. It was Simon's own recipe, and while Abby knew that he meant well, she longed for the day when she wouldn't even need to touch the concoction.

Whenever her mind detached from her body and ascended to the spiritual plane, she always visualized it differently. According to Simon, this was because the Elsewhere was so vast and incomprehensible that any mortal mind that beheld it had to scramble the signals it received from the optic nerve. This time, when Abby opened her eyes, her brain told her that she was standing in a snow-covered clearing somewhere in a mountain forest. Conifers as wide as swimming pools and as tall as skyscrapers formed a ring around the clearing, in rows that stretched away to infinity. The sky above was purple above her head, fading to black as it dropped toward the horizon, and a dazzling aurora of yellow, blue, orange, and green light spanned from one end to the other.

Abby took a moment to appreciate her surroundings, as she always did when she cast her consciousness into the Elsewhere, before setting herself to the task. She spoke the ancient oath that signalled the official start of the Bridge, and then she called upon the ghosts.

"I seek the counsel of one who cannot lie at rest, a soul taken from the mortal life before their natural time. I would speak with Edward Alan Purdy!"

The lights in the sky undulated in a frenzied dance of passion. Thunder rolled and a high wind kicked up snow all around her. She shielded her eyes as the trees whispered Ted Purdy's name to each other. "Spirit, I thee name!" She shouted the words, barely hearing herself above the rushing wind. "In the name of the Holy Witness, the Earth-maker and the Glory-giver, I implore you to reveal yourself, that one in the future might gain wisdom from the past!"

A cyclone of dry cold stung her cheeks, her nose, and the tips of her ears. She blinked and saw a figure emerging from the ring of trees. It lurched unsteadily toward her and swept its left hand to and fro, like a scythe reaping the sheaves of winter. The figure's face was pale but for two dark rings beneath the eyes. When it stopped just on the other side of the vortex of snow, Abby nodded a greeting.

"Ted Purdy," she said. "Pleasure to meet you."

"What the hell is this?" asked the ghost. "Where am I?"

This was always the hard part. Especially in cases when death came unexpectedly, it often took the spirits of the departed a while to accept what had happened. Sometimes, they didn't remember the event at all. But it was a Band-Aid that had to be ripped off.

"You're dead," Abby said slowly. "This is what happens next."

"No. No fucking way." Ted Purdy's spirit backed off a step and shook his head. "That's not—there's no way. I'm not—"

"Ted. Look at yourself."

He did, only now noticing the rusty red streaks all down his front or the raw stump of meat an inch above his right elbow. With his one remaining hand, he reached up to his neck and gingerly felt the torn and twisted mess of exposed muscle, severed blood vessels, and broken skin. For a moment, he just froze, with his hand on the gory remains of his neck. "Wait..." he whispered. "Shit... I think you're right. Yeah, I... I remember now." His hand dropped to his side. "Huh. Funny how you forget a thing like that."

The words came out hollow and droning, like a record played over a phonograph that needed repairs. Ted Purdy's form blurred and became translucent at the same instant, as if knowing what had happened made him move closer to ghosthood.

"So, what are you?" he asked without humour. "An angel? The Grim Reaper? Only you don't see many angels with tattoos, do you?"

Abby shook her head. "No, I'm not an angel. And I'm not the Grim Reaper." *I'm pretty sure I've met the Grim Reaper,* she thought to herself. *And there's no mistaking me for him.* "I'm human," she explained. "I can… speak to the dead."

"Like that Bruce Willis movie?"

"A little bit. My name is Abby Normal. I need to ask you some questions about Jack Kang."

"Kang?" the ghost said dismissively. "Never heard of him."

"I know that's bullshit, Ted. I've asked around. For two years, Jack Kang was paying you a regular sum every month. That smells like blackmail to me. I want to know what you had on him."

The ghost made a noise that, from a living mouth, might pass for a scoff. "Yeah? Why do you think I'd tell you anything?"

"The thing that killed you, it seems like someone sent it after you on purpose. There's a possibility that whoever did that also played a part in Jack Kang's death earlier this year. You tell me what was going on between you two, and maybe I can figure out who sent the creature that killed you."

"That's your theory, is it? Pretty flimsy stuff."

"If you cooperate, I could make it less flimsy."

Ted Purdy took a moment to think it over. "If I tell you what I know, you got to do something for me."

"Do I?"

"Yeah. If you're right, and somebody did have me killed on purpose, and you do figure out who did it, then you've got to send them my way."

"Kill them, you mean?"

"Damn straight. If some sonofabitch wanted me dead, he should've done the work himself. So, if you find him, I want to look the coward in the eye and finish whatever beef we've got like men."

"I'll see what I can do," said Abby.

"No, no, not good enough, little lady. You gotta promise me, okay? Or I ain't telling you shit."

Abby narrowed her eyes. Making promises to creeps like this was exactly how she'd landed in such a mess with Whittaker. But on the other hand, what could Ted Purdy do if she promised now and reneged later? She was the Gospel here, and he was just the ghost of another dead gangbanger. He didn't have the power to make her life hell like Josiah and Isaac Harcourt had.

"Okay," she said at last. "I promise." *I promise that monkeys will fly out of my butt before I keep my word to a thug like you,* said her inner monologue.

Ted Purdy nodded. "Now we're getting somewhere."

"I hope so. Now, why were you blackmailing Jack Kang?"

Ted Purdy smiled a humourless smile and shook his head. "Man wasn't who he said he was. Not one bit."

"What does that mean?"

"Oh, he talked a big game, didn't he? The son of first-generation immigrants, who came to this country to make a better life!" His voice became grandiose and exaggerated, and he made several ironic sweeping gestures with his hand. "Yeah," he said with a sneer, "they were immigrants, alright. Only one of 'em came from a lot further away than he said."

She wished she'd started with the spirit of Jack Kang himself. "Ted," she huffed, "can you give me a straight answer here?"

"I just did. Jack Kang's parents, they're the key. You want a straighter answer than that, ol' Ted's gotta get his beak wet." He extended a hand to her.

"You want a bribe? You're a ghost! What the fuck are you going to do with a bribe?"

"Old habits, little lady. I don't give anything up for free. You talk to ghosts, right? Well, from what I hear, folks who talk to ghosts can do a lot of other shit. You can channel 'em, right? Summon 'em into your body?"

Abby crossed her arms. "You want me to channel you?"

"Just for a bit. If I'm dead, if this is all I've got to look forward to, I want to take one more walk on the mortal side. Just… tie up some loose ends on Earth. I won't do anything with your body that you wouldn't like, I promise." He laughed and gave her a very appreciative once-over. "It'd suck to damage a package as *fine* as that one."

Abby suppressed a shudder. She had a feeling that somewhere very far away, her physical form was gagging. "Not. Happening," she said.

"Fine," Ted Purdy replied. "But that's all you're getting out of me."

He turned and walked back through the swirling wall of snow. Abby shouted after him, ordered him to come back, but he was gone.

"He could have been more helpful," said a voice behind her.

Abby turned. Karen was there, her arms crossed and an unamused expression on her face. Abby stomped through the snow toward the hallucination and jabbed a finger in its chest. "No. No, you do *not* get to play this game. Not here. I have tried so hard to reach my mother here. My real mother. I won't have some fucking figment of my imagination just waltzing in to pour salt in the wound."

"Then get rid of me," replied Karen. "If I'm just your hallucination, then you can send me away, can't you?"

Abby pursed her lips. She imagined a great hole opening in the ground beneath the vision's feet and swallowing it up. She imagined a geyser propelling the thing that was not her mother a thousand feet into the air, so that it would fall way on the other side of the trees. She imagined it dissolving into a thousand motes of grey dust and being carried away on the wind, like an Avenger that got on the wrong side of Thanos.

None of this happened. The vision remained exactly where it was, never blinking or flinching. Abby turned away from it and shut her eyes. She still had options here. She just hoped she could ignore the walking delusion behind her long enough to run through them all.

"What will you do now?" asked Karen.

"I'm going to call up Jack Kang." Why was she answering this thing? It wasn't here. She was just talking to herself. "Maybe he'll be more upfront than the man who was blackmailing him."

"Hmm..."

"What's that supposed to mean?"

"Jack Kang was paying Ted Purdy for two years to keep his secret. Somehow, I doubt he'll just give that secret up to you."

"He's dead. What harm could it do him now?"

"Well, if that's what you think is best."

Abby winced. That was the line her mom had always used when she wanted to argue an idea without arguing it. But just like with the Wilde quotation the other night, the delivery was all wrong. There wasn't an ounce of Karen Henderson's soul in it.

She shook her head and walked back toward the centre of the snowy cyclone. She couldn't think about that right now. "I seek the counsel of one who cannot lie at rest," she began. Lights flashed across the sky and the spinning snow picked up speed as she made the call to Jack Kang. For a moment, the only sound was the howling wind, and she had to squint to keep the flakes out of her eyes. Then he came.

Jack Kang moved with great caution, his eyes bulging and his shoulders bunched up in a defensive gesture. He reminded Abby of nothing so much as a housecat cornered by hungry dogs, and she wondered what the hell had happened to him to turn the handsome, confident man in Jacquie Swann's photos into this.

When she addressed him, he looked at her with an expression of pure terror. He backed off a step and stammered, "What do you want?" One side of his face sagged and seemed to fall in on itself, as if the bones beneath were not solid. Abby remembered that the cause of Jack Kang's death was blunt force trauma. But what kind of trauma could have reduced his bones to shards like that without damaging the soft tissue?

"Mr. Kang," she said slowly, "my name is Abby Henderson. I need to ask you some questions."

He flinched. "They sent you. Didn't they? Y-you're not—you can't be here! People can't be here!"

"I can. Nobody sent me, Mr. Kang. I'm a Gospel. I can speak to the dead. My mind is on this plane right now, but not my body."

"A… a Gospel? They didn't, then! They couldn't have! They wouldn't have sent a… a…"

"Sent a what? Who's they?"

"A half-breed," he whispered, as if the word were forbidden knowledge. "They'd never send someone… impure."

Abby said nothing. There were questions that needed asking here, and none of them were the ones that she'd come to ask. The blackmail seemed like small potatoes compared to whatever had so traumatized Jack Kang.

"Who do you think would have sent me, Jack?"

He looked behind him and shook his head. "No! No, I—I can't say! Not here! They've got ears!"

"Dammit, *who*?"

"Them! The ones who… who did this." He touched the fallen side of his face and massaged the sagging skin with the tips of his fingers.

The wind slowed for a moment, and Abby heard another noise over the roaring storm. Somewhere in the distance, a great stallion whinnied, and the snow crunched under the weight of four thundering hooves. Jack Kang sank to his knees with a whimper. "Oh God! Oh God, no! They heard us! They heard me!" The hoofbeats were getting closer. Kang crawled toward Abby and seized the front of her shirt.

"Listen to me! Go, now! You don't belong here! You can go! You have to go! Before they find you!"

Abby tried to pry him off, but his grip was solid. "I can't go! I have to ask you about—"

"It doesn't matter!" shouted Jack Kang. "Nothing matters as much as running!"

The horse whinnied again. Abby heard a noise like gas escaping a pipe and saw two jets of orange flame cut through the whiteness around her. She remembered the wet noise that Agent Fourteen's head had made upon the concrete after it fell from his shoulders.

Another whinny. Abby heard the crack of a whip. As the hoofbeats came ever closer, she freed herself of Jack Kang's grip. She lost her balance and fell on her ass in the snow. The Dullahan's grating laughter split the air as she scooted backward on her elbows. Black hooves and a black snout cut through the wall of snow. Abby closed her eyes. She cried out.

CHAPTER 11

PRETTIEST EYES

AND THEN she woke up.

At first her brain couldn't register that she was in the apartment. She flailed and kicked the candle over. Her arms swept across the coffee table and knocked over the potion. Mug and candle collided as they fell to the floor together, dousing the flame and making a waxy, potion-y mess on the carpet all in a single moment. As Abby's rational mind yanked control over her limbs away from her anxiety, something or someone came running from the bedroom. It jumped over the back of the couch, seized Abby in a bear hug, and said in her ear, "You're okay. Abby, listen to me: you're okay. You're safe."

She stilled, the only sound her rapid breathing. Eventually, she coaxed up enough saliva to speak properly. "Lee? When did you get home?"

"About an hour ago. I figured you were Bridging and I didn't want to wake you too early, so I laid down on the bed and did some sudoku. I guess some stuff went down up there, huh?"

Abby felt the brush of Leanne's lips on her cheek. She looked into her partner's eyes until her heart slowed to a regular rhythm and she stopped hyperventilating. *Leanne's eyes,* she told herself. *That's all that matters. Those are safe eyes. Those are kind eyes. And if you concentrate on them, you're safe. You're not going have your head cut off or get eaten by a monster dog or suffer the wrath of an old god. That stuff doesn't happen in the world of these prettiest, most wonderful of eyes.*

Leanne smiled. "You good?"

Abby kept her focus on those magical eyes and nodded. "I'm good."

Leanne kissed her. "I'm glad."

When they pulled away from each other, Abby noticed the mess she'd made on the floor and mouthed a silent curse. She started to rise, but Leanne pulled her back down. "Don't you move. You just got back from another plane of existence. Just relax and I'll deal with the cleanup."

Abby smiled and let herself fall into her partner's eyes all over again. "Have I ever told you that you're too good for me?"

"Yes." She grinned and winked. "But I still like to hear it."

*****

Twenty minutes later, the cleanup was finished, the tea was ready, and Abby and Leanne sat on the couch together. It was almost seven in the evening by now, and they were eagerly awaiting the delivery of a large pepperoni pizza with their names on it. While they sat and drank their tea, Abby caught Leanne up on her conversations with Jack Kang and Ted Purdy.

"That's really all that Purdy said?" asked Leanne. "Look at Jack Kang's parents?"

"Yup. And I was going to, before all the Bridge-us interruptus."

"But what would a Dullahan be doing in that part of the Elsewhere? Why would it come after you?"

"Damned if I know. I'll ask Simon first chance I get."

"You know, I wonder if you should ask Natalie instead? She's actually been dead. She knows what happens on that side, and she definitely seems like she knows a thing or three about the Dullahan."

"Hm. Point."

As Abby sipped her tea, her eyes flicked over to the corner of the room. Her mother was standing there. Watching her. Judging her.

"Abby," Leanne said softly, "what's wrong?"

She turned from her mother's dead, expressionless gaze to Leanne's bright and brilliant one. Her own vision blurred and her cheeks suddenly felt wet. "Everything. Everything's wrong, Lee."

Leanne set down her mug and squeezed Abby's hand. "Tell me. Tell me and I'll listen."

Abby sniffed and wiped her eyes. "Foreverways, right?"

"Foreverways."

Abby's jeans soaked up the tears that dripped from her face. "I think... I think I might actually be going crazy. I keep seeing my mom everywhere."

"I thought you said you couldn't summon her in the Bridge."

"I can't. I've tried and tried and tried, and nothing's happened. But... I see her. Everywhere, and not just when I'm Bridging. When I'm at work, when I'm in bed, when I get out of the shower..." She pointed to the corner. "I see her right now. And it's not her ghost or anything, because I know what a ghost looks like, and this thing isn't a ghost. But she's just... there. And I can't get rid of her." The words came out as an admission of defeat. Abby drew her knees to her chest, made herself into a ball on the couch, and wept into her torn denim. "I need help, Lee. Real help."

Leanne made small circles with her thumb across the back of Abby's hand. "Thank you, Abby. For being honest with me."

"I've wanted to tell you for weeks. I needed to tell you. But... all this stuff keeps getting in the way. Work's nuts and we're doing our self-defence stuff with Natalie and we're picking up Simon's slack while he recovers and this whole

Holly thing... we've almost lost a week already. There's so much happening, I feel like I'm drowning."

"That doesn't surprise me," Leanne said. "I've been watching you ever since we got back from Delapore. You've been... all over the place. Jumpy one day, withdrawn the next, super irritable the day after that. I don't blame you. We've both had a lot going on over the last year."

"I just can't keep going this way," Abby said. "I feel like a rubber band that someone just keeps pulling and pulling."

Leanne dug around in the pocket of her sweater and fished out a business card. "I might have an idea about that, actually."

Abby took the card and read it. "'Dr. Ken Duthie - Licensed Therapist.' You know I'm not good with shrinks, Lee."

"I know you've had bad experiences before, but I think this could be different. I was talking to Simon about this a couple days ago. He recommended this guy. Apparently, his specialty is people like us."

"A therapist for magic-users?"

"Is that so crazy? There's a lot of really nasty stuff lurking in the shadows. I bet tons of people have seen it and haven't been able to tell anyone." She smiled. "It makes as much sense as a woman who fights demons and then writes a blog about it."

One corner of Abby's mouth turned up. Damn it. Leanne had her there.

"Look," Leanne said, "I've been giving this a lot of thought. When I say I've been talking to Simon, I don't mean I was talking about you. If you want the truth, I'm not sure I'm having the best time dealing with this past year myself. Don't forget, I was at Applegate. I was at the Harcourt House. You've seen a lot of things I can't imagine, but that also works the other way."

Abby passed the card back to her. "Simon recommended this guy for you."

"Yeah. I need to talk to someone about what we've seen. Our support network for all this stuff is pretty small—basically just Simon, Natalie, and Kelly. Two of them aren't really mortal, and the third's in the Faroe Islands. So, I thought I'd give this a try. I already sent him an email: he's got an open spot this Saturday. Come with me?"

Abby thought about it for a long moment. She had been burned by therapists before, as a kid and as an adult. Before she learned the truth about herself, one shrink after another had given up on her. She'd been told she was making it up. She'd been prescribed pills she could never spell. But Simon trusted this Dr. Duthie. That was a badge of honour that few could wear. Certainly, none of her previous therapists had reached such heights. What did she have to lose, besides an hour out of her Saturday afternoon? She was working until three that day, anyway, so she doubted she'd be able to do much for the *Ci Annwn* investigation.

She nodded. "Okay, Lee. I'll give it a shot."

"That's all I ask."

They embraced. Karen watched them with an expressionless face, and Abby tried not to think about the cold burn of the unmelting ice crystals on her palm.

BOOK TWO:

BÊTE NOIRE

And graven in diamond with letters plain
There is written, her fair neck round about:
Noli me tangere, *for Caesar's I am,*
And wild for to hold, though I seem tame.

*

"Whoso List to Hunt"
Thomas Wyatt

IT'S DARK. The lights are on at the ends of their long metal stalks. Raindrops flit through their beams like tiny comets, before disappearing and dashing themselves against the surface of the street. When they hit her, the cold magic wafting from her body flash-freezes them and grips them tight, creating ice crystals up and down her black pelt. By the time she reaches the end of the block, her coat sparkles with a thousand diamonds.

She lifts her head. Sniffs out her prey. Advances. Her front paws spread white frost across the grass, toward a line of gormless, grinning orange faces staked into the ground outside the front door. She has seen faces like this before, when she has joined her master on The Hunt. They are a festive human decoration, meant to honour the old gods during Nos Galan Gaeaf. Illustrations of a green creature with metal bolts in its neck and a pale figure with a cape and pointed fangs smile at her from the window on the front of the house. She hears the command from the monsters. She snorts an angry breath that emerges as a cloud of frosty vapour.

The monsters command her to run, and she runs. Leaps. Shatters the window. She catches the royal blue curtains in her front claws and her momentum rips them from the rod. Inside the house, she shakes off the broken glass clinging to her fur. Takes another sniff.

She follows the scent out of the living room and up the stairs. A light comes on at the top and a man appears. He's pudgy, balding, and holding a long club with a curved metal head.

"Jim?" says a voice somewhere down the hall. "What is it?"

The pudgy man looks into her cold eyes. His hands shake, but for his wife's sake, he keeps his voice level. "Peggy, get Lisa! Lock the door!"

"Jim?" The voice sounds fearful.

"Do it! Just let me deal with th – "

In two leaps, she's at the top of the stairs. Her teeth enter his soft thigh and his words become a scream. He swings the club down across her back. She responds by snapping his femur. He collapses with a terrified howl and her jaws come down on his trachea next. With his arterial blood gushing into her mouth, she pulls away and runs down the hallway.

The wife appears in a doorway to her right. Pretty, blonde, and fat. She screams and starts crying when she sees the mess at the top of the stairs. She breaks for a doorway at the end of the hall and throws it open, pulling back bedsheets and hauling the prey out of bed. The girl is six years old with blonde curls. Her pyjamas bear the image of a black-haired, brown-skinned child with a purple shirt and a red travelling pack on her back. She holds a floppy, unwashed plush toy to her chest with both hands like a talisman of protection.

The door is ajar. A sleek, low body streaked with blood and rain shoulders its way through the gap and snarls, demanding that the fat woman turn to face it. She does not want to hunt for the monsters, but if she must, then she will try to find some honour in it.

But instead, the fat woman runs for the closet. She opens it, hauls out a large tub that reads "FIRE ESCAPE," and pulls out a ladder made of flexible rope and metal. She runs toward the window with the ladder in her arms.

She doesn't make it halfway. Sweeping claws cut across her thick thigh. She drops to one knee and the next sweep of claws tears away an entire ear and half of one cheek. As the mother's arms go limp, the child tumbles to the floor. She's crying and screaming and calling for help. She's squeezing her plush toy to her heart and burying her face in its squishy tummy, pleading with the thing to make the monster go away. The hunter wants to show the child that she is not the monster. The monsters are the ones who sent her here. She, the hunter, is simply hungry. The child is kicking her feet and backing herself into the corner and sobbing because her mother is still clinging to life, trying to crawl toward her. But that doesn't last long once the hunter's teeth puncture her throat.

The child wails and shuts her eyes. A dark stain spreads across her pyjama bottoms as the hunter turns and pauses for a moment. She hears the monsters' command. They tell her to leave none alive. She wishes she could spare this child. Children ought never be touched by war, famine, or The Hunt. But the monsters do not see it that way.

With grief in her heart, the hunter strikes.

CHAPTER 12

BETTER HOMES AND GARDENS

ONCE MORE, Abby awoke with the taste of blood on her tongue, even while the rest of the dream slipped out of memory. She went through the next few steps on autopilot without even bothering to open her eyes. Out of bed. Dresser. Crystal. Bathroom. Aspirin. Ignoring the spectre of her mother as it loomed in the corner of the mirror, she brought Natalie up to speed on the latest attack. It had happened somewhere suburban this time. Abby thought it was the North Shore. Natalie said she'd call back when she'd got her gear ready.

As Abby returned to bed, Leanne sat up and turned on her reading light. Even before she'd got her glasses on, Abby's distress was obvious. "What did you see?"

Abby's voice shook. "It was a kid, Lee. This thing's killing kids now."

Leanne reached out and seized the small silver crucifix that hung on a chain from her lampshade. "Jesus Christ."

"Get dressed. We're going."

Leanne put the necklace on. "Now?"

"Now. I have to see this for myself. If Gwyn ab Nethe wants me to find his hound, then I have to start from the scene of the crime. Natalie's car is still stuck full of arrows, so you're driving."

Leanne nodded and got out of bed. As the two dressed, Abby's crystal began to glow around her neck and a male voice said, "Miss Henderson. I assume you were already awake."

Abby gritted her teeth. "Agent Six. Still piggybacking on our frequency, I see."

"A phone call's too risky. My people have more ears than you'd think."

"What do you want?"

"The Department's satellites just picked up a massive spike in electromagnetic activity on the North Shore. We saw a similar fluctuation last time the *Ci Annwn* was active. We're mobilizing a field team now, but I'm prepared to lay odds on what we'll find."

Abby scowled. These Ministry creeps just thought they were *so* smart, didn't they? "You can save yourselves a trip, Six. I saw what happened. Every blood-soaked second of it."

"Figures. Do me a favour, Miss Henderson, and stay clear of this one."

"No can do. I'm the one who's supposed to be looking for this thing, remember? My friends and I need to get on its trail while there's still a trail to get on, and we can't do that by sitting around at home."

"Look, do you understand what you're walking into? The police will be swarming the scene, and my people are going to have enough of a headache pulling the investigation away from them before too many of the wrong questions get asked. If you come barging in, that headache becomes an almighty clusterfuck. I'm telling you: stay back."

"And I'm telling you: no fucking way. I saw what happened, Six! This creature just ate a *kid*! I… I can't walk away when there's kids involved."

A pause on the other end of the line. "I know," Six said more softly. "We interviewed Will and Mona Brady."

"Then you know what it means to me to find this thing."

Another pause. "Okay, listen, because this is the best offer that I can give you. Hang tight for now. I can't stop the field team walking over the scene, but I can be with them when they do. Once we've got the cops and the neighbours settled, I'll call you. Then you can have a look and do what you do."

Abby gritted her teeth. "That's really the best you've got?"

"That's it. Take it or leave it."

"Fine. I'll wait for your call."

"Good." He hung up without a *thank you* or a *goodbye.* Still only half-dressed, Abby flopped onto the bed and stifled a frustrated growl behind a pillow.

"I guess we're staying put?" said Leanne.

"Yup. Guess we better let Natalie know."

*****

It was pushing five in the morning before Agent Six called back to give the all-clear, and quarter to six by the time Abby and Leanne had picked Natalie up from the Letterbox and got across the bridge to the scene of the crime in North Van. After Leanne parked, Natalie produced two thin black wands from the inner pocket of her long trench coat and passed one to each of them. "Simon wants you to have these," she said. "Keep them close."

Simon, as it happened, was listening in over the Vokarion crystal, and was happy to answer the inevitable question before it was asked. "I asked Mother Hyld to make these wands up for you two. They've been imbued with a finite amount of magical energy, and they can produce certain enchantments on command. After what happened the other night, I don't like the idea of you going out without a magician to back you up. Unfortunately, the Order of Wulfredda do not practice the kind of combat magic this situation requires, and obviously I'm no use to you in my present state, so these are the best we can do."

"So, we just point and shoot?" Abby said.

"Do you see those runes engraved along the length of each wand? Those are spells rendered in the language of the Vanguard. If you wish to perform one, simply wave the wand in the air in the pattern of the corresponding rune and speak the spell aloud." At this, Natalie reached into another pocket and produced two folded sheets of paper, upon which the same runes were drawn. Each one had a one- or two-word spell written out phonetically below it, together with a bullet-point list of the spell's effects.

"You get one shot per rune," Simon continued, "and there's five runes upon each wand, so choose your moment carefully if it comes to it."

"Okay, good tip," said Leanne. "Thanks, Simon."

With that settled, the three crossed the road to the scene. A wall of eight-foot-high privacy screens had been erected all around the property, with collapsible white tents covering the Ministry equipment that still littered the yard. It had rained earlier in the morning, and muddy footprints criss-crossed the paving stones leading up to the front door. Agent Six stood at attention on the soggy welcome mat, wrapped in a long beige trench coat to protect him from the elements. (As if anyone didn't already believe he was a G-man.) Beside him stood a short, freckly, frizzy-haired woman wearing a white lab coat over a too-large argyle sweater. Six introduced her as, "Dr. Phillipa Susan Turner. We call her Phil. You can trust her."

"Agent Six has explained the... unique situation you find yourselves in," said Phil. "And he's made it very clear that I'm not to speak of it to anyone else."

"Phil's with the forensics department," explained Six. "She's our junior cryptopathologist."

"And cryptopathology is... what, exactly?" Abby asked.

"The study of injury, ailment, or death as a result of supernatural forces." As she said this, Phil saw Abby extending a hand to shake. She raised her hands above her head, sucked in a breath through her teeth, and backed away as if Abby were trying to pass her a live snake. "Er, thanks, but… I don't."

Abby drew back her hand. "Don't?"

"It's nothing personal. It's just… I don't do well with germs."

"I thought you were a pathologist."

Phil sniffed primly. "Yes, and I work in a sterile environment, so I know I can't catch a cold from some poor unfortunate who gets on the wrong end of a warlock. But I don't know where your hands have been for the last few hours, do I?"

"Apologies for Phil, by the way," said Agent Six, in the tone of a man who'd had this exact conversation a dozen times.

"So, are we going in or what?" asked Natalie. "It was a long drive out here and your people have already delayed us."

Phil sucked air in through her teeth again. "I'd prefer if it was just one of you. My team have made their inspection, but I'd like to preserve the integrity of the scene as much as possible. If the Ministry knows you were here, it's our jobs on the line."

"You go in, Abby," said Leanne. "Natalie and I can stand guard while you do your thing."

"Sure. I'll try to be quick." She took a step forward, only to be met by another suck of air from Phil.

"Um, do you mind…?" She pointed over her shoulder to one of the folding tents. Beneath it stood a moveable clothing rack with several white forensic oversuits hanging upon it. "The clean-up crew won't be in until morning. Germs, you understand."

*****

When she'd clad herself in her cut-rate Michelin Man cosplay, Abby went into the empty house. Phil followed her, identically dressed, in order to assure herself that Abby wouldn't mess up the scene too badly.

"Germs" was underselling the true extent of the horror. Though the victims' remains had been removed some hours before, every drop of blood or shard of bone lay exactly where Abby had seen it fall in her dream. She fought an urge to vomit behind her facemask and asked, "What's the story on the victims?"

"James and Patricia Nichols," replied Phil. "Jim and Peggy to their friends. Their daughter's name was Lisa. He was a fourth-grade teacher at the same school his daughter attended; she was a receptionist in a pediatrician's office. And before you ask: we are checking for any connection with Jack Kang and/or Ted Purdy. Nothing's come up yet."

"What about the kid? Could there be a connection there?"

"I wouldn't have thought so. Should there be?"

"I don't know. In my dream, when I saw this all happen, I... I almost felt what the creature was feeling. And it didn't feel like the parents were the targets."

Phil's gingery eyebrows went up behind her rigid facemask. "Really?"

"I can't explain it very well, but it felt like the adults were... incidental. The hound only went through them because they were in the way. I think it was the kid it wanted."

"I'll pass that on to Agent Six. If there's a connection, I'm sure he can find it."

"Yeah," Abby grumbled, "I bet he can."

Phil cleared her throat. "Miss Henderson, may I be frank with you?"

"Go ahead."

"I recognize that you have issues with how my colleagues conduct themselves—and I assure you you're not the only one—but at some point, you'll have to accept that you and Agent Six and I, we're all allies here. He didn't have to let you in here in the first place."

"Yeah, well, he also didn't have to threaten to have my memory erased. Not a great look on him."

To this, Phil had no response, so Abby left her behind in the entranceway and let her second sight take over. If the thick, coppery odour of blood had made her queasy before, then it almost knocked her flat on her ass now. Her knees wobbled as she traced the hound's path of destruction, and she nearly keeled over at the sight of the agitated red streaks that zig-zagged the stairs to the second floor.

"Are you sure you're prepared for this?" asked Phil, coming to stand beside her.

Abby took another few breaths and swallowed the sour bile rising in the back of her throat. "One hundred percent," she lied. Then she climbed the stairs.

Every step was worse than the one before it. As she climbed, the dark thoughts and desperate emotions hammering at Abby's sixth sense grew and grew. The hound's rage and hunger; its' victims terror and lack of understanding; their grief as, one after the other, they saw this thing tearing their family unit to literal shreds. None of it could show on her face. No muscle could twitch in her hands or her shoulders.

After what seemed like a solid week of climbing, she reached the top of the stairs. Phil was three steps behind her. For a brief moment, Abby just stood there, her head reeling and her stomach churning. She looked to the end of the hall, where the *Ci Annwn* had muscled its way into little Lisa Nichols's safe haven. A crescent-shaped section of the door had been bashed in when the creature made its last charge, and the bottom hinge was ripped right out of the frame. Ignoring every instinct that told her to turn and run screaming into the night, Abby looked down at the rust-red pawprints soaking into the carpet and followed them to the child's bedroom.

The prints stopped suddenly, on the far side of the bed. The sky-blue dresser that had once sat in that corner looked like somebody had taken a sledge hammer to it. On the wall behind, the paint had stripped away where the faerie ring had formed. The winter caps and Judas's ears sprang out of the very drywall, with flecks of peeled paint speckling them like the flakes in a child's snow globe. The carpet was soaking wet, reeking of blood and urine, and Abby was suddenly grateful for the blue booties that came with her oversuit.

Something tugged at the corner of her consciousness. Phil had stepped forward to examine the faerie ring and was saying something about subsonic magical resonance and recalibrating satellites, but Abby didn't hear a word. The something that held her attention was like an echo or a mist of breath upon a window—some vestige of a life that had no form or substance of its own. She began to shift from one foot to the other as the shade tugged at her mind, and when she moved a certain way, the tug became stronger. So, she moved closer.

Phil had stopped talking by now, and Abby followed the tugging sensation downward, onto her hands and knees. She looked beneath the bed on the side nearest the door, and there she saw the cotton-ball innards of a savaged stuffed toy. Small flaps of fabric skin still clung to the cotton here and there, the whole mess being held together by a paste of Lisa Nichols's viscera. Two little discs of black plastic and a chipped triangle of pink sat among the plush remains—the eyes and nose of the ex-toy. It was from these that the tugging sensation was strongest, so Abby reached beneath the bed and picked them up in her gloved hand.

"I have an idea," she said to Phil. "Mind holding onto these for a second?"

"What are you going to do?" the pathologist asked as she caught the plastic fragments in the palm of one glove.

"Probably something inadvisable." She peeled off her left glove, keeping her scarred right palm covered. Then Phil made a noise of protest as she laid her bare hand over the remains of the plushie and shut her eyes.

*****

It had started raining again, so Leanne and Natalie were sheltering in Leanne's little blue Golf. Natalie had pushed the seat back as far as it would go and still didn't have enough leg room, but that wasn't Leanne's main concern right now. "Tell me about the Dullahan," she said.

Natalie looked over with those grey, unblinking eyes of hers. "Tell you what about the Dullahan?"

"Whatever you think Abby and I need to know. Whatever's not in Simon's library. You have history with them, Natalie. Gwyn ab Nethe said it himself."

"Whittaker does, too. You can talk to him."

"Talking to Whittaker is like getting a root canal, with the added bonus of knowing that the dentist is probably going to ask for your firstborn child as payment. I'd rather not give him any more leverage than he already has."

"Would it make any difference if I said 'no'?"

"It wouldn't." When Natalie made no reply and turned to look out the windshield, Leanne pressed on: "If this is about what happened in the Letterbox, I get it. Something got out that wasn't supposed to, and the Dullahan are the reason why. I know they've hurt you, Natalie, but I want to make sure we know what we're dealing with before they hurt us." Still no answer. As a final stroke, Leanne added, "One of them came after Abby in the Bridge."

That got Natalie's attention. "What?"

"She went to talk to Ted Purdy and Jack Kang in the spirit world. Mid-interview, a Dullahan came for her out of nowhere. The way she tells it, she barely got back to Earth with her head on her shoulders."

"One Dullahan?"

"Abby thought so."

"That's not right. The Dullahan always travel in raiding parties. Three or four at least. Like those ghouls who came after us the night this all started."

"So why would one be coming after Abby in the Elsewhere? Come on, Natalie, you know these things. Tell me what we're dealing with."

Natalie looked at her again. "Do you know what a psychopomp is, Leanne?"

"Spiritual guides, aren't they? When a person dies, it's a psychopomp's job to take their soul into the afterlife."

"You got it. And it used to be that there were a lot of psychopomps. As many different kinds as there are different kinds of bugs living in one forest. And then one day," she shook her head and snapped her fingers, "there weren't."

"What happened to them all?"

"War. War like nobody alive today could even begin to imagine. Human beings… we think we know what war is, we think we've cornered the market on war, but Simon's told me stories. Four years of fighting in a Belgian trench wouldn't match one day of slaughter during the Last Great War of the Ancients."

Leanne was silent for a moment. That was the first time she could remember Natalie counting herself as a human.

"The way Simon tells it," Natalie said, "death came to town in a big way during the War of the Ancients. Not just for the people. For the demons and the faeries and the angels and the psychopomps. There was a backlog of spirits needing to be guided into the afterlife and no one to do it. So, the King-Among-the-Holly stepped up. His court is already the hub of snow and decay, so it was a lateral move."

"The Father of Winter decided to take responsibility for the winter of people's years," said Leanne.

Natalie nodded. "The fae of Holly guide the dead into the afterlife. They take that job seriously. But they also take liberties with it. If they find a lost soul that can't make it to the afterlife, they'll press it into the King's army or make it one of his servants in Carcosa. They'll still kill humans if a human offends them, but then they'll smile and shake that human's hand while they guide them to their rest. And the powers that be pretty much let Holly do the job in their own way, because all the other psychopomps got wiped out."

Leanne clutched the silver crucifix that hung around her neck. "There has to be some power that they're answerable to. You can't tell me God would just… outsource a job like that to something like Gwyn ab Nethe."

"Careful, Leanne. That's twice you've said his name. You don't want to go drawing his attention."

Leanne put a hand over her mouth. There was old magic attached to the true names of the Fair Folk. If a mortal spoke a faerie's name thrice, that faerie could be summoned. "Right," she whispered. "S-sorry. I shouldn't have… I'll be careful."

Natalie nodded, as if to say that was for the best.

"But why does Holly have it out for you?" Leanne asked after a moment. "What 'crimes' have you committed against them? Why would Gw—why would *the King* want you destroyed?"

"Think about it, Leanne. Yes, the fae might be killers and tricksters. Holly might play fast and loose with the rules of their job. But the chronology of life and death? They don't play with that. Mortals live, and then they die, and then they move onto what's next, whether that's Hell or Paradise or servitude in Carcosa. Things that break that nice, straight line—things like me—are a slap in the face to them. In their eyes, I'm committing a crime just by walking around."

"But you didn't ask to be raised!" Leanne protested. "That's insane to hold you responsible for something like that."

"You're not getting what I'm saying. 'Insane' is what the Fair Folk do. It wasn't our gods that made them. They are *different* on the most basic level of their brain chemistry. And I know how that sounds, to hear a Black woman talking scientific racism, but with the Fair Folk, it's *true*. That's why I don't like dealing with Whittaker: he's been on Earth long enough that he's started to think like a human, but he's only started. You can't predict what he's thinking. You can't predict what any of them are thinking."

"Then how do we keep ahead of them? How do we hold our own?"

Natalie lowered her seatback, stretched herself out, and closed her eyes. "Good question. If you figure it out, let me know."

*****

Ba-boom, ba-boom, ba-boom.

Ding-dong.

Thumpthumpthumpthump.

The chime of the doorbell and the pounding of tiny footsteps momentarily masked the mini-explosions blasting off in Abby's brain. When she opened her eyes, she was standing in the front hall of the Nichols house. There was no clock visible from her vantage point at the bottom of the stairs, but the pink light coming through the front window suggested the dinner hour. The loose dress worn by the suntanned little girl who ran past her suggested late summer.

In the vision, Lisa Nichols smiled a gap-toothed, the-Tooth-Fairy-just-paid-out smile, and her blonde hair bounced in two long pigtails behind her. She looked over her shoulder and cried, "I'll get it!"

"No running in the house, Lisa!" The mother's voice—Peggy, Abby reminded herself—came from deeper inside. The girl paid no attention, reaching the door in another three steps and pulling it open excitedly. On the other side, Jacquie Swann pulled the sunglasses off her face and bent low to pick the girl up in a hug.

"Auntie Jacquie!" Little Lisa Nichols laughed and squealed as the brain behind The Green World Initiative stepped into the house and spun her around in a warm embrace, then passed her off to the man standing half a step behind her on the front porch. While Jacquie set down the large silver gift bag she carried over one arm, Jack Kang gave the child an affectionate noogie.

Peggy Nichols emerged from the kitchen, wiping her hands on a dishtowel draped over her shoulder. "I guess you guys didn't have too much trouble following Jim's directions, eh?"

"Only got lost twice!" Jack Kang said with a grin. "Speaking of: where is he?"

"He's out getting the barbecue fired up. I bet he wouldn't mind another set of hands."

"I'll see what I can do." Kang exchanged a kiss with Jacquie, gave Lisa Nichols a high-five, then headed for the back of the house. As soon as he was gone, the child ran to the gift bag and started pulling out the multicoloured tissue paper.

"Whatcha bring? Whatcha bring?" she demanded.

Jacquie scooped up the gift bag and handed it off to Peggy Nichols. "Not anything you need to worry about, little miss," she said, as Peggy removed an expensive bottle of wine from the bag and looked at it with awe.

The child's face threatened a tantrum of disappointment, but Jacquie saved the day by reaching back onto the front step and presenting a second gift bag, this one decorated all over with My Little Pony characters. Lisa Nichols tore through the paper in a frenzy of excitement, and soon extracted the same plush rabbit that would one day fail to save her from the savagery of the *Ci Annwn*.

"I love him!" she exclaimed, as she buried her face in the rabbit's squishy tummy. "Look, Mama, look what I got!"

Peggy smiled. "What do you say, Lisa?"

The child darted forward for another hug. As she threw her arms around Jacquie Swann's lower half, the plush toy's floppy ears swatted the faerie on the bum. "Thank you, Auntie Jacquie! Thank you, *thank you*!"

Jacquie laughed and kissed the girl on the top of the head. "You're welcome, munchkin."

Peggy smiled and gently prised the girl off, allowing Jacquie to breathe again. "Sweetheart, why don't you go show your dad what you've got there?"

Lisa Nichols turned and bolted from the room, holding her bunny for dear life. "Daddy, Daddy, look what Auntie Jacquie brought!"

When Lisa was gone, Peggy let out a breath and sat on the bottom stair. "Good *grief*, but that kid can move. I think this is the first time I've sat down since breakfast."

Jacquie winked. "Buyer's remorse, Peg?"

That got a laugh. "Not a chance! I may be exhausted, but I've never felt so alive."

"Hard to believe it's been a year already, huh?"

"It feels like she's always been here." A pause, and then Peggy Nichols looked up at Jacquie Swann with wet eyes. "You don't know what you did for us, Jacquie. You and Gareth both. Without you, we'd still be wading through the adoption paperwork."

"Don't give me more credit than I'm worth, Peggy Nichols. Gareth did most of the legal heavy lifting."

"You found Lisa for us in the first place. I'll never be able to thank you enough for that."

Jacquie sat on the step beside Peggy and wrapped her arms around her. "You'll never have to, Peg. Seeing that little monster smile, that's all the thanks I need."

The vision broke. The remains of the stuffed rabbit fell from Abby's numb fingers. With her other hand, she reached up and felt the cold tracks of tears running down her face, sneaking in under her mask and making her cheeks itch. She hadn't even realized she'd started crying.

Grief quickly gave way to an incandescent rage that burned the lining of her stomach. The Nicholses had gone the extra mile to build a loving home fit for a child to grow up happy and healthy in. And whoever was controlling Gwyn's hound had just walked right in and deliberately—*deliberately*—torn that hard work to pieces.

Wherever that person was right now, Abby wanted them to *hurt*. She wanted to find them, look them in the eye, and call all the fury of the Court-Among-the-Holly down on their head. And more importantly, she wanted this evil motherfucker to know exactly why she had brought the wrath of God to their front doorstep.

As she scrubbed away those tears that hadn't yet taken refuge beneath her mask, she noticed that Phil was studying her like a museum piece. "Fascinating... psychometric perception in response to tactile signals... I had no idea the process was so instantaneous." Darting forward, she placed the back of one gloved hand against Abby's forehead and stared deeply into her eyes. "No rise in temperature... no dilation of the pupils... Tell me: do you feel any light-headedness in the aftermath? Nausea? And how do these impulses manifest? Are they full visions? Or are they closer to a sense-memory? A sound, a smell?"

Bewildered, Abby swatted away Phil's hand and took a step back. "Dude! Time and a place."

For a second, Phil looked equally confused. Then she seemed to remember the crime scene in which the two of them were actively standing. "Of course, yes. I couldn't run any tests in here even if I wanted to. All my equipment is out in the car and the residual magic in here would completely skew my readings. Controlling for that faerie ring alone would require an entirely different set of calculations."

"Not exactly what I meant," Abby said. "Look, let's just get out of here and call it a morning, okay? I'll buy you a coffee some time and answer all your questions then. Just... not right now."

She turned and started back down the stairs. Once again, Phil seemed to need a moment to recognize she was being given the brush-off. Then she hurried to catch up. "Can I just ask: what did you see back there? Or I suppose 'feel' might be a better word, if that's how it works?"

"Not as much as I expected," Abby replied. "But enough to know Jacquie Swann's got a lot more explaining to do."

CHAPTER 13

THE GOLDEN HAND

WHEN HIS business burned down around his ears and the kings of Faerie put a bounty on his head, R.G. Whittaker had been forced to make a very quick exit from the city he'd called home since World War II. Once the bounty hunters came out of the woodwork, that quick exit became the first in a series, which only ended when Ætheriċ, son of Wulfrecg, son of gold-giver Hroðmund—AKA Simon Lockhart, the Last of the Vanguard and Nosy Parker *extraordinaire*—had tracked the imp down and put him to work as an informant and errand boy.

Whittaker's many quick exits had meant he needed to travel light. When he bolted from Vancouver that first time, almost a year back, all he had to his name were his two best suits, one extra pair of cufflinks, three grand in large bills, and a spare key to the pile of burned-out rubble that used to be his nightclub.

He was down to just the one suit on his back now: the other had been ripped up and soaked with ectoplasm and other people's blood during the whole Harcourt business. He'd burned through the three grand trying to keep ahead of his pursuers, and he'd lost the cufflinks down a storm drain the night Ted Purdy jumped him. The spare key was all he had left of the imp he'd once been. It was in his pocket even now, and he worried it between his thumb and forefinger as he scurried past the cop shop and adjacent Police Museum on East Cordova.

He didn't think anyone would see through the glamour he was wearing—to any outsiders looking in, he was just one more of the grimy unfortunates sleeping out on the sidewalks of the Downtown Eastside, pushing along his shopping cart full of bottles and cans. All the same, it didn't hurt to be on his guard. The word was getting out that he was back in town. How could it not, now that the Vanguard had him putting his feelers out? More than a few folks in the Nocturn knew that the corner of Gore and Cordova had once been the heart of R.G. Whittaker's empire, and he couldn't be sure how many eyes the Court-Among-the-Oak presently had in the VPD. Walking right past them with "KNOWN FUGITIVE" flashing in neon letters above his head was a risky move.

He reached the corner and tucked himself into the pre-dawn gloom of the Firehall Theatre's doorway. Checked his watch. Scanned the street ahead of him. Felt his heart skip a beat when he realized his contact was late. Reassured himself that this was typical for Fearghal Fuckin' Molloy.

Little bastard probably just forgot to set his alarm. A little tardiness didn't mean someone had paid Molloy to lead Whittaker out in the open and then close the net around him.

He hoped.

For days after he started asking about Holly's hound, he hadn't heard a thing. He was ready to drop the whole project as a dead end when Molloy crawled out of whatever hole he usually slept in. Said he might know something about the initial theft from the heart of Carcosa. Whittaker didn't know if Molloy showing up when he had made things better or worse for himself. On one hand, the lead gave Whittaker something shiny to dangle in front of Ætheriċ's face, to prove that he was doing his bit and get him one step closer to removing this particular millstone from his neck. On the other hand, it meant that he now had to follow up on the lead. Stick that same neck out and risk getting in even hotter water than he already was.

Fearghal Fuckin' Molloy. Always with the bad timing.

He was getting really jumpy by the time Molloy finally showed, some ten minutes after they'd arranged to meet. As the little man came bustling up Gore Street, Whittaker leaped around the corner and hissed, "Where the fuck have you been?"

There weren't many folks in the city who were smaller than Whittaker, but Fearghal Molloy was one of them. As a baseline, leprechauns didn't get much more than four feet high, and Molloy was on the small side even for his race. But he was wide, by leprechaun standards, with a head like a bag of flour that was only three-quarters full and ears like radar dishes. That width wasn't puppy fat either: Molloy lifted weights that were half as big as he was, and he was a surprisingly skilled boxer. When Whittaker appeared from around the corner and loomed over him, Molloy just shook his head and gave a pitying laugh. "Jaysus, Whittaker. You're not doing yourself any feckin' favours with that glamour."

"Don't change the subject. I've been standing here for ten minutes shitting myself because I thought you were going to sell me out to Oak! Where were you?"

"Ah, I picked up a tail at the edge of Chinatown, didn't I? Had to lead the fecker down about six blind alleys afore I lost him."

Whittaker gulped nervously. "Did you see his face?"

"Nah, he was wearing a ball cap down low over his eyes. But I don't think he was one of Oak's."

"How do you know?"

"Cuz he was wearing a feckin' jean jacket and tennis shoes with pink and blue laces. That doesn't seem like any hardened mercenary to me."

Whittaker exhaled. "Okay. Okay, you're probably right. Just had to be sure."

Molloy softened and shook his head. "Ah, feck. I heard what happened with Ted Purdy. I don't blame you for being on your guard."

"Speaking of which... " Whittaker jerked his head in the direction of St. James Anglican, on the opposite corner. "Let's go somewhere private and have a chat."

Molloy followed as Whittaker crossed the road and removed the key from his pocket. In all truth, "key" was something of a misnomer: the thing was a smooth pink stone about three inches long and shaped like a teardrop. But when used properly, it opened a door that was otherwise closed and got you where you needed to get, so Whittaker didn't know what else he could call it.

He crouched and tapped the stone four times on one of the concrete steps in front of the church. With each impact, the stone chimed like a bell. After four chimes, there came the rumble of thunder and a tinny female voice on the wind. "Ground floor," it said. The squawk and crackle of a sound system on the fritz drowned out the next few words, and then the voice began to repeat itself. "Ground floor. Ground floor. Ground floor." With a twinge of sadness, Whittaker pocketed his key and turned to the source of the voice: an antique elevator car that stood in the middle of the road, attached to no cables or weights. Once upon a time, this had been the express route to Avalon, his own personal kingdom in the sky. Now it was a monument to his ruination.

The windows in the back of the elevator were smashed, the gilding on the scissor gate was cracked and peeling, and the overhead light was dead. The speaker kept chirping, "Ground floor. Ground floor. Ground floor." It only stopped only when Whittaker gave the car a solid kick.

"Now boarding for Avalon," the speaker drawled.

"Looks like yer wan there's had a rougher year than you have," said Molloy, not unsympathetically.

The imp scowled. "I've been away too long, Molloy. I never should have let her go to seed like this." The pair of them stepped into the elevator, and Whittaker took bitter notice of the fact that the gate did not automatically shut behind them, as it once had done in the heady days of yore.

As the elevator began its slow ascent into the grey clouds above the city, thunder rumbled once again. A light rain began to fall. In one of the shadowed doorways along Gore Street, a young man in a jean jacket and tennis shoes with mismatched laces turned up his collar against the weather. His eyes followed the elevator car until it disappeared through the clouds.

*****

After a few worrying jolts, a teeth-rattling grind of invisible machinery, and the *creeeeeak* of an unoiled elevator gate, Whittaker and Molloy at last stepped out into what remained of Whittaker's castle on a cloud. Only then did Whittaker stop holding his breath and break the illusion.

They had to tread carefully. The enchantment keeping the cloud together—packing the water vapour into a superdense and theoretically impermeable surface—had not been reinforced since the night Whittaker fled the scene. There were breaks that hadn't been there the last time he was here. Wet patches that dripped rainwater onto the rooftops below if he trod on them too heavily. Wispy stalagmites of vapour trying to pull away into the upper atmosphere. Thankfully, it wasn't a long walk to where they were going, and after a couple minutes of pussyfooting the imp and the leprechaun stepped off the cloud onto the white marble steps of Avalon: Whittaker's last legitimate business venture.

At least the building's impressive façade had survived, more or less. Okay, the front doors and the club's sign had been reduced to ash in the supernaturally supercharged fire that had ripped through the building on its last night in operation. And yes, the glass dome of the roof was gone, with only a few melted girders left over to suggest where the frame had once been. But it was still his place, warts and all. It was home, and there was nothing missing that he couldn't rebuild.

The tables and chairs had all held together about as well as his plans to stay off Holly's shit-list, so he and Molloy sat themselves down side-by-side on a pile of slag that had once been one of the dome's support girders. The bar and the liquor shelves were totalled, so they shared a drink from Molloy's own hip flask. The stuff was a sour, fiery brew from the peaks of the Svartryggr, the icy mountain range that cut through the northeastern extremities of Holly's lands. Whittaker grimaced after the first sip, waited for the burn in the back of his throat to subside, then said, "You couldn't bring something from more… neutral territory?"

"There's no such thing as neutral territory where you're concerned. Any taste of home is a taste of somewhere where someone wants your head on a stick. I could have brought gildflower wine from the heart of Ardenne itself, and it'd still be bitter with the taste of some Oak gobshite's spit."

"Thanks for the reminder." He took another pull from the sourbrew. "So, what's the story, Molloy? Why'd you drag me out here?"

The leprechaun took back his flask and fortified himself with another swallow of booze. "Few months ago, a tale starts going around among our lot. Somebody has a job needs doing, and they're ready to pay to get it done. No one said what the job was, exactly, but I put my name forward, same as half the operators in town. Got a meeting with a bloke to see if I was 'the right fit,' he said. This was… end of May, start of June or so."

Whittaker started paying a little more attention. That wasn't long after Jack Kang had been killed. "Did this guy you met with have a name?" he asked.

Molloy shook his head. "Yer man told me, 'We don't need names. If we likes ya, we lets ya know.'"

"'We'?"

"He wouldn't talk about it, but I got the feeling he had someone pulling his strings. The operation had plenty of moving parts, like, and he was just one. It took us fifteen minutes of dancing around it before he let me in on what the work actually was."

Oh, goody gumdrops, Whittaker thought. *Here it fucking comes.*

"They were opening a door from here into the Otherlands, and they needed someone to walk through it. Into feckin' Carcosa itself. Well, I heard that and I told yer man to go stick his head in a puddle. I wasn't wanting to get in that kind of trouble."

"What did he say to that?"

"Said he understood. It was dangerous work he was wantin' done, and the price might be too high for some. He was sorry we couldn't make a deal, but he wasn't short of offers, and there was no hard feelin's. Then we shook hands and I was off. Only… "

"Only what?"

"Only something about the meet bugged me, didn't it? He was too eager by half, was yer man. Once he finally told me what the job was, I mean. Here's him asking for some poor fecker to stick his head in a damn noose, and one look in his eyes tells you he almost wishes he was doing it himself. Whole thing smelled like trouble, and I thought I ought to know who yer man was answering to, so I could warn folk off from dealing with him, like. So, when we shook hands and made our peace, I went fishing, didn't I? For a wallet, ID, anything." In one movement, the leprechaun grabbed Whittaker's hand and shook it heartily, whilst with his other hand he reached around the imp's back.

Whittaker had to give Molloy his due. He didn't even feel the leprechaun's other hand slip in and out of his pocket until it was already done. The only reason he knew Molloy had made the move was because he'd been the one to teach it to the little sneak.

"That was all he was carrying," Molloy said when Whittaker retrieved the object that the leprechaun had just slipped into his pocket: a gold coin, slightly bigger than an old English sovereign. The reverse face showed a blazing sun rising over the snow-capped peaks of a mountain range. Patterns of miniscule, interlacing oak leaves and holly berries were painstakingly engraved upon the mountain slopes, giving an impression of rolling, uneven topography. On the observe was a hand, fingers parted and palm facing outward. The same pattern of oak and holly woven together played across the "skin" of the palm.

"This week just keeps getting worse," said Whittaker.

Molloy said nothing. His face was screwed up in an expression of distaste, his eyes on the coin as though it had slapped his mother.

The gold *lau* wasn't a coin that circulated in the Otherlands anymore. It hadn't been for a couple hundred years at this point. That wasn't anything to do with value or rarity. It was more what the imagery connoted. The golden hand—the hand of Nethe the Fair, the first king of the Fair Folk—meant something very different now than what it did when the coins were first struck.

There was a particular philosophy popular among certain elements in the Otherlands. The old and reactionary, mostly, but some of the young and impressionable, too. Just enough to keep the movement alive. The thinking went that the Fair Folk had lost their way some time in the past two or three centuries. More and more of them had started migrating to Earth about that time, with a decent number integrating or interbreeding into human society. And there were some faeries—assholes, Whittaker called 'em—who didn't like that one bit. The great race of the fae was diluted by the blood of mortals, the old magicks were at risk of being forgotten, blah blah blah. All of your standard "reject modernity" horseshit. At some point the assholes had latched onto the golden hand as the symbol for the "traditional thinking" they wanted their neighbours to embrace. Never mind that there were roughly six hundred fables about Nethe the Fair coupling with some human peasant and siring a child of exceptional beauty and guile. Facts didn't mean much to the assholes. One way or another, the golden hand was their symbol. The Golden Hand (capitalized) was the name on their letterhead. Nethe's was the lineage they supposedly fought to defend.

It was all Whittaker could do not to throw the coin right over the edge of the cloud. He reminded himself it was evidence and stuck it back in his pocket. There were any number of tracking spells that someone with Ætheric's experience could use to identify this coin's previous owner. That person, whoever they were, probably knew a thing or two about the King-Among-the-Holly's missing hound.

"I'm not too proud to say it, Molloy: this was worth the trip out here. Thanks for the tip."

"Happy to serve if it means stepping on some Golden Hand fecker's balls."

"No promises. But if I get a chance, I'll give 'em a swift kick for both of us."

The leprechaun laughed and raised his flask. "That sounds more like the Whittaker I know!"

He brought the flask to his lips. The sourbrew sloshed inside. Then, all hell broke loose.

Whittaker never heard the thrum of the bowstring. The first he knew of the danger was when Molloy let out a sharp gasp and dropped his flask. As the leprechaun rolled forward, Whittaker saw four inches of carved ebony sticking out of his back. Two more arrows came flying out of nowhere. Whittaker snapped his fingers and got himself out of the line of fire. One black shaft sank into the wall, and the second joined its brother in Molloy's well-muscled back.

The snap brought Whittaker to the front steps of Avalon. He stopped just long enough to breathe, and another arrow came flying at his head. The imp threw himself down the marble steps and laid flat on the cloud outside. He'd definitely heard that one, cutting the air as it flew past him.

He heard something else. Heavy footsteps racing across the marble. He looked back and saw a faintly silver shimmer on the edge of his vision. When that shimmer pulled down the hood of its riding cloak, it came into focus as a Dullahan in full sprint. The lower half of its face was obscured by a riding mask, and it was already reaching for another arrow.

Fucking invisibility cloaks. Whittaker hated fucking invisibility cloaks. He buried his face in the cloud, covered his head with his left hand, and curled up the fingers of his right. Before he could snap his fingers, something punched a hole through his hand, and his whole world became pain. He screamed, groped around until he felt the shaft of the arrow, snapped it off just above the head. Somehow, having an inch-and-a-half of steel and wood stuck between his metacarpal bones seemed marginally better than the full twenty-eight inches.

His hand felt cold, his fingers stiff and uncooperative. The wound had an acrid smell that he recognized as dragon venom. Eastern Frostspine, if he remembered his wilderness training from way back. The species had never evolved the fire-spitting glands of its larger cousins, so it fell back on a paralytic agent that it brewed in its second liver. There wasn't enough toxin on the arrowhead to shut down the rest of his system, but Whittaker could feel the muscles in his fingers seizing up. "Aw, fuck this!" he spat. He might not be able to snap himself out of danger, but he still had legs, didn't he? With the one hand that still worked, the imp pushed himself to his feet. Then he ran like hell. The bowstring *twanged* behind him and he ducked another arrow by a hair's breadth. He ran in a zig-zag, both to keep the Dullahan guessing and because the cloud was so patchy here. One wrong step, and that was that. He kept his eyes on the elevator sitting at the edge of the cloud. The King had all but admitted that the Dullahan didn't know these streets. If he could get back to the ground, he could get himself lost.

The Dullahan whistled, and time and space pulled themselves apart before Whittaker's eyes. One of those fire-snorting stallions jumped out of the void and reared up with a whinny. Its hooves seemed as big as hammers. Whittaker's eyes followed those hooves down to the cloud as the beast lowered its head and charged him. Then he looked at the cloud beneath the hooves: all patches and wisps, as thin in some places as muslin.

"Goddammit." The imp jumped out of the horse's path, aiming for a landing on the thinnest patch of cloud he could see. It held his weight for all of two seconds before it broke.

He fell face-down, the whole city wide open beneath his gaze. His city. In the old days, this had been his favourite way to look at her. He'd just stand at the edge of his cloud with a cigar and a good scotch and watch the lights shining below him. He'd always thought of each light as alive in its own right. Each light had been installed by someone, wired by someone, drew power from a river or lake dammed by someone. A car's headlight, a signal light on the bridge, a reading lamp in some millionaire's penthouse—every one had a switch that someone needed to flick. Every light in Vancouver was somebody's story.

The dawn had broken, and some of the lights were going out. Others were coming on, as folks got on the road to work. Stories ending and stories beginning, everywhere he looked. They were getting closer, too. No time to get wistful now. He needed to act. With the one hand that still worked, he reached across to the pocket where he kept the key. He withdrew it and tapped it against the splintered arrow shaft still sticking out from his other hand. It hurt like hell, but he needed a solid surface, and this was the most solid he could reach right now.

The ethereal bells chimed with each tap. Thunder rumbled. A second later, the elevator car plummeted through the cloud about ten feet away from him. It hit terminal velocity the same time he did, and he started tapping out a different rhythm on the key. He'd worked out the magic for this one only a few months before the fire, but he'd never tested it. It was real "In Case of Emergencies, Break Glass" material.

The scissor gate opened and the elevator sped toward him, swallowing him in one gulp. As the gate shut again, he slammed against the back wall, winded and achy. He dropped the key and sank to the floor. Then he heard the snort of horse-breath.

The stallion broke through the clouds at a full gallop, its hooves touching nothing but thin air, spitting flame as it raced for the elevator car. On its back, the masked rider uttered a hissing laugh and raised his bow. Before Whittaker even had his hand on the key, an arrow whistled through the gate and punched him in the abdomen. He gasped, closed his fingers around the key. A second arrow found its mark. His eyes watered and he bit back a scream as he picked up the key. The third sequence of taps was the longest yet. His muscles tightened as the Frostspine toxin leaked into his bloodstream. But as he tapped out the last beat, he heard the thunder again. The whole car rattled and his fingers froze, clawlike, around the key. Dark patches encroached on the corners of his vision. The last thing he saw clearly was the fast-approaching Dullahan on its flying steed, nocking the last arrow in the quiver. Then the air split with a teeth-rattling crack as Avalon, the Dullahan, and the distant pavement of Gore Street all disappeared in a flash. Where he ended up after that, Whittaker didn't know. He was already unconscious.

CHAPTER 14

TEA AND SYMPATHY

"GROUND FLOOR. Ground floor. Ground floor. Ground floor."

One second the road was clear, and the next someone had dropped an elevator car right in the middle of it. The impact smashed up the pavement and sent every car alarm for three blocks into panic mode. Behind the wheel of her little blue Golf, Leanne slammed her foot on the brake and shouted, "Jesus, Mary, and Joseph!" It had been raining for most of the hour-long drive back from the Nichols residence to the Letterbox, and the tires wouldn't get a grip. The Golf swerved, skidded, shot past the elevator and jumped onto the sidewalk. As her seatbelt knocked the wind out of her, Leanne straightened her falling glasses and tried to get a look at the blockage in the road.

"Is everybody okay?"

"Aside from the seatbelt punching me in the tits?" Abby coughed and groaned from the backseat. "Just dandy."

Natalie was already out of the car and going in for a closer look. "Holy shit," she breathed. "Abby! Leanne! Over here, now!"

That brought them running. Natalie knelt in front of the elevator and stuck one arm through the gate so she could check the pulse of the sprawling figure on the floor.

"What the fuck happened to him?" said Abby.

"Whatever lead he went to chase up, it looks like he found it," Natalie responded. She was silent for a few seconds before she drew her arm back with a sigh of relief. "He's got a pulse. It's weak, but it's a start." The scissor gate had buckled and jammed upon landing, so Natalie stood and got both hands on it. "We need to get him into the Letterbox, now."

"What are we?" Leanne asked. "Four, five blocks out?"

"Thereabouts." Natalie pulled on the scissor gate until it peeled open like a banana. Abby pulled Whittaker out of the elevator and laid him flat on the pavement.

"What did this? Dullahan?"

"No question," said Natalie. "See his hand? That swelling and the blue-green tinge of the skin around the wound? That's Frostspine venom. The Dullahan use it on their arrows sometimes." She ripped open the imp's shirt and saw identical discolouration surrounding the shafts in his torso. "Shit. If we leave the arrows in, the paralytic could hit his vital organs and shut them down. If we take them out, he'll lose a lot of blood he can't afford to lose right now."

"I've got it!" Leanne dug deep in the pockets of her sweater and extracted the Rent-a-Wand and the cheat sheet of spells that Simon and Mother Hyld had whipped up. Her eyes flicked over the page for a quick moment until: "Yes! Right here! 'To halt the motion of an object.' I mean, blood cells are an object, aren't they?"

"Worth a shot. Abby: you call the Letterbox while we deal with this."

As Abby stepped away to raise Simon on the Vokarion crystal, Natalie and Leanne set to work on Whittaker. Natalie got one hand as close to each arrowhead as she could and then pulled. As the first bursts of red appeared, Leanne pressed the wand close to Whittaker's chest and whispered, "*Forsete.*"

She felt something she couldn't describe, like a shockwave or a mild electrical current, but not quite. It came from somewhere in the air around her, passed through her in a rush, and came out the end of the wand as a burst of golden light. The flow of blood stopped as soon as it started, and she thought she could feel all the little cells hit the proverbial wall as they came running up toward her. The wand thrummed like a tuning fork in her hand, and the first rune glowed a deep, fireplace-ember red.

"Cavalry's on the way!" Abby reported. A few seconds later, Simon and Mother Hyld stepped out of a ripple in space and time. Natalie picked Whittaker up in both arms while Leanne kept her wand close to his wounds. Then they all hurried through the portal into the Letterbox.

*****

The Letterbox wasn't exactly well-appointed for major emergency surgery, so Mother Hyld made do with Simon's laboratory, down the distant corridor from the holding cell. Simon lent a hand where he could, but without his magic he wasn't much more than a sponge-holder. The others waited upstairs. Leanne made the tea.

It was a long ninety minutes before Simon came limping back up the stairs. He undid the top button of his shirt and groaned as he lowered himself into a chair.

"How's Whittaker?" Abby asked.

Simon exhaled. "I can't say. Mother Hyld has stanched the bleeding, but the Frostspine venom is another matter. One of the Dullahan's arrows perforated his small intestine. That could mean serious loss of organ function unless she's able to bind and extract the toxin from his system."

"Jesus," Abby muttered. Leanne just hugged herself and looked at her shoes.

"It could have been worse. That spell that Leanne cast over his wounds doesn't seem to have distinguished between blood cells and venom molecules. For the briefest moment, both were arrested. That stopped the toxin's spread and bought us a few blessed minutes."

Abby gave her partner an encouraging nudge. "Small victories, huh?"

"I guess. I just wish we knew what this was all about."

"We may have caught a break there," Simon said. He reached into his waistcoat pocket and held up a shining gold coin. "Whittaker had this on him when you brought him in. It's a golden *lau*—a faerie coin. And if I'm right, it's just given the whole game away."

"How do you mean?" Abby asked. Simon explained the *lau*'s history and its connotations among the more reactionary sort of fae.

"Wait," said Leanne, "you mean the Fair Folk invented fascism?"

"'Discovered' is rather more the word. I'm afraid that mode of thinking is all too common among sapient races. Humans, demons, the Fair Folk, even the Vanguard: sooner or later, some of us always start to think the world would be better off if it weren't for all of our neighbours' pesky variances." He leaned forward and held up the *lau* as if it were a museum piece, and he the expert invited to deliver a lecture upon it. "Whittaker set off earlier this morning to chase up a lead. He returns with this coin in his pocket and three Dullahan arrowheads stuck in him. The safe conclusion for my money—no pun intended—is that whomever stole the King-Among-the-Holly's hunting hound did so either in cooperation with or at the behest of someone with a connection to the Golden Hand. But then Whittaker came sniffing about, and so that person had a sudden need to cover their tracks."

"And then they sicced a Dullahan on him," said Abby.

Natalie spoke for the first time. She'd been sitting in the corner for the last while, sharpening the iron-headed bolts of her crossbow. "I'll give you two-to-one it's the same

Dullahan that came after you in the Bridge." Simon raised his eyebrows at this. Natalie blinked. "He does know, right?"

"Would you believe something came up?" Abby replied.

Simon cleared his throat. "Abigail, what exactly happened when you Bridged with Ted Purdy?"

She gave him the Coles Notes version, up to the moment the lone Dullahan came riding out of the storm. "Before the trance broke, Jack Kang said something that I didn't get at the time. He was afraid 'they' had sent me. But then I told him I was a Gospel. He trusted me after that. He couldn't believe that 'they' would send someone who was, and I'm quoting him here, 'impure.'"

"That adds up, doesn't it?" said Leanne. "It sounds like these Golden Hand types are pretty rah-rah master race. Gospels are humans with a drop of demon blood, so they probably wouldn't be too keen on that."

"We were working from the assumption that Jack Kang and Ted Purdy had a connection," said Simon. "Suppose for a moment that connection got them both on the wrong end of the Golden Hand." He looked back at the coin for a moment. The others could see the wheels turning in his head. After a short silence, he nodded and said, "Right. Now follow me here, but bear in mind this is an untested hypothesis. Proposition the first: we have a cell of Golden Hand sympathizers operating in the city. Proposition the second: Jack Kang fell afoul of this cell, perhaps because he was in a relationship with Jacqueline Swann. Our Mr. Kang was quite a name in local politics, so his death naturally made headlines. Proposition the third: the Golden Hand are emboldened by this. They believe they have fired the first shot in a righteous war of racial supremacy. And so, they make a power play."

Abby picked up the thread. "They steal one of the royal hounds of Carcosa. They start siccing it on humans. They frame humans for the crime, get the King-Among-the-Holly thinking the humans have blasphemed against him. Now he's ready to go scorched earth on Vancouver and wipe out the skin-apes completely."

Leanne's face twisted in disgust. "So all of this is in the name of an ethnic cleanse?"

"The evidence seems to point that way," Simon confirmed.

Leanne sat motionless a moment. Then she shook her head and rose from her chair. "I—I'm sorry, guys. I don't think I have the mental bandwidth for this. Not right now. You... you make your plans and assemble the war council and all that. I think I need a minute." Before the others could call her back, she turned and disappeared down the corridor.

*****

Abby found her partner deep in the library a half-hour later, at a chipped old reading table with a cup of tea and a tattered Pratchett paperback open in front of her. She didn't seem to be absorbing the words on the page, and the mug was cool when Abby touched it, although it was basically full.

"We missed you back there," Abby said, as she scooched a chair right up beside Leanne's. Leanne didn't say anything. "Simon and I both figure the next move is go talk to Jacquie Swann again. I was wondering if you were going to come with." Still no answer. Abby put her hand over Leanne's and leaned in to catch her eye. "Okay. You did the tea and sympathy bit with me the other day. Now it's my turn." Her thumb made small circles on the back of Leanne's hand. "What's going on?"

Leanne put her other hand on top of Abby's, making an Abby-hand-sandwich. "Don't you just... hate how destructive magic can be sometimes? I mean, think of everything we've seen this last year. The Enlightening. The Rite of Ka'thonn. Now this whole Carcosa thing. Why is everyone in the Nocturn so... so cruel?"

"You're thinking about the Golden Hand."

"Abby, I grew up in hardcore Christian territory. I went to a Catholic elementary school, a Catholic high school, and Mass every Sunday. I was the short, fat, closeted little gay girl with the big glasses in a place with way more Confederate flag bumper stickers than should be allowed in Canada. The world was scary enough for me growing up, and that was just everyday human bigotry. Now I grow up and find out that not only is there a whole other side to fascism, but that it has world-destroying magical powers on its side? That's a little more than I can process right now."

"We're going to get through this, Lee. We'll find Gwyn's hound, we'll find the twisted fuckers who set it loose on our city, and we'll make them sorry."

"*You'll* make them sorry. When it comes down to it, it's always you and Simon and Natalie. I feel like I'm standing at the bottom of a mountain looking up at you all sometimes." She raised her free hand above her head. "You're all up here: the undead bruiser who can lift a truck. The Saxon wizard-prince who knows every spell that's ever been written. The psychic who can rewrite the physics of the spirit world with one word." She held her hand an inch above the table. "And here's me: the short, fat little gay girl with the big glasses who makes the tea and helps with the research."

Abby took Leanne's other hand and kissed it. "Don't say that. Don't you dare say that. It wasn't Simon or Natalie who walked into the middle of Following HQ and threatened to blow them up with a Hellstroke. They weren't first on the scene when Isaac Harcourt broke into our motel and tried to kill us. And what did Simon say earlier? When we found Whittaker outside, you bought him some time he might not have had otherwise."

"By accident."

"Who gives a fuck, 'by accident'? You were there, Leanne. You're always there when it matters. You're there for me, you're there for the people we care about, and you do it all without any kind of gift from on high. I can't begin to tell you how incredible that is."

Leanne met Abby's eyes for the first time. "You really mean that."

"Foreverways. You're right up on that mountain with the rest of us."

Leanne smiled. "Thanks. I think I needed to hear that."

"No problem. Now, are you going to come re-join the party or what?"

"In a bit. I think I just need to sit for a little while, decompress."

"Don't be too long."

"I won't. I promise."

Abby kissed her partner, stood, and left her to herself. Leanne sipped her tea, smiled, and lost herself in her book.

CHAPTER 15

THE OL' ONE-TWO

ULTIMATELY, IT was Simon who accompanied Abby on her return trip to T.G.W. They stepped off the elevator a little before noon and told the kid at the front desk they wanted to see Jacquie Swann, and that it wasn't a request.

It was the same young man who'd been there last time. Curtis or Christopher or Connor, or some other 'C' name like that. He didn't seem very surprised to see the last of the Gospels and the last of the Vanguard rolling up to call on his boss unannounced, and he put the call through to Jacquie Swann's office without much argument. "She, uh, she might be a few minutes," he said. "It's been a rough few days over here."

As the pair took a seat in the waiting area, Simon gave Abby the side-eye and murmured, "I wonder if our friends in the dark suits have been in."

"Wouldn't surprise me," she answered. "It was Six who gave me the tip-off about these guys, remember?"

"A few minutes" slowly became ten minutes. Twenty. A half-hour. At minute forty, Abby got up and fixed herself and Simon each a cup of tea. Simon's eyes were on his watch when she returned and set his down in front of him.

"Blimey, they don't half keep you waiting around here, do they?" he said.

"Almost makes you think it's deliberate."

He blew on his tea. Took a sip. "Rather good, this."

"Leanne thought so. She must've had like a litre of the stuff when we were here last time. Barely stopped peeing the whole rest of the day."

He sniffed his cup. "I know that smell." He took another sip and smacked his lips together. "I know that taste. Yes... ealdorflower and... a hint of silversprig, if I'm not very much mistaken. Not a common blend on this side of the veil."

"You're saying this is faerie tea?"

"Silversprig only grows on the hillsides of Vael Ardenne—that's the great forest kingdom of the King-Among-the-Oak, off-limits to all but the most ancient elven clans and their distinguished guests. Jacqueline Swann must have some prodigious connections in the Otherlands to be able to get this brew imported."

"So, not something you can just buy a box of at Safeway. How do I break the news to Leanne?"

"It's best enjoyed in moderation, anyway. At high enough concentrations, silversprig is powerfully soporific. And the hangover is no fun either."

Before Abby could ask for that story, Simon set down his cup and looked at her seriously. "I want you to let me take the lead on this, Abigail. You handled yourself well with Dr. Swann last time, but the situation's changed. Her connection to this business is deeper than we realized, and she may have her guard up now. It's the nature of the Fair Folk to obfuscate and cajole when they come under pressure like this. I have more experience in these affairs than you do, so I hope you'll trust me to do the talking."

"I'm not just going to sit there and look pretty, Simon. You should know me better than that."

He smiled. "Oh, I do. You have a knack for speaking from the heart at the worst possible moment, so I want you to wait for that moment and then do what comes naturally."

She smiled back. "I get you. You talk Jacquie Swann into a corner, and then I hit her with the ol' one-two."

"Precisely."

"You set the tune and I'll play along, *maestro,*" Abby said.

Simon winked. "Top of the class, Henderson."

A young woman clutching a tablet and a stylus—both inlaid with the Shattergrip clan's peculiar crystal-and-rune-work—came to collect them a few minutes later. Well, "young" was perhaps a relative term in this case. Once again, Abby saw no aura, which meant the woman was full-blooded fae. She might be older than Simon, for all Abby knew. The faerie woman was as pale as a Dullahan, with long red hair that flowed down her back, sharp cheekbones, and a mouth that was just a little bit too wide. She wore a well-fitting grey pantsuit over top a forest-green blouse, and Abby could see the edge of a hair comb sticking out of one pocket of her blazer. It looked a hell of a lot like real ivory. Abby's mind jumped between a number of witty remarks—*Thanks! It has pockets!* and *Alright for some, isn't it?* were the frontrunners.

"Miss Henderson? Mr. Lockhart?" said the faerie woman. Abby looked up from the ivory comb, her witty remarks forgotten. "Iris Keane," the faerie announced, in a lyrical Dublin accent. "I'm Mr. Swann's personal assistant." She smiled, showing too many teeth, and shook hands with a grip as cold as death. Abby suddenly felt very grateful for her fingerless gloves.

"Mr. Swann?" Simon inquired.

"Dr. Swann's brother," explained Ms. Keane. "I'm sorry, you should have been told, but we all thought it was best to loop him in on this. He's with Dr. Swann in the office, if you'd like to follow me?"

Simon and Abby exchanged a look as they followed Ms. Keane down the corridor. Abby subtly touched the Vokarion crystal under her shirt and shot Simon a telepathic message. *Who the hell's "we"? And why does Mr. Swann need to know what's going on?*

Good questions all, Simon replied. *It may be that Dr. Swann already knows exactly why we're here. The Green World Initiative might be getting ready to play a spirited game of Silly Buggers with us.*

As they approached Dr. Swann's office, they could make out two emotionally charged voices within, speaking in what Simon identified as an eastern dialect of the elven tongue. One voice was male, the other female.

Hang on, Simon said, *I'd quite like to try something.* He whispered a short incantation in Anglo-Saxon and sparks of blue-green energy danced at his fingertips. Abby's ears popped and a rush of sound filled her head as the previously muffled voices became crystal-clear. Beside her, Simon sucked in a breath and clutched at his side. Bloody hell. I'll regret that tomorrow…

The old war wound? Abby asked.

Quite. At least we can hear what they're saying now. I might be able to translate.

I thought you didn't speak Elvish?

I don't speak High West Elvish. This is the dialect of the eastern valleys. Now, let me see…

Simon's Elvish was a bit shaky for a real-time telepathic translation, but the gist of the conversation, as far as he could make out, was this:

"You can fight me on this all you want, Jacqueline." That was the male voice, presumably Mr. Swann. "The best thing for the Initiative is if you're not part of it until this all dies down. We say you've suffered a personal tragedy; you need time to focus on your own well-being. We let the board handle the day-to-day for a while, and you take some time away. No interviews. No statements to the press, the constabulary, anything."

"That makes it look like I'm running away!" Jacquie Swann replied. "I haven't done anything wrong, Gareth. T.G.W. hasn't done anything wrong! And don't call me 'Jacqueline.' I hate when you call me that."

"Jacquie, two people are dead who can be linked back to T.G.W. That looks bad. That could shake confidence in the work we do here, and neither of us want that."

"Are you saying this as my brother, or as my attorney?"

"Both. Jacquie, I'm so proud of this place you've made. Mother and Father would be so proud of it. And I just… I just don't want anything to spoil that. But we have knights of the realm at our front door now. If these rumours are true… Dullahan and the hounds of Carcosa and everything they're saying in the Nocturn… this could be a massive problem for us."

Ms. Keane had led Abby and Simon right to the door by this point. She raised her hand, uncertain whether she should knock or not, then typed a quick message on her tablet.

"I won't hide from this, Gareth," Jacquie said. "I'll do whatever I can to stop this horror. It's our people who are dying out there."

Almost under his breath, Gareth Swann muttered, "Are you sure about that?"

There followed a long, icy pause. At last, Jacquie hissed, "What did you just say?"

Ms. Keane turned to look at Abby and Simon, smiled nervously, and then furiously typed out another message on her tablet.

"Auberon king, Jacqueline, you know what I mean," Gareth shot back. "Not 'our people' like our people. In the organization, I mean! I didn't—that wasn't me talking."

"No," she answered, still icy. "It was Grandfather. It's always Grandfather who comes out and says that shit, isn't it?"

Another pause. Abby guessed that Gareth had just checked his phone, because the next thing he said was: "Dammit. Ms. Keane. She's right outside with that Gospel you talked to."

"Well, let's pray to Nethe-on-High that 'that Gospel' doesn't speak Elvish."

"Just let me do the talking here, Jacqueline."

Abby's ears popped again as Simon reversed the spell, leaving her with a faint ringing that muffled the sound of the door opening and the first few words of Gareth Swann's introduction.

This was indeed the narrow-jawed, platinum-haired man she'd seen in those photos the first time she was here. He wore a three-piece suit, clearly bespoke, with a gold oak leaf pendant hanging from a Double Albert watch chain on the waistcoat. The pinky ring on his right hand was inset with a small emerald, and his shoes had a shine to them that would have put many a Royal Canadian Army Cadet to shame. He smiled, shook Abby and Simon's hands, and welcomed them into the office as though he hadn't just been dropping microaggressions left and right. "Coffee? Tea?" he asked. "Ms. Keane will be happy to accommodate you, I'm sure."

"We're good, thanks," said Abby.

"I'm chief legal officer here," Gareth explained as Abby and Simon took their seats. "I thought it was best if I sit in for this conversation." His eyes flicked over to his sister. "Frankly, Jacqueline should have brought me in the first time you were here, Miss Henderson, but I've received a full debrief from her on the content of your conversation then."

"I didn't imagine we were expected," said Simon. "The young man out front was certainly on the back foot." He shrugged and gave a *mea culpa* sort of smile, as if the element of surprise hadn't been exactly the point.

"I'm afraid you're not the first people to come asking around in the last few days, O Ætheriċ, Wulfrecg's son," Gareth replied. "It's more prudent for me to stick close by at all times, in case someone gets the wrong idea about us."

"Provided you're only here to observe and advise, of course. There's many an inquiring mind out there who's inclined to get suspicious when a well-connected person like your sister lets their lawyer do all the talking for them."

"Presumption of innocence, sir. It's one of the most wonderful notions ever dreamt up by the human race. I think we can all agree that my people's sense of justice leans a little too heavily on the sword and the bow before it reaches the 'beyond a reasonable doubt' phase."

"No argument there," Abby muttered.

Simon's tone became more serious. "You're obviously trying to get out ahead of a certain narrative, Mr. Swann. That leads me to believe that you and your sister both know exactly why we're here."

"Yes," Gareth said, "we know about what happened to the Nichols family."

"What was the exact nature of your and your sister's relationship with Peggy Nichols?"

The siblings looked at each other. Gareth seemed to be looking for the diplomatic, attorney's answer. Jacquie looked like she wanted to scream, to cry, to throw something. After her vision, Abby wanted to let after, but Gareth shook his head ever so slightly before looking at Simon again.

"Patricia Nichols worked the front desk here between 2016 and 2018. She left the Initiative that summer when she and her husband moved to the suburbs up in North Van, so they could be closer to his parents, I believe. She asked for a reference when she started looking for jobs on that side of the bridge, and she received it. I believe Ms. Keane has pulled her employment records, if you'd care to look." He gestured to his assistant, who proffered her tablet.

"Well, that all seems quite in order," said Simon, "though I should like to have a hard copy of this to look over at my leisure. Crossing the t's, what?"

"Of course. We'll have that ready for you before you leave." He looked expectantly at Ms. Keane, who typed a note on her tablet.

"I was also rather hoping you could tell me where Lisa Nichols fits into the picture, since we're on the subject," Simon added. "From all that my young colleague here has gathered, you played a significant role in the adoption process, Mr. Swann."

"I offered my perspective as an attorney. Unofficially, of course. Family law isn't my field, but I gave James and Patricia Nichols advice where I could. You know: checked over paperwork, made some calls to colleagues... to use your phrase, I crossed the t's."

"And when approximately were you crossing the t's for the Nichols family?"

"Well, it was my sister who first found Lisa in the foster system. That would have been... September or October 2018, I think, and then she reached out to ask me for advice in early November." He looked to his sister for confirmation. "I think I have that right?" Jacquie nodded, and Gareth looked back to Simon. "But these things take time, of course, and the adoption wasn't finalized until June of the next year."

"Did you continue to provide advice to Peggy Nichols even after she was no longer employed by The Green World Initiative?"

"Perhaps two or three times. I had developed something of a... personal interest in the matter by then. It felt too much like unfinished business."

Simon looked over at Jacquie. "And what about you, Dr. Swann? What was your 'personal interest' in the Nichols family?"

Gareth stepped in front of his sister. "I'm afraid Dr. Swann is not at liberty to answer that."

"Is that your opinion or hers?"

"I'm my sister's legal representative. Any questions you have for her, you can ask me."

"If she'd formed any sort of a friendship with Peggy Nichols, then I rather think she's better positioned to describe the nature of that relationship than you are."

"I never said there was a friendship."

Abby recognized the chance to put in her two cents. "If somebody buys a toy for a kid, and then that kid calls the person their aunt, what do you call that other than a friendship?"

Jacquie flinched at her desk. Gareth paused, his charming lawyer's smile tightening ever so slightly. He looked at Ms. Keane for just a second, but she appeared lost for an answer. Simon patted Abby's arm in a manner that seemed to say, *I'm so sorry, she's from Barcelona.* Over the Vokarion link, he said, *I couldn't have picked a worse moment myself. Well done.*

After an excruciatingly long pause, Gareth fixed his tie and his smile in the same breath. "I'm sure I don't know what you're talking about, Miss Henderson."

"Don't sweat it, big guy. Your sister does." She looked Jacquie dead in the eye. The woman tried not to flinch again.

"I found the rabbit, Jacquie," Abby said softly. "I found that fluffy rabbit that you gave Lisa Nichols, lying there under her bed after something tore through her and her family like a hurricane. I saw her reaching for it in my dream, when that thing came into her bedroom. It was the last thing she turned to before she died. The ultimate, most desperate act of a scared little girl was to look for safety in a token of your love for her."

Jacquie blinked. A tear made tracks down her cheek. "Gareth," she whispered, "could you and Ms. Keane give us the room for a moment?"

Gareth shook his head. "Jacquie, as your attorney and your brother, I can't let you—"

"Gareth." The same icy tone from before reared its head again. "Give. Us. The room."

"We'll be right outside if you need anything." He snapped his fingers at Ms. Keane and pointed to the door. Then the two of them made their exit.

When the door had closed, Jacquie Swann clasped her hands in front of her and bent her head low, until her brow was almost resting on her knuckles. "What do you want from me, Abby Henderson?"

"The truth. All of it. Peggy Nichols wasn't just your employee, Jacquie. Lisa wasn't just collateral damage in an animal attack. And what happened to Jack wasn't a random coincidence. All these things are threads in the same very ugly web."

"What happened to Jack has no bearing on the rest of this." She paused. Looked Abby in the eye. "Doesn't it?"

"I'm sorry, Jacquie, but I think it bears very much on the rest of this." She laid out the short version of Simon's Golden Hand theory, minus the Carcosan connection. That was her trump card, and per Simon's lead, she was saving it for the worst possible moment. As Abby kept talking, Jacquie went pale. She reached for the ring that she kept around her neck, seemed to think better of it, and let her hand drop. She blinked away tears. By the end of it, she looked like she was about to throw up.

"I looked through this creature's eyes went it went for the Nichols family," Abby concluded. "In my dream, I felt everything it was feeling. And I'm as sure as I can be that Lisa was the target. I don't know why. I'm hoping you do."

"Lisa Nichols was the sweetest little girl in the world," Jacquie whispered. "Why—how could someone mark her for death?"

Abby thought suddenly of Will Brady and Josiah Harcourt. "Could it have been something to do with the birth family? Someone might have been holding a grudge against Lisa's bloodline and took it out on her."

"I—I really don't know. Maybe? I have to tell you, I didn't look too much into Lisa's birth parents. She'd already been bounced around the foster system for years."

Simon's voice came over the Vokarion link. *She's lying.*

You sure? Abby thought back.

Trust me. I've had enough dealings with the elves of the eastern territory to know when they're speaking truthfully. She's lying about the birth parents.

Why would she do that?

Search me. But that's the fact of the matter.

Abby was reminded of Ted Purdy's cryptic reference to Jack Kang's heritage, when she'd called to him in the Bridge. *Hmm. If I had a nickel for every time someone got cagey about parents in the course of this case…* To Jacquie, she said, "I don't think you're being honest with us."

The elf blinked. "I promise I'm telling you everything I know."

Abby leaned forward in her chair. Jacquie Swann had no aura she could study, but one hard look into her eyes revealed plenty about her. Perhaps that was one of the drawbacks of being an elf raised among humans: one didn't learn to speak as artfully as their Fair Folk kin, nor to dissemble or cajole quite as effortlessly. When Jacquie leaned back in her chair, when she blinked, and when she tried not to move her eyes away from Abby's, the humanity she'd been raised to appreciate came through loud and clear.

"Somehow," Abby said softly, "I don't think you are telling the truth. Neither does Simon, and between the two of us, he would know better. One more time: what do you know about Lisa Nichols's birth parents?"

"I told you, I don't know anything." It wasn't quite the same tone she'd used with Gareth, but it was sharper than anything Abby had heard during her first meeting with this woman.

"Okay. Then what do you know about Jack Kang's parents?"

Jacquie's hands twitched on the desk. "Jack never talked about his family," she said. "I know they came over from Hong Kong in the late '70s, but other than that… he never said."

"Are you sure?"

"I'm positive." As she spoke, she reached across the desk for a pen and paper and scribbled a note, in big enough letters that both Simon and Abby could read it.

Can't talk about this, it said. Gareth's right outside.

Simon and Abby looked at each other. Abby tapped the front of her shirt, over the spot where her Vokarion crystal hung. Simon gave her a wink and nod, then pulled his own crystal out of his shirt and offered it to Jacquie. She looked at it for a moment, considering, but then she shook her head. Turning her paper over, she wrote another message on the back.

Too risky. Taboos all over the building. Cut through even a Vokarion crystal.

This didn't mean a thing to Abby, but Simon seemed to get the gist. He put the crystal back down his shirt, stood with a wince and a groan, and signalled to Abby that it was time to go.

"What?" she said. "Simon, we didn't wait all that time just to—"

"I think we've found out all that we can here, Abigail." As he said this, Simon threw a hard look at Jacquie. On "here," one eyebrow quirked up. Abby got the picture at last, and stood with a shrug.

"If you say so."

Jacquie stood as well. Abby thought of a scene from a Marvel movie. *Here we are, a bunch of jackasses just standing in a room.* While she was mid-intrusive thought, Jacquie came around the desk and took one of Abby's hands in both of hers.

"Please understand, Miss Henderson," Jacquie said, "I want to help you put an end to this horror. I promise you: I want nothing more than that in the whole world. But there's only so much I can do. This place… the work we do here… if I put one foot wrong, everything I care about could come crashing down."

Abby looked Jacquie in her jade-green eyes. So much pain, so much want, and yet so much love still to give. The elf's hands were as warm as a mother's. Abby reminded herself that, despite Jacquie Swann's youthful appearance, she was older than any living human in the city. Not as old as Simon or Whittaker, to be sure, but she'd seen a lot. She gently drew her hand away. "I sympathize, Jacquie. I really do. Your work helps so many people. If something comes along to upset that, it could damage who knows how many lives." She removed the glove that concealed the icy scars on her palm. "But I'm answerable to people too. And if *I* put a foot wrong, it could kill everyone I care about."

Jacquie flinched and whispered an Elvish oath when she saw the mark. Then she repeated a few lines of the Carcosan mantra in English. "*Long is the storm. And long is the slumber. But longer still…*"

Abby lowered her hand. Nodded. "Yeah. I think I know a thing or two about his wrath at this point."

"So you face a trial by anoeth," said Jacquie. "How long?"

"Halloween."

"Auberon king…"

"Pretty sure it was the other guy I met."

Jacquie didn't laugh. "The first time we spoke, you told me you'd been tasked to recover a missing weapon. A *Ci Annwn*?"

Abby nodded.

"Auberon king… Someone stole a *Ci Annwn* from the heart of Winter itself and set it on Lisa Nichols?"

"I'm so sorry, Jacquie, but that's what happened."

She turned away. Ran her hands through her hair. Turned back. "I wish I could be more help. I do. But there are treaties. Taboos." She was silent for a moment, lost in thought. Then she ran to the desk, grabbed a pencil, and took a business card from a stack in the top drawer. "I'll put you in touch with someone. Someone I trust, who's not bound by their oaths like I am." She wrote down a date, time, and address on the back of the business card, then pressed it into Abby's hands. The appointment was three days hence. Not terribly helpful with the kind of ticking clock Abby had hanging over her, but then she didn't know exactly how these faerie politics worked.

"It's the best I can do," Jacquie said by way of apology. "I'm sorry, but if this is a Holly affair, then I truly cannot intercede as a child of Oak."

"I understand." She didn't—not completely—but that was what you said in situations like this. "Thanks for this, Jacquie. You've been a big help."

Jacquie stepped back, laid a fist over her heart, and spoke a blessing in the language of the Fair Folk. Then she repeated it in English: "May the blessed hands of Nethe the Fair guide you on this quest."

Simon made a similar gesture and said something back in the ancient language of the Vanguard. Abby, slightly caught off-guard, did likewise and said, "Um. *Slàinte mhath* to you too, I guess."

*****

Ms. Keane secured the paperwork Simon was looking for and then saw them out of the office. On the elevator down, Abby looked at him and said, "What was that you were saying about Silly Buggers?"

He looked up from Peggy Nichols's employment record. "You're not wrong. For all her talk of wanting to be an open book, Dr. Swann played it pretty close to the vest once you brought up the family question."

"There's definitely something there that we're still not seeing. And what was all that stuff about taboos? As soon as that came up, you got a little cagey yourself."

"Yes, I'm sorry I didn't explain that earlier. You recall, of course, that the Fair Folk ascribe great magical potential to certain words and ideas."

She nodded. "That's why I'm in such hot water with this eulogy."

"Quite so. Well, one discipline of faerie wordsmithing involves attaching powerful curses or countercharms to particular phrases, so that no one may speak of them freely without inviting terrible repercussions. The kings of Oak and Holly were the first to put this into practice—they're the reason why one may summon a faerie by speaking its name thrice. In days of yore, summoning a faerie was usually dangerous enough in itself to scare folks away from doing it. But there are many other spells one can attach to a word in order to create a magical taboo. Some of them forbid speaking the actual name of the thing itself, and others govern speaking it in a particular location. Speak the forbidden word within the perimeter of the taboo, and things get ugly, but step outside it, and you're safe."

"Like if you shouted 'Go Canucks' in a Calgary Flames bar?"

"If you like. Evidently, there's something that Jacqueline Swann and her inner circle don't want spoken of on Green World property. Whatever knowledge it is that's been tabooed, I'm guessing it crosses lines that the Court-Among-the-Holly doesn't want crossed. You notice she hid behind treaties and oaths as soon as you mentioned the King was involved?"

"You think she's working against Holly on something? Something the Golden Hand wants to stamp out?"

"It's possible, I suppose. The Court-Among-the-Holly's reputation for xenophobic, isolationist politics is well-earned. I can't say for certain if The Green World have any Hollykind on their payroll, though that Ms. Keane certainly looked the part. That blending of cultures might be enough to earn Holly's ire and the Golden Hand's in equal measure. But I suspect there's something more… I just can't place what it might be."

Abby looked at the date and address that Jacquie Swann had given her before they parted ways. "Well, there's one way to find out. Assuming it isn't a trap."

"Oh, don't kid yourself, there's an excellent chance it's a trap," Simon said nonchalantly. "And if it is, then springing it will provide us with some very useful data."

CHAPTER 16

THE CIRCLE

THE DATE and time Jacquie Swann had set was Sunday, shortly before midnight. That left Abby with Friday and Saturday wide open, and no good excuse to get out of meeting Dr. Duthie. There were a handful of threads to pull on in the case, but not many. Whittaker was still unconscious but stable at the Letterbox, working the Frostspine venom out of his system. Simon and Agent Six each had a handful of contacts in the Nocturn whom they could lean on for more intel on the Golden Hand, but news of Fearghal Molloy's murder had spread fast, and none of those contacts wanted to risk a meeting with what Abby and her friends had started referring to as The Lone Dullahan. Between them, Simon and Mother Hyld had subjected the gold *lau* to every tracking spell they could think of in hopes of finding the Golden Hand's hideout, but the farthest back they got was the tavern where Molloy and the Golden Hand's point man had met. Beyond that, the signal was too scrambled.

There was also the lingering question of Jack Kang and Lisa Nichols's mysterious family histories, which a lot of people seemed weirdly determined to lie about. Some gentle prodding by Dr. Phil Turner was enough to get her colleagues at the Ministry looking down that rabbit hole, and thinking all the while that it was their idea. By similar means, Agent Six was able to get some man-hours directed toward the re-examination of a possible link between Jack Kang and

Ted Purdy. But with all of that happening on the watch of a government agency that thought she'd gone dark, Abby knew it was in her best interest to keep herself well away from those inquiries.

So here she was, stepping out of Leanne's car at 4:00 on Saturday afternoon, bunching herself up under an umbrella that the wind kept threatening to take right out of her hands. She should have twigged that something was wrong when she watched Leanne input the destination into Google Maps, before they left their apartment. They weren't heading for an office block in the downtown core, but rather a multipurpose room in a church basement in the south end of Burnaby. Only when she saw the circle of twelve folding chairs, the coffee station against the back wall, and the sign-in table with its permanent markers and stick-on nametags, did she fully appreciate what she'd gotten herself into.

"You didn't tell me this was a group thing," she whispered to Leanne as they got their nametags. A note on the sign-in table politely asked them to write down their pronouns if they were comfortable doing so, so she stuck "ABBY" over the left side of her chest and "SHE/THEY" over the right.

"I'm sorry," Leanne whispered back, sticking a "SHE/HER" to herself. "If I had, there's no way you would have agreed to come."

Fuck. That was probably true. It didn't stop it from stinging, though. "That's a dirty trick coming from you, Lee."

Leanne took her by the hand and blinked those prettiest eyes of hers. "One hour, Abby. That's all I ask. One hour to try and... straighten out some of this mess up here." She reached up and brushed a lock of Abby's hair off her forehead. "If it isn't your thing, that's fine. We don't have to come back. But let's at least be able to say we gave it an honest shot, yeah?"

"Don't you feel weird dumping out all our baggage in front of a bunch of randos?"

"You don't have to dump out all of it. I'm not going to. But if you let off a little bit of the pressure, it might make tomorrow and the day after that a little bit easier."

Abby felt an itch in her palm. She saw her mom standing over by the coffee station. The scars on her left side ached and a familiar melody marched uninvited through her head.

Give me that old-time religion
Give me that old-time religion
Give me that old-time religion
It's good enough for me...

Somehow, she doubted very much that this would make a tangible difference. But she put on a brave face for Leanne and said, "Screw it. Nothing ventured, right?"

They weren't the first to arrive. About a half-dozen folks had already grabbed their nametags and their coffee, and one or two of these had found their places in the circle. In no particular order, Abby spotted a beefy, short-haired man with a greying moustache; a young man—almost a boy, actually—in a toque, torn jean jacket, and tennis shoes with pink and blue laces; a pale, middle-aged woman with big round glasses, a turtleneck sweater, and mom jeans; an older South Asian couple who sat together and spoke to each other in whispered Punjabi; and a balding, bookish-looking, bespectacled man dressed in corduroy, whose collared shirt had been ironed to within an inch of its life. According to his nametag, he was Ken (pronouns: he/him).

Her eyes returned to the kid in the jean jacket, whose nametag identified him as Chris (pronouns: he/they). Something about him pinged in her memory, but she couldn't think why. After a moment he noticed her looking, and started in his seat like he recognized her too.

She turned to Leanne and tried to make it look like no big deal. Now she remembered the kid. "That's the receptionist from T.G.W., isn't it?" she whispered. "The one in the toque?"

Leanne looked without looking. "You're right. Small world."

"Is it?" Abby muttered.

"Abby, relax. So one of Jacquie Swann's employees tries to look after his mental health. That doesn't mean there's a conspiracy. Honestly, I'd be surprised if there weren't a few Green World folks who came to see Dr. Duthie."

Abby glanced back at Chris. He'd pulled out his phone—fitted with the same crystal-and-rune arrangement that adorned every electronic device in the T.G.W. office—and was now idly texting someone. Or at least he was trying to make it look like it was idle. She was pretty sure he was making as big a deal out of not making a big deal out of things as she and Leanne were. She shook her head and gave Leanne a smile that was more reassuring than she felt. "You're right, I'm being paranoid. But can you blame me, after the month I've been having?"

"No, I can't," Leanne admitted.

A few more stragglers came in. The man in corduroy waited until everyone had secured their nametags, their seats, and their refreshments, then cleared his throat. "Well," he said with a bland, easy smile, "it looks like all of us are here, so we might as well get started."

A few folks smiled back. One or two nodded. Abby supposed that these were the regulars. A couple others—particularly the big guy with the moustache and the woman in the mom jeans—looked around them uncertainly. It was a relief to know she and Leanne weren't the only fresh fish.

"You've probably all figured it out by now, but I'm Dr. Ken Duthie," said Dr. Ken Duthie. With a glance at one of the regulars, he added, "I know some of you have heard me give this spiel before, but I see some new faces today. I think it'll help if we all start off on the same page." He leaned forward, rested his elbows on his knees, tented his fingers together in his lap. The easy openness of his posture loosened some knot of tension in Abby's gut.

"We're all here," Dr. Duthie said, and on this point, he was emphatic, "every one of us, because we've... experienced things we can't explain. Sights. Sounds. Feelings. For some of us, it might have been one day, one moment, when we were kids. For some of us, it might be everyday. But at one point or another, each one of us has run up against something that doesn't fit with what we thought we knew about the world, that doesn't gel with logical or scientific thinking. There's only one word for what we've felt: supernatural."

This word sent a ripple through some of the newbies. The big guy with the moustache—Ron, according to his nametag (no pronouns given)—shifted in his seat and crossed his arms over his expansive belly. The lady in the mom jeans (Caroline; she/her) stifled a nervous hiccup.

"Supernatural," Dr. Duthie repeated. "It's not a dirty word, my friends. It's a technically accurate descriptor for what we've seen, at some time or another. There are things out there that science can't explain. Forces. Creatures. I know that's a scary thought. Believe me," and here his calm mask cracked for just a second, "I know. But that's why I do this. That's why I bring people together to talk about the things we've all faced. Because I know, as I'm sure you all know, that talking about it can be the hardest part."

He stopped for breath. Leanne reached over and squeezed Abby's hand. When Abby looked at her, she gave a little smile.

"We can't tell people about these things," said Dr. Duthie. "When we try, they laugh at us. They call us crazy. And if we hear that often enough, we start to think we are crazy. We start to doubt our senses and our place in the world. That's an incredibly isolating experience, and it can lead to much darker things. Again, I'm speaking from experience here." He paused to let the implications settle in, and received a few sober nods for his troubles. Abby belatedly realized that she was one of those nodding soberly. "And so," Duthie finished, "that's why I want to bring us together like this. Because we're not alone in the world. We're not crazy. And if we share our experiences—our griefs, our anxieties, hell, maybe even our triumphs—if we start to find that common ground with each other, we can build our collective fire a little bigger, burn away a few more of the shadows on the wall of the cave, and cut a path through the darkness together."

He sat back in his seat. All around the circle, people exchanged glances, some apprehensive, but others hopeful. A couple looked perturbed by his use of the word "everyday." What kind of fucked-up did you have to be that you ran into the supernatural every single day?

Ron uncrossed his arms and leaned forward in his chair, unconsciously mimicking Duthie's posture from a moment ago. "So, um…" He cleared his throat. Rubbed at the back of his neck with one hand. "So, how does this work? I mean, who starts now, after that pep talk?"

"Whoever feels comfortable doing so," Duthie responded. "If nobody does, that's okay too. We can wait. Somebody will eventually."

"Okay. Well. I don't know about feeling comfortable, but…" Ron cleared his throat again. "Well, somebody has to start at some point, I guess." He raised one hand and waved uncertainly. "So, I'm Ron. I gotta be honest, I don't really know why I'm here. Not yet, I mean. But well, see, the thing is… Okay, so it's like this: I work campus security out at SFU. Harbour Centre. Night shifts, mostly. And I guess about nine, ten months ago, it, uh… it started for me. So, I'm there at the end of the night, and we're about to lock up, and I see this face at the door. A girl. Maybe nineteen. Twenty. But she comes running, pounding on the door, like, 'Not yet, not yet!' kind of thing, you know? And it is pouring rain out there, and this kid, she's got no umbrella, no jacket, so I go and I let her in. And she doesn't even take a breath, she just starts talking at me. Late getting out of class, missed her last bus home, it's pouring rain and she wants to call a taxi, but she realizes she left her phone in the library, all that kind of thing. And I mean, I'm not a dick or anything like that, so it's not like I'm going to tell her she can't go grab her phone or anything. So, I let her into the library, tell her to calm down, take her time, I'm not going to kick her out or anything, but just, y'know, swing by the security desk and let me know when you've found your phone. Then I can lock the place up."

He paused. Smacked one fist into his open palm. Shook his head like even he didn't believe the next part of the story.

"So, I'm back at the security desk. Far as I know, this kid's in the library looking for her phone. But I can't see her from where I'm sitting. Five minutes goes by. Ten. I don't see her. So, I get up to check." He shook his head again. "Not a soul in that fucking library." He looked over at the older couple and reddened slightly. "Um, 'scuse my Frahn-kays. But like I say, that library is empty. And I know I let this kid in. I held the door for her, and there's only the one of them. But you know, after a while, you just start to think, 'Well, I'm getting tired, kinda zoning out, maybe she walked past me and waved, and I didn't notice.' And you know, if that was all that happened, that would have been fine. But then, two weeks later, I'm on shift again, and the rain's coming down. And there's that knock on the door. Same girl. Same routine. Late getting home. Phone in the library. I hold the door for her. Then ten minutes later she's gone. My hand to God, this happens to me three more times over the next month. Same girl every time, and she never once seemed to recognize me. Never said anything like, 'I can't believe I keep doing this.' It's as if it's starting over every time. After the last time it happened, I said something to one of the cleaning staff, like, what the fuck's going on here? Again, pardon my French. Turns out she's done this to a few security guys. Always on rainy nights in March and April." His face fell a little, and he sank into himself in the chair. "She was an undergrad. Got taken out in a hit-and-run right outside the building, about five years ago. It was raining and… she was on the phone trying to get a cab. Twenty-eighth of March. I… I don't really know where I was going with that story, but… yeah. That led me to this." He looked about him and blew out a breath, clearly unsure whether he was more relieved or embarrassed to have unburdened himself like that. "My name is Ron, and I've seen a ghost. Not an alcoholic, though."

The joke only registered one or two charity laughs. Ron shrugged and lowered his head, like he hadn't expected much more. "Sorry for… for rambling."

"Don't be sorry," Dr. Duthie replied. "It's why we're here. Our stories, our experiences, they don't divide us from the rest of the world. Telling our stories brings us a little closer together. It helps us to normalize, let's be honest, some pretty abnormal things."

"I've seen a ghost." That was Caroline, the woman in the mom jeans. She looked apologetically at Dr. Duthie, like she was afraid she'd offend him by speaking out of turn. He just smiled and motioned for her to proceed.

"Well, I mean, I've seen… something," Caroline continued. She looked at Ron, clearly as unsure how to begin as he'd been, and seemed to come to the same conclusion that just starting was the best option. "So, I used to have this neighbour across the street, right? Older lady, lived alone. Lydia… something. Clinton or Collins or something like that. I think she ran a bookstore not that far from here. But she had this big dog. Samson, he was called."

Leanne sat straight up and squeezed Abby's hand tight.

"About a year ago," Caroline said, "this lady just… I don't know, she disappeared one day. Someone on our block had seen her go out that morning with the dog—maybe she was taking him to the vet—but she never came back home. One of my other neighbours called the police. They did what they could to find her, but I guess whatever happened, she just didn't want to be found. I worried about her, though, because I heard her store was a wreck when they went to check it out. The story that went around was meth heads or bikers or something, but that never made a lot of sense to me."

Abby extracted her fingers from Leanne's vicelike grip and patted her on the shoulder. The neighbour whose name Caroline didn't remember was Lydia Clifford, Leanne's old boss at the Olde Curiosity Shoppe. She had been taken by the Deacon to be a vessel for one of his Following acolytes, and Samson had been magically transformed into an awful, vicious hybrid of canine and demon. Leanne and Kelly had been forced to put the creature down at Applegate Asylum, and Abby had done the dirty work on Mrs. Clifford herself.

"But none of that's the really weird part," said Caroline. "A couple weeks ago, I was in bed, asleep, and I guess the noise must have woken me up, but I hear a dog walking around and growling outside this lady's old house. It's a new family that lives there now, and I know they don't have a dog. Neither do the people who live beside them. The folks on the other side do, but it's only a little wiener dog. This was something big. And it was growling this deep, deep growl. But you could hear there was just... just something wrong with it. Like it was sick or hurt. So, I went to the front window and tried to get a better look at it in case I had to call animal control, and it runs away. I saw a flash of light and heard something like fireworks going off, and that was it. I talked to the neighbours who live in that house the next morning, and one of them said their son had woken them up to tell them about a big doggy walking around outside just about the same time I saw it. In the spot where he said his son had first seen the dog, the husband found the grass all dead and a circle of ice at least three feet across."

Abby and Leanne shared a wide-eyed look. Caroline, misunderstanding the gesture, went on: "I know! It sounds nuts. And you can laugh all you want. But like you do, I went on the internet, because I didn't know what to think of any of this. It turns out there's a whole tradition in the UK of ghosts appearing in the shape of dogs, in graveyards or other places where death has struck or is about to strike. And that got me thinking about how this old neighbour of mine just vanished last year. I don't know if the two things are connected but... I don't know, it's weird, to say the least."

One of the regulars (Dennis; he/him) shook his head and said, without an ounce of judgement in his voice, "There's some freaky things out there, man. Now that everyone's got a phone in their pocket, people are noticing. And Big Brother can't keep up, for the first time in his life."

Another regular (Charlie; he/him) pointed and nodded enthusiastically. "I found a blog with a whole bunch of stories about this kind of thing. Ghosts and vampires and lotsa other shit that was way more out there than that. Most of it right in our backyard, like you're saying." He nodded at Caroline. "I'm not sure I believed half of it, but there was some stuff there that made a whole bunch of sense. Too much, if you ask me."

"Makes you think," Dennis agreed. "How much else have they been keeping from us?"

"Like that old mental hospital out near Hope," said Charlie. "The one that got torched last year. I read something said there were devil worshippers out there back in the '60s or something."

Abby wanted to curl up and die in a hole somewhere. There was every chance Charlie had been reading a *different* blog dedicated to supernatural happenings up and down BC, but it seemed like pretty long odds. The conversation kept going in this direction for several more minutes, and Leanne reached over to squeeze Abby's hand in sympathy.

But gradually, she started to notice something. The rest of the circle was opening up. Those who'd seemed the most apprehensive at the start of the hour were more relaxed in their posture, their tone of voice. Caroline and Ron, who'd so bravely broken the ice despite being two of the most nervous newbies in the room, were animatedly bouncing ghost stories back and forth. The Punjabi couple—Waris and Amrita (he/him and she/her, respectively)—interjected with some of their own understanding of shape-changing *bhootas,* which they thought could account for Caroline's dog. Nobody laughed at anybody else's theories. Nobody called bullshit. They listened, they gave serious consideration to the theories that made sense to them, and they agreed to disagree about the ones that didn't. Dr. Duthie was an even-handed moderator, and made sure everybody felt heard and respected in their course. He never forced someone to talk if they didn't want to, and he didn't interrupt if they did.

In his own way, Dr. Duthie had achieved what the Abby Normal Blog had always strived for. In the beginning, all she'd wanted was to start a dialogue, so that people that they could guard themselves against threats like the Deacon. So that they wouldn't feel as alone as she had when she was a kid. And even if these perfect strangers right here weren't always hitting the bullseye the first time, they were having that dialogue. As Simon had once said, they were opening the door and looking through to the other side. Abby had no idea if Dr. Duthie had ever seen her blog. It didn't matter. He and she were united in their cause. Her eyes flicked to Leanne. Leanne looked back and smiled, and Abby thought there was just a *little* twinkle of "I told you so" in those prettiest eyes.

Goddammit. You did tell me so, didn't you, Waller?

She looked across the room, to where Karen Henderson still stood, expressionless, by the coffee station. She shifted in her chair and blew out a breath.

Dr. Duthie raised a hand, and the conversation died away after a moment. "I'm glad to see us all getting comfortable," he said over the silence, "but I think someone else would like to share something." His eyes flicked ever so briefly to her nametag. "Go ahead, Abby."

She smiled awkwardly and gave the circle a little wave. "Hey. I'm, uh, I gotta be honest, I wasn't sure about all this. But… I'd probably be sleeping on the couch tonight if I'd said 'no.'" She put her arm around Leanne, and heard Waris chuckle at the joke. "Yeah, this guy knows what I'm talking about."

No chuckle this time. She dropped her head into her hands. "Ugh. I don't know why I said that. I'm just feeling a little awkward here."

"I think we all do, a bit," Ron said.

"Take your time," said Dr. Duthie. "You're not alone here, Abby."

"No, I'm not, am I? It's taken me…" She looked at the clock on the far wall. "Jesus, it's taken me the last twenty minutes of sitting here listening to you all to actually believe that." She exhaled again. Where to begin with these people? She knew there was no judgement in the room, but she couldn't just push these poor folks right into the deep end of the pool, where the Deacon and Josiah Harcourt and Gwyn ab Nethe swam beneath the surface. That was more than any of them had signed up for. And she thought it would be nice—God, oh so nice—to not be the main character for once. But she'd opened her big, stupid mouth now, and *something* had to come out of it. What was the phrase? *I've started, so I'll finish.*

She looked back to the coffee station and met her dead mother's gaze. Blew out another breath. Rubbed her hands together. "Okay," she said, "if I'm going to do this, I might as well do it right. So, I've been… seeing things pretty much my whole life." She paused. For maybe the first time in her life, nobody rolled their eyes when she said that. "Yeah. There it is. I can see things. Dead people. Things that haven't happened yet. Things that have happened, but to other people. And I've heard every *Sixth Sense* or *X-Files* or *Final*

Destination joke you can think of, since I was a little kid. I got picked on a lot when I was younger, and after a while I started pretending like this wasn't a part of me. I just wanted to be…" She paused before she said "normal." Somewhere deep down, those old wounds started to ache again. *Abby Normal. Abby the Freak. Abby the Psycho.*

"I just wanted to be ordinary," she said at last. "Boring. But I also wanted someone to listen to me. To hold my hand and tell me I wasn't the crazy psycho bitch all the other kids thought I was." She squeezed Leanne's hand. She sniffed. She wiped her eyes. When the hell had she started crying?

"And I think that's where my mom comes in." She looked at the apparition on the other side of the room. "Because I guess she wanted the same thing for me. She wanted me to be just another kid. But she went about it all the wrong way. Because she knew. She knew what you all know, what we're all sitting here reassuring ourselves we're not crazy for knowing. My whole life, my mom knew about the things out there in the dark, that we can't talk about with other people. She knew, but every time I had a nightmare that was just a little too real, or I saw something that science couldn't explain, she pretended like she didn't. She'd tell me it was just a dream, and I was safe in bed with her standing there beside me, and all that." She sniffed. The tears kept on coming. *Fuck it,* she thought. *Let 'em come. Because this is what you did to me, Mom.*

"She lied to me. Over and over and over, for *years*. My own mother, who should have been that guiding hand I needed more than anyone else. And that wasn't all she lied about. There's other stuff—way bigger stuff—but I'm not ready to get into that. And eventually, I grew up. I found out she was lying. We fought about it. And then she was gone. Just… gone."

Leanne reached into her purse and found a packet of tissues. Abby took them and composed herself over the course of several long, quiet moments.

"Before my mom died, she told me it was all for my own good." She heard someone scoff at this. It was Chris. "I know," she said, turning to look at him. "That old excuse, right? 'I'm just trying to protect you.' And I think in her mind, she was. But..." She returned her attention to the ghost across the room. "You can do a lot of damage trying to protect someone. My mom loved me. I know she loved me. And I love her. I miss her. But I'd give anything to sit down with her just one more time, and tell her that she really fucked up."

She stared at the ghost. The ghost stared at her. Was she imagining it, or was there a touch of regret in those flat, empty eyes?

Dr. Duthie leaned forward in his chair. "Thank you for sharing that, Abby. I can see that wasn't easy for you."

"Those kids you went to school with didn't know a thing," Caroline offered. "You're not some crazy you-know-what."

"I think what Abby's done here is hit upon something very important," Dr. Duthie said, "and that's that sense of isolation I talked about at the beginning. Everybody noticed, didn't they, that she used the word "listen"? That's all any of us want, at the end of the day: to be listened to. We want to be heard, to have our feelings and perceptions validated."

Chris shifted uncomfortably in his seat. "And parents can kind of suck at that sometimes. That's a really lonely way to live, when you get the runaround from the people you trust most."

Abby looked at him, and he at her. That was the first thing he'd said since the circle had gathered. Leanne was probably right. This was just a kid with a lot going on upstairs. T.G.W. and Lisa Nichols and the Court-Among-the-Holly didn't enter into it at all. She made an effort to smile, to meet him where he was. "Honestly, it's kind of a relief to know I'm not the only one here with 'rental issues."

He smirked. Chuckled. "You don't know the half of it, sister." There was something weirdly familiar in the expression, in the tone of voice. There was also something a little artificial, like he was flipping a switch someone had told him to flip without ever explaining why he should flip it. Abby wondered who'd taught him to do that.

She focused on the young man's aura: a thin, solid band of off-white, like the light from a single forty-watt bulb. That was the boring old colour of the non-magical human race. And yet… there were cracks in the light. Spots of blackness and threads of nothing that chewed parts out of the whole. The puzzle was incomplete. *What could do that?* she asked herself. Every earthborn creature projected an aura. Even ghosts did, and she'd met enough to know that for a fact.

But the Fair Folk don't. Was that the big twist, then? Was Stripy-Haired Chris half-human and half-fae? She saw a glimmer of scattered thoughts racing through his aura like fish at the bottom of a muddy pond. Stressors and anxieties, mostly. Things that needed sorting out in the next few days. He needed to pay his cell phone bill. That thing in the car was making that noise again. He'd had a text from one of his roommates just before this session with Dr. Duthie started: *Pharmacy say's my E's ready for pickup. Can you do that after your thing? It's on your way, and I'm stuck at work.* And that reminded him, he still had a buttload of his own paperwork to sort out first chance he got. Finally get the passport changed.

One of those big red-and-white nametags appeared before her mind's eye. The first letter was legible, but the rest had been scratched out by an agitated pen. She realized what she was looking at and quickly turned her attention elsewhere. Chris's aura, all his deepest secrets, slipped out of her grasp and she made no effort to recapture them. There were some things that neither man nor Gospel were meant to know, and Chris's deadname was one of them.

She felt a poke in the side and realized Leanne was trying to get her attention. The conversation around them was still moving apace, and a glance at the clock told her she'd tuned out the last several minutes of it trying to get a read on Chris. She could see him out of the corner of her eye, still studying her. Jacquie Swann had clocked her a few minutes after meeting her. She wondered if Chris had figured her out that quickly himself.

Eventually, the meeting came to an end. A contact sheet went around to all the newbies, so they could get a hold of each other or Dr. Duthie outside the appointed time, if need be. "An extra layer of community," was his reasoning. "So, if you feel like you're alone, you just have to make one phone call and remember you're not." Abby put her number down right below Leanne's. Leanne herself was at the coffee station by this point, making small talk with Caroline and Waris. Abby got up to give her a poke back, and then they said their goodbyes and headed for the car.

"So, how do you feel after that?" Leanne asked, as they stepped out the front doors into the rain.

Abby pulled Leanne beneath her umbrella and said, "Honestly? Not the worst way I could have spent that hour."

"Think you'll be coming back?"

"Maybe," Abby admitted. "It was nice to talk to someone human for once. Someone who's not as deep in the shit as we are."

Leanne nodded. "Gives you some perspective on things." She looked Abby in the eye, and saw something there that made her ask, "So, how's… everything? Upstairs?"

"Everything?"

"I mean… is your mom still hanging around?"

Abby looked down the street. Behind her, to the church. Karen was nowhere in sight. Hadn't been since Abby had tried to get a read on Chris. "Huh. Not right now, I guess. I hadn't even noticed that."

Leanne smiled hopefully. "That sounds almost like progress to me."

Abby felt a lightness that she hadn't in a long while. "It does kind of, doesn't it?"

They reached the car. As Leanne unlocked the door, Abby saw a face behind her, reflected in the window. She turned around sharply, but it wasn't her mom.

"Whoa, sorry! Sorry!" Chris blurted out. "I didn't mean to sneak up on you. But I… I think we need to talk." He looked at Leanne and added, "All of us."

"What about?" Abby asked.

"Well, I mean, you're… *her,* aren't you? You're Abby Normal." He went for his phone, opened the Notes app, and showed them a memo containing a date, a time, and an address. It was the same time and place that Jacquie Swann had written down for her the last time they'd spoken at T.G.W.

"Dr. Swann wanted me to meet with you?"

"Yeah." He put his phone away. "But we're all here now, so we might as well get it over with."

"Can we do it somewhere inside, maybe?" asked Leanne. "My feet are getting soaked."

CHAPTER 17

CHRIS

THEY DROVE to an authentic Chinese restaurant that Chris knew of, just across the river in Richmond. When the server came, he ordered for the table in Cantonese. "I grew up like eight blocks from here," he said when she'd left. "This place has been around for… God, forty years or something? It's a little out of our way, I know, but a lot of the staff, their English isn't great, so less chance somebody'll hear something they shouldn't."

"So, it sounds like there's something to Jacquie Swann's whole hush-hush act," said Leanne, who'd heard all about Gareth Swann and the taboos.

"Oh man." Chris shook his head. "You two don't even realize what you've stepped into here."

"I think I have a pretty good idea, actually," Abby replied. She removed her gloves and laid her scarred hand palm-up on the table. Chris looked uncomfortable at the sight of it, but not surprised.

"The moon has many phases," Chris said, "and a story many threads. Old faerie proverb."

"What do you know about faeries, Chris? 'Cause I'm guessing it's more than a lot of people might realize."

"You must learn a thing or two," Leanne added, "working at a place like T.G.W."

Chris reached up and took off his toque. The hair beneath was short and black, except for a thick white streak in the middle. Abby had noticed it on her first visit to T.G.W., but hadn't thought it noteworthy at the time. After all, she was hardly in a position to throw stones when it came to turning one's body into modern art. It was obviously important to Chris, though, because he tugged at one of the white locks and asked, "Do either of you know what this signifies? My skunk stripe?"

Abby and Leanne exchanged a look, a shrug. "Can't say we do," Abby admitted.

"This is the mark of someone who stands on the threshold between Earth and Faerie," Chris said. "A half-blood, or else a mortal who's been so touched by the Otherlands that they might as well be a half-blood. To put it less poetically, a changeling."

"And which is it with you?" Abby asked. "Are you a half-blood, or a fae-touched mortal?"

"The first one. My mom's from Guangzhou. My dad's from somewhere way farther away than that."

"Guess it makes sense you'd end up working for Jacquie Swann," said Leanne.

Chris nodded. "Yeah. That job kind of saved my butt, honestly. I never would've lasted working among the Zeds—"

"Zeds?" Leanne asked.

"As in 'zero,'" he explained. "Zero magic. You know, the normies."

"Gotcha."

"So, like I say," Chris continued, "I never could have worked for a Zed. Hiding what I am just isn't my thing. But on the other hand, it's not like there's a lot of Knocks out there lining up to read a changeling's resumé, either. It was pretty much T.G.W. or nothing. It's a great job, though; don't get me wrong on that. Everyone gets along. The work we do actually matters. Dr. Swann's super nice."

"And she obviously trusts you," said Abby. "Or else she wouldn't have set us up like this."

"Let's drill down on that for a sec," Leanne said. "Why did she set things up like this? What's the big secret that she couldn't talk about at T.G.W?"

"Well, to put it bluntly, I am. Me and all the people like me."

"The changelings?"

"Yeah. You gotta understand: it's rough out there for halfbreeds. A lot of folks in the Nocturn really don't like humans poking around in their business. They think mankind should be on one side of the fence and Knocks on the other."

"And never the twain, *et cetera,*" Abby said. She'd run into this sort of thing herself; for some of Whittaker's old associates, even the one tiny drop of demon blood running in her veins had been a bridge too far.

"And never the twain," Chris agreed. "Now for changelings, take all that and multiply it by ten. Twenty. A hundred. A halfbreed's one thing. A half-fae is a whole other ball game. Lineage still counts for a lot among the Fair Folk, more than with most other races. And the best lineages are the pure lineages. Humans? Not so pure. There are places in the Otherlands where interbreeding with a human still gets you locked up. And if any live offspring are caught walking around, it's death. They call us mutts. Skunks. That's all we are to them: stray animals that need exterminating."

The food arrived just then. Chris had bitter melon with eggs. Abby and Leanne both had the *char siu*. For a few minutes, they ate in silence. Chris looked like he was working up to the big reveal, and the girls both figured it was best to give him the time he needed to get there. After a spell, he wiped his mouth with his napkin and carried on where he'd left off. "So, it's no surprise that not a lot of changelings spend much time in the Otherlands. But life on Earth's no picnic for the diaspora, either. That's where Dr. Swann and The Green World come in. You've probably guessed it by now, but I'm not the first skunk who ever walked through that office."

"Jack Kang," said Abby.

Chris nodded. "Right in one. He was a lot quieter about it than some. Pretty sure he started shaving his head the minute his skunk stripe came in."

"That was what Ted Purdy said," Abby recalled. "Jack Kang's parents were immigrants, but one of them came from farther away than anyone realized. That must have been what Purdy was blackmailing him with!"

"That would have done it," Chris agreed. "Mr. Kang made a lot of connections on both sides of the fence, so to speak. But some of those were pretty delicate. He never let on to anyone in the political sphere what he really was. If he was, all his connections in the Nocturn would have evaporated like… " He flicked his wrist with an airy gesture.

"Did Jacquie Swann know her fiancé was a changeling?" asked Leanne.

"She knew, but she never repeated it. She had her own connections to think about, and she'd have been tainted by association if the word got out. She even kept it from her brother at first." He shook his head. "That didn't last."

Abby frowned. "Gareth Swann didn't strike me as the most tolerant sort when I met him."

Chris winced. "Mr. Swann is… I mean, he makes an effort, at least. He tries to keep an open mind. But Dr. Swann's told me it wasn't always that way. He was never exactly Hitler Youth, but he was close. The two of them were on thin ice for a lot of years. I think the whole 'So I Married a Changeling' thing was almost another breaking point for them. But he settled down, eventually. He usually does."

"Don't take this the wrong way, Chris, but you seem pretty well-informed for a humble receptionist."

"I do a lot more than work the phones, Miss Henderson."

"Abby," she said. "I think we're past the formalities now."

"Fair enough."

"So, what do you besides answer the phones, exactly?"

He pushed his plate aside. Leaned forward. Folded his hands on the table. "Okay. This is where we get into the big stuff. The 'whole building's under a taboo just so we don't say the wrong thing' kind of stuff. See, people like me and Mr. Kang, we're the lucky ones. All the blackmail, job discrimination, all of that, it means we've made it to Earth and the Nocturn, yeah? We can fade into the diaspora and get on with our lives. But a lot of changelings just don't make it out of the Otherlands. They get found out. Put away. Put to work. Put down. That's why I choose to wear my skunk stripe loud and proud. They usually grow in at puberty, see. And four in ten changeling kids born in the Otherlands don't live long enough to get theirs.

"Now, Dr. Swann, she's not the kind of person who's going to read a statistic like that and then sit on her hands. Neither was Mr. Kang, for that matter. And a couple years ago, they started networking with some folks on the other side. Full-blood fae who want a change for the half-bloods that they brought into this world. And they started working to get the next generation of changelings out of the Otherlands to somewhere safer."

"Earth?"

"It was just a few at first. Then it grew. Because the skunks who make it on the other side, they stick together. They talk to each other. And word got around that Dr. Swann and Mr. Kang were smuggling young skunks out of the danger zone. The network got bigger. And now it's a machine. Last year, we got almost a thousand changelings to Earth. But that's only the first step, because a skunk still has to eat and have a bed to sleep in. They need a job to keep them afloat."

"So it's pretty goddamn lucky that the woman at the top runs an aid organization," said Abby.

"Ten percent of T.G.W.'s budget goes into relocation and support for changelings every year," Chris acknowledged. "Under the table, of course. If the wrong people found out what we were up to, we could open ourselves up to reprisals. Most of the staff know it happens, but there's only a handful of us in the office who really focus on keeping the machine running. The dirty work is contracted and subcontracted and sub-subcontracted to folks Dr. Swann trusts."

"You said 'us,'" Leanne observed.

Chris shrugged. "Takes a skunk to talk to a skunk, doesn't it? I do a lot of the mediating between the changelings and Dr. Swann's network. Make sure everyone's taken care of, knows who to talk to and what to say. I get the, um, payments sorted out."

Abby raised an eyebrow. "It sounds a bit like you're a people-smuggler, Chris."

"It sounds *exactly* like I'm a people-smuggler. I'm under no illusions about some of the folks in the network. Not all of them do this out of the goodness of their hearts."

"Equal pay for equal favours," Abby and Leanne said at the same time.

"Ain't that the truth," he agreed.

"So you need to taboo any talk of changelings in the office to keep Oak and Holly from finding out," Abby said. "Because if they find out you're sneaking a bunch of living crimes out of their reach, they might take it the wrong way. Is that about right?"

"That's half of it. At first, the taboo was just for the sake of Dr. Swann's legit business contacts in Faerie, like you said. But about nine months ago, we started getting some pretty nasty messages in the office. It started as just phone calls. Spam emails and anonymous letters. Accusing Dr. Swann of blood treason, calling her a skunk-fucker, that kind of thing. Then it got worse. Our servers got hit with a DoS attack for three days in February. In March, Dr. Swann found a package on her desk when she came in one morning. A dead skunk in a shoebox. Mr. Swann hired a private security firm to sweep the office, just so he knew there weren't any more surprises. They did background checks on all the staff, too."

"Did he think the threat was internal?" asked Leanne.

"He had a feeling. Some of the messages got pretty personal. And there are electronic alarms and spells of warding in the office that reset every night at seven PM. The skunk-killer didn't trip any of them. At that point, we locked things down like Fort Knox. Mr. Swann's the expert at defensive magic, so he went in to all the wards and the taboos and really beefed them up."

"We've dug pretty deep into T.G.W. on our end," said Abby. "How is this the first time we're hearing about all this?" *More to the point,* she didn't say, *why didn't Agent Six ever mention any of this?*

"Did you hear the part about Fort Knox?" Chris said. "I'm not kidding around; the security was *tight*. And radio silence was the official policy as far as the authorities were concerned. The VPD wouldn't understand what we're doing, and they leak like a sieve to the worst parts of the Nocturn anyway. And don't get me started on the Ministry of Uncommon Knowledge. They had the knives out for Mr. Kang way back when he was in the legislature. They'd have shut him down at T.G.W. in a second if they could."

"You know the Ministry's been looking at you?" asked Leanne.

"Of course we know! Our whole mission statement is bringing the Zeds and the Nocturn together, and the Muckers are all about keeping humanity in the dark. If we gave those spooks an inch of rope, they'd find a way to hang us. So, obviously, when this harassment campaign started, we made the call that we'd handle it internally."

"Because otherwise, someone might start asking why you were being harassed. And then your under-the-table work would come to light."

"Exactly. So, we locked things down like I said. And for a little while, it seemed to work. The phone calls and emails stopped coming in. There weren't any more surprises on people's desks or waiting for them at home. And then things came crashing back down in May."

"When Jack Kang was found dead in Oppenheimer Park," said Abby. "And harassment escalated to murder."

"Yeah. And this is where you and your friends come in, 'cause you've put a whole new light on the shit we were dealing with at the start of the year. The hack, the shoebox, all that's got Golden Hand written all over it." He sat back and shook his head. "It seems so obvious now."

Abby saw the puzzle pieces falling into place. "Chris, I have to know: Lisa Nichols. Was she… one of the lucky few?"

He nodded. "True blue skunk. We think her bio dad was a nixie or a puca, but it's hard to trace these things a lot of the time. We'd have known for certain if her magic ever kicked in and she shapeshifted into a horse one day, but…" He shrugged. The gesture seemed incalculably painful.

"That's what we were missing," Abby whispered. "The changelings are what this is about. Not T.G.W. Not Jacquie Swann's people. The Golden Hand are ramping up a campaign of extermination against half-breeds."

"Pest control," said Leanne.

That thought hung heavy over the table for a moment. Eventually, Abby broke the silence. "Go talk to Jacquie, Chris. Tell her it's time to lock things down like you guys did before. If the Golden Hand were able to get to one of the kids you relocated, they'll be able to get to more. Triple-check all your people again, because you've clearly been infiltrated. If you keep any lists of the changelings you've helped, destroy them. That info's toxic right now. And keep a close eye on Gareth."

"You think he could be involved in this?"

"You said yourself he used to be pretty extreme. You sure he isn't still?"

Chris shook his head. "There's no way. Mr. Swann and the Golden Hand? Nuh-uh. He'd never do that to his own sister."

"Can you take that chance right now?"

"You're not listening to me, dammit. This whole thing hurts Dr. Swann as much as anyone. Gareth can rub people the wrong way, sure, but he loves his sister. It was for her sake that he broke out of that bubble he used to live in. He's not behind this."

"Abby's right," Leanne said, "you can't afford to take things on faith right now. If there is a Golden Hand mole inside T.G.W., it's best to be thorough."

"Okay, okay!" Chris threw up his hands in surrender. "You're probably right. It's just... you think you know people, yeah?"

"I get it," said Leanne. "You don't want to think the worst of the people who've given you so much. But these are innocent lives that are at stake."

Chris checked his watch. It wasn't battery-powered, Abby observed, but a good old, wind-up, analogue timepiece. "It isn't even seven yet," he said. "I can probably ring Dr. Swann at home. She told me to debrief her on everything I said to you."

"I think that's the right call," said Abby. "We'll do the same with our friends, and then we can get a proper war room going. Find Gwyn's *Ci Annwn*, stomp on the Golden Hand, and make sure this city doesn't turn into a blasted heath."

"Fuck," Chris whispered. "I forgot about that part."

Leanne turned to look for their server, then swallowed nervously. "Uh, guys? We might have a problem." She directed Chris and Abby's attention to the wall of muscle in the dark suit now approaching their table with purpose. Without breaking his gaze from them, the Ministry man said something into his wristwatch, listened for a second, and nodded.

"Muckers?" Chris whispered. "What are they doing here?"

"Goddammit," Abby said. "This is because of me."

"What?"

"Those goons told me to stop chasing this thing, or else they'd drag my ass over the coals. I didn't listen, so obviously it's ass-drag-o'clock. Six must have told them we were running around behind their backs."

Chris recoiled. "You've been giving the Ministry of Uncommon Knowledge the runaround? When the hell were you going to mention that?"

"Ideally, I wasn't, or else we never would have gotten this far."

The young man gritted his teeth. "Do you have any idea how much shit you've just dropped on me and my people?"

"I'm sorry, Chris, but this was the only way to do this."

The wall of muscle was within arm's reach now. There wasn't any point in running anyway. He was armed, and he was clearly in contact with someone nearby. When he reached the table, he put his hands ever-so-casually in his pockets, pushing his open jacket just far enough back to make the hip holster obvious. Except for his hair, which was more of a chestnut colour, he was cut from the same cloth as Agents Six and Fourteen. *Seriously,* Abby wondered to herself, *do they grow these guys in a lab or something?*

"Well, well, well," said the wall of muscle. "You don't take 'no' for an answer, do you, Miss Henderson?"

"I don't know what you're referring to, Agent…"

"Twenty-four," said the Ministry man. "Special Agent Twenty-four. That's all the identification you need from me."

"We're just having dinner with a friend, Agent Twenty-four."

He laid a hand on Chris's shoulder and pressed him down into his seat. "Your 'friend' here is connected to multiple persons of interest in an open departmental investigation. Isn't that right, Miss Mah?"

Chris's face twisted up in shame and pain. Ignoring his squirming distress, Agent Twenty-four pulled the changeling to his feet. "It's time to wrap it up, girls. All three of you are coming in for a nice long chat."

"Can we at least settle the bill first?" Chris asked.

"Not how this works, Miss Mah." There was that face again, like Chris had just swallowed something cold and wriggling. Abby wanted to stick her chopsticks in the Ministry asshole's eye. "There's a car waiting outside," Twenty-four said, "and you three are getting in it. Now you can come out quietly, or I can call in my back-up and we can turn this into a whole song-and-dance. But either way, we're leaving here together."

"Okay, but can we please go out the back way? They know me here, and I don't want to be seen getting marched out by the secret police. We'd just be going over there. The fire exit, past the bathrooms. Second door on the right."

That sounded like a hint to Abby. It must've also sounded like a hint to Agent Twenty-four, because now his free hand was moving to the hip holster. "I'm not going to repeat myself, you little—"

Chris snapped his fingers. The air whooshed and whip-cracked as it filled the space where he and Agent Twenty-four suddenly weren't, and Abby and Leanne bolted for the exit before their ears had stopped ringing.

"Since when can changelings teleport?" Leanne gasped.

"Their parents can!" said Abby. "Makes some kinda sense, doesn't it? Anyway, a chance is a chance!"

The fire exit opened onto a narrow alley behind the restaurant. Directly opposite was the back wall and fire exit of a twenty-four-hour laundromat. To their left, the alleyway was blocked by a chain-link fence about fifteen feet away. To their right, it opened onto a busy street. If Agent Twenty-four had backup, that was probably the first place they would look. The laundromat it was, then. Abby tried the door. "Shit. Doesn't open from this side."

Leanne drew her Rent-a-Wand and the corresponding cheat sheet. "I think Simon had something for this!" She checked the available spells, found the one she wanted, and flicked the wand toward the door. "*Incantō clāvis*!" The second rune on the wand glowed for a moment, then faded to black. The door swung open like someone had kicked it hard from the other side. Leanne squeezed Abby's hand, and they bolted into the laundromat.

Abby shouted over the clanging fire alarm: "You're getting pretty handy with that thing, huh?"

"Turns out magic powers make life a lot easier! Who knew?"

The patrons stared as they ran for the front entrance. An older Chinese woman shouted at them in grouchy, managerial tones. They didn't catch a word of what she said. Abby fumbled around down her shirt for her Vokarion crystal, found it, and called out to the Letterbox. "Hey, Simon! Natalie! We need a quick exit pronto!"

"Abby?" Simon replied. "What in blazes is going on?"

"Okay, short version, Lee and I moved up this meeting with Jacquie Swann's contact. Good news, he gave us the full picture on the Golden Hand, bad news, we have the Ministry of Uncommon Knowledge on our asses! Our teleporter's gone AWOL, so we could use a pickup!"

"I can have Mother Hyld there in two shakes. Whereabouts are you?"

She saw a street sign through the front window but couldn't read it clearly. "Hell, I don't know where we are! North end of Richmond!"

"Get yourselves outside," Simon answered. "Get out of sight, and keep this line open. When you've got your bearings, we'll come for you."

A black Crown Victoria jumped the curb and hit its brakes just as Leanne got her hand on the door. Abby pulled her back and turned the way they'd come. Two walking refrigerators climbed out of the car, weapons hot. Agent Twenty-four came through the open fire exit, gun in one hand, badge in the other.

"Department of Advanced Research and Special Defence!" he hollered over the alarm. "Nobody move! You two: on the ground, now."

The backup walked in, flashing their badges and raising their guns. One agent plucked the wand from Leanne's hand. The other pulled the crystal from around Abby's neck. Abby and Leanne raised their hands and spoke as one: "Lawyer."

CHAPTER 18

UNCOMMON KNOWLEDGE

THE MINISTRY of Uncommon Knowledge maintained two facilities in Metro Vancouver: the "North Campus" was somewhere in Gastown, near Waterfront Station, while the "South Campus" was spread over an otherwise unused block of warehouses in Richmond. It was to the South Campus that Abby, Leanne, and Chris had been brought.

Outside, the South Campus was industrial-district standard issue. The kind of place you might drive past on the way to a doctor's appointment that would make you think, *You never see anybody going in or out of there, do you? I wonder what they get up to in there.* Then you'd keep on driving, and the thought would fall out of your head until you passed the place again on your way to the follow-up appointment six weeks later. Inside, it was something out of a Bond film. The décor was sterile, businesslike, with a bare minimum of frills to pretty up an overreliance on Brutalist cement. The tech looked like army surplus from the latter days of the Soviet Union. Fat CRT security monitors. Wall-like computer banks with tape reels and big, chunky square buttons all up and down their fronts. Plenty of the devices sported the kind of wood panelling that had been *de rigueur* throughout the 1970s. Abby had only ever seen that kind of thing in pictures from when her parents were kids.

"Magic doesn't screw with analogue tech as badly as it does digital," Chris explained, once the three had been shut up in the holding cell. "If you're dealing with folks like us 24/7, it helps to keep things retro." He rubbed at his wrist. His fancy watch, like all the trio's personal effects, plus belts and shoelaces, was in a secure lockup. Even Abby's gloves were gone, and the sigil of the Court-Among-the-Holly burned into her palm was exposed to every prying eye.

The holding cell was a bulletproof glass-fronted box lined with a fine steel mesh like a Faraday cage. The universal energies that the ancients, in their peculiar and grandiloquent way, referred to as the "True Magic" had a lot in common with plain old electromagnetism, and what was good for the magical goose was good enough for the Ministry gander. Chris wasn't snapping his way out of this one, and Abby wasn't astral projecting. The three sat together in the one box, which could have comfortably housed another three or four bodies without feeling cramped. There were two army cots and a metal prison-style toilet in the corner, and that was about it. A pair of armed security men kept the watch on the other side of the bulletproof glass, as immovable as the guards outside Buckingham Palace.

"This is bad," Chris said, still rubbing his wrist. "This is really bad." He shook his head, his breathing quick and anxious. Leanne moved closer to him and put a hand on his, trying to calm him.

"This isn't ideal," she said. "But we're not dead and buried yet. There are people out there who know we've been scooped up. They'll raise holy hell when they come to find us."

"This is my fault," Chris moaned. "I've never been good with the teleport. I zapped that agent right into plain view of all his buddies, right there on the sidewalk. If I'd gotten him farther away, you two could have…" He didn't finish the thought. He just brought his knees up to his chest and dropped his forehead upon them. "Some kind of Fair Folk I am."

"This isn't your fault, Chris," said Abby. "It's mine. I heard the Ministry's ultimatum loud and clear, and I didn't listen. Agent Six warned me what would happen if I fucked around too much behind the Ministry's back, and I still waited to find out."

"If only every confession came as easily as that one, my job would be so much easier."

They all looked up to see a new face on the other side of the bulletproof glass, making notes on a clipboard. He was a tall, slender Black man with a shaved head, small rimless glasses, and a dark suit that fit better on him than Six's or Twenty-four's did on them. When he raised a hand to adjust his glasses, Abby caught a glimpse of the silver cufflinks he was wearing. Definitely not another workaday, off-the-rack ensemble, then.

"Dr. Gilbert Harkness," the man announced. "Director of Operations, Pacific Station. Locally, I'm known as Theta. And you've been making all our lives very difficult of late, Miss Henderson."

Abby shrugged and gestured to her cellmates. "What can I say, Gil? I couldn't have done it alone."

That got a half-smile in return. "Of course I don't mean to downplay Miss Waller's contributions," said Dr. Harkness. "Nor Mr. Mah's, or indeed any of your further associates. But we all know who's the biggest worm in our apple."

"I'm not sure if I should be insulted or flattered."

"Take the comment how you wish," Dr. Harkness said with a shrug. "But your continued interference in Department affairs puts you in direct violation of the Security of Information Act, not to mention several articles of the Criminal Code and Amendment Eight of the Vael Ardenne Treaty. The plain fact is that I have more than enough cause to order the immediate seizure of the Abby Normal domain name, a full wipe of all your memories within the last twelve months, and the swift relocation of your drooling, incontinent husk to the darkest, coldest part of the Canadian north that I can possibly think of."

Abby stood and smacked her palms against the glass. "Then why don't you just fucking do it?" she snapped. "I'm running myself ragged trying to save this city from Armageddon, and you guys are just standing there, ticking off every fucking man in black cliché! Dark suits, memory wipes, extralegal detention! Please just come up with some original material, you hack *fucks*!"

"This is not a joke, Miss Henderson."

"I'm right there with you, Gil!" She smacked her palms against the glass once more, so Dr. Harkness could see Holly's icy mark. "And it sure as hell ain't no party, disco, or fooling around, either. So I would love for you to explain to me, in very simple language, why the three people in this box are the only ones taking this remotely seriously. My friends and I have been out there for the last two weeks trying to stop this thing, and so far, you guys are just getting in our way."

"Since the murder of Agent Fourteen, the Department has devoted every local resource to finding and containing this extraplanar entity," Dr. Harkness replied. "Just because you cannot see us doing the work, Miss Henderson, does not mean we are sitting idle. In fact, I would venture to say that our ability to do the work quietly is precisely the reason why I'm standing on this side of the glass and you're in the box."

She wanted to snap back at him, to kick the glass and flip him both middle fingers. But that wasn't going to accomplish anything fast. Because for the time being, she was the one stuck in the goddamn box. And for all her previous talk of Simon and Natalie strutting in with their ass-kicking boots on, Abby wasn't totally sure what they could actually do right now. Simon wasn't punching anywhere near his usual weight class until his injuries from the Harcourt House healed. Mother Hyld's oath to the Order of Wulfredda prevented her from taking the fight to mortal opponents. And Natalie was just plain outnumbered, for all her charms.

Choking on a mouthful of her own venom and bile, Abby took a step back from the glass. "So what happens now?" she grumbled. "Memory-wipe time?"

Dr. Harkness adjusted his glasses again and let out a slow breath. "No."

Abby blinked. Looked at Chris and Leanne. Blinked again. The two of them had mostly let her get on with it the last few minutes, but now their full attention was on Dr. Harkness. Abby turned back to him. "What the hell do you mean, 'no'?"

Dr. Harkness extracted a microfibre cloth from his pocket. Removed his glasses. Cleaned them. Put them back on. He was trying to drag this out, as if anticipating that the next words out of his mouth were going to be particularly unpleasant to say. "Your methods to this point have been wildly unacceptable, Miss Henderson, but the uncomfortable truth is that you have achieved remarkable success as a self-appointed protector of the innocent. In the last twelve months, you have not only survived two encounters with Category Five extraplanar entities, you have successfully neutralized those entities as credible threats to the Canadian public."

Jesus, this guy *was* just running through all the clichés, wasn't he? She could almost picture the sweaty eighties police chief in her head. *Gawddammit, Henderson, you're a loose cannon, but you get results!*

"More to the point," Dr. Harkness continued, "the unique suite of abilities you possess presents a significant tactical advantage that few of our field agents can match. Reading the case reports from our people in the field concerning the Applegate and Delapore EPIs, I can see that you and your… team occupy a singular position between the ordinary and the extraplanar. Though I hate to admit it, it's a position where the Department has never been able to maintain as firm a footing as we would like."

And there it was. The great, looming hand of the puppeteer in the sky was shortening the strings yet again. She'd already been the Deacon's hobby, Whittaker's bargaining chip, and Gwyn ab Nethe's trophy. Why not be the Ministry of Uncommon Knowledge's ventriloquist dummy?

"You want to use me," she said. "You want to use us."

"Please understand, Miss Henderson, I had no say in your previous interactions with us. Those orders came directly from Ottawa. But I have been briefed on the *Ci Annwn* situation and I have argued your case with my superiors. In light of this new information, Her Majesty's Government of Canada is prepared to make you an offer. You abandon the Abby Normal Blog, permanently. You submit to full oversight by the Department. You continue your activities as a firebreak against extraplanar incursions, but you do it in our facilities, using our resources and funds, and according to our regulations. Anything that you have discovered independently, you turn over to us. In exchange, you will receive a salary and benefits as befits a consultant to the Department of Advanced Research and Special Defence, and all currently outstanding charges against you will be dropped." He nodded toward Leanne. "Miss Waller will be afforded the same terms, of course, as will Mr. Lockhart and Miss Arnaud."

"And if I refuse?" She hardly needed to ask, but she figured it was best to have it all out in the open.

"If you refuse this offer, you and Miss Waller will be prosecuted to the fullest extent Her Majesty permits. You will receive psychological conditioning to remove all memory of your interactions with extraplanar entities as a precaution against the further spread of that information among the public, and you will serve a lengthy sentence at Her Majesty's pleasure, following which we will relocate you to another jurisdiction with new identities. Simon Lockhart and Natalie Arnaud will be designated hostile entities and enemies of Her Majesty's Government, and warrants will be issued for their arrest or extermination." He shrugged. "Depending on how feisty Miss Arnaud feels that day."

She bit down on her thumbnail and looked back at the others. Then Dr. Harkness again. "What about Chris? He's not a part of this. He's just a kid who was in the wrong place."

Dr. Harkness smiled a little. "You're not a very good liar, Abigail. I've spoken with Special Agent Six. I know he tipped you off about Mr. Mah's employers pursuant to your unauthorized investigation into the missing *Ci Annwn*. You pressed Mr. Mah for information about The Green World Initiative during your dinnertime chat, of that I have no doubt. And I have every intention of learning what Mr. Mah told you in that time."

Chris's whole face was as white as his skunk stripe. He stared past Dr. Harkness, no doubt watching the whole world tumble down around him. Raw guilt stabbed Abby in the gut. If she accepted the Ministry's offer, she'd have to tell them everything she knew about T.G.W.'s off-the-books work. If she refused, they'd chuck her in a deep, dark hole somewhere, but probably not before a lengthy interrogation that would drag the truth out of her anyway.

"I… I'm gonna need time to think about this," she said at last. Stall. Defer. Make a plan. That was all she knew how to do right now.

Dr. Harkness looked at his watch. "Three hours. You have until 11:15PM exactly to consider my offer, at which point it will be rescinded. Think carefully, Abigail." Without waiting for her reply, he tucked his clipboard under one arm, turned, and left her and the others to stew.

*****

The cavalry showed up twenty minutes later, not wearing their ass-kicking boots, but waving the white flag of surrender. Dr. Harkness led Simon and Natalie through the door single file, followed by the four security guards who'd done the frisk-and-disarm routine on them. He was infuriatingly polite as he brought the two to stand before the bulletproof box and presented Abby and the others like the star attraction at the zoo. "As you see, your friends have come to no harm, Mr. Lockhart. As I promised you."

Simon's eyes blazed. Abby had seen this look only a couple times before, and every time it had presaged some incredible act of property destruction. He obviously wanted nothing more than to bring the whole Campus crashing down, but at this stage in his convalescence he'd only end up hurting himself in the attempt. "You had no right, Gilbert. The terms of our agreement—"

"There is no 'our' agreement, Mr. Lockhart. The Pax Arcana is an expired contract which you entered into with my predecessor, and the original terms say nothing about your… protégé. In a functioning human society, federal law takes precedence over outdated gentlemen's agreements. If you have any complaints, you can take them to the Minister of Public Safety. Now, if there's anything you wish to say to your friends, I advise you to do so within the next—" He checked his watch. "—two hours, thirty-nine minutes."

"I suppose it would not be too much to ask for some privacy?" Simon said.

"I have no objections," Dr. Harkness said. To one of the security guards: "Please transfer Mr. Mah to Interview Room Three. I have a number of questions I wish to ask him."

Two of the guards escorted Simon and Natalie away from the cell door, guns very much at the ready. A third opened the door. Numbers Four and Five led Simon and Natalie into the cell, giving Abby and Leanne the stink-eye, and walked out again with an unresisting Chris between them. Abby mouthed the words *I'm sorry*, but he just shook his head. She wasn't sure if he was telling her not to be sorry, or if he was telling her it was too late to apologize. Either way, she felt like shit.

Dr. Harkness left Abby and the inner circle to their devices with only the original two guards standing watch outside the cell—obviously, that was as far as "privacy" extended around here. As soon as the door was shut behind them, Simon scooped Abby and Leanne up in a long hug. "Have they hurt you?"

"We're fine," Abby answered. "Just a bit shaken up."

"Bloody hell," Simon said, taking a step back, "I was concerned things could get sticky if the Ministry got involved, but I didn't think... I mean, to deny the Pax Arcana..."

"What was all that about?" Leanne asked. "What is the Pax Arcana?"

Simon and Natalie shared a look. Abby recognized it as the *We should have told you this ages ago but we were hoping it wouldn't become relevant* look. "Simon," she said a little more urgently, "what's the Pax Arcana?"

"A foolish old man's attempt to control a desperate situation," he replied. As he sat on one of the cots, his face was coloured with regret. "The Pax Arcana goes back to when you were a child, Abigail. It came out of the Dead Man's Pledge your parents made with the Deacon. You see, a young Gospel just coming into her abilities is an impossibly rare and precious thing. Once the Cult of the Following took an interest in you, it wasn't long before other factions in the Nocturn started getting curious themselves. A number of those factions made attempts to win your power for themselves. Natalie and I did what we could to protect you from these attempts, as we had sworn to do."

"But once, we didn't intervene in time," Natalie interjected. "And then the Deacon stepped in."

Abby shivered. The Deacon's claim upon her soul had been his driving force for twenty-five years. If he thought he had any rivals to that claim, he would have killed them on the spot. And probably not quickly, either.

Simon picked up the thread again. "All this turmoil in the Nocturn eventually caught the eye of the Ministry. They identified the Following as the most immediate threat to Her Majesty's Government and the great Canadian public and attempted to take them off the board. I'm told they lost an entire field team that way. At this point, the situation had become thoroughly untenable. A summit was held, with representatives from all the concerned factions attending. I was there, as was the Deacon, and agents from the Ministry of Uncommon Knowledge. We instituted a pact of total nonaggression between all local factions, along the same lines as the Dead Man's Pledge. Interference in the affairs of mortals was strictly prohibited as well, in exchange for the Ministry's withdrawal from Metro Vancouver. In effect, the Nocturnal society of this city became a law unto itself. And so arose the Pax Arcana."

"But now I'm all grown up, the Deacon is dead, and whatever terms the Pax was settled on are right down the shitter," Abby concluded.

"Apparently so," Simon sighed. "I remember Gilbert Harkness from the night the Pax was settled. He was never happy with the arrangement, but he was the low man on the Ministry ladder then, and he was overruled. Obviously, he's ascended since last I saw him."

"New sheriff, *et cetera*," said Leanne.

Simon ran his hands through his hair, thinking. "*Metodes miht*. I'm sorry about all this, girls. I should have told you long ago about the Pax, about the Ministry. I should have thought of what would happen when the Dead Man's Pledge and the Pax expired! I just got too damn swept up in all that's happened this last year."

"You didn't put us in the box here, Simon," said Abby. "And there's not much that self-recrimination is going to do to get us out of it."

"And that's coming from Abby Henderson, I might add," said Leanne.

"What sort of deal is Harkness offering you?" Simon asked. "There must be something, or else he would have already started on your psychological reconditioning."

"It's a full blank slate," Abby said. "Forgive and forget, if I shut down The Abby Normal Blog and we all bend the knee to the Ministry."

"And if we don't come work for them," added Leanne, "Abby and I get the memory-wipe and hard time, and you two are on the Most Wanted List."

"It gets worse still," said Abby, and here she lowered her voice below the level the guards could hear. "If we come in from the cold, we have to turn everything over to these guys."

Simon matched her whisper. "And I suppose you've found something you don't want the Ministry knowing."

"Let's just say Lee and I know a few things about what T.G.W. have been doing off-hours. It's a good cause, but it could sink Jacquie Swann if the news gets out. A lot of folks could be at risk."

"I see. Well, that is an awkward spot to be in."

"Any ideas?"

He rubbed a hand over his mouth and chin. "Well, possibly one or two. I got Jacqueline Swann's number from that business card she gave you, and I was able to reach her on the way down here."

"Hardest part of that was finding a working payphone in this town," said Natalie.

"Quite so," Simon nodded. "Anyway, I told her what you told me, that the Ministry were on top of you and one of her people was involved. I'm rather relying on that to light a fire under her and that legal-eagle brother of hers."

"You think Gareth Swann can help us here?" Abby asked.

"I think he can certainly talk circles around Gilbert Harkness long enough to give you a stay of execution."

Outside the cell, one of the guards touched his earpiece. Then he tapped on the glass and made a "wrap it up" gesture with one hand. "I suppose we'll have to table this conversation for now," said Simon, as the other guard unlocked and opened the cell door.

"Okay, you two," the guard said. "Theta says that's long enough. Outside."

"I presume you have a reception area prepared for us?" Simon asked, with a touch of forced bravado.

Standing behind him, topping the guard by six whole inches, Natalie added, "We're not leaving until they do."

"Theta said you might say that." The guard met Natalie's cold, unblinking stare. That was something few people managed to do. "Don't worry. You'll be looked after." He made a gesture with the barrel of the submachine gun he was packing. "Now come out of there, and we'll get someone to escort you."

Simon and Natalie exited the cell, and the guard shut the door again. As his partner called for an escort, Simon looked back at Abby and put a hand upon the glass. "Brave hearts, both of you. We'll get you out of here."

Abby tried her hardest to believe him.

*****

Another twenty minutes brought Chris back to the cell. He was still pale, but he'd stopped shaking. A cold sweat had broken out on his forehead, and there were rings under his eyes that hadn't been there before. Leanne sat with him and held his hand as he tried to compose himself.

"You doing okay?" she asked.

"I… I think so. I don't think I told Harkness anything major. It's all kind of a blur."

"You think he whammied you with the Lethe crystal?" Abby said.

"He might've? I dunno. There was this blue light, and then I kind of spaced out. But faerie brains are built different, so I don't *think* it stuck." He dropped his head into his hands. "I don't know. Could be nothing, could be the sky falling on our heads."

"Our friends have told Jacquie what's up. Even if Leanne and I are stuck, hopefully she can spring you. It doesn't matter what Dr. Harkness said; your hands are clean here, Chris. They can't pin a damn thing on you right now."

Chris didn't respond. Abby didn't blame him. Before she knew it, three hours had ticked down to two hours. Then an hour forty-five. She was lying on one of the cots, staring at the ceiling, when she heard a commotion in the corridor. Multiple sets of footsteps. Angry voices. One of the guards touched his earpiece and then nudged his partner. "Get Theta. Now." The other guard nodded and set off into the unknown depths of the Campus, moments before the Swann siblings, Ms. Keane, and a small train of armed security men came bustling down the corridor.

"Where is he?" Jacquie Swann demanded. She pointed at the remaining guard and snapped, "You have one of my people in there. I want him released *now*."

"Dr. Swann?" Chris jumped up and pressed his nose to the glass. "Oh, thank Auberon. I thought I was going to be in here all night."

The mama bear crept back into her den for a second as Jacquie put a hand against the glass and gave the young changeling a reassuring smile. "I'm sorry, Christopher. I wanted to be here earlier. But we're getting you out now. All of you." Her smile graced Abby for a second, and a great weight was lifted. Seemed like there were no hard feelings about the whole "blowing up your illegal humanitarian aid" thing.

Jacquie's eyes flicked back to the guard. She pointed at the earpiece he was wearing. "You're in touch with the big boss, yeah? Tell him to get his butt out here now."

"He's been summoned, ma'am. There is a reception area for civilians if you would care to wait—"

"I'm not moving from this spot, buster. You're holding one of my employees illegally, and I'm standing right here until you either show cause or get him the hell out of there."

The guard didn't respond, but instead looked past Jacquie to where Dr. Harkness and the other guard were now coming back down the hall. Jacquie followed the guard's eye and wheeled around to bear down on Dr. Harkness. "You look like the man in charge here. Mind telling me why you've arrested my receptionist?"

Gareth Swann, who hadn't been able to get a word in edgewise for the last several minutes, gripped his sister by the arm and pulled her back a step. "Jacqueline, this isn't the way to handle this."

That seemed to have an effect on her. She drew back from DEFCON 1 and glowered at Dr. Harkness as he came into the holding area. He showed not a flicker of emotion as he stood before her and offered a hand to shake.

"Dr. Jacqueline Swann, I presume. And this will be your brother Gareth? My name is Dr. Gilbert Harkness. As you've correctly surmised, I am the 'man in charge.'"

Before Jacquie could lose her cool again, Gareth stepped around in front of her. He made a point of not shaking the offered hand. "Dr. Harkness, may I inquire on what grounds you're holding these people?"

"Unauthorized possession and publication of information related to extraplanar phenomena, not to mention civilian interference in official investigations of extraplanar phenomena, have been designated as acts prejudicial to the safety and interests of the Canadian government, per Section Three of the Security of Information Act. Abigail Henderson's public blog is a clear example of unauthorized publication, and her continued, unsanctioned investigation of the *Ci Annwn* phenomenon has repeatedly impaired the security and intelligence capabilities of Her Majesty's

Government. Six days ago, our agents notified Miss Henderson that she had been designated as a person permanently bound to secrecy under Section Ten of the Act, and that further communication of protected information on her part was a prosecutable offence. Yet the Abby Normal Blog is still live as of this date. According to dispatches from two of my agents, it was at Leanne Waller's encouragement that Miss Henderson left the blog up, despite full knowledge of the legal consequences. Miss Waller is therefore being charged as an accomplice to Miss Henderson's criminal actions. She is also being charged with resisting arrest earlier tonight."

"Christopher Mah has neither publicized nor interfered in any case relating to extraplanar phenomena. Why is he being held?"

"Mr. Mah is being held on suspicion of attempting to communicate information related to extraplanar phenomena to Miss Henderson and Miss Waller. Also an offence under the Act."

"But Abigail Henderson was not acting as a private agent when she spoke to Mr. Mah." Gareth turned and looked squarely at Abby. "Miss Henderson, please show Dr. Harkness your hand."

Abby, unbalanced by the legalese flying past her at a mile a minute, pressed her palm to the glass again. It fogged up where the ice crystals made contact.

"Do you know what that sigil represents, Dr. Harkness?" Gareth asked. He didn't wait for an answer. "It is the symbol of a contract made between Miss Henderson and a citizen of the faerie nation of Holly. In this particular instance, the citizen in question is Gwyn ab Nethe, the lawful monarch of Holly. The 1964 amendment to the Vael Ardenne Treaty, which your government is a signatory to, officially recognizes the sovereignty of Faerie, its citizens, and its deputized representatives."

"Her Majesty's Government may be a signatory to the 1964 amendment," Dr. Harkness shot back, "but the Court-Among-the-Holly was not, as you well know, Mr. Swann. We have never recognized the sovereignty of Gwyn ab Nethe and his subjects."

Abby banged on the glass. "Hey! Watch your language, jackass. You say that name again and you'll recognize his sovereignty pretty fucking quick."

They ignored her. "You're exactly correct, Doctor," said Gareth. "The Court-Among-the-Holly never signed the amended Treaty. But the Court-Among-the-Oak did. And before she entered into a contract with the King-Among-the-Holly, Miss Henderson received a boon from one Robyn ab Godfelwe, a scion of the noble house of Godfelwe, in exchange for which she pledged to him her permanent vassalage, in the form of her heart's words. The house of Godfelwe swear themselves to the King-Among-the-Oak, and their members are therefore recognized as citizens of the sovereign nation of Oak according to the Vael Ardenne Treaty."

Noses against the glass, Chris and Leanne had come to join Abby in watching the fireworks. "Wait a sec," said Chris, "did he say Robyn ab Godfelwe?"

"Whittaker is *nobility*?" Leanne spluttered. "*Our* Whittaker?"

Dr. Harkness pursed his lips slightly. "I'm not sure what exactly you're implying, Mr. Swann, but if you mean to say that Abigail Henderson is not responsible for her actions by dint of some arcane statute of your people—"

Gareth raised one hand and pinched his fingers together in what Abby could only describe as a "shaddap-a-you-mouth" gesture. "I imply nothing, Dr. Harkness. According to the faerie traditions of fealty and vassalage, as codified in the Court-Among-the-Oak's Declaration of the Rights of Sovereignty and Citizenry, Abigail Henderson was legally bound as a vassal to a citizen of Oak between the dates of

November 2, 2019, and October 3, 2020, the day when Mr. Godfelwe transferred his right of suzerainty over Miss Henderson to the King-Among-the-Holly. According to both the Declaration of Rights and the Vael Ardenne Treaty, faerie vassals are afforded certain legal protections when operating in foreign territory, a term that is here defined as any nation other than the place of the faerie suzerain's birth." He gestured to Ms. Keane, who tapped at the screen of her faerie-enchanted tablet and then pushed it into Dr. Harkness's hands. Gareth allowed himself a triumphant little smile as Dr. Harkness began scrolling through what must have been a veritable wall of faerie statutes and legal citations.

"At no point before October 3 of this year," Gareth said, "was Abigail Henderson operating as a private agent. Even if her involvement in the Applegate and Delapore incidents did not plainly meet the standard for a plea of self-defence, her so-called 'interference' constitutes the action of a faerie vassal exercising her legal right to enact martial justice against the foes of her suzerain, the aforementioned Robyn ab Godfelwe. Her actions after October 3 are protected under the laws of *anoethau*, the tradition of trial by deed, which the Vael Ardenne Treaty recognizes as a protected act of Faerie culture or heritage."

"We can still charge her for offences against the Security of Information Act."

"According to subsection 11(1) of the Act, an individual is only designated as a person permanently bound to secrecy as of the moment that they are personally notified such a designation has been made. You just told me that notice was served six days ago." He turned his head back to Abby. "Miss Henderson, have you made any posts on the Abby Normal Blog in the past six days?"

She shook her head. "I've been kind of preoccupied."

"Legally speaking," Gareth went on, "Abigail Henderson has neither wilfully communicated nor confirmed any privileged information since she was notified of her designation as a person permanently bound to secrecy. Any posts she made before that date are non-prosecutable, and there is a reasonable case to be made that she was acting or believed she was acting in the public interest when she made them. That would constitute a defensible disclosure under section 15 of the Act."

Dr. Harkness had fully stopped listening. He was scrolling furiously through the documents Ms. Keane had compiled, trying and obviously failing to find a loophole. Gareth stuck his hands in his pockets and broke into a full, sharklike grin. Given what Chris had said about the Ministry's scrutiny of T.G.W., Abby could only imagine how much Gareth was enjoying sticking his thumb in their eye.

At last, Dr. Harkness looked up from the tablet. Through tightly gritted teeth, he said, "We can still bring charges against Leanne Waller."

Gareth shook his head. "The protections afforded to a vassal automatically extend to the vassal's family in the event that those persons are also found to be operating in the interest of the suzerain. Family members are further granted certain rights pertaining to the sharing of privileged information, say for example if they discover the existence of extraplanar phenomena as a result of their family member's actions or behaviour. The nature and duration of Miss Henderson and Miss Waller's relationship more than meets the requirement for common-law status under both federal and provincial law, to say nothing of the relevant statutes of Faerie. Anything that Abigail Henderson knows and acts on, Leanne Waller is permitted to know and act on." When Dr. Harkness opened his mouth, Gareth made the "shaddap-a-you-mouth" gesture again. "And don't tell me you'll bring charges against Mr. Mah. In the first place, I very much doubt you can prove what he spoke to Miss Henderson and Miss Waller about. In the second place, if he did communicate information relating to extraplanar phenomena, it was to two people who are already privileged to know that information."

"He resisted arrest! He performed an unlawful demonstration of a supernatural ability in a public place!"

"Summary charges, and to the best of my knowledge, Mr. Mah's first offence in either case," Gareth said with a shrug, "punishable by fines not exceeding $5000 each, in lieu of jail time. Mr. Mah is well-liked in the office and a highly competent employee. The Green World Initiative's legal fund will happily foot the bill for any missteps he has made tonight."

Dr. Harkness scrolled as far down as he could scroll, then started scrolling back up. Gareth reached out and gently pulled the tablet from his hands before giving it back to Ms. Keane. "To put the matter quite simply, Dr. Harkness, you have nothing to charge these people with. Now I suggest you release them from custody, or I will take this matter higher."

Dr. Harkness adjusted his glasses very, very slowly, then turned his deadly cold stare upon one of the security guards. "Well, Mr. Flannegan?" Apparently, the low-level security grunts didn't warrant codenames around here. "You heard the man."

The guard sprang to attention and unlocked the cell to let Abby and the others out. Dr. Harkness couldn't quite keep his eye from twitching as he gave the order to: "Send someone to collect Mr. Lockhart and Miss Arnaud from the waiting room. Then escort these people off the premises. And have Agent Six brought to my office. There are a few things I'd like to say to him."

Abby and Leanne fell into a natural huddle with the faeries once they were out of the cell. "Jesus," Abby said to Gareth, "I am glad you're on our side."

Gareth raised one finger. "Let me make something very clear, Miss Henderson. I've done some research on 'Abby Normal' since the last time we spoke, and for what it's worth, I think Dr. Harkness has a point. Your methods are highly questionable, and based on our interactions thus far, I find your personal style to be overly crass and impulsive. You and I are not on the same 'side.'" He paused for a look back at his sister, whose eyes fixed him with a look somewhere between gratitude and admonishment. "However," he said, turning back to Abby, "your goals are presently in alignment with the goals of The Green World Initiative. I want to see the *Ci Annwn*'s rampage brought to a decisive end just as much as you do, and though I cannot in good conscience support the decision, the King-Among-the-Holly has appointed you as the last, best hope of finding the creature. So, I suggest you take what you have learned tonight and get back to work very fucking quickly."

She returned with a two-fingered salute. "Coming from you, Gareth Swann, I think that's practically a kiss on the cheek."

Dr. Harkness cleared his throat. "If you've concluded your tearful reunions, then I will remind you all that this is an active government facility. We have a great deal of work to do, and I think it's time you were on your way."

With half a dozen security guards standing around them packing submachine guns, how could they say no to an invitation like that? Dr. Harkness called three of the guards to his side, and together they escorted the gaggle of civilians down the bare, concrete corridors of the South Campus. Every one looked very much like every other one, possibly in a deliberate attempt to disorient the hypothetical intruder or nail home the idea of no escape for the hypothetical prisoner. As they walked, Dr. Harkness fell into step beside Abby. Unheard by the others over the echo of footsteps, he leaned over and whispered in her ear, "You have been fortunate tonight, Miss Henderson, but be advised: I will be keeping a very close eye on you from now on. Put one toe over the line, and you will regret it."

She didn't answer. It was easy, in a weird way, to abstract herself from threats like the Following or the King-Among-the-Holly. That was fantasy, comic-book stuff. Institutional paramilitary power, on the other hand, was in the news every damn day. She'd never treated the Deacon or Josiah Harcourt's violence as anything less than deadly serious, but it still felt less real than a gun in the hand of her own government. So, lesson learned. Save the biting wit for another day, take the W where she could get it, and be very, very careful when playing with the Ministry of Uncommon Knowledge.

The corridor branched off in a 'T' shape. Abby heard footsteps coming from the other branch and turned to see Simon and Natalie being escorted by another guard. Apparently, the Ministry had not seen fit to position the waiting area anywhere near the front entrance when they converted these warehouses into their South Campus. Simon and Natalie fell in step with the rest of the pack, and now it was Simon's turn for a word in Abby's shell-like.

"I take it Gareth Swann had the law on his side tonight."

"You were waiting for this the whole time, weren't you?"

"I may have politely suggested that he inspect the relevant judicial precedent for a loophole that would let us get on with our work."

"Well, he found it. Apparently, I've been living in vassalage to fucking Whittaker for the last eleven months."

"I did warn you there'd be consequences if you struck that bargain."

"Yeah, well, those consequences saved my ass tonight, so who's laughing now?"

They came to a security checkpoint. According to the signs on the wall, this gate and the heavy, hospital-style double doors beyond it were the last barrier before sweet, sweet freedom. One by one, everyone went through the scanner—like every other piece of tech here, it was big, clunky, probably Soviet surplus, and capable of sterilizing a man at fifteen paces. Everyone got patted down, spent several minutes picking their shoes, belts, and other effects out of the relevant plastic bins, and waited until the light above the door turned from red, for "locked and secure," to green, for "get the hell out of here." The doors swung open, and a chill rippled through Abby's body.

The main entrance hall was painted in frenzied splashes and smears of wet, stinking blood. It oozed like a kinked garden hose from the gaping, headless neck of the guard who'd been on front desk duty, now slumped across his security terminal. Two more guards lay glassy-eyed on the linoleum floor, the black shafts of arrows puncturing their ragged bodies. Standing in the middle of it all, hands resting upon the pommel of its gore-soaked longsword, was the masked figure of the Lone Dullahan.

CHAPTER 19

E.P.I.

FOR ALL Dr. Harkness's faults, he was no coward. As soon as the Lone Dullahan adjusted its grip on the sword, he pushed to the front of the crowd and reached for the Colt Detective Special hidden under his jacket. He tapped the trigger at one of the Lone Dullahan's eyes, then the other. The creature hissed and staggered back a step, weeping blood.

"Hutchins! Thornton!" Dr. Harkness shouted at two of the security men. "Light that thing up! The rest of you, get these civilians to safety!"

Hutchins and Thornton poured round after round into the Lone Dullahan, while the others pulled Abby and the others back behind the security checkpoint. The shower of lead wasn't anywhere near fatal to the creature, but at point-blank range it sure slowed it down. The Lone Dullahan took two halting steps forward before recognizing that it wasn't going anywhere fast, then pulled its riding cloak up across its body with a vicious hiss. The last of Hutchins and Thornton's rounds bounced off the cloak like hail off a windshield, and the two security men fell back beyond the security checkpoint. As soon as they were clear, Dr. Harkness hammered a big red button on the wall next to the scanner. Warning lights flashed, an alarm whined overhead, and a heavy metal security shutter descended from the ceiling.

It didn't descend nearly fast enough for Abby's taste. She could still see the Lone Dullahan as it threw back its cloak and extruded bullets from the holes in its body onto the gory linoleum tile. *Plink. Plink. Plinkplinkplink.* The Lone Dullahan unfurled the ghastly white bone-whip hanging at its side, and Dr. Harkness ordered a tactical retreat. The whip snaked under the still-falling security shutter and snapped around Thornton's ankle as he lagged behind the fleeing group. He fell. Grunted. Then the Dullahan yanked him backward onto the killing floor.

The security shutter met the floor with a *clang*. Beyond it, they could hear Thornton's screams. The Dullahan's laughter. "He's dead," Dr. Harkness growled. "There's nothing we can do." He led the group down the long corridors at a run, not even pausing for breath as he made a call on the radio receiver in his watch. "Attention, all personnel, this is Director Theta! Category Five EPI in progress in main entrance hall! All special operational and security personnel are to assume immediate action stations! All other personnel will observe strict lockdown procedures until otherwise notified!"

Abby huffed and puffed until she caught up with him. "You know that gate won't hold that thing for long."

"Longer than you imagine, Miss Henderson. All the security barriers in this facility are lined with iron filaments. There's iron in the walls and floors at each security checkpoint as well."

She caught on immediately. "When the barrier comes down, the filaments make contact! You create a closed loop of cold iron."

"Impenetrable to fae-kind, not to mention a host of other extraplanar entities. They can't even teleport past it." He rounded a corner and hugged the wall, huffing and puffing for breath. The others fell in step with him. Abby joined Dr. Harkness for a peek around the corner, flinching when something heavy impacted the security shutter on the other side. Twice. Three times. The metal bulged, buckled, but did not break, and at last the hammering stopped.

"The Dullahan can find other ways through the facility, but this route is effectively closed to it," said Dr. Harkness. He looked at the three remaining security guards. Every one was ready to curb-stomp the Lone Dullahan for what it had done. "Spread out," he ordered. "Make sure the other checkpoints in this wing are sealed."

The guards checked their weapons, but before they could move out, a tinny voice came over Dr. Harkness's watch-radio. "Director Theta! Come in, Theta! Do you copy? This is Agent Forty-nine!" The voice was deep, female. Well, at least they weren't growing all the field agents from the same clone batch, Abby thought.

Dr. Harkness spoke into his watch. "Forty-nine, this is Theta. Give me a sitrep."

Static. Gunshots. In the background, someone screamed. Agent Forty-nine said, "I'm in the infirmary, sir! I have eyes on the hostile. It… Jesus, it just tore through the wall! We didn't even get the shutters down." More static. More gunshots. "Agent Twelve and Dr. Lomax are down. I had eyes on Nineteen, but I've lost her now."

"Listen to me, Forty-nine: get yourself behind the nearest checkpoint as quickly as possible. If you can, find your way to the armoury. I am issuing blanket authorization to deploy F-1 countermeasures as of this moment. This Dullahan won't feel so smart with ten grams of iron in its skull."

A pause. Even more static. "A Dullahan? Sir, did you just say Dullahan?"

"Yes, Agent Forty-nine, a Dullahan."

"I'm sorry, sir, but that wasn't a Dullahan that just ripped a hole in the infirmary wall."

The *Ci Annwn*'s howl nearly blew the speaker on Dr. Harkness's watch. Through the static, Agent Forty-nine said, "Shit! It's seen me! I'm withdrawing, sir!" Two more gunshots. Heaving breath and stamping feet. Then the feed cut out completely.

They heard the second howl not through the watch, but as a deep, echoing note that rattled through the air vents and shook the ground beneath their feet. The alarm box on the wall and the heavy scanner at the security checkpoint went dead silent, and Chris raised his hands above his head with a cry of surprise as the fluorescent ceiling lights exploded in a shower of hot glass and sparking wires.

"Oh, Nethe-on-High!" cried Ms. Keane. "Oh, Golden Father and Blessed Sons, I didn't sign up for this!" She pushed her tablet into Gareth's hands and ran back toward the security checkpoint, hammering on the button on the wall in some vain hope that it might raise the shutter. "Get me out of here! Someone, please, just get me out of here! I'm just a fucking paralegal! I'm not part of this!"

Dr. Harkness holstered his weapon and bore down on the panicking fae. He pulled her back from the shutter, then gave her a hard slap when she kept pleading to be let out. "Listen to me, goddammit! The Department has protocols for scenarios like this one. If you people do as I tell you, you stand a better chance of leaving here alive. If you go off on your own, if you panic and act like idiots, I can make no such guarantees. Now, which is it to be?"

Abby's stomach turned. The sudden spike of adrenaline had made her forget for a moment who this asshole was. But all the threats of memory-wipes and prison time felt like a secondary problem right now, so she bit her tongue and let Dr. Harkness say his piece.

"This is a two-pronged attack," he said, after Ms. Keane had gone quiet. "*Ci Annwn*. Dullahan. Both sent here to eliminate a single target." He looked directly at Abby. "The King-Among-the-Holly has appointed you as his champion, Miss Henderson, and that makes you the most immediate threat to the people pulling the strings here. How they discovered you were here is an open question with some very disturbing implications, but it is presently of secondary importance. What matters right now is getting you and the rest of the civilians to safety and neutralizing the extraplanar threat."

The sudden glow of emergency lighting along the floor signalled the activation of some backup power source, though Abby couldn't guess how it was holding up against the *Ci Annwn*'s magic. Maybe the Ministry of Uncommon Knowledge had struck their own bargain with the Shattergrip clan. The spinning red warning light on the wall started up again, but the alarm was still silent. Dr. Harkness took Ms. Keane's tablet without asking and spent a moment connecting to whatever secure, retrograde intranet the Ministry used. Eventually, the screen filled with a map of the South Campus, in all its teal, 16-bit glory. An array of red dots pulsated at various points on the screen, mostly at doorways and junction points. "Now look," said Dr. Harkness, "in the event of a power failure, all the security barriers drop automatically. Full lockdown, no passage between different departments." He circled a portion of the western corridor with his finger. There was a red dot at either end, which he tapped with his finger as he spoke. "Right now, we're here, between the front entrance and the security room. Shutters in front of and behind us, locking us off from either. With the iron filaments lining the shutters, we're safe from fae incursion for the moment."

"Unless the fae start busting through these walls," Leanne observed.

"Unless they start busting through the walls," Dr. Harkness agreed. "That's why I do not advise that we stand here for very much longer." His finger traced the route they had all come. "The cell block is the most secure part of the facility, with shutters at every entrance and wall-mounted machine guns that are controlled from the security room. The steel mesh lining the cells means the fae can't get in no matter how hard they try, so long as the doors are shut. I suggest you all return there and shut yourselves in a cell until the threat is neutralized."

"What about me?" Natalie asked. "I can fight this thing, extraplanar entity to extraplanar entity."

"You got absolutely thrashed last time," Abby pointed out. "Plus, that was just the one Dullahan. Now we've got a Dullahan and an angry *Ci Annwn*."

"I'll last longer than just about anyone here. These things are cutting people down before they can get a shot off. Do you think the rest of the security staff will be much more of a deterrent? Get me some iron weaponry and some raw chicken from the fridge, and I'll be okay."

"Out of the question," said Dr. Harkness. "I'm not letting a rogue undead walk around this facility, lockdown or no lockdown. If you lose control, we'll have twice as much trouble. But you make a reasonable point about weapons. We have a number of countermeasures in this facility that are effective against hostile fae."

"Like those dart guns your men pulled on Whittaker," Leanne said. "You pump enough shots into the Dullahan, and it'll go down like a bag of sand."

"I was thinking of a more permanent solution," Dr. Harkness admitted.

"Well, unthink it, bub," said Abby. "We have a golden opportunity to take the *Ci* alive. Then we can get it back home before the King-Among-the-Holly buries the city under eight metres of snow."

"And if we can capture the Dullahan," Leanne observed, "we can question it about the men—faeries—upstairs. Find out where they're hiding and lay them out permanently."

Abby smiled. "Ruthless and tactical, Leanne. I love everything about it."

Dr. Harkness uttered a little growl of frustration. "Very well." His finger traced another line on the map toward a small, rectangular room near the southeast end of the South Campus. "There is one option which may satisfy you. The

HVAC system is linked to a suite of atmospheric deterrents. In the event of an EPI, we can pump in various aerosolized agents that are proven effective against a variety of extraplanar entities. One of these agents is particularly high in iron oxide. In a fae entity, it induces dizziness, shortness of breath, and eventually unconsciousness in less than five minutes."

Jacquie gave Dr. Harkness a cold look. "And I presume we're better off not knowing how you tested these deterrents."

Dr. Harkness ignored her. "There's a set of controls for the atmospheric deterrents in the director's office. If someone can get there, they can pump the compound full of iron oxide and put these creatures out in no time at all."

"And how does someone get there?" Abby asked. "You just said that full lockdown means all the shutters are down." She nodded at the map, where at least a half-dozen red dots flashed between the group's current position and Dr. Harkness's office.

"That's the difficult part," Dr. Harkness admitted. "There are manual overrides for all the security shutters in the security room, but the system won't allow more than three shutters to be opened at once. Any more defeats the purpose of a lockdown. Someone has to get in there and override the shutters to allow the rest easy movement through the facility, but someone also has to reach my office so they can activate the atmospheric deterrents."

Abby looked at the shutter that stood between them and the security room, and then at Simon. "What do you think? You got enough in you to teleport to the other side of that barrier and hit the override?"

"I can try to open the way," he said, "but I don't know if I should make the crossing myself. The energies could tear me to pieces."

"What about our Rent-a-Wands?" Leanne said. "I thought I saw a spell of intangibility on there. One of us could just walk right through the shutter! You said the security room's just on the other side, right?"

Dr. Harkness considered this. "It's worth trying." To one of the security guards: "Pryce, you took possession of those wands when our guests here were processed, correct?"

Pryce blinked. "I did. I was going to run them down to the lab when my shift ended, but..." She gestured at the chaos all around her.

"So you still have them?"

"Affirmative. But, sir, you said you wanted them destroyed after the boys in the lab checked them over."

"I'm countermanding that order. Give Miss Waller her wand back."

Pryce opened a pouch on her bulletproof vest and out came the two Rent-a-Wands. Leanne immediately made her way toward the second security shutter. "First door on the right on the other side," Dr. Harkness told her.

Leanne stood about a metre away from the shutter, shoulders square, feet shoulder-length apart, wand straight out in front of her. Abby watched in breathless anticipation as her partner lifted her chin, cleared her throat, and spoke the spell in the most self-assured tone she could.

"Iċ ðurh-fare."

For a couple seconds, nothing happened.. Then the fabric of Leanne's jeans, the strands of her hair, the knit of her fuzzy cardigan all seemed to pull apart, connected only by the loosest thread. Leanne took one slow, careful step forward. When her foot came down, it sank half an inch into the floor. She took another and sank another half-inch. One more step, and she passed through the heavy security shutter like a fog.

For a moment, silence, and Abby wondered if her girlfriend had just vaporized herself. Then a clank and a groan as the shutter rose to the ceiling. Leanne's voice came from beyond: "Hurry up, slowpokes!"

The security room was only just large enough for four or five people to occupy comfortably. One wall was entirely covered in bulky CRT screens that showed a variety of CCTV angles. Below this bank of monitors was a fat security console—the best 1980s NASA surplus that money could buy. As soon as everyone was past the security barrier, Dr. Harkness seated himself in the rolling office chair positioned before the console, switched the feeds, and made a diagnostic check of the Campus's security systems.

"All the security is run from the emergency power supply," he said, not that anyone had asked. "I should have visual on our houseguests… now." He stopped flicking through the security feeds when an image of the Dullahan came up on one of the monitors. Another feed showed the low-slung black form of the *Ci* as it loped under a security shutter that had jammed four feet off the ground. Both moved slowly, tactically through the Campus. Hunters on the prowl. Dr. Harkness checked the feeds for the corresponding camera number. "Looks like the Dullahan found its way to the northwest quadrant. The hound is near the armoury now." He turned his attention to a row of switches in front of him. Each had a little red or green light below it, as well as a label bearing the name of some section of the Campus. He cycled through the security feeds again and saw multiple security shutters that hadn't close all or even most of the way. One looked like it had had a tube light from the ceiling jammed right up underneath it. "Dammit. Barriers have failed at Checkpoints Nine, Twelve, and Twenty-Two."

"How much of a problem is that?" asked Jacquie.

"Remember how I said the system won't allow for more than three shutters at once to be overridden during a lockdown? The system also doesn't know the difference between a shutter that's been overridden and a shutter that's failed to engage properly." He pointed at the green lights. "These barriers currently register as overridden, according to the computer's understanding."

"So we can't open any more shutters until we close the busted ones," said Abby. "It'll take forever to get to the countermeasures in your office."

"And that's assuming none of the other shutters fail when whomever we send out tries to raise them. Unless someone in the vicinity is able to properly engage the shutters that have already failed, we're as good as stuck here."

"Can't you end the lockdown?" Ms. Keane asked. Her eyes flicked about the room as if she were looking for Dullahan behind the walls.

"A full override of the lockdown means there's nothing between us and the hostiles," Dr. Harkness replied. "That is not happening." He cycled through the feeds again, looking for any signs of life in the right places. There were security personnel poised combat-ready behind sealed checkpoints, a few dark-suited operational personnel on the prowl in the hallways, and research and admin staff hunkered down where shelter was available. No one was in striking distance of an open shutter.

He stopped cycling when the feed for his own office came up. It was a small room, but well-appointed: mahogany desk, leather-backed chairs for meetings, oak panelling and bookshelves, and a portrait of Her Majesty on the wall. At least, that was how Abby imagined it was supposed to look on a good day: for now, everything that wasn't nailed down was shoved right up against the door, and the mahogany desk had been tipped over on its side to give cover to Agent Six and the security guard who was with him. They must have made it to the office just as the lockdown order came through.

Dr. Harkness scooted his chair over to the intercom at the far end of the security console and tried to connect to his office. "Attention, Agent Six. Come in, Agent Six. This is Director Theta. Do you copy?" No answer. On the security feed, Six and the guard stayed exactly where they were, shooting the odd wary glance over top of the desk. "Who is that with him?" Dr. Harkness asked. "I can't make out the face."

Pryce stepped forward and squinted. "Looks like it's Bradley, sir."

"See if you can raise him."

Pryce tried her radio, with no more success. "Nothing doing, sir. They can't hear us and we won't hear them."

Dr. Harkness looked at Simon. "I don't suppose you saw fit to imbue those wands of yours with any teleportation spells?"

"Alas, no. That's slightly more advanced magic than such a simple package can handle."

"And Chris can't teleport past the iron in the shutters," said Abby. "Simon, how long does that intangibility spell last?"

"Two minutes exactly. That's the maximum amount of magical potential the wand can hold."

Abby took her own Rent-a-Wand from her back pocket. "Well, there's five charges for five different spells on these things, right? What if you redistribute all that energy? Throw out four spells with minimum charges in favour of one supercharged spell?"

She could see the wheels turning in his head. "That might get you as much ten minutes."

Abby smiled. "You feel up to it?"

He took the wand, considering. "I could reset the charges here and now, but I'll probably be flat out on the sofa for the next three days. Mind you, the alternative is that we stand in an iron-enclosed box playing 'I Spy' until our fae friends come bursting through the wall."

"What's that line from *Master and Commander*? Something something the lesser of two weevils?"

"Yes. Yes, you're quite right, Abigail. Dr. Harkness, I'll have that chair, if you don't mind. I'll need to sit down after I'm through."

Dr. Harkness ceded the chair. Simon pushed himself as far back from the security console as he could manage so he wouldn't blow the circuits, then laid the wand across his knee with both hands upon it. He shut his eyes, and a long, twisting incantation in a dead language rolled off his tongue. The five runes carved down the side glowed orange and twisted together like a flowing river, rearranging at last into one symbol. Abby's hair stood up, and a few of the security feeds cut in and out under a pattern of white noise. At last Simon opened his eyes, pale, shaking, and breathless. He slumped over in the chair and held up the wand in one white-knuckled fist. "Bloody… hell… that's going to set me back a fortnight… Here. One supercharged spell of intangibility… "

Abby took the wand and put her arms around him in a gentle embrace. "You did great, Simon. You've earned a week on the couch for this."

Natalie laid a hand on Simon's shoulder. "She's right. As soon as we get through this, you just put your feet up and rest. I'll keep things running the next little while."

Abby straightened and looked thoughtfully at the supercharged Rent-a-Wand. "Welp. Here goes nothing, I guess."

Dr. Harkness shook his head. "Oh, no. You're not going out there. You're a civilian."

"I'm also the reason this is happening, according to you. I'm not about to let someone else risk their ass for my sake. I've been in that situation before. Historically, it hasn't turned out great."

Jacquie spoke up. "If you get hurt out there—Auberon forbid, if the worst happens—it will be tantamount to failing the *anoeth*. Do you have any idea what Holly will do then?"

"I don't imagine it'll be worse than what they'll do if we don't return the *Ci* to Carcosa before the clock runs out."

"Enough," Dr. Harkness snapped. "This is not an open debate, Miss Henderson. Hutchins, confiscate that wand until she comes to her senses."

Hutchins made a move, but Abby was already backing out the door. With the wand held high above her head, she shouted, *"Iċ ðurh-fare!"* This time, the effect was instantaneous. She felt a surge of energy throughout her whole body, tugging at every atom that made her up. A million magnets pulled her in a million different directions, and a breeze with no discernible origin rushed through the newfound spaces where she wasn't. Hutchins tried to grab her wrist, but his fingers closed on nothing at all.

Its magic spent, the Rent-a-Wand clattered to the floor. The rune faded to black, the slender wood bent in on itself, and then it snapped down the middle. Abby shrugged. "Well, I guess that settles that argument."

Dr. Harkness might well have tried to strangle her if she wasn't intangible. Without taking her eyes off her, he seized Ms. Keane's tablet once again and pulled up the map of the South Campus. "Very well. If you're going to be a child about this, we may as well make the next ten minutes count. My office is here, on the northern end of the Administration Wing. Third floor, room 316. The code to activate the atmospheric deterrents is 4-9-3-5-7. No one but a head of department is supposed to know that, but these are extraordinary circumstances. We're on the first floor of the West Block right now, so this is the route you need to follow." He traced a line with his finger, slowly enough that Abby could commit the path to memory. It looked like a pretty direct shot, especially without all those pesky walls and security checkpoints getting in her way. All the same, it was no small distance to cover, and she wasn't totally sure how intangibility would stack up against two flights of stairs. She'd probably have to move fast to beat the traffic.

"You're intangible," Dr. Harkness said, "but not invisible. If you run into one of the houseguests, they will come for you. I suggest you keep a low profile and watch the doors and corners carefully. No sense in wasting what little time you have dancing with the fae."

"Speaking of not wasting time," Abby replied, "I better get going while the getting's good."

Dr. Harkness managed to choke out a very strained, "Good luck." Abby nodded to him, to her friends, and then jogged right through the security console into the unknown belly of the South Campus.

CHAPTER 20

HUNTED

THIS WASN'T anything like astral projection, she decided. When Abby untethered her spirit-self from her physical form so the former could walk the earth unchecked, she always felt a pull from above as the Elsewhere tried to draw her into a Bridge, and she had to concentrate like hell to keep her spirit-self from rocketing off to the place where the spirits dwelt. Right now, she had the opposite problem. She was no mere thought in this moment; she still had form and a mass that responded to gravity. If she concentrated, she found that she could convince a few particles at a time to pull themselves together and make something like an impermeable surface—one hand here, a foot there, just enough to keep herself from falling straight through to Shanghai. But she'd had a couple missteps already, her feet sinking through the linoleum like she was walking through a marsh, and she hadn't even come to the first flight of stairs.

When she reached the Administration Wing, she heard something that made her breath catch in her throat. Come to think of it, did she even need to breathe right now? There was nothing to stop the air passing right through skin and muscle into her alveolar sacs as she walked. That was a question worth unpacking later. Because right now, there was a noise coming from down the hall. She crept toward the source and saw a door hanging ajar. An arcing streak of blood on the tiles curved through into the room beyond.

Abby picked up the pace and ran toward the source of the noise, her footsteps as quiet as falling snow.

"Listen..." It was a male voice on the other side of the door, raspy and racked with pain. "Just... just listen to me, goddammit!" Abby crouched outside the door and poked her head inside. She saw an overturned conference table, smashed chairs, the remains of an overhead projector, a torn screen hanging onto the ceiling by a couple threads. There was a man slumped against the back wall, one leg straight out in front of him, the other bent back at a grotesque angle. His dark jacket was open, his white shirt stained with blood from hip to navel. He had one hand clapped firmly over the wound, the other upon his 9mm.

The Lone Dullahan stood three steps away from the wounded agent, saying nothing. It just tapped the point of its sword upon the floor in a way that Abby took to mean, *Tick-tock, tick-tock, motherfucker.*

"It doesn't... it doesn't have to go this way," the agent gasped. "You and me... we can make a deal..."

Abby squinted. The only illumination in the smashed conference room was the deep, dusky red of the warning lights, but she definitely recognized that voice. It was hard not to; it had been misgendering Chris only a few hours ago.

"I can... I can get you the Henderson girl..." gasped Agent Twenty-four. "She's what you're here for, right? I can give her to you, if you just leave my people alone." No reply. Just the *tap-tap-tap* of the Dullahan's sword. "That's how you people operate, isn't it? Equal pay for equal favours?" *Tap-tap-tap*. "Talk to me, goddammit!"

"That is a law made by false kings," the Lone Dullahan hissed. "The Golden Hand does not extend favours to lesser blood."

With one sword-stroke, the Lone Dullahan sent Twenty-four's head flying like it was driving a ball across the eighteenth fairway. The bloody pound of flesh rolled toward Abby, who made a sudden, nauseous retreat as the dead face flashed her the whites of its eyes. She set off down the hall at a run, concentrating on pulling together the molecules in her feet into solid mass that could grip the floor. Only too late did she realize that solidity meant noise, and she pumped the gas when she heard the Lone Dullahan give a low hiss.

Leather riding boots squeaked on the tiles behind her as the creature burst out of the conference room. Abby looked back as the Lone Dullahan took a low stance, drew the longbow from its back, nocked an arrow. She felt a chill as the arrow *whooshed* between the molecules where her small intestine should be and *shnnked* into the next security shutter. She remembered Whittaker, bleeding and broken on the streets outside the Letterbox.

The Lone Dullahan wasn't giving chase. It must have known it couldn't, with the iron-reinforced security shutter blocking its path. Instead, it had its bone-whip in hand. The business end was already entwined in the grating of a nearby air duct, and with one great tug, that grate came free of the wall. The Lone Dullahan's body twisted, lengthened, compressed in a way that Abby knew bones shouldn't be able to, and then the creature squeezed itself into the duct and disappeared. As she sprinted through one security barrier after another, she could hear the Lone Dullahan clanking along behind the walls, through ducts that she knew she could never normally have hauled herself through no matter how skinny she was. "Note to self," she muttered, "tell Gil to line the air ducts with iron."

She finally reached the first flight of stairs. How many minutes had she used up by now? Seven? Eight? She concentrated on the soles of her feet, the palms of her hands, until she was pretty sure she could get a solid grip on the banisters. She put one foot on the first stair. Then she saw a flash of movement in the air duct on the first landing.

Step One: the Dullahan kicked the grate right off the wall. Step Two: the grate flew toward, through, past her head. Step Three: the Dullahan squeezed out of the vent and rolled.

Step Four: it swept its sword through her chest, and ice and electricity rippled across every one of her many particles. Thank God she wasn't solid enough to process the terror, or else she was pretty sure she would have pissed herself.

She jumped when the Dullahan lashed out with its bone-whip, all sense of density and form abandoned. A sudden weightlessness sent all her particles rushing toward the ceiling and she felt that same cold, buzzing sensation in the empty spaces between her as she rose through the second floor and kept going, past a trio of very confused security personnel. She was just particles of carbon now, floating upward under the last of her momentum, and as she passed through the hard cement that separated the second floor from the third, some part of her brain remembered the mission. She saw the third-floor ceiling racing toward her and raised her hands, screaming at the various molecules to get a grip on one another. They did, just in time to stop her from kissing the ceiling. When she'd found the balance of solidity versus formlessness in her feet, she pushed herself back down to land on the third floor, just on the right side of the first security shutter and another group of very confused security officers.

"Long story," she told one of them. "Look, your director and some civilians are holed up in the first-floor security room, comms are down, you've got a hungry *Ci Annwn* and a rogue Dullahan crawling around in the air vents, and I need to get to Dr. Harkness's office ASAP so I can pump the compound full of iron oxide and put these things down. Any questions?"

The security guards looked at each other, shrugged, then looked at her. "Fuck it. This ain't the craziest day I've had in this job," said the first guard.

"I shudder to think. Doc Harkness's office?"

"Down this hall, a left, two rights, and a left."

"Thanks. Watch the air ducts. If the Dullahan comes after me, odds are it'll be coming that way."

She took off running again as the first guard barked at the rest: "Alright, you heard the lady! Eyes on the vents until we get the all-clear. And be sure to mask up. We'll have countermeasures coming through the HVAC in a minute." As she rounded the corner and clapped eyes on Room 316, she tried not to reflect on the fact that she'd wound up following Dr. Harkness's orders anyway. Somewhere far behind, one of the guards gave an order, and a burst of live ammunition ripped into the air vent. She put on a last burst of speed and jumped headlong through Dr. Harkness's steel office door.

"Movement! I've got movement!" As Abby tried like hell to bring enough of her molecules together to create a solid braking system, two gun barrels and two heads popped up over top of the overturned desk like gophers from their holes. She raised her hands, closed her eyes, and felt all her molecules race back into the place they'd started with an audible crackle. The clock ran out on the intangibility spell, and she suddenly remembered what mass was as she slammed hard against the desk. The impact knocked her back on her ass, and she covered her head with her hands as she none-too-proudly begged the Ministry men not to fire.

"Jesus Christ… " said Agent Six. "Henderson?"

She opened her eyes. Six stood, holstered his gun, and motioned for Bradley to do the same. "What," he asked, "and I cannot stress this enough, the fuck are you doing?"

He looked like he was having a worse night than her. His sweat-stained shirt was open to the second button, his face and chest only a little less white than it was (in stark contrast to his bloodshot eyes). Instead of the usual highly gelled high-and-tight, his hair was messy and limp across his forehead, and when he came around the desk to offer her a hand up, she noticed a tremor in the muscles that he clearly didn't want her to see. Dr. Harkness had said that he'd already had words with Six, and he'd meant to have more once Abby and her friends were out of the building. She didn't know the full scope of what that entailed, but she wouldn't be surprised if there was a Lethe crystal involved. She chanced a quick look at his aura, and the fatigue oozed out of him so strongly that Abby felt her own knees starting to wobble a bit. Adrenaline was the only thing carrying him through the attack, and she almost wanted to tell him to take a nap while she and Bradley figured out what came next.

Instead, she leaned in and whispered, "Is Phil okay?" Sure, the little pathologist was a bit on the quirky side, but Abby didn't want to see her dragged into the middle of this shitshow.

"Phil's fine," Six whispered back. "Up to her eyeballs in paperwork at the North Campus for the last two days. As far as Theta's aware, she doesn't know thing one about our little arrangement."

"Let's keep it that way." Her eyes flicked over to Bradley as she said this. "She doesn't deserve to get dragged over the coals for helping me."

Six nodded, winked, then turned and went to sit on the edge of the desk. He opened another button on his shirt and shook out his collar to get some air flowing. "What's the situation out there? We locked down when the order came in, but we don't have a live camera or comm feed in here. I don't even know what we're dealing with."

"That's why I'm here," said Abby. She told him about the rogue fae wandering the halls, and the casualties she'd already seen.

"So you want to activate the atmospheric deterrents," Six concluded. "Knock them out and put this nightmare to bed. Smart. I had the same thought when we shut ourselves in, but neither of us has the clearance to activate them."

"Dr. Harkness gave me the code. Just point me to the controls."

Six pointed to one of the bookshelves set into the west wall. "Hidden switch in the back. Third row, four books from the left."

She found the button and pushed it. There was a muffled click somewhere inside Dr. Harkness's desk, and then the leather blotter opened on a hinge, revealing another chunky security console, the baby brother of the computer bank in the security room, inset in the mahogany. Abby saw a chubby screen and a speaker on one side, and on the other, a keypad above two rows of switches that were labeled "A-1" to "L-1." She knelt before the desk and tilted her head so that the console looked most of the right way around, then put in the code Dr. Harkness had given her.

"What's the switch for rogue faeries?" she asked Six.

Officer Bradley piped up. "The fae are Class F entities. You want F-1 countermeasures for them."

She thanked him and flipped the switch labeled "F-1." After a few seconds, the ceiling vent started to hum as the HVAC kicked in. Agent Six covered his nose and mouth with his shirt and Bradley pulled a cloth mask from one of the pouches on his belt. Abby followed their lead and pulled her own shirt up over her nose. "This stuff's not dangerous to humans," Six told her, "but it'll give you a mean headache if you breathe too deep. Best keep your mouth shut for a few minutes so you don't get a lungful."

She gave him a thumbs-up.

"And if it stops you talking for a bit," Six muttered to himself, "so much the better."

The thumbs-up became a middle finger. "I heard that."

The console's bulbous speaker cracked and warbled. "—ome in—Henderson—read me?" Dr. Harkness's voice was drowning in static, so Bradley bent over the console and pounded on it with a closed fist until the interference cleared. "Come in, Henderson, come in. Do you read me?" His face came up on the chubby little monitor, upside-down from Abby's perspective. It was like a special effect from *The Matrix*: all green scan lines and a waterfall of descending pixels. Abby bent herself around so they were roughly eye-to-eye and felt the blood rushing to her head.

"Hey, Gil!" she chirped. "How's it hangin'?"

Even in scan-line-and-pixel format, the scowl was plain on his face. "If we could dispense with the gadfly act for a moment, Miss Henderson?"

"Sorry. It's a fear response thing. What's the situation?"

"We lost visual contact with the houseguests a few minutes ago. There was a short skirmish with the Dullahan near your position, but then it disappeared."

"Yeah. I saw it squeeze into an air duct a few minutes back. Stupid thing's, like, quintuple-jointed or something. By the way, iron filaments in the vents. Write it down."

"No, I mean it quite literally disappeared in front of our eyes: one second it was standing in full view of the cameras, and then it pulled up its hood and suddenly it wasn't. That riding cloak it's wearing obviously bears some sort of invisibility enchantment."

"Great. And you said "houseguests," with an 's,' so I guess you don't know where Gwyn's pet is either."

"I'm afraid not. Last confirmed sighting was in the second-floor dining hall. That was ten minutes ago."

"Well, good thing I got your precious F-1 deterrents running."

"Indeed. We're going to wait another few minutes here until they've had a chance to do their work, and then I will kindly ask you to input the lockdown override code into the console in my desk. That will deactivate the alarms and the security shutters, and I'll be able to send out a security team to sweep up the houseguests when we know they're neutralized."

"So, sit down and shut up is what you're telling us up here."

"Essentially. The director's office has a built-in panic room hidden behind the west wall. Iron filaments in all four walls and the door. You can sequester yourself in there if it would make you feel secure until the lockdown ends.

There's a comm link in there, so I would still be able to reach you."

"Aww, Gil, I didn't think you cared!"

"I have a duty to protect Her Majesty's citizens, Miss Henderson. Even when I find those citizens personally distasteful in the extreme."

"You know, somebody else said something like that to me tonight. You and Gareth should talk."

Dr. Harkness looked down, and she heard the clicking of buttons on his end. "The override and lockdown codes should appear on your monitor in a second. Please try to be more responsible with them than you were with your borrowed magic." Dr. Harkness's face disappeared from the monitor, replaced a second later by two five-digit numbers.

"I don't think that guy likes me very much," Abby said as she punched in the code for the panic room.

"He might be more favourably disposed to you if you didn't keep treating all this like some kind of game," Six answered.

"I have to laugh, Six. Otherwise, I'll just start screaming, and I won't ever stop."

There was a deep clunk of moving tumblers somewhere behind the bookshelves, and then one section of the wall slowly opened on a hinge. Agent Six suppressed a grunt as he pushed himself off the desk. "That door looks heavy. I'll need some help opening it the rest of the way."

Abby and Officer Bradley joined Six beside the false bookshelf and got all their weight behind it. "On three," said Six. "Ready?" He counted them in, and on 'three' they gave it their all. The panic room door was heavy, and the three of them together only just managed to keep it scraping along the carpet.

"Jesus," Abby gasped. "Shouldn't this thing be motorized?"

"It should be." Dr. Harkness's reply came over the security console's speaker. "The motor must have jammed when the *Ci Annwn* knocked out the power."

"I hope you're paying the complaints department overtime, Gil, because I got a few things to say to them when this is finished!"

Something rattled in the vent above their heads. Abby's hand started to itch, and when she looked up, she saw two pinpricks of icy blue light among the gloom of the air shaft and a trail of icy vapour falling to the floor. The *Ci Annwn* uttered a low warning growl.

"Contact!" Six barked, and he and Officer Bradley had their guns out before Abby knew what was what. She ran to get behind them, behind the not-quite-open panic room door, and covered her ears as the first shots went off. The vent cover clattered to the floor, and the *Ci Annwn* came tumbling ignominiously after it. It landed side-on to the hail of bullets and only managed to stand after a concerted effort. It snorted, growled, shook out its coat, anything to try and psych itself up enough for the final push.

The creature bared its teeth and jumped at Officer Bradley, sinking its teeth into his forearm. "Fuck!" Bradley howled. The *Ci* planted its feet and tugged. At its full fighting strength, it might well have ripped his arm off, but the lungful of countermeasures had it some distance away from full fighting strength. It was probably somewhere in junkyard-Rottweiler territory right now, which wasn't a huge improvement, and Abby broke cover to do something very stupid. She ran around behind the *Ci* and locked her arms around its chest. Six holstered his gun and came around beside her, trying to prise open the *Ci*'s jaws with both hands The itch in Abby's hand turned to a burn as she tightened her grip on the raging beast. She heard a rush of whispered, indistinct chatter from somewhere close by, felt a low thrum of energy. As the *Ci* strained against her grip, she realized that vibration, that resonance, wasn't coming from the creature itself. But then where… ?

Six got the *Ci*'s jaws off Bradley, and the security officer kicked it hard. Abby was still clinging tight to the beast, and she and it both went tumbling ass over teakettle toward the other side of the office. Her hand brushed against its throat and she felt a solid band of cold metal there. As soon as she touched the collar, her hand and forearm exploded with pain. Bitter, bitter cold surged up her arm, and all the sounds of the natural world assaulted her ears. Stars spoke to sky spoke to cloud in the cold night outside. The moon spoke to the tide, the trees spoke to the earth, the rain spoke to the river, and Abby heard it all. As the *Ci Annwn* scrambled to its feet once more, the sigil on her palm glowed an eerie blue in the emergency lighting. Besides the thousand voices of the magic coming at her from all directions, she heard that same rush of indistinct chatter from a moment ago. A secondary enchantment from a secondary source, latched onto Holly's magic like a flea.

She saw the next few moments as a series of snapshots. The *Ci Annwn* leaped at her. Agent Six and Officer Bradley reloaded their weapons. Her hand glowed like a cold, blue star. The *Ci*'s collar shone with a pale light of its own. Words appeared in the silver, rendered in the language of the high elves. She read them, and all the forces of nature whispered a translation in her ear. The moon and stars told her to put her hand upon the *Ci*'s collar. The rivers told her to speak the mantra aloud. The wind told her to have faith.

She did as nature commanded.

"Long is the winter!" she screamed. *"And long is the Hunt!"* The *Ci* tilted its head. *"And long is the night in –"*

Before she could finish, the whole world turned white.

BOOK THREE:

TOOTH AND CLAW

The grete greundes in the greves so glady thei go;
So gladly thei gon in greves so grene.
The King blowe rechas
And folowed fast on the tras
With many sergeant of mas,
That solas to sene.

*

The Awntyrs off Arthure
at the Terne Wathelyne
Anonymous

SHE IS falling fast. White oblivion whirls all around her. Snow clings to her fur, and she hears a voice. It is not an unfriendly voice. It is the voice of her master, and yet she has forgotten it. The monsters made her forget it.

The girl is falling with her. The Gospel-child, who helped her remember her master's voice by invoking the ancient magicks. She is a mere hand's breadth away, her fingers still outstretched as if to once more hold the sacred silver that entwines her throat. The fall through oblivion has separated them, and yet the hunter is sure that if she tried, she could reach the girl again. Bite down on that outstretched hand. Sever the muscles and nerves that would presume to tame her.

No. No, that is not who she is. The monsters twisted her power to a crueller purpose. They turned her upon the bald man, and the child with the rabbit, and so many others. They took her from her home, starved her, caged her, and then sent her after those who had not offended Winter's sight. She was starving and maddened, and when they sent her out, she would eat. She would eat, and eat, and eat. Any meat that crossed her path was suitable. She is ashamed of this. She has always known it is an aberration, and she will abide it no more.

It is not this Gospel-child who is her enemy. It is not the mixed-bloods. It is the monsters. The bearers of the coin. They who carried the totem of the Golden Father and sang praises to him when they sent her into the world to murder their enemies.

The Golden Hand have committed terrible, nameless sins against her master. They have abused her. But now she is free, and she will not be satisfied until she feasts upon their flesh.

CHAPTER 21

COOLDOWN

W-WHAT HAPPENED?" Leanne stammered. "What the hell just happened?"

They had all watched it play out on the security feed. Abby, holding tight to the *Ci Annwn*. Her hand upon its collar. An incantation upon her lips. Then a flash, and the camera cut out.

White snow on the screen now. No response when Dr. Harkness tried to connect to the intercom in his desktop security console. He was flicking every switch, pushing every button trying to raise Agent Six or Officer Bradley. Nothing worked.

"It can't have... gone, surely?" asked Ms. Keane. "The creature. It wouldn't... it couldn't have just..."

Dr. Harkness pressed another button on the security console. "Attention, Agent Six. Come in, Agent Six! This is Theta. Do you copy?"

A buzz of static. A few broken chirps of sound. Then a noise of someone pounding upon machinery and cursing it back to life. "—stupid piece of—dammit—I'll—"

"Agent Six! Come in, Agent Six! Do you copy, over?"

The static cleared, and they heard his voice. "Theta, this is Six. I read you, over."

"Status update, Agent Six."

"I'm glad you're safe, too, sir." Six paused like a man who doesn't know whether to start with the bad news or the bad news. "I had a rough few minutes trying to re-jig the speaker in the panic room. Door took most of the blast, but that was the largest surge of extraplanar energy I've ever seen. Probably turned most of the circuits in here to slag."

"What happened in there, Agent Six? Is everyone okay? Is the *Ci Annwn* subdued?"

"It's... sir, it's gone."

"Gone?"

"I mean 'poof.' I mean vanished. Henderson, too. They're gone into the place between places, or into the land of wind and ghosts, or however you want to romanticize it. They're not here, sir. I don't think they're in the building anymore."

Simon leaned forward and pushed the 'talk' button. "Agent Six, do you see any residue of fae enchantment?"

"There's a six-foot-wide faerie ring sprouting from the carpet, if that's what you're asking."

"Indeed... tell me, what did Abby say before she disappeared? What were her exact words?"

"It was that mantra again. *Long is the winter...*" Six intoned.

"And long is the Hunt, et cetera," Simon replied. He turned away from the intercom for a moment, pursed his lips, and thought hard. Then he hit the 'talk' button again and said, "I think we've all been played for suckers."

"What do you mean?" asked Leanne.

Simon guided Dr. Harkness's thumb to the 'talk' button while he held court. "I mean that universal truths like time and causality are mere toys in the hands of a being as powerful as Gwyn ab Nethe. It would be the work of moments for him to cast his eye toward the future and foresee everything that has happened tonight. But faeries can be fickle, indolent." He turned to reassure Chris, Ms. Keane, and the Swann siblings. "Present company excepted, of course." Even so, none of them objected very strongly to the characterization. "It must have frustrated the King to no end," Simon went on, "watching as his knights failed to find the *Ci*. But then, here comes a human blundering into the middle of the scene. Not just any human, either, but the one human in this city who can see farther than her fellows. Who can see farther than all the powers of Winter, even. He runs the calculations. He deduces that if he makes Abby his agent, she will succeed where all others have failed." He took Leanne's hand in his, laid the other softly over top, and looked her in the eye. "And then he shakes her hand. He places within her the smallest fragment of his power. A power that will lie dormant until the moment that Abby and the *Ci Annwn* set eyes upon each other. And when they do, that power erupts. It issues forth a command, against which both Abby and the *Ci* are helpless."

A tear prickled at the corner of Leanne's eye. "It calls the servants back to their master. Back to Carcosa."

"I am sorry, Leanne. I am so very sorry."

"You're saying that the King turned yer wan into… what? A fast-return button?" asked Ms. Keane.

"The direct route. No waiting." Simon let go of Leanne's hand and raised one palm to the gathered masses. "That scar on Abby's hand was not just a mark of her oath to him. It was a spell, written in blood and ice. Old magic to call both her and the *Ci Annwn* to his side when the time was right."

Leanne removed her glasses and wiped away her tears. Took a breath. When she found her voice again, it was angry. "Okay. So, let's get her back."

"I don't think it's that simple, Leanne."

"Like hell it isn't. The *Ci* may be gone, but we have a rogue Dullahan zonked out somewhere in this building. The way I remember it, the King demanded the return of his hound and the rotten SOBs who stole it in the first place. Well, Abby's just handed him the first. We can give him the second, in exchange for Abby. Alive. Unhurt. Here."

"Leanne, one does not simply summon a King of Faerie."

"But me no buts, Simon Lockhart! We've been dancing to Gwyn's tune this whole time and we haven't got a word of thanks back. If you're right, we've just handed him everything he wants, so it's time he gave us something in return! Equal pay for equal favours, right?"

Simon gave a half-smile in response to this. "You're starting to sound like her."

"Someone has to remind you Nocturn types that the human race doesn't like to be pushed around."

"And quite rightly, too." He turned to Dr. Harkness. "Any chance of finding our Lone Dullahan, Gilbert?"

But Dr. Harkness was already hard at it, his fingers flying across the chunky keys as he flicked through camera feeds, activated the infrared overlay, the whole nine yards. After a few minutes' work, he landed on a thermal outline of a prone body on the floor. Its core temperature read as fifteen degrees less than the average human body temperature, yet it was most certainly alive. He switched off the infrared, and the prone body was suddenly invisible to the naked eye.

"Found it," he growled. "I'll dispatch a security team now to pick it up and throw it in a cell."

"How far did the Dullahan get?" asked Leanne.

Dr. Harkness pointed to the corner of the screen. "Do you see that door there? That leads to the alcove directly outside my office. Another thirty seconds, and the hostile would have been within arm's reach of your partner and Agent Six."

*****

After a quarter of an hour, the Lone Dullahan started to stir in its bulletproof Faraday cage. Dr. Harkness stood before it with clipboard and pen, flanked by two security officers. In the viewing gallery one floor up, the civilians observed through bulletproof, floor-to-ceiling windows. They in turn were observed by two more guards standing at the one and only door. Cameras on the ground floor delivered a live feed to a bank of chunky security monitors on the wall opposite the bulletproof windows, so that a watcher in the gallery could look away from the overhead view to a closeup and see all the nuances of the Lone Dullahan's hateful expression.

At first, the Lone Dullahan looked confused. It hissed when it had taken the time to process the four walls around it, and it automatically reached for its sword. It wasn't there. The creature reached for its bone-whip. That had been confiscated as well. Same with its boots, belt, and cloak. The creature bared its teeth, growled, and lunged. The blink of an eye brought it right up against the glass. It hissed again and scored the bulletproof material with its long nails.

Dr. Harkness clicked his pen and made a note on his clipboard. "My name is Dr. Gilbert Harkness," he said, as if the Dullahan had asked. "I am the Director of Operations, Pacific Station, for the Canadian Department of Advanced Research and Special Defence. You have engaged in hostile action against official representatives of Her Majesty's Government on sovereign Canadian soil. You will state your name, place of origin, your current allegiance, and the nature and number of your force. If you have allies planning any further hostile action, you will give me their identities and current locations."

"Little man," the Dullahan growled. "Do you think to frighten me? Dispense with this bondage, and let us test your mettle in the honourable way."

Dr. Harkness made a motion to one of the guards, who pulled something like a garage door opener from one of the pouches on his vest. When he pressed the button, the floor of the cell glowed an electric blue and the Dullahan curled in on itself, slamming its fists against the bulletproof glass as four hundred volts raced through it.

The guard took his finger off the button and the current stopped. "I'm sorry," said Dr. Harkness, "did I give the impression that was a request? Name. Place of origin. Allegiance."

The Lone Dullahan spat on the glass. "Vermin. What manner of creature are you to make demands of your betters?"

The guard put his finger on the button again. The Dullahan's long tongue lolled out of its mouth, and it bit down hard to stop itself from screaming.

Up in the viewing gallery, Leanne turned away from the window, her stomach in a tight knot. She found herself looking directly at the monitor bank, grimaced, and shut her eyes. To the guards, she said, "Can you turn that off, please?"

"Security protocol, ma'am. All interactions with prisoners must be recorded in case of psionic disturbance, memory interruption, or non-visible phenomena."

"You can see everything that's happening down there. Can't you bend the rules this once? It's sick!"

"It's protocol," the guard repeated.

"It's justice," said Gareth Swann. He was leaning against the window, watching the scene below with a fascination that Leanne didn't consider healthy. Ms. Keane had his jacket neatly folded over her arm, and his crisply ironed shirt sleeves were rolled up past the elbow. "If that thing is part of this conspiracy, then how can it deserve less than this?"

While the Ministry men had been processing the Lone Dullahan, Chris and the Swann siblings had been talking. Whispering, really, in Elvish. Leanne didn't think the guards had taken much notice, but she had, and she had a guess that Chris had been passing along everything he, Abby, and Leanne had discussed over dinner. Good. That meant they knew the stakes, even if they didn't necessarily have the most perspective on things.

"How can you say the Dullahan deserves *any* of this?" she asked Gareth. "Even if it is working for the enemy, that doesn't justify torture."

"The enemy tortures us, we torture them," Gareth returned. "Equal pay for equal favours, Ms. Waller. In terms you might understand, karma."

"That is a living being down there," she insisted. "One of your own kind, Gareth Swann. Do you really imagine that Dr. Harkness wouldn't do the same thing to you if he thought you were a threat to him? He was happy enough to turn up the pressure on Chris, and he's half-human!"

"The Dullahan are *not* 'our kind.'"

"And that makes it okay? God, it's just so easy, isn't it? Find one degree of difference between yourself and the Other, and you can abstract them right out of the race! That's not me and I'm not that, so the bullies can just go right on ahead and do whatever the hell they like. Because at least they're not doing it to me!"

"I didn't say that."

"You didn't have to. It's the rationale of every coward and bigot in history."

He bore down on her, poking a finger in her chest and grinding his perfect teeth. Vivid red tinged his pale, silky elven cheeks. "Who in all the hells are you to speak to me like that, Leanne Waller? I can understand why your friends are here, even if I disagree with it. But what are you? A Zed with no mystical talent, no military training, not even a pair of working eyes. You don't know one thing about me, and you have no right to speak to me like that!"

He was tall. It wasn't until just now that Leanne had really processed how tall he was. Standing at only five foot two herself, he seemed even taller. And she had pissed him off worse than she guessed even Abby could have done. But Abby had been taken into the Perilous Realm, and that left a void that needed filling. Someone had to speak truth to power. Put the jerks and the monsters in their place.

"You think I don't know you, Gareth? Look at me: like you said, I'm a Zed with nothing to offer. Just a short, fat little gay girl with bad eyes who went to Catholic school." She swatted his hand away, just a little harder than she needed to. "I've been dealing with creeps like you since I was eight years old."

For a long moment, he said nothing. Then he looked at his hand and slowly drew back his extended forefinger. Smoothed down his hair. Straightened his tie. "I apologize." The words took a minute to come out, but at least they sounded earnest enough. "Maybe you do have something to offer your friends." Looking to one of the guards, he asked, "Is there somewhere around here where I would be allowed to step outside? Perhaps get some peace and quiet?"

One of the guards pointed to a door on the far wall. "There's a coffee station through there. But we'd have to escort you."

Gareth glanced down at Leanne and spoke through a grimace. "Then escort me."

The guard escorted him. As automatically as breathing, Gareth snapped his fingers at Ms. Keane on his way out and gestured for her to follow him. When the three of them were gone, Leanne went and sat in one of the revolving office chairs that was bolted to the floor by the security console. She blew out a heavy breath, spun in a slow circle with one foot, and found herself face-to-face with Jacquie.

"Sorry you had to see all that," Leanne said.

Jacquie took off her heels and sat cross-legged on the floor beside Leanne. "Don't be." She leaned back against the security console and gave an apologetic smile. "As much as I love him, my brother can be a dickhead sometimes. I won't act like he didn't have it coming."

Leanne smiled back. "Is that a faerie term? 'Dickhead'?"

"It sounds more poetic in Elvish."

Leanne laughed. On the security feed, Dr. Harkness had paused the Dullahan-torture, and for a moment all was quiet. After a beat, Leanne filled that space by asking, "So Chris brought you up to speed?"

Jacquie's expression darkened. "Yes. And he passed along your suggestion about a security audit. From top to bottom." She looked to the door that Gareth and Ms. Keane had just left through.

"Do you mind if I ask...?"

"What's the full story with Gareth?"

"Chris made it sound like there was some serious unpleasantness there. If there's the least chance your brother is involved with the Golden Hand..."

"I know. I know." Jacquie put her head in her hands. As she drew them down past her chin, a deep, defeated groan rushed past her lips. "The first time we met, I told you that my parents came out of Faerie looking for something different. I didn't mention what their normal was before that."

"Golden Hand?"

"Not by that name. Not at that time. But the beliefs were the same. Our grandfather was called Tristeyn ab Cullhwch. That name means nothing to you, I'm sure, but there was a time when it meant everything to certain folk in the Otherlands."

On the other side of the viewing gallery, Simon stirred. He had been lying across two chairs, trying not to move after his recent exertions, but now all his attention was on Jacquie. He signalled to Natalie, and she helped him into a sitting position. After he caught his breath, he said, "Hang on; *your* grandfather was Tristeyn ab Cullhwch?"

"Did you know him?" Leanne asked.

"I'm pleased to say I never had the pleasure, but I knew his reputation. Tristeyn ab Cullhwch was a rabble-rouser in the Otherlands, some centuries back. A propagandist, a populist, an advocate of pan-Faerie nationalism and isolationism."

Jacquie nodded. "The Court-Among-the-Oak has always been more welcoming of humankind than our Holly cousins. In bygone centuries, we traded stories with your people. Songs, crafts, knowledge." She shrugged bashfully. "Flesh. Most of the changelings now alive are Oak's fault. And my grandfather hated that. He thought it polluted our own culture, to intermix so freely with another. He was always seeking court appointments, trying to get into the inner circle of King Auberon so he could put things right in his own way. When that didn't work, he renounced his allegiance to Oak and sought the favour of Holly. And when that didn't work, he took his case to the people. He styled himself the voice of the common faerie and gathered grassroots support. Protests turned into rallies turned into riots until Oak finally outlawed his gatherings. It wasn't very long after his arrest that my parents came here."

Leanne nodded at the Lone Dullahan on the security monitors. "But obviously the ideas grew beyond the man—elf—whatever."

"When Gareth and I were young, Grandfather died in prison. It's a rare thing for an elf of the green places to die, let alone to die like that. People talked about him. Remembered him. Remembered what he said. The organized Golden Hand movement began there. It found its following in the dissatisfied and the downtrodden. The young males were the first to turn out in numbers."

Leanne sighed. "When are they not?"

"Some of Grandfather's papers came into our parents' hands when he died. It wasn't their choice. The last will and testament of a faerie is a hard thing to fight. My father destroyed most of them, but Gareth read just enough to start thinking that Grandfather was onto something. Gareth had never been happy growing up among the humans. We changed schools every couple of years, and he never had many friends. How do you explain to the other parents that the pale kid at the back of the room won't hit puberty until he's thirty? So, he latched onto a culture that he felt he'd been deprived of. This was only a couple years after the Soviets had liberated Auschwitz, so he had a lot of reasons to think that humans were as ugly and brutal as Grandfather always said you were.

"Mother and Father never looked at Gareth the same way after they found the golden *lau* in his dresser. That only pushed him further away. He left home, took passage back to the Otherlands. He attended the rallies, learned the chants, all of it. He came back now and then and sought like minds here, among the diaspora. Even faeries have a concept of Lebensraum."

"What changed?"

"Me. I was the only one who never gave up on him. I hated the ideology he'd fallen into, but I couldn't bring myself to hate him. He was my baby brother. I worked so hard to break him out of that cycle. Before T.G.W., that was the great undertaking of my life. And I got through to him, I really did."

"Are you sure? That didn't sound like much of a breakthrough just now."

Jacquie shook her head. "I know my brother's not perfect. Some of the rot is still in there, and I call him on it when I need to. But I promise you: he has changed for the better. He knows more about human law than the Supreme Court, and he's been one of T.G.W.'s greatest assets since he joined us. And I'm talking on and off the books."

Leanne cupped Jacquie's hand between both of hers and looked in her eyes. "I know you want to believe in your brother, Jacquie, but you have to be realistic about him. Some part of your grandfather is clearly still rattling around in his head. You have to consider that part might be big enough to drive Gareth to something like this."

Jacquie looked away, toward the door Gareth and Ms. Keane had disappeared through. She slowly pulled her hand back. "I hope you're wrong. I hope by all the stars above and the grass below that you're wrong. But I'll do as you and your friends suggest. Gareth won't get a free pass when we do our next security audit."

"I think that's really for the best."

Jacquie sat silently with this decision for a moment. Then she stood and slipped her high heels back on. Hailing the remaining guard, she asked, "Is there a restroom nearby? I'd like a minute to gather my thoughts. And I don't think I'm ready to talk to my brother quite yet."

The guard told her to stay put while he radioed for someone to escort her. While they were waiting for the backup to arrive, Leanne let the silence linger. She cleaned her glasses. She twirled her chair in a slow circle. She stifled a yawn and saw from the clock on the wall that it was pushing eleven PM. She needed a pee and a cup of coffee, and she thought of tagging along when Jacquie's escort showed up. On the floor below, Dr. Harkness and the Lone Dullahan had picked up their old routine, and she didn't know how much more of it she could stomach.

Dr. Harkness signalled once more to the guard to kill the power. The Lone Dullahan looked at him through gritted teeth and spat a mouthful of blood onto the floor, where it began to steam from the electric heat. "I am a patient man," Dr. Harkness said. "And as I understand the situation at present, the extraplanar entity you've been using to attack people in this city has returned to its place of origin. I begin to doubt that your allies have any intention of retrieving you, or they would have done it by now. You have nothing to threaten us with, and I have no reason to cut this interview short." The guard started the flow of electricity once again. "Name. Place of origin. Allegiance."

The Lone Dullahan spoke a name, but it was lost amid the buzz of electricity. Dr. Harkness signalled for the guard to cut the power again and said, "I didn't hear you."

"Owain ab Gwylem," the Lone Dullahan repeated. "My name is Owain ab Gwylem."

Up in the viewing gallery, Leanne's attention snapped to the security monitors. "What did it say?"

"Owain ab Gwylem," the Lone Dullahan said again. "Knight of Holly and Huntsman-in-Ordinary of the Wild Hunt."

"You serve the King-Among-the-Holly," said Dr. Harkness.

"I serve the blessed will of Nethe-on-High!" snarled Owain ab Gwylem. "The King Who Sleeps, who sowed the stars in the sky and strung the first bow that ever killed beast or man! Gwyn ab Nethe is a cringing pup compared to him!" He clenched his teeth and held back a scream as the electricity started to flow again.

"You will control your temper whilst you are in my custody," said Dr. Harkness, "or I will be forced to pacify you."

"'The grave-walker fled,'" Leanne said, "'and Owain ab Gwylem hunts it even now.'"

"What did you say?" asked Natalie.

"I was watching the Vokarion feed when Abby was taken before the King the first time, remember? That's what one of the other Dullahan said: 'The grave-walker fled, and Owain ab Gwylem hunts it even now.'"

Natalie came closer to the security monitors and studied the face carefully for a moment. Then a spark of recognition flashed in her eye. "You're right! I didn't see it before—it was so dark, there was so much going on—but you're absolutely right, Leanne. That's the Dullahan that came after me that night."

"That's how the Golden Hand did it! Abby said way back that there must have been someone already inside Carcosa who helped smuggled the *Ci Annwn* out. It must have been Owain ab Gwylem!"

Natalie nodded. "And you wonder why Gwyn's knights could never find the beast once they came here. Someone inside was leading the searchers off-course the whole time."

"Or telling the Golden Hand when to relocate."

Natalie's face twisted into a bitter expression. "I hate to say it, but... we need to tell Dr. Harkness. This is leverage that he can use to get Owain ab Gwylem talking."

As if awaiting his cue, the Dullahan's eyes snapped to the camera. They seemed to look right through the security monitors at Leanne and Natalie. His lips peeled back in a grimace, and the points of his sharklike teeth grated one against another.

"I smell you, grave-walker. You and the stinking apes you serve. I smell you up there. You would appease Gwyn ab Nethe by offering him my head?" Owain ab Gwylem reached up and clenched his hands around the sides of his skull, then twisted and lifted. The seam in his throat split wide like a mocking grin. "Take it!" He held his head high above the stump of his neck and roared over the disturbed Dr. Harkness: "Take it, for all it is worth! Spilling my blood will not gain you the day." Dr. Harkness gave the order to pacify again, but even as the electricity began to flow, Owain ab Gwylem rammed his head back down into place and leaped to the ceiling. His nails dug into the plexiglass like pitons and he clung there while the floor buzzed, a skittering spider with its head on a three-hundred-and-sixty-degree swivel.

"I am nothing, but we are many! We are the Golden Hand! We watch you from the dark places of the world! We strike like a blade in the dark! And we shall not rest until Faerie and the Mid-lands are pure!"

He let go of the ceiling and landed on his feet. The electricity was still flowing, but he didn't seem to notice it anymore. On the monitors, Leanne saw the Dullahan's long tongue rolling around in his mouth as he worked something forward. Then she heard the crunch as he bit down. His whole body spasmed once. Twice. He spat out a mouthful of bluish-black bile. Then he collapsed to the floor as stiff as a board.

"Something's wrong!" Natalie said, and then she was running for the door. The guard tried to stop her from leaving the gallery. He might as well have tried to stop a freight train with a toothbrush. Leanne gasped out a breathless apology as she stepped over the groaning guard and chased Natalie down the stairs.

"What the hell are you doing?" Natalie demanded as she pelted toward the cell.

"I don't know!" Leanne exclaimed. "Seems like the kind of thing Abby would do!"

Dr. Harkness had the cell door open by now, and the guard killed the power to the floor and ran to the aid of Owain ab Gwylem. As soon as he was in reach, Owain ab Gwylem's tongue shot forth from the half-open mouth and raked a long cut down the guard's cheek. The guard fell back screaming, and Natalie cleared the gap between the bottom of the stairs and the open cell in two seconds. Leanne hung back, huffing and puffing as she watched her friend enter the cell, plant a heavy boot on the lashing, prehensile tongue, and rip it free of Owain ab Gwylem's jaw through main strength alone. Blood poured from the wound as Owain ab Gwylem twitched in death, and then all was quiet.

Natalie dropped the Dullahan's tongue on the floor of the cell and backed away, clenching and unclenching her hands into fists. "How do you feel?" she asked the guard.

The man shook his head and pointed to his cheek. The cut was already turning the colour of sea-glass, and the side of his mouth near where he'd taken a literal tongue-lashing was stiff in a rictus of fright. Natalie looked him over, then patted him on the shoulder. "Frostspine venom," she said. "Not enough to do real damage. You'll need a muscle relaxant, a hot compress, and sutures for that wound, but you'll be fine in a couple hours."

After she'd caught her breath, Leanne approached the scene with caution. "What, and pardon my language for saying this, the fuck was that?"

"Indeed." Dr. Harkness held his clipboard tight. "I'm rather curious myself." He played it off like it was nothing, but Leanne recognized a frightened man when she saw one. The guy had struck her as a control freak from the word 'go,' and this obviously was not his night for keeping control of the situation.

"Another wonderful trick of faerie biology," Natalie growled. "The Dullahan's tongue is barbed. A hundred teeth on each side, smaller than the head of a fishhook, and capable of cutting three times deeper." She held her hands palm-up, so they could watch as the long wounds there closed up. Then she clenched and unclenched her fingers again. "Our friend in there chose the easy way out. A capsule filled with Frostspine venom, is my guess. But enough ended up on his tongue for him to play one last trick before he checked out." Clench. Unclench. Then she shook her hands back and forth in front of her. "I got some too, when I jumped in."

"Frostspine venom's a paralytic, right?" Leanne said.

Natalie nodded. "I can feel it trying to lock up my hands. My healing ability will purge it from my system in a few minutes, but it's gonna cramp like a bastard." To Dr. Harkness, she said, "You do a necropsy on your houseguest, and you'll find respiratory and heart failure caused by a lethal dose of tetrodotoxin. That's why your man needs a muscle relaxant."

Leanne crossed herself. "Jesus... he chose *that* over letting down the Golden Hand?"

"Or," Natalie said grimly, "he chose that over answering to the King's justice."

CHAPTER 22

LITTLE GIRL LOST

TEN INCHES of fresh snow softened Abby's landing. Mostly. Her ankle turned, made a sound like a firecracker. She opened her mouth to scream and got a mouthful of the white stuff. She thrust her arms up, to the side, down, trying to find ground and sky. She shifted her hips and jagged pain ran from her left foot all the way up to her brain. Something gripped the back of her shirt, and then she was being hoisted out of the snow like a plushie in a claw machine. She bit her tongue and hastily shifted her lower half despite the pain, so she could sit upright in a position that didn't make her want to die.

The pressure eased off the back of her shirt and she hugged herself tight to stop from shivering. The *Ci Annwn* loped around her in a slow circle until it was directly in front of her. Then it sat and just stared at her.

"G-go-good doggie?" she said hopefully. The hound blinked once but remained otherwise motionless. "W-well," Abby continued, "you've got me d-d-dead to r-rights." Her chattering teeth dragged every syllable out twice as long as it needed to be. "If you w-w-want to rip my th-throat out, I c-can't stop you."

The hound stood and loped through the snow toward her. She didn't even try to back away. Any movement would just mean fresh agonies from her ankle. The hound came up right beside her, turned a hundred-eighty degrees, and sat down again. Then it leaned over and pressed its cheek against hers. The creature blew out a heavy breath. Then another. It shuffled nearer in the snow until its whole bulk was pressed right up against her. Instantly, Abby felt warmer.

"Th-thanks," she said, a little surprised. "I n-needed that."

The hound puffed out another breath in agreement. She felt the warmth spreading. There was a slight hum of magic in the air, and she knew it was the hound doing this. She pressed herself as close to the creature as she could and the warmth spread some more. The snow started to liquefy in a five-foot circle around them. Tentatively, she stretched out her arm and wrapped it around the creature's muscular shoulders. The hound didn't resist, and she scratched it underneath the foreleg. She heard its tail thumping on the rocky ground beneath where the snow had melted.

She couldn't help laughing. "Huh. I guess you're not such a bad guy after all, are you?" The hound let out a haughty, offended breath. Abby shifted, tried to get a look between the creature's hind legs, realized her mistake. "Sorry. Not such a bad girl," she amended.

The hound raised her head and gave one short, approving *woof*. As she did so, Abby caught a flash of silver in the corner of her eye. The hound's collar thrummed with magic yet, but the sensation wasn't half so strong as it had been in Dr. Harkness's office.

She remembered also the second enchantment she'd felt. It was there still, riding piggyback on the energies coming from the collar. She asked the *Ci Annwn*, "Do you mind?" The hound tilted her head to one side to better expose the collar so Abby could have a closer look. She ran all ten fingers over the collar's surface. Nothing out of the ordinary there, so she slipped one finger between the collar and the *Ci*'s neck to check the underside.

The hound growled and jerked her head away. Abby felt a sharp prick on the tip of her finger. When she drew it out, it was bleeding. With pats and soothing words, she tried to calm the agitated *Ci Annwn* as she searched for the collar's clasp. Eventually she got the thing off. The *Ci* immediately stopped fighting against her and gave a long sigh.

The inside of the collar was a fine steel mesh, with sharp barbs jutting out at regular intersections that would have constantly dug into the *Ci*'s flesh when she moved. Abby could see solder marks, and she knew this wasn't part of the original design. Someone had added this. She had a pretty good idea who.

There was something else fixed to the inside of the collar, just where it would have closed over the *Ci*'s throat. It was a small ivory disc about the size of a loonie, polished smooth and rimmed with a thin outer ring of delicately carved gold braiding. The hitchhiking secondary enchantment felt strongest when she looked at the disc, and she didn't need to see the image of the open palm and five extended fingers etched into it to confirm her suspicions. She shut her eyes and closed her hand around the disc, to see if she could get some kind of psychometric reading off it.

She opened her eyes to a world in greyscale. Thick iron bars cut across her line of sight, making her feel slow and stupid. She knew they would hurt her if she touched them, so she kept her body curled up tight against the opposite wall, which was of cold, wet concrete.

Cell. Cell was the word men used to describe boxes like the one she was in. Ten paces from front to back and twelve from side to side, with one wall of concrete and thick iron bars on the other three sides. The ceiling was just high enough for a man to stand comfortably. There was a metal dish in one corner of the cell—copper, not iron. It held water stained red with blood. They had brought her the carcass of a lamb some hours ago, and when she had eaten, she had become thirsty, and the blood on her lips had fallen into the water. She remembered all this, but she did not remember how she had come to be in the cell. She had woken up here. When last she had gone to sleep, she had been in her own kennel, in the ebon halls of Carcosa. Her master had been there. He had praised her for her great skill at the hunt that day. Now she was here, and she was afraid. Cowardice was not the way of Winter, not the way of the court of Great Gwyn the Pale Rider, but she could not deny the feelings of her heart. She was afraid.

Two figures stood beyond the bars. Darkness consumed their features, but they were shaped like men. One figure turned its head to look at its partner. "You sure that fuckin' thing's calmed down?"

"The iron will keep it docile," the second figure responded. "Its last meal was worked with certain craft to make it doubly slow."

"Just say you drugged it," snapped the first figure. "I'm not getting paid to listen to your poetry slam."

"Neither are we paying you for your, how do you say it, 'honest opinion.' Do as you are bidden, Purdy."

"And you're *sure* you can control this thing? I'm also-also not getting paid to get my face eaten off by the hounds of Holly."

Looking through the eyes of the *Ci Annwn*, seeing her first memories of Earth and knowing what was to come, Abby could almost hear the second figure trying to keep the smirk out of its voice. "As you say."

Ted Purdy slowly melted out of the shadows, holding the collar at arm's length in front of him. He jangled a key in the lock and pushed the cell door open, then waited a moment for the hound to spring to life. When she didn't, he untensed his shoulders and took a nervous step into the cell. A second. A third. In time, he reached his quarry and closed the collar around her throat.

Abby instantly felt a searing ring of pain about her own neck. She opened her mouth to cry out, but the cry emerged as a deeply mournful canine howl. Ted Purdy backed away faster than she imagined any person could move and pulled the door shut again. The baying continued until a third voice in the darkness breathed a single word, in the language of storms and snow and death. "*Stop.*"

The word cut through the darkness like a note plucked on a harp-string: long, melodious, painfully sad, and totally captivating. The *Ci* didn't just stop, she felt herself *wanting* to stop. *Needing* to stop. Hell, *Abby* felt the urge to stop whatever it was she was doing.

"*Come forward.*" Two more words, in the language of wind and rain and falling leaves. But more than words. A song. Abby had heard the language of magic before—this was the same thing, now elevated to the level of music. A third figure moved in the shadows, not man-like as the first two were. This shape—the shape of the singer—was more graceful. When it sang, its chin pointed to the sky and its arms made elegant sweeps through the air. Its song—*come forward*—rang in her ears, at once a funeral dirge and an irresistible command. She needed to step forward, and so she did. She stepped forward until her nose was right up to the bars. Then she stepped forward again. The iron burned her skin, made her want to cry out again, but she would not move until the singer permitted it.

Ted Purdy crept forward out of the shadows once more. He ran a hand over his bald scalp, his eyes shining with amazement. "You did it… you crazy fuckers actually did it…"

The second figure smiled from the darkness, and Abby could see the white glint of its sharklike teeth. "This," hissed the Lone Dullahan, "is but the start, Mr. Purdy."

The vision broke. Abby started, let go of the collar, grabbed it again before it hit the ground. She looked at the *Ci*. The *Ci* looked back at her.

"Jesus…" she whispered. "This is how they did it, isn't it? Ted Purdy and the Dullahan… they pulled you out of Carcosa. They controlled your mind with this and made you kill those people." She held the collar out. The *Ci* bunched her shoulders, growled, backed off a step. Abby drew the collar away. "I'm sorry. I'm sorry, I don't want to... I have to understand. So I can stop all this. Look. Look, I'm putting it away now, okay?" Taking care to avoid the barbs on the collar's inside, she bunched it up and stuffed it in her jacket pocket. It was material evidence, and if she could figure out how the hell to get back to the Letterbox, she was sure Simon would be able to do something very clever with it and trace the Golden Hand right to their front door.

When she'd pocketed the collar, she raised her hands, palms open. "Look," she said to the *Ci*, "it's gone, okay? It's not coming back."

The hound un-bunched her shoulders and stopped growling. Then she took a cautious step forward and laid a paw on Abby's outstretched leg. Despite herself, Abby cried out. The hound backed off again. With tears of pain in her eyes, Abby croaked, "Sorry. That wasn't for you. I don't blame you for any of this." A chill wind howled past her before she could get another word out, and she curled the parts of her that didn't hurt like hell into an upright ball. "L-listen to me." Her teeth were chattering again, and she rubbed her hands furiously on her biceps to find some warmth. "I have to get back to m-my friends. My w-world. Otherwise, I'm going to f-f-fucking freeze to death out here with a busted ankle. You c-can zap back and forth whenever you want. Do you think you could help me out?"

The hound cocked her head to one side. "P-please try to understand," Abby continued. "I n-need you t-t-to zap me home." The hound still didn't move. "Do you get it? H-O-M-E. *Home*."

The hound turned and walked a few paces away. She seemed to be weighing her options, as she looked into the churning snow and freezing wind that whited out the world. She looked back at Abby, who pleaded silently for any sign of understanding or sympathy. For the briefest of moments, the storm parted. Abby looked up and saw against the white sky the hazy, faraway silhouette of a city. High black walls ringed around spiked and twisting towers. Atop one of the highest, she saw the flutter of a dirty yellow pennant. She had no sense of detail or scale at this distance, but an itch in her hand and a pain behind her eyes told her what she was looking at. *He* was there, in one of those towers. Her ears rang and she curled in on herself, wincing at the grinding, throbbing, thrashing pain in her head. She felt the heat of two terrible blue stars beating down on her. Against all sense or logic, she remembered a fragment of poetry she'd read in university.

Lurid and lofty and vast it seems;
It hath no rounded name that rings,
But I have heard it called in dreams
The City of the End of Things.

The hound looked back at Abby. Ahead, to the City of the End of Things. Back at Abby again. Then she lowered her head and ran into the snowstorm.

Snow and cloud veiled the black outline of the City once more. Abby couldn't speak. Couldn't move. She felt like someone had opened her up and scooped the heart out of her chest. Surely, this was death: sat alone in a snowstorm beneath an alien sky, ankle broken, home beyond reach.

A minute passed. She hugged herself for warmth. Two minutes. She rubbed her hands together. Blew on them. Jammed them under her arms. Three minutes, and she clenched her jaw tight to keep her teeth from chattering.

Ten minutes (maybe twelve). Something moved in the distance. Abby squinted as the shape came running at her out of the mist and snow. A low-slung body on four powerful legs, black as black could be. A second figure followed it. Bipedal, not tall, but wide and sturdy. The quadruped burst out of the storm and heaved its full bulk at Abby, knocking her flat. It laid itself down atop her and licked her face furiously. Those licks were so blessedly warm that she didn't even notice the jagged pain in her ankle. Abby reached up and gave the *Ci* Annwn a scratch behind the ear, crying grateful tears, shaking with laughter, smiling like an idiot. "You went and got help? That's a good girl. That's a *very* good girl!"

The stout, bipedal haze in the distance drew closer. Resolved into a familiar shape. If Abby hadn't been crying before, she sure as shit was now.

"Abigail Henderson." The voice was feminine, with a thick Yorkshire accent that could drop aitches with the best of them. "Pardon my French, but why is it I'm always picking you up from flat on your arse?"

Margaret McAllister. Meg. Beloved grandmother of Karen Henderson, eponym of Abigail Margaret Henderson, and the previous Gospel in the family line. The *Ci Annwn* moved so that Abby could sit up, and the old woman closed in to embrace her great-granddaughter.

Abby buried her face in Grandma Meg's cardigan and got it soggy with her tears. "Hi, Gran. Sorry I haven't called in a while."

*****

With Grandma Meg supporting her weight, Abby was able to get up on one foot and hobble. The *Ci Annwn* walked some paces ahead of them, and Abby could feel the rippling magical energy that the creature exuded. She got a similar whiff of magic off Grandma Meg. She wasn't cold anymore. Her ankle didn't hurt. The wind and snow both seemed to settle, and the knee-deep drifts on the ground might as well have been cloud vapour for all the resistance they gave. A prickle of heat at the back of her neck hinted that Gwyn ab Nethe's neutron-star gaze was still upon her. How much of this was his doing? Had he called this storm up in the first place, or was he calming it down to give the travellers a clear path? She'd seen his wrath, but now that she'd fulfilled part of her oath to him, could she count on his mercy?

Abby had thought that Grandma Meg would have questions galore while they walked—it had, after all, been nearly a year since she had made contact with the old woman's spirit here in the Elsewhere. They'd said their tearful goodbyes on the day the Deacon and the Cult of the Following were destroyed. And now Meg was here. But to Abby's surprise, she didn't seem to need much catching up.

"I've kept my eye on you this last year," Meg said, in answer to the question Abby hadn't yet voiced. "Always meant to drop you a line during that Harcourt business, but that bloody Josiah put out too much psychic interference. I could never break through his walls." She shifted her weight to give Abby a better hold. "And talking of walls, you know you could have contacted me any time you were having troubles." Her voice and the knowing glance she gave held no trace of judgement. Her sympathy was total. Yet Abby couldn't help feel the guilt wriggling inside her like an eel.

"I should have," she said. "I'm sorry I didn't. I just… it felt like my own drama, this thing with Mom. *I* was the one who couldn't call her up, so *I* had to figure it out. After what you and I went through with the Deacon, calling you for any less just felt… I don't know. Is 'small' the right word?"

Grandma Meg stopped. Turned her head. "Abigail Henderson, I want you to look me in the eye. You and I are blood. More than that, we are the only two people who know what this burden is like. All the other Gospels, the ones who came before us, they've passed beyond the final veil. Their names have been forgotten and their works are dust. Even I can't talk to them, and believe you me, I have tried. I never had a chance to know the people I inherited this power from. You do. That is a treasure beyond imagining, but if you'll pardon my French, it means bugger all if you don't use it. It doesn't matter how small the problem is: if you have one, you come to your old gran, and I will answer."

Abby turned and threw her other arm around the old woman. Suddenly her face was in Meg's cardigan again, soggy with more tears. Meg held her tight and let her get it all out. "You're such a brave girl, love. I don't think you know how strong you really are. But you don't have to do this alone."

The wind howled around them. Abby felt the chill of her own tears on one cheek, and the warmth of two neutron stars upon the other. The sky seemed to clear as she straightened up and dried her eyes. As cloud and flurry receded, a structure showed on the distant horizon. This was not the cold black walls and high towers of Carcosa. This was smaller and altogether warmer. A simple, one-floor log cabin with a moss-covered shingle roof. A couple shingles had fallen, and Abby remembered the long, dark night of the soul she'd experienced in her first year of university, when she'd tried cutting her own hair into bangs. Yet for all its dubious charms the cabin suggested warmth and comfort. Smoke curled from the red-brick chimney. A light shone in the front window. The *Ci Annwn* uttered a happy bark and ran to the front door, then gave it a gentle but resounding scratch. Meg shifted her weight again, got herself back under Abby, and marched them both to the door just as it opened.

Abby was already an emotional wreck just from seeing her gran. Eyes red, cheeks wet, nose snotty. If the old woman hadn't been supporting her, she would have fallen over flat when she saw the face that answered the cabin door. It was small, round, and feminine, with a slight upward turn in the nose. And it was beaming at her with a smile that could melt glaciers. The eyes were wet and ready to laugh. The upper lip was slightly stained by hot chocolate, a steaming mug of which the figure held in its hands.

This was the mother Abby remembered. Not that flat-eyed spectre that had haunted her morning and night. Karen Henderson patted the *Ci Annwn* on the head and took two steps out the front door of the cabin. Abby was sobbing like a baby as she let go of Meg and hopped the rest of the distance under her own steam. Karen set her hot chocolate down on the cabin's front windowsill and held her arms wide. Abby threw herself into them, and mother and daughter cried together.

CHAPTER 23

SITREP

IT WAS pink, dewy morning before Leanne and the others stepped into the fresh air outside the South Campus. Simon and Natalie stuck close by her, as they had done for the past few hours. Chris and Jacquie formed their own cluster nearby, as did Gareth and Ms. Keane. The Swann siblings maintained a civil air when they spoke, but the scant metres separating them seemed like miles.

It was Sunday now, Leanne realized. The day before Thanksgiving. As of two weeks ago, the plan had been for her and Abby to drive out to Leanne's parents' house in White Rock for dinner with all the Waller siblings and their families. There'd been a seat saved for Abby's father Don, too. After the King-Among-the-Holly reared his head, Leanne had never actually called to cancel those plans. There'd been too much on her mind. That conversation seemed terribly necessary now, and a lump formed in her throat now as she started to conjure a suitable excuse.

A fleet of black SUVs, transit vans, and nondescript sedans filled the central lot, and more were coming through the main gate minute by minute. It seemed like Dr. Harkness had called in every operative he had on reserve to help clean up the mess that Owain ab Gwylem and the *Ci Annwn* had left behind. As two security men wheeled a Dullahan-sized body bag out the front entrance on a stretcher, one of the transit vans opened its back doors and Dr. Phillipa Susan

Turner jumped down onto the pavement. She pushed past the security guards, past Dr. Harkness, marched straight up to Agent Six, and threw her arms around him in a tight hug. Shock froze him to the spot, and before he'd worked out the proper response, Phil had detached herself, pulled a bottle of hand sanitizer from her pocket, and given herself two squirts. "I am *very* glad you're not dead, Agent Six," she stated emphatically.

Six blinked, took another moment to shake off the confusion. "Um, so am I, Phil."

Dr. Harkness tapped his pen against his clipboard. "Dr. Turner! If I might trouble you for your expert opinion?"

Phil extracted a pair of blue surgical gloves from her pocket and put them on before she pulled down the zipper of the body bag, just enough to see Owain ab Gwylem's face. "Self-inflicted?" she asked.

"I watched it happen," Dr. Harkness replied. "Miss Arnaud suspects a tetrodotoxin of extraplanar origin."

Phil zipped up the body bag and spoke to the two guards working the stretcher. "We have a refrigerated truck bringing up the rear. When it arrives, put the houseguest in there with the other casualties, and see that they all make it safely back to my laboratory at the North Campus."

"I expect your report within twenty-four hours," Dr. Harkness said brusquely. "Comprehensive toxicological analysis, and be sure you save some blood and tissue samples for the Chemical Engineering department."

Leanne's skin crawled at the clinicality of it all. Nine Ministry operatives were dead or missing. More were hurt. And for all anyone knew, Abby might be worse off still. Simon sensed her unease and put an arm around her. "We'll find her," he whispered. "If I must delay my recovery another three months, I promise you I will find the spell that brings her home to us."

"I suppose bargaining with You-Know-Who is out of the question now."

"It was a desperate hope in the first place, Leanne. Abby's the one who got the *Ci Annwn* back to the Perilous Realm, however inadvertently. If the King were interested in granting favours, she's the one it would go to. And letting her pass through his realm alive would be ample payment for services rendered, in his eyes. We, on the other hand, have nothing to bargain with. We've exposed a traitor in the ranks of the Wild Hunt, but we still don't know with whom that traitor is working, and he lies too far beyond the reach of mortal sight for us to ask."

"But Gwyn's a god of death. Can't he reach out and... you know?" She extended a hand and balled it into a tight fist. "Pull him back?"

Simon shook his head. "The faeries are not made as we are, of body and soul. That's why they live so long as they do. Mortal bodies are made to be fallible, to wear down as the spirit gestates, so that one day it may shed its imperfect shell and begin a second life. But the body of a faerie is that perfect inner essence. The primordial energies of Creation made tangible. When it's gone, it's just gone." He looked at the body bag containing all that remained of Owain ab Gwylem. "A part of me's always suspected that's why the faeries' auras are not visible to Gospels. It's not that they don't have them; they are simply so large and burn so bright that they're impossible to see. After all, how many of the sun's rays can you actually see when you stand outside on a summer's day?"

Dr. Harkness turned away from the troupe of guards to whom he was issuing orders. "Far be it from me to interrupt your poetic interlude, Mr. Lockhart, but I think the time has come for us to discuss next steps."

Simon dropped his arm and positioned himself between Leanne and Dr. Harkness. Natalie, saying nothing, moved in close and shifted her weight to a loose, ready stance. "We've already been through the legal how-d'ye-do once tonight, Gilbert," Simon said coolly.

Dr. Harkness pressed his clipboard into the hands of a nearby guard and removed his glasses. For a long count of ten, he cleaned the lenses with a microfibre cloth he pulled from the inner pocket of his jacket. Then he exhaled and put his glasses back on. "I know you disapprove of our organization, Lockhart. Believe me, the feeling is perfectly mutual. But I think we can agree that the events of the last few hours represent a clusterfuck of epic proportions. Your chief asset is lost in an unmapped extraplanar space. My internal security has been significantly compromised. Agents of a fascistic terrorist cell have infiltrated this city and very probably this organization as a first step toward igniting a supernatural race war. As much disdain as we have for each other, we both feel a certain responsibility for the well-being of this city and its people. You spoke earlier tonight of the Pax Arcana. I propose revisiting that arrangement."

"Didn't we already have this conversation?" Natalie interjected. "We're not working with your jack-booted thugs."

Dr. Harkness ignored her. "I'm not making threats this time. I am telling you that neither party benefits if we continue to argue like children while this enemy remains active. They have lost the *Ci Annwn*, but they are organized, and they will re-mobilize before long. Does it not make more sense that we organize and respond in kind?"

Simon looked at Natalie. Then at Leanne.

"It's my understanding that Agent Six has been communicating with your people for some time now," Dr. Harkness put in. "This is merely an extension of the existing *détente*."

"Only now you're asking us to place our trust in several dozen armed and paranoid government agents, instead of merely one," Simon answered.

"I will consider myself personally responsible for the conduct of my subordinates. If you have any trouble with them, you report it to me." He closed the distance and lowered his voice. "You know me, Lockhart. You know I would not propose something like this unless I thought it were the only way."

Simon considered Dr. Harkness in silence for a moment. "Your material resources," he said at last, "my insider knowledge. Your operational efficiency, my methods. This has to be done ethically and humanely, Gilbert. No shooting first, no extreme countermeasures. No torture."

"I won't grant you blanket autonomy. When it comes to arcane matters, yours will be the final word, but during normal field operations, I expect you to submit yourself to my authority. You follow departmental procedure and regulations, and you wait for authorization before you take action. 'No shooting first' goes both ways."

Simon considered this for a moment before extending his hand. "Agreed." He and Dr. Harkness shook. Natalie and Leanne exchanged a wary look with each other, then directed it at Simon. The look he shot them back might have meant either *I know. Just trust me,* or *Just do as I say.*

Dr. Harkness took back his clipboard, clicked his pen, and started jotting down notes. "Agent Six will act as your primary liaison," he said, "since he has already seen fit to perform that role in an unofficial capacity. I understand you have a… headquarters of your own?"

"The Letterbox, but it's not equipped—"

"We will set up a temporary mobile operating base in the vicinity of your Letterbox for ease of communication and coordination. I'll arrange for a field team to mobilize as soon as we finish the clean-up here. If you have any enchantments on-site that may interfere with our equipment, I suggest you de-power those forthwith. As to the other matter…" Still scribbling away, he turned his gaze upon the Swann siblings and their retainers. Chris noticed Dr. Harkness looking, and shrunk into the trauma blanket he'd been given by the Ministry's medical team. "Your fae friends over there are currently all persons of interest in an ongoing investigation. After tonight, they may be in several more. It is my intention to question them all thoroughly as soon as time permits."

"And presumably," Simon broke in, "you would prefer they remain alive long enough for that to happen."

"You take my meaning exactly, Mr. Lockhart. Until this crisis is resolved, I must insist on placing Jacqueline Swann and her associates in protective custody. Twenty-four-hour surveillance, total communications blackout. The Golden Hand will not take kindly to their survival tonight, but we cannot be sure when or how the next attack will come. Unfortunately, as I'm sure you will agree, the Department's own security measures fell woefully short of expectations tonight. And that's where I'm hoping your knowledge of defensive magic will prove handy."

"The Letterbox can be equipped for this sort of thing," Simon agreed. "And it wouldn't be the first time. We have the resources to make Dr. Swann and the others safe and secure, but I will not be anyone's jailer. If you wish to interview them, it shall be under my supervision, and I will not tolerate any of your more extreme tactics."

"No Lethe crystals."

Simon nodded. "No Lethe crystals. In the interest of transparency and security, I will allow a limited number of your personnel to operate within the Letterbox, but so long as they are in my space they shall conduct themselves according to my rules."

"Very well," said Dr. Harkness, gesturing toward Jacquie and the others. "I will leave you to extend the offer."

Simon shared a last look with Natalie and Leanne, then stepped over to speak to the Swanns. The words that passed between them were inaudible. Gareth looked skeptical at first, but eventually he nodded his consent. "I don't suppose you could lay on an escort, could you, Gilbert?" Simon called out. "We'll have to see everyone safe back to the Letterbox."

"What about T.G.W.?" Jacquie asked. "We have a lot of active projects that can't afford to stall out at this time. Someone has to steer the ship if my brother and I go underground for a while."

"Ms. Keane will reach out to the board," Gareth said. "They can arrange a remote meeting and elect an interim chair. Williams and Robichaud are reliable enough; they can be our proxy votes."

"Make it fast," said Dr. Harkness. "When I say communications blackout, I mean cell phones in the drawer, and you will receive them back after class. Now, I'll see about that escort."

"And I'll make some calls," said Ms. Keane. Gareth nodded and waved her away, and she crossed the central lot typing out messages and memos on her tablet. Silence fell. Instinctively, Leanne reached out her hand. Then reality came crashing back in on her when Abby didn't grab it. Trying to smooth out the lump in her throat, she motioned subtly toward Gareth and whispered to Simon, "Are you sure about letting all these guys waltz through the Letterbox? We don't know who we can trust."

"The Letterbox's defensive magicks are robust. If things go pear-shaped, I'd greatly prefer it to happen in an environment I can control. We'll put the siblings Swann down on the lower level and tell them it's for their own safety."

"But if anything happens… I mean, you're not exactly fighting fit."

Simon reached up and threw an arm around Natalie. "And that's why I keep this great lummox on retainer."

Natalie smiled at this. "Yeah, fuck you too, Lockhart."

Leanne couldn't help smiling herself, but it was subdued by the painful sight of that empty space beside her. Simon put his other arm around her, pulled her in close, and kissed the top of her head.

"We'll find her," he repeated.

*****

With Karen supporting her under one arm and Grandma Meg under the other, Abby hobbled her way into the cabin. The furnishings were spartan: a rickety twin bed in one corner, a nightstand and lamp beside it, a low pine chest against the opposite wall, next to a stone-mantel fireplace. Someone had been tending the fire only recently—Abby could hear the pop of a fresh log. Beside the mantel, there was a wrought-iron stand with a wide base and hooks branching out for the poker, brushes, and tongs. Atop the pine chest were two more mugs of hot chocolate and an open bottle of fine single-malt scotch. Abby had always heard that Grandma Meg enjoyed a scotch in the evening, practically up till the day she died.

Karen and Meg eased her down onto the bed. There were extra pillows there, which they stacked in order to keep Abby's leg elevated. As Abby lay her head back, the *Ci Annwn* padded into the cabin and curled up on the floor beside the bed. Abby felt a rush of sense-memories she didn't think were her own. Cold rain on a stony beach. Sea salt mingled with petrichor. A wind whipping through a copse of fir trees. The cry of an infant taking its first breaths. Something felt familiar about the place, though she could not imagine when she would have been here before.

"What is this place?" she asked, looking around.

"A memory," Grandma Meg answered. "Of times long gone."

"Of good tidings," Karen said, taking Abby's hand, "and bad."

The sound of a blade scratching on wood made Abby turn. Above her head, the number 25 had been carved into the bare log. She felt goosebumps rise on her neck and the lyrics of a familiar hymn marched through her head.

It was good for Paul and Silas
It was good for Paul and Silas

Abby shook her head to push away that thought. She turned back to Karen and squeezed her hand. It was as warm as if she were alive. "I called out to you so many times. Why didn't you answer?"

"I'm sorry, baby. I'm so sorry. But I was so scared. What could I say to you? What would you say to me? What I did... giving you over to him... that was unforgiveable." She kissed Abby's hand and squeezed it tight. "I never wanted to hurt you, sweetie. But I did. I was afraid you'd hate me if you saw me again."

"Hate you? Mom, you signed my soul away to a monster before I was even born. You torched any chance I had of a normal life before I got a chance to live it, and you lied to me for decades." She embraced her mother. "I hate that you did all of that, but I don't hate you because it happened. He never gave you a choice. You, Grandpa Bram, Meg, you spent your whole lives in the Deacon's shadow. Yeah, you fucked up, because he fucked you up. If I started hating you for that, it'd just be another victory for him."

Karen held her tight and close. "I'm sorry I hurt you, Abby."

"That's all I ever wanted to hear, Mom."

"No more running away. I promise you that, here and now. The next time you call, I'll come."

"Thank you. You don't know what it means for me to hear that."

They parted. Their eyes met, and some sliver of ice melted in Abby's heart. She saw something likewise thawing in her mother. The *Ci* looked up, her wagging tail thump-thump-thumping upon the floorboards. After a moment, Abby became aware of Grandma Meg, standing by the pine chest and nursing her scotch. Saying nothing, but smiling knowingly.

"You brought her here, didn't you?" Abby said. "You gave her the push I couldn't."

Meg winked. "Are-haitch-eye-pee, love."

Abby smiled and nodded. "Rank has its privileges." She stretched out on the bed and nodded to her ankle. "Come on, then, O Wise One. What do we do about this?"

Meg sipped her drink and made a face. "That's above me pay grade, unfortunately. Have to call in the experts on that." She made a move toward the door. The *Ci*'s ears perked up. Two seconds later, there came a knock. Abby straightened up as Meg opened the door to let in the duo who stood on the front step.

They were tall enough that they both had to stoop to gain entry to the cabin. The gentleman wore rimless pince-nez spectacles; the lady carried an umbrella to keep the snow at bay. They were richly dressed in thick furs, gloves, and scarves, like something out of an illustrated edition of *A Christmas Carol*, and as they came in the gentleman removed his top hat and brushed the snow off the brim.

"Well," said Brother Dearest, in his cut-glass, RP tones, "here we all are at last."

"Charming place," said Sister Dearest, in a manner equally posh, as she took in the scenery and closed her umbrella. "Perfectly charming."

Grandma Meg nodded her thanks.

Abby looked from the newcomers to Grandma Meg and back again. She'd grown used to the idea that the old woman had secrets, but this was pushing it. She didn't know exactly who Brother and Sister Dearest were—or what they were—but she had put together a pretty solid case that they were supernatural heavy hitters. They came and went as they pleased (through her dreams and visions, mostly), they possessed insight that blew her own out of the water, and they never seemed the least bit phased by the horrors that plagued her day-to-day. She'd met them a few times before, during the Following and Harcourt incidents, always just long enough for them to give her a nudge in the right direction. They seemed to have her best interests at heart, but whether they were gods, ghosts, fae, or something else entirely, she couldn't work out. And now they were here, deep in the King-Among-the-Holly's territory, where neither Karen nor Grandma Meg seemed at all surprised to see them.

"Whuh—" she inquired astutely. "Buh—who—how...?"

"I've told you before, love," said Grandma Meg, "are-haitch-eye-pee."

Brother and Sister Dearest strode toward the bed with purpose. The *Ci* gave a nervous whine. Abby backed herself into her pillows. "What the hell is this? Gran, how do you know these two?"

"That's a long story," Meg replied. "One that'll be told someday."

"But there is another story you must finish first," said Brother Dearest, sitting on the edge of the bed and laying a hand upon Abby's ankle. She winced and tried to pull away, but Sister Dearest came around on the other side and put a firm hand upon her shoulder.

"Come, come, child, don't be tiresome," she chided. She extended her other hand to Brother Dearest, who took it with his own free one. Each met the other's eye and they nodded their heads as one, a silent signal of readiness.

Raw power surged through Abby's body, from the tips of her toes to the top of her head. Something snapped, crackled, and popped in her ankle. She could feel the shards of bone grating against each other as they knitted back together, hurried along by the magic flowing out of Brother Dearest's fingertips. The energy ebbed and flowed like the tide, one minute filling her up and awakening all her senses, the next minute sucking the vitality out of her and stretching her thinner than she'd ever been stretched. She looked at her hands and saw her nails growing, then chipping away and falling onto the bedspread. Something tickled the back of her neck, and she reached up to feel her hair creeping down toward her shoulders and over her ears. As her ankle bones pulled themselves together, her leg muscles burned with the ache of a thousand miles walked all in an instant. Her head swam with feelings of fatigue as a hundred sleepless nights raced by, her stomach cramped and cried out for so many meals uneaten, her clothes clung to her skin with sweat and stink as she missed shower after shower. At some point—she couldn't say when—she started screaming, overwhelmed by the sensory onslaught. Then Brother Dearest pulled his hand away, and the world stopped racing around her.

Karen was on one side of her, Grandma Meg on the other, each squeezing one of her hands. She was still screaming, she realized. The *Ci* howled in sympathy. Abby cut herself off with a rapid inhale of breath—her lungs were burning like she hadn't properly taken a breath in weeks. She tried to speak, but her mouth was so dry. There was ice in a bucket near the scotch. Grandma Meg grabbed a cube and wetted Abby's lips with it. After a moment she opened her mouth so Meg could tip the ice in. She rolled it around on her tongue for a bit, like she used to do during the hot summers of her childhood, then swallowed what remained. There was just enough moisture in her mouth to ask, "What—what the hell did you do to me?"

"Time, my dear," was Brother Dearest's reply. "Simply time."

"On its own," Sister Dearest expanded, "that ankle would have wanted seven weeks to heal properly. We simply expedited the recovery period."

"Quite so. Time, my dear girl, is a luxury that you do not have right now, so we pushed your body through the necessary interval at something rather more than the normal rate."

"We did try to compensate for the, ah, metabolic necessities as best we could. Though you may have experienced some side effects."

"S-seven weeks?" Abby gasped. "You pushed me seven weeks into the future?"

"Seven weeks further into your personal timestream, in point of fact." Brother Dearest said this as though it were the most obvious thing imaginable.

"Linear time in the broader sense," said Sister Dearest, "continued around you at its normal pace. So you won't have missed a trick by the time you return home." She smiled brightly, like she and her brother had just done Abby a huge favour.

"Home," Abby groaned. She wiggled her toes inside her sneaker, then rolled off the bed and tried to stand. "Hafta—gotta—get home!" Her ankle, when she put her weight on it, was sturdy and painless. But her knees and calves had other plans, and she didn't make it two steps before she fell. Meg caught her and eased her back onto the bed.

"Easy, love, easy! You've not stood up in seven weeks!"

Abby shook her head and tried to push herself up. One firm push back from Meg and she sank right into the pillows. "The Golden Hand… still… they're still out there. I got the hound back, but I still have a job to do for Gwyn. I have to get home."

Meg leaned over and planted her hands on Abby's shoulders. "You, my duck, are lying right there until I say otherwise. Don't forget: I've been watching you, Abigail, and even I can't remember when's the last time you had a proper night's sleep. I can keep this memory solid for as long as I please, and right now, it would please me to see you get some shut-eye."

Abby tried once more to push herself up, but her gran was a tough old bird. "I can't waste time here!" she pleaded. "Not while the clock's still ticking out there! Otherwise, I might not have a home to go back to!"

Karen laid a hand on Meg's arm. "Gran… she's right. Days could have passed already, and she still has part of the job to do. You know he wouldn't accept half a result." Meg looked at Karen. Her grip loosened. "Besides," Karen went on, "do you really think you're going to convince her? She's a McAllister, for God's sake."

Meg looked back at Abby, chuckled, and let her go. "Aye. As bloody-minded as the rest of us."

For a fourth and final time, Abby tried to get up. Smaller steps this time. Incremental changes in elevation. She kept one hand on the bed, on the wall, on Meg's shoulder. Eventually she made it, and when the blood had had enough of a chance to flow back down to her feet, she let go of that last support and tried to stand under her own power. She was still a little woozy, but at least she wasn't faceplanting on the first step anymore.

"How do you feel?" Karen asked.

Abby checked in with herself. "Good. I think I'm ready to go." She paused. "Just one problem. How do I, uh, go?" She knew that, theoretically, it was within a Gospel's power to open a physical gateway between the mortal realm and the Elsewhere and walk between worlds in both body and soul, like a supercharged version of the Bridge. But after the Harcourt House affair, she'd run the raw calculations on how much power it would take and concluded that, practically speaking, she wouldn't be able to handle it herself without running the risk of a brain aneurysm. Not without another decade's hard training, at any rate.

"We'll pool our collective power, you and I." Meg saw the mental math Abby was doing and answered the unspoken question with a wink. "Like we did when we fought the Deacon."

"Channel your spirit?" Abby asked. "Would that even work here?"

Meg raised a hand. The outline of her fingers grew hazy and her outstanding veins took on a silverish, ghostly quality. "You're the only flesh and blood here, love. Don't forget that."

Brother Dearest doffed his hat. "We shall see the *Ci Annwn* the rest of the way home."

"Oh, let's do, Brother Dearest!" Sister Dearest agreed. "And perhaps we can call upon her master when we are in the city. A visit from two old friends should brighten his disposition."

"Ah, I do fear that you're teasing again, Sister Dearest. Though I confess I am of your opinion in this. It is too long since we broke bread in Winter's court." Brother Dearest whistled, and the hound stood and trotted obediently to his side. Then, bowing to Abby and the others: "We take our leave of you, dear ladies."

"All our best wishes go with you, child," Sister Dearest added with a curtsy.

And like that, they were gone. Abby didn't see them turn to leave, didn't hear the door close. She didn't even blink. It was like the whole world just skipped a frame as brother, sister, and hound all disappeared from the cabin. They even took with them the snow they'd trod on the floor.

Meg harrumphed. "Not much for teary goodbyes, those two."

At least they said goodbye this time, Abby thought.

Meg led Abby into the middle of the cabin. "Right, that's them off. Now let's see about you, love. Time and tide, et cetera. Karen, love, you'll want to stand back for this next part."

"In a minute," Karen said. "I need to do this first." She stepped forward and caught Abby up in a tight hug. Kissed her cheek. Ran a hand through her hair. "I love you so much, baby. I'm so sorry that I hurt you. You were the greatest adventure of my life, and I'm so proud of what you've done with the time you took back from *him.*"

Abby sobbed out a weak, "Thank you." Meg gave them the space they needed until Abby had dried her eyes. Then Gospel joined hands with Gospel and Karen stepped back.

"Now, then," Meg said. "Back straight, shoulders relaxed, and remember your breathing." Abby readied herself as instructed. When Meg told her to close her eyes, she did.

A cold shock ran up her arm, like she'd just dunked it in a bucket of ice water and then dropped a toaster in after it. Her heart skipped a beat, and on the next breath in she felt a warmth spread through her lungs and her belly. The force of another spirit entering her.

"Reach out," Meg said. "Feel this place around you."

Abby's psychic senses probed outward. Her brain buzzed as her mental energy bounced off the raw magic that shaped the Elsewhere. She felt Meg's psychic signature beside her, around her, within her, guiding her and filling her up and holding the cabin construct together all at the same time. "Think of this place as an electric field," said Meg. "Charged particles racing all around us. Try and grab hold of the space between those particles." Abby checked her breathing, felt the rush of the Elsewhere's energy. She told that energy to slow, give her some time to think. The Gospels controlled this realm, she reminded herself. Reminded the realm. She commanded the Elsewhere to slow down, to keep time with her steady breaths. The Elsewhere obeyed her. Now she had a clearer view of the spaces between each charged particle. The fabric of her reality sitting just beyond the veil of magic in which she was enshrouded. She put out two psychic fingers and plucked at that fabric.

Something buzzed louder in her brain. She raised a hand, mimicking the motion she imagined her psychic senses making. When she pinched the air, she felt that thin, soft fabric between her fingers. "I think I've got something," she told Meg.

"Aye, I feel it too. Now this is the hard bit. You need to pull, like you're pulling a thread from a sweater. Be careful not to break the thread or rip out more cloth than you need. The Elsewhere won't like either."

Abby worried at the fabric between her fingers until she found something like a loose thread in spacetime. She eased her grip so that that one thread was her only tether. Then she started to pull.

Another cold jolt up her arm. A cramp in her stomach. She winced, checked her breathing, kept pulling. "You still there?" she asked Meg.

"I'm here, love, I'm here. You're doing fine."

She thought she heard her mother say something, but all that reached her ears was an inscrutable buzzing. She kept pulling. She felt a wetness in her left nostril. Sniffed. Tasted blood in the back of her throat.

"Steady, now," said Meg.

She felt the thread give way, the fabric start to unravel. She breathed in, out, in, out, pulled her hand back and back and back. The thread followed her. There was a pressure behind her eyes. Meg was squeezing her hand, reassuring her that she was still on track. All was still normal.

Warmth on her face. Red light behind her eyelids. She snuck a peek and saw, through a gap in the open air, sunset drawing down over a city street. Her breathing quickened, and she pulled a little harder.

"Slow down, Abby, slow down," Meg warned.

The fissure in reality was only two or three inches wide. She wanted to pull it wider. Slip a hand through. Tell her world, "I'm here! I'm alive!" She tugged on the thread. She heard the fabric rip.

The fissure widened, and the pain behind her eyes increased. She gritted her teeth and pulled again. Another ripping sound. More pain. Meg was squeezing her hand with maximum force. "You're going too fast, love! You need to ease up, or you'll burn out!"

Abby thought of everything that was waiting for her on the other side of that fissure. Leanne and Chris and the Swanns. She'd left them behind with a killer. God knew how long she'd been away, or what she'd find when she got back. She tugged. The fabric ripped. The pain swelled.

Her stomach cramped violently. Blood shot forth from her nose. Her knees trembled. All of it just pissed her off. The Elsewhere was resisting her efforts to tear it a new one, and after the day she'd had, she was in no fucking mood for resistance. She reminded the spirit world who was the boss, followed the loose thread back to its source, and took a whole fistful of the fabric of reality.

The whole Elsewhere screamed around her when she rent it asunder. Meg's hand let go of hers. She heard logs splinter and crack. The ground quaked. She opened her eyes. Before her, the slit in spacetime stood nearly five feet high. She could see the base of a lamppost and a newspaper box on the corner of a street somewhere. She held a lump of silvery, jagged-edged mist in her hand.

All around her, the cabin shook. Dust fell from the rafters. The scotch bottle rattled itself off the pine chest and shattered on the floor. Meg and Karen had braced themselves in the open doorway. Meg opened her mouth to say something. Abby thought it was the word Go, but it was lost over the noise of the quake.

The roof groaned. Abby looked up as one of the timbers cracked. Her stomach kicked like a spooked horse, and she looked back toward the cityscape. She took a breath and plunged headfirst through the hole she'd torn in the world.

CHAPTER 24

NIGHT-THOUGHTS

CHRISTOPHER MAH hadn't slept in forty-eight hours.

That was how long it had been since he'd been arrested, searched, locked up, and grilled by Gilbert Harkness's thugs. Since the agents of a racist death cult had tried to kill him and the people he worked for.

He understood that Leanne's friends had good intentions, confining him and the Swanns to the Letterbox. All the same, he couldn't shake the feeling that he'd swapped one cage for another, albeit with slightly better gilding. His quarters on the Letterbox's lowest level were never locked, but they were majorly lacking in creature comforts. He had to climb two flights of stairs just to use the bathroom. And with Dr. Harkness's forced comms blackout, he couldn't text his housemates to tell them he was okay.

He was coming back from the bathroom now, swaddled in one of the fluffy pink bathrobes Simon apparently bought in bulk for all the Letterbox's guests. Towel bunched up in one hand, toothpaste and toothbrush in the other, keeping one arm out against the slick stone wall at all times so he didn't trip going down the spiralling stairs. He passed Dr. Swann going the other way. Remembered he wasn't wearing his binder, and cinched his robe shut up top out of embarrassment. She smiled at him but said nothing. He let her pass, thought he ought to say something, and called back to her, "How's Mr. Swann handling all this?"

She paused. Turned. Smiled again like it hurt. "He's… he's being Gareth."

Chris nodded. That was about as much as he'd expected, and all he needed to go on. Hardly anyone had seen Mr. Swann outside his cage or the Letterbox's vast library for the last two days. He'd saved himself the trouble of talking to anyone by using Ms. Keane to relay the simplest messages. Even Dr. Harkness was having trouble pinning him down long enough to conduct an interview.

"If I didn't know better," Dr. Swann continued, "I'd almost say he feels a little guilty. This is everything he bought into when we were kids, taken to its logical extreme."

Something cold wriggled in Chris's belly. He swallowed. "You know what they're saying about him, right?" He blurted out the question before he could process his own discomfort.

Dr. Swann nodded. "That he might be involved in this. I don't want him to be. Nethe-on-High knows I don't want him to be. But I'll be prepared to hear the worst, if it happens."

"What do we do if he is? He knows, like, everything. He could nuke us with that info."

"We'll regroup. Reorganize. I've seen you at work, Christopher. I know you have a head for the logistics of it all. You and I together could remake the network so that the Golden Hand could never touch us."

He nodded, trying to decide if he believed that. It was true, he'd never struggled to keep track of the fine details of T.G.W.'s underground network, many though they were. Some of that, he supposed, came from the fae side of him. Imps like his father were a pain in the ass to get a straight answer out of, but once they put their minds to a singular task, they could retain and sort information like nobody's business. Still, two people wasn't a lot to run an underground railroad.

Dr. Swann gave him a long, considered look, as though his whole train of thought was written on his face. She descended the steps toward him. Put a hand on his shoulder.

"Chris, I… you know I don't look at you the way my brother looks at Iris Keane, right?"

"What do you mean?"

"I mean, I ask a lot of you. I know I do. First with our off-books work and now with this Golden Hand business. If I hadn't made you my go-between with Abby Henderson, who knows, maybe the Ministry wouldn't have snatched you. I put so much on your plate in this job, and I want you to know it's okay if you ever need to say 'no' to me. That's your right if you wish to use it, and I won't hold it against you."

He considered this. He ventured to reach up, put his hand on hers, and then thought better of it. He wasn't sure if that was a line he was ready to cross yet. "It hasn't got to that point," he assured her. "I hope it won't get to that point. Everything T.G.W. does, everything you do, I'm lucky to be part of it. Our 'off-books work' saves people's lives—saves my people's lives—from assholes like the Golden Hand. I'm glad to break those laws for you, Dr. Swann."

She smiled. "When we get through this, I think you and I should sit down and discuss your future prospects within T.G.W., Christopher. A young man with your drive could go very far in the organization."

He smiled back. "I think I'd like that. Although…" Shrugged a little. "Maybe we could talk about getting *me* an assistant?"

She laughed and patted his arm. "I think we can find something in the budget for that."

He wished her a warm good night, and she him. Then they turned and went their separate ways. At the bottom of the stairs, he came out into a circular stone alcove with passageways leading off in several other directions, like spokes on a wheel. His appointed quarters were at the two o'clock position from where he now stood. He stopped on the threshold, thinking for a moment, then turned and walked down the nine o'clock passageway. There was something he needed to say to the resident of that chamber, and it had waited long enough. Over half of Chris's twenty-three years, in fact.

*****

Whittaker didn't stir when Chris came into the room. Chris hadn't expected him to. The scuttlebutt around the Letterbox was that the imp hadn't so much as opened his eyes since the day they'd scraped him out of Avalon's elevator.

Chris had seen some of it go down that day. Whittaker and Molloy going up. Whittaker coming down. The elevator coming after him. The Dullahan. He hadn't been able to suppress the rush of pride he'd felt when he saw the elevator blink out of sight, leaving the frustrated Dullahan behind. It was quickly washed away in a wave of anxiety when he realized, in no particular order, that: there was a homicidal faerie in the skies above him; he was a material witness to a hit that faerie had just carried out; he had no clue if the main target had gotten away alive.

Never in a million years would he have guessed they'd both end up at the Letterbox. Part of Chris had wanted to come down here to see the imp as soon as the Ministry escort had brought him and the Swanns in two days ago. The fact that Whittaker was still unconscious was something of a blessing in disguise—it both meant Chris could postpone the inevitable on the pretext of giving the patient time to recuperate, and he wouldn't have to have this conversation face-to-face the first time around. He could rehearse.

A single chair sat to the left of Whittaker's metal-frame hospital bed. The seat was warm before Chris lowered himself into it. He guessed Mother Hyld had been ministering to her patient in the last little while. Chris cringed as the chair scraped along the floor when he pulled himself closer. Then he wondered who he was trying to be quiet for, and he started to laugh. Wasn't like he was going to disturb Whittaker, was he?

He chewed on that for a moment and stopped laughing. Wondered if he should start again. That was exactly the sort of pitch-black joke Whittaker would appreciate.

The imp was wrapped tight in his coarse white bedsheets, right hand still bandaged from where he'd been stuck with a Dullahan's arrow. He'd produced a healthy growth of hair on his face since he'd been unconscious, but Chris could see beneath it to the hollow cheeks and tired expression. Veins rose up beneath slack skin, faintly blue and green in colour. When Chris touched the imp's unbandaged hand, it was cold. The nails needed trimming. Chris made a mental note to see to that first thing in the morning. If Whittaker awoke dishevelled as all this, he wouldn't be a happy camper.

He let out a slow breath. Where to start? He thought of his mom, of the "Eastern wisdom" routine she would start whenever she had too much wine and wanted to make white people very uncomfortable. *Confucius say that journey of thousand mile begin with single step.* Chris knew it was actually Laozi who'd said that, but you didn't argue with Melinda Mah once she got going. And besides, the sentiment was good.

Start simple, then. Chris took another breath, squeezed Whittaker's cold hand, and said, "Hi, Dad. Been a long time, huh?"

Chris had only been nine or ten years old the last time he'd properly seen his father, and this was not the same being he remembered. He'd been at an age then when he was starting to get queasy at the thought of long hair and butterfly barrettes, although he wouldn't have the language to explain his feelings until his last year of high school. Whittaker had noticed, though. The three of them—Chris, Melinda, and

Whittaker—had gone out for a nice dinner, during one of those rare and glorious periods when Whittaker stayed put for more than a few weeks. It was the same restaurant, funnily enough, where Chris would be arrested by the Ministry of Uncommon Knowledge thirteen years later. Chris had been looking at this handsome, mysterious figure who came and went out of his life a couple times a year, with his pinstripe suit and his French-cuff shirt and his emerald cufflinks. He'd wondered to himself if his mom would ever buy clothes like that for him. At one point his mom got up to go to the bathroom, and the imp wasted no time leaning across the table, tapping one cufflink with his finger, and whispering in conspiratorial tones, "You like these, do you, Chrissy?"

"Chrissy" wasn't the name Whittaker had used. But it was the name Chris liked to imagine he'd used, when he thought back on this moment. He nodded and said he did like them. That made Whittaker smile a wry, shark-toothed smile.

"Used to be a tailor in Chinatown," the imp said. "Mr. Chow. Always gave me a good deal. Retired years before you were born. Your mom takes you up to Chinatown sometimes, doesn't she?"

Chris nodded. "I like the garden up there."

Whittaker smiled. "That's my boy." He didn't say "boy." Again, Chris took some creative licence on that part of the memory. "I was there when they first opened the garden for Expo," Whittaker continued. "Beautiful place. Your mom ever tell you that's where she and I met?"

"Really?"

"Scout's honour. I might tell you that story one day." He grew quiet then. Spent a moment looking out around the restaurant, thinking. Then he went to adjust his cuffs.

It took Chris a moment to realize Whittaker was taking his cufflinks off completely. Then he was taking his jacket off and rolling his shirtsleeves up to the elbow. He held the cufflinks in one hand. Shook them twice, like the world's smallest maracas. Then he set them down on the table and pushed them toward Chris. "Take 'em," he said.

"Really? J-just like that?"

"I want you to have 'em. A kid should have something of their old man's."

Chris felt a hole open up down deep in his belly. "You're going away again, aren't you?"

The imp nodded. "Yeah, I'm going away. The thing you gotta know about me, Chrissy, is I'm not good people. The people I work with aren't good people. You and your mom are good people. Last thing you need is to get caught up in my bullshit. Last thing I need is to... to watch you get caught in it." Somehow, Chris didn't think that last part was what Whittaker had really wanted to say, but he couldn't find the strength to call him on it right now.

"I know," Whittaker said. "It sucks. But one of these days, you're going to understand that this is best for all of us."

Chris put his hand on the table. Closed it over the cufflinks. "Doesn't feel best."

Whittaker laid his hand atop Chris's. "I know. But that's the hand we were dealt. We just gotta play it." He sat back, manful and stoic, and sipped his wine. "Now, eat your rice, and don't tell your mom I was swearing, okay?"

In the cold of the Letterbox, Chris blinked away a tear and held Whittaker's hand a little tighter. He still had those cufflinks squirreled away in a box in the back of a closet somewhere. He'd never worn them. He'd never even been in a menswear section with French-cuff shirts. Maybe one day.

One day.

*****

Leanne wasn't sleeping either. For the past two days, she'd been in the library, stuck in a loop of research, strong coffee, and lower back pain. Bathroom breaks (which were frequent, thanks to all the coffee) were the only times she took any exercise. If she was lucky, she might remember to eat something on the way back, and then she'd grab a granola bar or a cold plate of last night's leftovers from the icebox. Once or twice, she saw Gareth Swann perusing the stacks, but got nothing more than a curt nod of greeting and a stony expression from him.

She was sure there was something they'd missed. Somewhere, amid all the written knowledge Simon had collected over the centuries, would be some formula, some spell or enchantment that would open the door to the Elsewhere and to Abby. Otherwise, what was all this magic for?

Opening the way wasn't the problem. Any faerie worth their salt could do that, and they were up to their eyeballs in faeries right now. Finding Abby in the Otherlands, way on the far side of the Elsewhere, was where it got complicated. If Gwyn had spirited her away to his realm, odds were good he'd stymie any attempt to breach his borders and retrieve her from this side of the veil. More likely, he'd characterize the separation itself as part of the anoeth: just another hurdle that Abby had to figure out in her quest for the truth.

Leanne pushed herself back from the reading desk she'd adopted as hers, shutting the book she'd been consulting and returning it to the pile at her feet. Then she stretched until the joints went pop and checked her watch. Nearly one in the morning. It was time for another cup of coffee and a pee break. Probably not in that order. As she stood, her eyes went to the Vokarion crystal sitting on the corner of the desk, and that oh-so-persistent lump in her throat returned. They'd discovered Abby's crystal abandoned in the wreckage of Dr. Harkness's office during the clean-up, likely torn off by the whirlwind. Leanne had been holding onto it since then. Not because she expected to get any messages on it, but because it was Abby's. Keeping it safe gave her a reason to think there was someone to keep it safe *for*. Abby would be back soon enough, and she'd thank her partner for having kept the crystal warm in her absence.

Before she left the library, she laid a hand on the crystal and whispered to it, "I'll find you. I promise." Just like she'd done the last two nights.

When she'd emptied her bladder and refilled her coffee cup, she took the scenic route through the Letterbox's winding corridors, to give her restless legs a workout. As she turned a corner, she saw Mother Hyld coming the other way, hobbling on her staff. Leanne raised her mug in weary greeting and said, "I didn't think anyone else would be awake now."

"I was ministering to friend Whittaker," replied Mother Hyld. "He progresses... slowly, but I do see improvement."

Leanne smiled sadly. "I couldn't stand the little creep when he was up on two feet making snide comments. Now I think I'd give anything to have him back to his old self."

"Grief charts strange paths for us all," Mother Hyld agreed. She turned in the direction Leanne was going and gestured with her staff. "Will you walk with me?"

They fell into step together, saying nothing for the first few moments. Then Mother Hyld asked, "How long is it since you slept?"

Leanne looked down and took a sheepish sip of her coffee. "Long enough that I'd rather not give an honest answer to a healer."

"I know what you are thinking, Leanne Waller. You were raised to believe that God's will was intractable. Absolute. But then you saw beyond, and you began to doubt. Now you believe there are no absolutes, and everything is possible."

"Ever since the Following... everything I've seen with Abby and Simon and Natalie... I... I haven't been sure what to think. I have seen the impossible, but I'm not sure if it defies God's will or backs it up. I don't even know if it's an either/or answer. I trust that He is out there somewhere, but whether he's absolute? I don't know."

"And if He is not, then that means He can be overcome, yes? The answers to the great mysteries must be out there somewhere. Anything less is unacceptable."

"But if *that's* true, then why can't I find a way to fix this?" Her eyes stung with fresh tears, and she lifted her glasses to wipe them away. "Why can't I bring Abby home?"

"It is a cruel lesson, but it is one we all must learn who walk this road in life. Even when the borders of the possible are sundered, there will always be something beyond our reach. Before I swore my vow to the Order of Wulfredda, I was an ER nurse in Montego Bay. I saw things terrible to speak of, and I prayed every night that God would shine a light for me, give me the strength to work that little bit harder and faster. I still do."

"You were a Christian too?"

Mother Hyld chuckled. "'Were'? I have convened with many gods, Leanne Waller. I have played chess with devils." She reached down the front of her long gown and fished up a small gold cross that dangled at the end of a chain about her neck. "But I know of only one who was a help to Daniel in the lions' den."

Leanne choked out a sad, spluttering laugh. "What's your secret? How do you square those two circles? God's absolute except for the times when He's not, and magic has killed Him and ceded the ultimate power to Man, but sometimes it hasn't and we're still the playthings of uncaring deities when it suits their fancy?"

Mother Hyld shrugged. "There is no secret, child. There's just a whole bunch of bullshit that we have to shovel out of the way."

Leanne laughed again, more warmly than before. Mother Hyld's lips quirked into a smile, and Leanne laughed harder. She fell against the wall crying tears of mirth, and Mother Hyld laughed with her.

After the spell had broken, Mother Hyld put a hand on Leanne's shoulder and said, "It is difficult to accept, I know.

Even we sisters of Wulfredda lose patients, for all our craft. But you must understand that there is a difference between the working of wonders and the working of miracles. True Magic allows for the one, but the other remains the province of the divine. We cannot change that, and we hurt only ourselves by trying to force it."

Leanne clasped the hand that held her and nodded mute thanks through a fresh flood of tears. "Serenity," Mother Hyld advised. "Courage. Wisdom. Some answers will not come easily. This, we must accept."

Leanne squeezed Mother Hyld's hand. "Can… can I ask… I mean, is it possible…?"

"What, child?"

"Your vows… your magic… did they ever make any of the answers easier to find?"

"Some," Mother Hyld allowed. "Not all."

She sniffed. Wiped her eyes. "Then teach me. Please."

CHAPTER 25

CRY HAVOC

A FLUORESCENT glare burned Abby's retinas when she opened her eyes. Her back ached, her stomach ached, her limbs ached. Her head felt like a scene from a Patrick O'Brian novel: a squadron of Royal Navy frigates all beating to quarters and launching their broadsides within her sinuses. There was an overwhelmingly bitter taste in her mouth. Had she thrown up? She turned her head—all three hundred pounds of it. The chunky, acidic soup smearing the toilet bowl said she had.

She shut her eyes, threw her arm across her face for further protection. She was lying on a thin mattress with unevenly distributed lumps, atop a metal frame chained to a blank cement wall. The toilet was stainless steel—okay, eighty-six the stainless part for now—with a sink built into the top. All of that together spelled "jail cell" in big, blocky letters.

"Jesus, please don't let me be in Delapore again," she groaned. "That's all I fucking need."

With a grunt of effort, and no small number of cracks from her joints, she eventually pulled herself up to a sitting position. The motion jostled her stomach, and she stuck her head over the toilet bowl to expel what was left. It wasn't much, and in a short time she was spitting clear bile onto the steel.

She flushed twice for safety, then sat on the cell floor and rested her head against the toilet tank, the cold steel soothing against her cheek. She tried to piece together the chain of events that had led her here. The cabin. Karen and Meg. Double Trouble fixing her ankle. Her and Meg ripping a hole in the Elsewhere. And then… and then…

[SCENE MISSING.]

She shook her head, as if she could knock the memory loose. The motion just made her queasy again, and she stopped before she barfed up her stomach lining.

She took in the surroundings. Hers was just one of a half-dozen barred cells in a bare concrete hallway. Except for hers and the one directly across from her, they were all empty.

She raised her voice in a bid to rouse her fellow inmate. "Hey. Hey, over there!"

The bunched-up figure on the mattress stirred and sat up on his elbows. He was unshaved, with lines of orange makeup badly applied down both cheeks and across his forehead, a battered brown fedora, and a red-and-green striped sweater that was a little too big. He was wearing one glove wrapped in duct tape. Two cardboard blades flopped pathetically at the fingertips, and a third lay forgotten on the cell floor.

"Oh, shit," said Discount Freddy Krueger. "You're awake! I wasn't sure you were going to make it through the night."

"You saw them bring me in?"

The man hooted with laughter. "You must have been on a fucking tear, kid. It took two of 'em to drag you in here, and they couldn't get a straight answer out of you 'bout who you were. Didn't sound like you knew your own address. Muttered something about a box and a gold hand. Then you tossed your cookies and dropped off. That was… good ten hours ago, probably."

Abby thunked her head against the toilet and groaned.

"Hey, hey, I'm not judging," said Discount Freddy. "I know

what Halloween ragers are like." He waggled his DIY killer glove.

Halloween. The word sent a jolt through her. She ripped off her fingerless gloves and looked at her hands. Holly's sigil was puffy and red on her palm, the skin cold to the touch. Distant storm clouds whispered in her ear.

"Listen, Elm Street," Abby said, "I need you to tell me where we are and what day it is, right now."

"You telling me you don't know?"

She slammed a fist against the toilet. "Would I be asking if I did?!" Discount Freddy recoiled. Abby sighed and ran a hand through her hair. "Jesus, I'm… I'm sorry about that. It's been a really rough last couple of weeks. Work stuff. Deadlines. I… let's just say I wanted to blow off some steam last night, and things got out of hand. I just want somebody to know I'm here, but I'm not even sure where here is."

"Yeah, yeah, sure," said Discount Freddy. "Langley. We're in Langley. The ol' drunk tank. It's the nineteenth. Wicked early still. 'Bout… five in the morning's my guess."

She breathed a sigh of relief and ran the calculations in her head. Five or six days had passed her by in the Elsewhere, but there was still time to find the Golden Hand conspirators and deliver them to Gwyn. "The nineteenth," she said, as much to herself as to Discount Freddy. "So, I guess it was an early rager for you."

He looked at his sweater. "Yeah. Couple buddies and I, we're doing all the haunted houses on the Lower Mainland this year. Gotta look the part, right?"

Abby nodded. "Sure do. You get up to the PNE yet?"

Discount Freddy grinned. "Fright Nights is always the grand finale. Donuts, a freak show, get the crap scared outta us in the Doll Factory, then lose our lunch on the Coaster."

Abby smiled back. "Sounds like my kind of party." Her palm itched, and a shiver ran up her right forearm when she put her gloves back on. "I hope you have fun this year, Elm Street. I really do."

The metal door at the end of the corridor opened with a heavy creak, and a heavy woman in an RCMP uniform walked in reading from a clipboard. "Henderson, Abigail!"

Abby crawled across the cell and stuck her hand out through the bars. "That's me! Over here!"

"Someone's here to pick you up," the cop said. "Back from the door, please."

Abby scooted away on her butt as the cop unlocked the door. Then she stood, dusted herself off, and walked out.

"Look at that," said Discount Freddy, "someone knew you were here after all."

"First thing that's gone right for me in a long time," Abby said, relieved. She turned to follow the cop back down the hall, then thought better of it and gave Discount Freddy a last look. "I mean it. Truly. When you go out on the town this Halloween, you have yourself a whale of a fucking time. Do that. For me."

He gave her a strange look for a moment, then smiled. Nodded. Tipped his battered fedora. "I will, thanks. I hope you get that work stuff figured out."

"So do I." Then she walked out with the cop.

*****

Agent Six sat in the reception area, his G-man's trench coat laid over his lap, nursing a travel mug of steaming coffee. Despite herself, Abby flashed a smile when she saw him. "Jesus. Didn't ever imagine I'd be glad to see you."

He took a long sip of coffee, stood, and put on his coat. "Believe it or not, the feeling is almost mutual."

She flagged down the desk sergeant so she could collect her personal effects. Wallet. Phone. The *Ci*'s doctored collar. Six had stopped by the Letterbox on his way down and grabbed her Vokarion crystal. "I tried to wake your partner, let her know we'd found you, but she was dead to the world.

Apparently, she's barely let go of that thing since you vanished."

Abby donned the crystal. Held it close to her chest. She could almost feel Leanne's hand upon it. God, she couldn't imagine what these last days had been like for her.

"How'd you know I was here?"

"Department satellites caught an energy spike in the area last night. We thought it might be the hound at first, but then someone down here had the bright idea to run your ID after a few hours. That brought up your B&E prior from Delapore this summer. Anyone in civilian law enforcement tries to call up those files, the Department gets an automatic notification. Eventually, they give me a call, and I haul my ass out of bed at four in the morning and drive halfway across Metro Vancouver to bring you home."

"Well, I appreciate it. A taxi from here would've been crazy expensive."

Six didn't smile. "Very funny."

"I try my best."

As he led her through the parking lot back to his Cadillac, Six brought Abby up to speed on what she'd missed the last few days. "Fortunately, the Golden Hand have been quiet since you and the hound vanished into the Elsewhere. We still haven't found where they've been hiding, but I wouldn't be surprised if they've taken the chance to relocate and come up with a new strategy. And we've finished our security audit on Jacqueline Swann and her outfit. No red flags there, which means either your inside man theory's a bunch of bull, or someone forged their credentials extremely well. For my money, I don't think it's the first one. Theta's still pushing your friend Lockhart to let him deploy more extreme interrogation techniques."

"You mean Lethe crystals." Abby shook her head. "Simon wouldn't greenlight that in a million years. He hasn't even used the Mind Lock since the Deacon got in my head to lure me out to Applegate last year."

"Then we'll lock you in a room with these people and get you reading them one by one. Someone in T.G.W. is hiding something. And I'm not talking about the Swanns' little underground railroad."

Abby stopped in her tracks. "I... what?"

He stopped. Turned. Stared her down. "Don't play stupid, Henderson. You're not as good at it as you think. It's obvious what Jacqueline Swann's been doing if you look closely at her books, which we have. Theta hasn't jumped on it yet, though. Maybe he's looking at the Golden Hand as the bigger picture, maybe he's looking at you."

"You think he'd use this... against me?"

"He still wants you onside. If he thinks threatening to blow up Jacquie Swann's refugee pipeline is the way to get you to play nice, he'll do it."

"Jesus, Six, how do you sleep, working for a guy like that? Is there no line in the sand for you, or did they zap that out of your brain with a fucking Lethe crystal as well?"

"I took an oath to protect this country from the things in the dark, Henderson. The line in the sand for me is that neofascist thugs from another reality don't get to kill Canadian citizens with a magical superweapon. Beyond that, I will do whatever is necessary to preserve human life and give us a leg up in the fight against the darkness, no matter how uncomfortable it makes a few idealistic bleeding hearts. If Theta thinks that you're the leg up we need, then it's my duty to get the hell out of his way and let him ratfuck you any which way he pleases until you play ball."

"When this all started, you went against Ministry orders to help us. Where's that Agent Six now, huh?"

"I went against the grain when I realized there was no strategic benefit in our attempts to remove you from the field. Now my superiors have caught up to me on that, I'm following their lead."

"All for the greater good, huh? Yes, Dr. Harkness. No, Dr. Harkness."

There was no humour in his voice. "Three bags full, Dr. Harkness. Now, you are going to get in my car, and you are going to tell me exactly what you saw in the Elsewhere while I drive your ass back to the Letterbox. Understand?"

"Fine," Abby growled. "But we're stopping at a Shopper's Drug Mart and a McDonald's on the way back. I need some deodorant and a goddamn Egg McMuffin."

"Deal."

*****

After breakfast and a quick whore's bath in the McDonald's bathroom, Abby felt a lot closer to human. Her anger toward Agent Six cooled somewhat while he was topping up his coffee and she was washing her pits and tits, and after she'd freshened up, she found him in the parking lot, perched on the hood of the Cadillac and watching the sunrise.

"Thanks for the stop," she said. "I hadn't eaten anything in seven weeks."

Six shook his head. "I never know what's going to be the next thing out of your mouth, do I?"

"I'll explain on the road, I promise."

It was a long haul between Langley and Vancouver even before the rush hour commute, and Abby filled the time with a play-by-play on her recent trip into the Elsewhere. Based on her vision and what Six had said about Owain ab Gwylem, a possible timeline of events was starting to take shape in her mind. It started with Owain ab Gwylem opening a door into Carcosa for Ted Purdy, who did the actual kidnap job and left the stink of human all over the kennels, which in turn was what got Gwyn ab Nethe's attention.

"And then the Dullahan worked from the inside to lead the King's knights down the wrong path at every turn," Six offered. "That's what your partner thought, anyway."

"And she was onto something. Holly's wrath goes unsatisfied, the Golden Hand keep working the *Ci* over until they can control it, and then they set it loose on prey Gwyn never chose."

"He hits the boiling point—"

"And muggins here gets pulled into the middle of it."

"And what was Purdy's motive? The money?"

"I spoke to Ted Purdy in the Elsewhere, once upon a time. Wasn't a long conversation, but I got the feeling he didn't think about much past his own gratification."

"Hmm. Every man has a price."

"Yep. And apparently the Golden Hand were able to match Purdy's. Then I guess they iced him when he was no longer useful. Had to keep the ranks pure."

"Explain to me again how the Golden Hand got control of the beast."

"With this." Abby laid the collar on the dashboard. It was tightly sealed in a Zip-loc baggie she'd purchased at the Shopper's. You never knew what kind of magic could leak out of evil mind-control devices. She told Six about how the collar had been tampered with, about the funeral song she'd heard in her vision. "My two cents? That logo, disc, thingy on the inside there is some kind of a receiver. When the Golden Hand sent the *Ci* out to do their dirty work, that thing broadcast their mind-control murder song into its head. I guess the connection broke when the hound and I got yanked into the Elsewhere."

"Any idea who the singer was?"

Abby shrugged. "Still haven't worked that out. I'm pretty sure it was a female voice, but that doesn't really narrow it down."

"Hmm." Six scanned the road ahead, then hit the turn signal and pulled onto a side street. Open fields and distant farmhouses on one side, dense forest on the other. Hardly a car to be seen in any direction. For several minutes, he drove in total silence, his eyes locked on some point in the middle distance. Abby looked at his reflection in the rearview mirror and saw something glassy in that thousand-yard stare that she didn't like. The colours of his aura were dulled too. Patchier than she remembered, like someone had been too overzealous with the pruning shears. Or perhaps... shadowed? She thought of Chris's half-human aura, with the bits missing where his fae parentage rounded up to a big metaphysical zero. This was kind of like that, but not quite. Those bits were there, but something was blocking them. Like an eclipse. Faerie sunspot activity blacking out an otherwise clear visual signal.

Something twisted in her gut. She'd seen metaphysical whammies like this before. Historically, things hadn't gone smoothly after someone near her got hit. "We're, uh, going a little off the beaten path, aren't we?"

"Quick detour," Six grunted. "I just need a pit stop."

Even coming from him, the explanation was too mechanical. Like a theatre kid at the first table read for their high school play. She tried to keep her voice light, although her gut kept twisting with worry. "Shouldn't have had that second coffee, huh?"

"Something like that." He turned to open his door. Abby put a hand on her seatbelt buckle.

"Mind if I come with?" Keep calm, Henderson. Breathe. Ignore the jerk playing paddleball on your heart. "I haven't, uh, powdered my nose in a few weeks, if you know what I mean."

Six hit the lock button and reached into his jacket. Then the butt end of a Glock broke Abby's nose.

CHAPTER 26

THE SINGER

SIMON WINCED, the pain from his scars radiating up his torso like an electric burn. He was going to pay dearly for casting this spell of silent passage on himself. Creeping through the darkened halls of the Letterbox, he whispered an apology to Mother Hyld. She had worked hard to mend him after the Harcourt House affair, and he kept spoiling it for them both. Even a spell this minor would likely push his full recovery back past Christmas.

He had been a light sleeper all his life. But ever since the ghost of Isaac Harcourt had gouged out a pound of his flesh with a Cutting Curse, there were nights when he'd be lucky to get forty, fifty minutes—a damn sight short of the four hours an adult Vanguard required. Tonight had been such a night, the pain keeping him tossing and turning in his chambers from midnight onward. He supposed he should thank the High Celestial for his agonies. Without them, he might not have been awake to welcome Agent Six and receive the good news that Abby was safe and sound. Without them, he might never have heard the music.

It came from the front lounge, low and slow and terribly sad. A funeral march in the key of dying leaves and sons lost in wartime. He reached the end of the corridor and stood motionless at the edge of the lounge, watching the singer from across a distance of twenty feet or so. She knelt barefoot on the cold stone, her three-inch heels neatly arranged beside her. Beside this lay an open briefcase containing a thick manila folder and a black smartphone inlaid with the runes of the Shattergrip clan. As she sang, she drew a comb through her luscious red hair, lifting it and letting it fall like water down her shoulders. Simon watched and waited until the singer concluded her performance. Then she kissed the bone-white comb and whispered, "Take care, you brave soldier boy." At last, she slipped the comb into a pocket of her grey blazer, shut her briefcase, and stood with it in one hand and her heels in the other.

She raised a hand and snapped her fingers. Nothing happened. She cocked her head to one side and looked quizzically at her hand, then tried again. Simon cleared his throat and stepped into the lounge.

"Little-known fact about the Letterbox," he said. "While I will permit a modest amount of teleportation within its walls, movement between this dimension and the outside world by any other means than the front door is strictly forbidden. It took me months to design the counter-enchantment, and by the time I'd finished laying it down, even I couldn't break it. You're not going anywhere, Ms. Keane. Not that way."

Iris Keane turned and batted her lashes at him, a coquettish smile playing on her face. "And I suppose you'll tell me next you've sealed the front entrance."

"I raised the wards as soon as I smelled a rat. If you touch that wall right now and try to pass through, there won't be enough ashes to fill a measuring cup."

"I would accuse you of bluffing, but I know the Vanguard of old."

Simon blew out a chagrined breath. "I won't lie, I was rather hoping you would. This floor needs a good sweeping anyway."

"Well, I won't quarrel with you on that, Mr. Lockhart."

Simon reached into his waistcoat pocket and flipped the golden *lau* at her. She caught it before it hit the ground. "I've been meaning to return this, by the way," he said. "I know what they're worth to people like you." She nodded her thanks. "I've seen the Ministry files, Iris. You passed their security audit with flying colours on the first day. T.G.W.'s, too. You've been at the heart of the Swanns' operation for months, eating away at them from within, and they've never smoked you out. I suppose what I'm asking is, who does your work for you?"

"A more talented forger than your imp friend, I can tell you that." She sighed and gave a disappointed shake of the head. "You really should have let them use the Lethe crystals on us."

Ms. Keane opened her mouth, and the shriek of a thousand frenzying harpies bounced around the chamber. The wall-mounted torches guttered, the stones cracked, the mirror above the fireplace shattered to bits. Simon mouthed a spell that he didn't hear: "*Āhefe mūr*!" Blue lightning crackled in the air between them as a concussive shockwave of pure noise slammed into his magical barrier. He felt the impact in his bones and bit his tongue to distract himself from the angry burn of his wounds.

"Yes," he said, raising his voice above the ringing in his ears, "yes, I thought as much. Keane. Keening. The Gaelic lamentation for the dead. Bit on the nose for a *bean sí*, don't you think?"

She walked a predatory semicircle around him, a long scarlet tongue licking hungry lips. "Would you believe you're only the second person to call me on that? I had to kill the first." She screamed again. Simon adjusted the barrier and felt the rush of pure sonic force driving past him on either side, to carve deep fissures in the stone behind him.

"The unfortunate Jack Kang, I presume! I couldn't fathom what must've happened after Abby told me what she'd seen of him in the Elsewhere. This is rather advanced magic for your lot, though, isn't it? Sonic attacks and… what? Can I presume you found some way of infecting innocent minds with your filthy agenda by means of your song? That's rather more in the sirens' line than the *bean sí*'s."

"I had an auntie from Paestum. Don't tell anyone." She winked.

"It was you all along, wasn't it? The scare tactics at T.G.W. Jack Kang. The attack at the South Campus, naturally." He chuckled and shook his head. "That must have felt like the luck of the gods to have all your problems lined up in a row on one big killing floor. You rather overplayed your hand on that one, though."

Ms. Keane shrugged. "Perhaps we did. But I didn't fancy Owain ab Gwylem's odds alone against all those big, strapping soldiers. How was I to know the King would put a part of himself into your Gospel friend?" She aimed her next scream at the archway above Simon's head. He stumbled as he sprinted out of the path of the rubble, his arms windmilling at his sides, trying to keep his balance and maintain the barrier all at once. His knee scraped hard on the floor while falling stones crashed against the barrier like baseballs striking a gong. When their eyes met, she smiled. He cursed his failing body, genuflecting at the altar of hatred.

Cold sweat prickled at his brow and on the back of his neck. He gritted his teeth and fought to keep up the façade. "It's been an admirable performance, this meek, browbeaten assistant routine. Am I right in thinking that the odious Gareth Swann was just a convenient smoke screen?"

"The man's an arse," Ms. Keane admitted, "but he was never able to do what was necessary. He's no good to the cause."

"You make him sound like an abject failure. But I'd take his imperfect empathy over your poison any day of the week."

"I wonder: are you this chatty with everyone who tries to kill you, or are you just trying to flirt with me, you dirty old man?"

Simon did something unexpected for a man on his knees: he grinned. He grinned, reached down his shirt, and flashed his Vokarion crystal at her. "Don't flatter yourself, lovey. I just need your attention on me until Natalie gets in position."

Another scream, but this one didn't come from Ms. Keane. The stones in the ceiling parted wide, vomiting a spitting mad zombie in combat boots directly over the banshee's head. Ms. Keane dropped her briefcase and her high heels and leaped for dear life, landing with a roll that flowed seamlessly into a splay-legged crouch. Natalie's fist made a dent in the stone floor where Ms. Keane had been. When she looked at the banshee, her eyes spelled murder.

"Oh, didn't I mention?" Simon chirped. "The Letterbox is, apart from all its other charms, ever so slightly alive." He picked himself up with a grunt, cracked his back, and rolled his shoulders. "Sorry. Should've added that to the previous fun fact."

Natalie leapt at the banshee. The banshee leapt at Natalie. They met in a hail of feet, fists, teeth, and nails. Simon lowered his barrier and tapped his foot on the floor. A stone bucked two feet in the air, launching the briefcase into his outstretched hand. "And what have we here?" he asked, forcing the lock with a minor spell. The phone and folder fell out and he caught them in his other hand. All Ms. Keane's attention snapped to him, and in that moment of distraction Natalie punched out three of her teeth.

Simon flicked through the contents of the folder. "My, my, talk about enough rope to hang yourself. I dare say Jacquie Swann's entire life story is in here. Names of children, the families she's matched them with, dates of transfer... a particularly bad actor could use this information to hunt down and kill every changeling refugee she's ever helped." All remaining humour fled his voice in an instant, and he fixed Ms. Keane with a look of the blackest hatred. Natalie held the banshee prone, grinding a knee into her spine and her face into the floor. She bent back the index and middle fingers of Ms. Keane's right hand so she couldn't snap her way out of trouble.

Simon waggled the phone in the air. "Tsk, tsk, Iris. Trying to beat the blackout, are we? I presume this contains the rest of the information you've collected?" He dropped the phone to the floor and stamped on the remains.

Ms. Keane spat blood onto the floor. "Haven't you heard of cloud computing, you Luddite? It's the magic of the twenty-first century! Everything I've gathered on Jacqueline Swann's project of pollution is backed up on a secure server. Silence me if you dare, but a thousand others like me await their chance to carry our mission forward! The Golden Hand will cleanse the blood and make Faerie a word to be feared, as it was in the time of the old kings."

The manila folder burst into flame in Simon's hand. "What was the plan after Abby and the *Ci* disappeared, if you don't mind me asking? Keep your head down and collect what information you needed to ruin Jacquie Swann, then drug us all to the gills and slip away quietly?" He dusted his hands together. "I did look in on Leanne and the others, by the way," he said to Natalie. "I was right: enough silversprig on their breath to drop a bull elephant."

"And when I tried the tap in the kitchen, what do you think I smelled?" Natalie growled in agreement. "You've been poisoning our well, Keane."

"It's just your bad luck that I have a far higher tolerance than the others and I spend my nights in sleepless agony," said Simon.

Ms. Keane snarled and struggled uselessly against Natalie's grip. "Am I supposed to be intimidated by this little two-man act? Even if you kill me, you won't stop what's coming for Jacqueline Swann!"

Simon looked at Natalie and shrugged. "Well, that's as may be, but the net result is still n-minus-one fascists in the world. Personally, I'm comfortable with those numbers. Natalie?"

She wrapped a massive hand around Ms. Keane's throat and flashed a bloodthirsty grin. "Fine by me. You know what they say about the only good Nazi."

Ms. Keane blew out an annoyed breath. "Alright, you called my bluff." She raised her voice and called out, "Oh, Soldier Boy!"

Simon and Natalie's Vokarion crystals both began to glow. Abby's voice screamed out in stereo, her voice thick with blood and panic. "Simon! Natalie! Anybody! It's Agent Six! He's—"

A gunshot. A shriek. Sounds of violence, and then Six's voice, distant and soulless. "I have her, Lockhart. Henderson's alive for now. That could change, depending on how smart you are."

Ms. Keane smiled. "Now, can we talk about this like civilized people?"

*****

Mud and morning dew soaked the back of Abby's clothes. Thick blood clogged her nostrils and the back of her throat. Agent Six had dragged her from the car toward the treeline. She'd tried to make a break for it. A single warning shot and a pistol butt behind her ear had been enough to dissuade her from that course of action.

Six kicked her in the stomach and ripped the Vokarion crystal out of her hands. "I have her, Lockhart. Henderson's alive for now."

Abby spat blood onto a mass of fallen leaves and rolled to one side. Tried to heave herself up on her elbows. She still felt rough from how Brother and Sister Dearest had handled her. Now she had a feeling Six had thrown a concussion and a broken rib on top of her shit sundae. She'd never win a straight fight like this.

"Abby, I need you to listen to me." Simon's voice was steady over the Vokarion relay. "Natalie and I are handing over our crystals now. Ms. Keane is going to keep a line open to Agent Six. For your own safety, I advise you to do exactly what he says. Please, Abby. For once in your life, don't argue."

Silence for a moment, then Ms. Keane's voice. "I'll make you a deal, Henderson. You've been a right royal pain in the backside from minute one, but you are not the bigger picture here. Right now, all I want is for your Vanguard friend to lower the wards around the Letterbox and give me the chance to walk away. You've stymied the Golden Hand's plans for the *Ci Annwn*, but you and I don't need to go to war over this. So, how about it? You let me walk, or my big, brave soldier boy there puts a bullet between your eyes."

"Fuck you, Keane!" Abby spat a mouthful of blood. "I'm not letting one more innocent person die for your dogshit race war."

"Be sensible, Henderson. You're not the only card in my hand. I could always kill you and see if your fat little fuck buddy will be a more compliant hostage."

"Try it and I'll rip your head off, you psycho bitch!" she screamed. "I'll shit down your neck! I'll pull out your eyes, I'll get the biggest strap-on I can find, and I will skull-fuck you six ways from—"

Six pistol-whipped her. She gagged on her own blood, teeth rattling and ears ringing. A little voice in her head screamed at her to just give up, to do as Simon said and not make things worse for herself once in her stupid goddamn life. Her body ignored her brain's commands and dragged it kicking and screaming through the dirt. Six dropped on top of her with a knee in her kidney and a hand on her neck. When he brought down the Glock, her ear went pop and blood trickled down her jawline. She scrabbled around in the dirt with both hands, looking for anything she could hit back with. Six flipped her over on her back, and her fingers closed around a rock the size of a grapefruit.

Hey. Ain't no school like old-school.

She swung the rock into Six's left temple and pulled herself out from under him. He hadn't hit the ground before she was on her feet again, and then she was running. Okay, she was staggering, but any distance between the two of them was good enough. The first shot went *phut* into the muddy ground beneath her feet. The second *cracked* into a tree branch. Then Six let out a primal yell and ran right at her. She hardly even saw what was happening as he closed the gap in about three seconds flat and took her down to the ground in a gold-star rugby tackle. Her head rang like a bell and she saw two Agent Sixes pointing their Glocks at her from four inches away. Her Vokarion crystal stuck out from a pile of leaves several feet away, forgotten sometime between when she'd beaned him and when he came at her like a bullet train.

She sniffed. Thick, hot blood poured down into the back of her throat, choking her as she tried to speak. "Six. Six, listen to me. I know this isn't you."

He punched her in her already broken nose and growled, "Shut up."

Her whole field of vision was a blinding void of pain, but at least that meant she wasn't looking down the barrel of the Glock anymore. Swings and roundabouts, really.

"Goddammit, Six, you can fight this!" She could barely hear herself over the ringing in her ears, but this was at least worth a try, surely. "Keane, she's… she's put a whammy on you! Just like she did the *Ci*! But you don't have to do this! The *Ci* didn't! I got through to her. I stopped her. Are you going to tell me an agent of the Department of Advanced Research and Special Defence doesn't have as much willpower as a fucking *dog*?"

The twitch in his wrist was almost invisible. But there it was. When it happened a second time, Abby smiled a wide, bloody smile. One kernel of doubt. That was all she needed. One second of hesitation.

"Just put the gun down, Six. We can talk about this."

"Oh, no, no, no." The voice was Ms. Keane's. Abby's Vokarion crystal shone where it lay, and she realized the connection to the Letterbox was still open. "You don't get out of this that easily, you little bitch. Soldier Boy: kill her!"

Ms. Keane's song swelled out of the crystal, and Six's arm went ramrod-straight. No trace of doubt in him now. She grabbed his wrist with both hands, pulled him down atop her, and rammed her knee into his balls. Sank her teeth into the delicate flesh on the back of his hand. He screamed. The gun went off.

CHAPTER 27

RECHASE

SOLDIER BOY?" Ms. Keane hollered into Simon's crystal. "Soldier Boy! Answer me, you stupid son of a hoor!"

No answer. Simon and Natalie were on their knees, hands clasped behind their heads. As the glow faded from the Vokarion crystal, Simon lowered his head and shut his eyes. Natalie ground her teeth and tensed her shoulders, ready to jump Ms. Keane at the first chance. Simon opened one eye and shook his head. He didn't know if Abby was lost or not, but there was no sense in chancing any threat against Leanne or the other innocents in the Letterbox.

Ms. Keane harrumphed and gave the crystal an annoyed look. "Plan B, then." She pursed her lips and gave a shrill whistle. Shadows moved in the corridor, and then Jacquie and Gareth Swann emerged from the dark with Leanne, Chris, Whittaker, and Mother Hyld heaped over their shoulders like sacks of grain. The elves' eyes were glassy and distant, their movement jerky like cheap theme park animatronics, as they hauled the sleepers into the centre of the room and dropped them uncaringly on the stones. They reached into their waistbands and drew forth a pair of long, ivory daggers with the hand of Nethe the Fair carved below the guards. Then Jacquie seized Chris by the hair and pressed her blade to his throat.

"I had a feeling yer wan would make more trouble," Ms. Keane said, "so I sang these two a bit of a lullaby earlier."

She looked at Simon. "You were half-right, Lockhart. I needed time to collect the rest of the files, but I figured it couldn't hurt to lash up a few more receivers like the one I put on Gwyn's beastie." She pulled a small ivory disc from her pocket and held it up to the light. "They do make my job ever so much easier. Now, are you going to drop those wards for me, or do I have to make your friends kill each other one by one?"

"I can drop the wards," Simon said, "but you won't make it ten feet. You saw the Ministry set up their command post, Iris. There are a dozen armed agents half a block from here. Cameras across the street, pointed directly at this building. You walk outside with two hypnotized drones and a suite of hostages, and they'll raise every alarm from here to Ottawa."

Ms. Keane rolled her eyes. "Yes, I had thought of that, thank you."

Somewhere in the Letterbox, a bell pealed a low note of warning. The double doors of the armoire flew open and blotches of colour swirled on the surface of the reflective silver dish, resolving after a moment into an image of the streets beyond the Letterbox's four walls. A window onto the world, and Simon's own private security feed.

In the surface of the silver dish, Simon and Natalie saw a line of three boxy, black trucks devoid of identifying markings—the Ministry's triple-wide mobile command station and liaison outpost. From beyond the perimeter of the dish, a half-dozen figures emerged, dressed in nondescript black street clothes and balaclavas and armed with bows, arrows, and broadswords. Each of the balaclavas was streaked with a five-fingered golden emblem across the face.

Armed Ministry agents kicked open the doors of their trucks and took their ready positions with their weapons hot. The silver dish offered no sound, but facial expressions were enough for Simon and Natalie to understand the general sentiment. The agents of the Golden Hand let off a volley of arrows, killing three Ministry men in the first round. The agents returned fire. Then Ms. Keane shut the armoire's double doors.

"You get the general idea," she said. "Those men out there are a fraction of our number. More will come if they fall, and if they do not see me on that street corner within the next few minutes, they will put every man, woman, and child they can find to the sword. Humans, skunks, fae, it really doesn't matter to them."

Simon bowed his head, accepting defeat at last.

*****

When the gun went off, the last vestiges of Abby's hearing fled for the hills. She had felt the rush of air as Six fired into the dirt beside her head, and she was suddenly really glad she'd used the bathroom at the McDonald's. Might have been embarrassing, otherwise.

He was groaning and grimacing on top of her, and gave no resistance when she pushed him off and yanked the Glock out of his hands. Sound was unknown to her as she legged it over to her fallen crystal and gave it two sharp taps to break the connection to the Letterbox. As she did, the ringing in her ears faded just enough for her to catch the tail end of some furious invective from Ms. Keane: "—upid son of a hoor!"

She shoved the crystal in her pocket and muttered, "Soldier Boy can't come to the phone right now, you cunt." She could barely hear her own voice right now, and that gave her an idea. The song in the hound's ears had been the driver for all this horror. Abby had stopped it by breaking the connection between the transmitter and the receiver. But what if she unplugged the connection between the ear and the brain?

"Sorry, Six," she didn't hear herself say. He was still in a daze on the ground, hands over his crotch, and he barely gave her a look as she shoved the pistol into the dirt beside his head and fired. He cringed and slapped his hands over his ears. She stuck the pistol down the back of her muddy jeans, then stripped off his G-man's coat and his dark blazer and ran her hands through the pockets. The collar was still in its baggie on the Cadillac's dash, so she guessed that Ms. Keane must have planted a spare ivory receiver on his person in order to hold the connection. Probably slipped it to him when he showed up at the Letterbox first thing.

She found the engraved ivory disc inside the coat's collar, fixed in place with a safety pin on the back. On the ground beside her, Six began to stir. Abby ripped the receiver free of his coat and hammered on it with the butt of the Glock until it was a fine white powder. Her hearing was starting to come back in fits and starts, enough for her to notice Six groan and sit up. He rubbed his forehead with a moan of, "Jesus Christ..." Then he saw her with his gun in her hand. "Henderson? Would you mind explaining to me why my groin is on fire?"

She pulled the gun out of her waistband and aimed at him. "One question first: do you hear any singing?"

"What? No, I don't hear any singing. Why—" Then it dawned on him. "The Golden Hand got to me, didn't they?"

"Yeah. We need to get to the Letterbox ASAP."

Six beat all possible speed records getting the Cadillac back on the main highway, but Abby knew it wasn't going to be enough. She smashed the collar's ivory receiver with the butt of the Glock, shoved the whole mess in the glove compartment, then pulled her Vokarion crystal out of her pocket and tried to re-open the connection to the Letterbox. "Hello, Simon? Simon?!"

Ms. Keane answered. "I'm afraid Simon's a little tied up at the moment."

"Keane! Listen to me, you smug bitch, when I—"

"Temper, temper, Henderson! This is no way to endear yourself to the woman who'll sing at your friends' gravesides." She chuckled. "Do you know, a *bean sí*'s lament does not only portend death in a family. If we concentrate hard enough, we can conjure it. Weave reality together from the notes of our music. They say Nethe-on-High sang the song that shaped the Otherlands in their infancy. Now we who guard his legacy will do the same across these Midlands."

"You're not guarding shit. You're manipulating innocent minds to force them into killing for you. It's sick."

"What's that phrase you humans use? To-may-to, to-mah-to. You know, I really have to applaud your resilience, Henderson. It is extraordinarily difficult to kill you. I'll be curious to see if your friends give me half as much trouble. Think I'll start with the little skunk..."

The line went dead. Abby pounded her fist on the dashboard and let fly a string of profanity that shocked even her. It didn't do anything to solve the problem. It didn't even make her feel that much better. "That's it." Defeat crept into her voice. "We're never going to make it. The Golden Hand's going to get away, and Gwyn won't give me half-credit for trying."

Six chewed his lip. Sighed. Slammed on the brakes. Then he hit the trunk release. "I really shouldn't be doing this," he said to himself. Then, to Abby: "Aluminum briefcase in the trunk. Grab it."

"What—"

"Just do it, Henderson."

As fast as she could, Abby ran around to the trunk and found the briefcase. It was too early in the morning for any serious traffic, but that didn't mean they weren't still parked in the middle of the highway, and she didn't want to add "getting steamrolled by an F-150" to her present list of sorrows. She climbed back into the passenger's seat with the briefcase on her lap. It was heavy. Jesus, it was heavy. Six said, "Open it."

The inside of the briefcase was filled with a mix of chunky Cold War electronics and arcane materials. A keyboard and eight-bit screen. Dials. Switches. A red crystal, alike in size and shape to a Lethe or Vokarion crystal, set in at the top with electrical nodes connected to each end. A circular pattern of magical glyphs, etched into a steel plate on the underside of the lid. "What the hell is this?" she said.

"For the past few years, the Department has been experimenting with portable teleportation technology," Six explained. "Seems like every magic-user and their grandmother has teleportation capabilities these days, and we didn't want to be left in the cold. After you disappeared into the Elsewhere, I borrowed this prototype from the North Campus. It might not even work. It'll probably fry the car battery. We could end up outside the Letterbox, or we could end up on fucking Mars."

Abby laughed nervously. "Well, if we do, at least we won't have to watch Gwyn ice the city."

Miracle of miracles, she actually saw Six smile at that. In a less desperate situation, she would have taken a victory lap around the Cadillac. Instead she asked, "How do you work this thing?"

"Punch in the coordinates you want. The device will do the rest."

She had to Google the exact coordinates of the Letterbox's post office façade before she punched them in. They appeared as blocky green text on the screen. When she hit ENTER, the crystal started to glow. She looked up and saw a storm of light on the road ahead of them. Blues, reds, greens, and beyond. Sparks of magical energy popped at the storm's edge. Six looked over his shoulder and cranked the Cadillac into reverse. "Need a bit of a run-up for this." Then he put the car into first gear and let 'er rip.

*****

Iris Keane glided through the Anointed Gate to the beat of the Letterbox's heavy, chugging machinery. As her heels touched down on the pavement of East 6th, she breathed deeply of the dewy morning air, then crooked one finger at the wall behind her. Simon and Natalie passed through the Anointed Gate first. Then Gareth, with his jerking, dreamlike gait. Next were Leanne, Chris, and Mother Hyld, rudely awakened from their heavy sleep and duct-taped at the wrists and mouth. Jacquie was last, with the deeply dreaming Whittaker held in a fireman's carry. The street was lined with the black-clad foot soldiers of the Golden Hand – perhaps two dozen, plus the strike team who'd taken out the Ministry's mobile command station. Each one carried a burning pine resin torch. When Ms. Keane appeared, they raised them above their heads and sent up a great cheer.

The end of the street became a shower of light in all the colours of the rainbow and beyond as Agent Six's Cadillac jumped out of pure nothingness. The V8 engine growled like a wild animal as the car jumped the curb, ran down two foot soldiers, and steered into a hard braking turn outside the Letterbox. Abby caught a glimpse of faerie balaclavas in the side mirror, each with their emblem painted across the face like the White Hand of Saruman. (If Saruman had bred the Uruk-hai to be a bunch of fascist shitkickers.)

The Golden Handers stormed the Cadillac, ripping open the doors, pulling Abby and Six onto the street, menacing them with swords and bows. Ms. Keane stayed them with a single word. "No!" She took Gareth's ivory dagger from him and pulled Chris from his place in the line. Then she threw him, spluttering and sobbing, into the gutter. She pointed the dagger at Abby and proclaimed, "She will watch this!"

The Golden Handers hauled Abby up to her knees. One got his hand under her chin and held her eyeline on Chris. Ms. Keane brushed a lock of Chris's hair back with the flat of the knife. He shut his eyes and flinched away, fighting tears as she spoke.

"Do you know how I know skunks aren't truly of the blood?" she hissed. "Nothing but cold iron leaves a lasting mark upon the fae, but you bleed as easily as any ape." She raked the blade down one side of Chris's face. He screamed behind his duct tape as the blood ran down his cheek. Ms. Keane licked her lips and drew the knife back for the final blow. Chris spat out a muffled cry for help.

*****

Deep in the fog of Dreamland, someone heard the changeling's desperate mewling. The signal was faint and the static plenty, but still the call came through. Whittaker wasn't sure he hadn't imagined the voice the first time he heard it, echoing off the stones way deep down in the Letterbox's belly. Here? After all these years? In his slumber, he had felt the soft warmth of a hand on his, heard the comforting but fumbling words of a voice trying to boil fourteen years of "I love you's" into something a coma patient could handle, and he'd chalked it up to a lack of oxygen. The last gasp of a half-dead brain throwing his great regrets at him, so he could atone before he went off to the halls of his forefathers. Was that days ago? Weeks? Who knew?

Now, hearing that long-forgotten voice again, he realized it had been no dream. Even in the faraway place where he was, the real world could leak through. And by the grace of the Golden Father and his Sons the Sun and Moon, the real world had seen fit to give R.G. Whittaker a second bite at this particular apple.

His child was here, now, crying out in pain and terror. They were hurting for no better reason than that someone didn't like how they'd been born. He heard this, and something happened to him that hadn't happened in a long time.

Robin Whittaker, son of Goodfellow, got mad.

*****

The imp's eyes snapped open. He saw cement. A pair of expensive—but sensible—heels. His gaze tracked up the long, elegant legs of the woman over whose shoulders he had been thrown like a fur stole. Some part of his brain cleared just enough to congratulate the artist's eye that had put this body together. Then his child cried out again, and the world before him turned red.

Whittaker's head shot up and he locked his eyes onto Ms. Keane. He wriggled out of Jacquie's fireman's carry with a throaty, sharp-toothed hiss and climbed over her, Gareth, Simon, and Natalie to reach his target. Abby couldn't follow the flowing movements of his skinny body as he closed the gap, and no one else seemed to notice he was there before he'd already jumped another two places. "I thought you said he was still in a coma!" she shouted back at Six.

"He was when I left!"

Whittaker pounced on Ms. Keane before she struck the killing blow. He'd grown thinner since the attack from the Lone Dullahan, but his strength seemed unchecked as he scratched, bit, kicked, and squeezed. He sank long, dirty toenails into the banshee's shoulder. His grasping fingers clenched around her throat. His teeth flashed like knives in the dark as he bit down on her ear and tore it loose. At the sound of Ms. Keane's agonized wailings, the foot soldiers of the Golden Hand drew their swords and nocked their arrows, but before they could get off a shot, Whittaker snapped his fingers.

With a sound like a gunshot, Whittaker and the bewildered banshee jumped from street level to the roof of the old post office two storeys above the ground. The Golden Hand let fly a volley of arrows in that direction, forgetting Chris entirely. Jacquie and Gareth stood as dumbstruck as everyone else, offering not the least resistance as Natalie tore herself free of her duct tape and set to work helping her friends. Obviously, Ms. Keane hadn't accounted for whatever the hell this was when she sang the elves her song, and the shock was overwhelming their hypnosis.

Whittaker got his hands on Ms. Keane's shoulders and drove his knee repeatedly into her soft bits. On the third blow she dropped the knife. Before she could draw in the breath for a killer scream, he picked it up and cut her throat from ear to ear.

She gasped and slapped a hand over the wound. Blood poured through her fingers and turned her green blouse brown. Whittaker kicked her onto her back and planted his foot on her chest. "I always thought it was a bunch of BS," he rasped. His voice was hoarse with disuse. "You know, all those stories about moms and dads summoning the strength of the gods in a moment of crisis. Turns out all you need is one fascist shitheel to pull a knife on your kid." He jumped and stamped both feet on the banshee's chest. "Really wakes you up in the morning!"

Ms. Keane coughed blood. Her words drowned in it. It pooled under her head, her shoulders. "Yeah, yeah, I know," said Whittaker. He straddled her and twirled the gore-slicked blade through her hair. "Strike you down and you'll become more powerful, blah, blah, blah. Problem is you're right. This rinky-dink potato peeler won't keep you down for long, and I'm not going anywhere near a blade of cold iron. Guess I gotta outsource this." He rose, wrapped his hands in her hair, and dragged her toward the edge of the roof, not minding the second volley of Golden Hand arrows that whizzed up toward him. The jagged edges of Ms. Keane's wound started to knit themselves together, and she was able to suck in enough air to scream out in pain.

"GWYN AB NETHE!" Whittaker hollered. Ms. Keane gasped and coughed out a flurry of "no's."

"Gwyn ab Nethe!" the imp shouted again. "No" was joined by "please."

"Gwyn ab Nethe!" Whittaker shouted a third time. "Thrice named, I summon you!" Then the lights went out.

CHAPTER 28

LONG IS THE WINTER

IT WASN'T just the building next door.

It wasn't just the streetlights on their block.

As far as Abby could see, the whole damn *city* was in a blackout.

Dark clouds were gathering fast in the sky, swallowing the sun and spitting rain on the back of her neck. Thunder boomed in answer to Whittaker's invocation. A freezing wind whipped between the buildings with a howl that could shame any banshee. More than a few of the Golden Hand foot soldiers simply dropped their weapons where they stood and ran like rabbits. Some of the more optimistic ones turned their bows on the coming storm. Simon shouted up to the roof. "Whittaker! What the hell are you doing?"

"Something you chickenshits should have done a long time ago!" the imp hollered back. Lightning flashed over his head. He spread his arms wide and cackled, blood staining his teeth and chin, wind whipping around his blue and white hospital gown. He gargled and spat with rainwater to clean out the taste of Ms. Keane's ear. "Come on, big man, show us what you got! The stage is lit and the actors are waiting for the curtain call! *La commedia* is fucking *finita*!"

The sky opened like a dark wound as a dozen faerie stallions came riding across the sky, snorting flame and fury, the silver swords and white bone-whips of their Dullahan riders the only contrast against the dark clouds. The riders split into two columns as a thirteenth steed, far greater in size and pallid in colour, came barreling down the middle, its rider's long hair and riding cloak billowing like black fire. The Golden Hand's arrows plinked off the pale stallion's hide like nothing. Gwyn ab Nethe raised a hunting horn to his lips and blew a long note as a half-dozen *Cŵn Annwn* passed between him and his columns of huntsmen and launched themselves at the remaining foot soldiers. Abby shut her eyes and plugged her ears against the baying of the hounds, the cries of the Golden Handers, the flurry of Dullahan arrows burying themselves in the stragglers. She'd seen enough of the Wild Hunt to last her a lifetime, and she was willing to leave this bout to the imagination.

Two hands on her shoulders made her start, and then Agent Six's voice was in her ear. "Come on." He led her across the street and up onto the curb into the shadow of the Anointed Gate. Still not daring to look at the carnage, she stuck a hand out in front of her and groped around to get her bearings.

A warm hand enclosed hers. Kissed it. Those same lips found her cheek. Her mouth. She wrapped her arms around Leanne and buried her face in her partner's shoulder, venting her relief with great, wet sobs.

Up on the roof, Ms. Keane wasn't quite so lucky. Her throat had healed, but she still couldn't summon the breath she needed. She looked at Whittaker, pleading, shaking her head, her hands scrabbling for purchase on his hospital gown.

"Please," she croaked. "Please! You can't give me over to them. I-I-I'll do anything you want! Money. Property. Women. Men! I-it's yours! Just don't let them find me!"

Whittaker tsked. "After all that? You come into my city and take a shot at me. Threaten my people. My *son*. And you think you can just cut a deal and walk away?" He shook his head and flashed her a vengeful grin. "Sorry, Red, but that dog just won't hunt."

He threw her off the roof. At the sound of the banshee's screaming descent, one of the *Cŵn Annwn* perked up its ears and took a running leap at her. She was a Frisbee in its mouth. A ragdoll. Dessert.

Abby didn't open her eyes until the screaming had stopped. The sight of the killing field almost made her lose her Egg McMuffin. Turned out there was something besides cold iron that could leave a mark on the high fae. She averted her eyes again as one of the Dullahan came riding up from several blocks away, two bodies trussed up on the back of its steed. In the reflection off a rain puddle, she watched as the Dullahan alit from its steed and kneeled. "Survivors, O Great Gwyn," she heard the creature say. "They ran without engaging in the fight."

"COWARDS..." The surface of the puddle froze over at the single word. "YOU DID WELL TO PURSUE THEM, TARACH AB TELG."

Abby turned. It was indeed one of the three Dullahan from that first night. Tarach ab Telg thumped a gloved fist against his breastbone in a gesture of courtly devotion, then stood and hoisted the two sobbing foot soldiers off the back of his steed.

Gwyn ab Nethe's pale horse stood nearly seven feet high at the shoulder, and its rider was proportional in the saddle. Abby could hardly discern the features of his face for the glare of those neutron-star eyes. Her ears rang just at the sight of him, and she realized with a start that her nose was starting to bleed.

"COWARDS..." Gwyn repeated the foul word and stretched out his hand. Thunder rumbled. "FEAR... NOTHING," he commanded. The foot soldiers raised their eyes to the sky. Without a sound, their bodies broke apart into a million snowflakes that floated away on the wind. The King then cast his eyes over the carnage his Wild Hunt had wrought. "THE SNOW COVERS ALL, AND REMEMBERS... NOTHING." He waved his hand again. The grim remains of the hunt turned to white powder and drifted into the sky. Arrows broke apart where they had stuck and bloodstains peeled themselves off the street, the walls, the skin and clothing of Abby and her friends. The storm stole away the least hint that the Golden Hand had ever been there, leaving the street cleaner than Abby had ever seen it.

At that final passing of Iris Keane from the mortal realm, the spell broke over Jacquie and Gareth Swann. They started as if waking from a dream and looked about them with eyes full of fear and wonder. Jacquie gasped and clung to her brother when she saw the King-Among-the-Holly before her. The noise made him turn, and the siblings quickly bent the knee, their eyes locked on the ground beneath their feet. Abby, Leanne, and the rest quickly followed suit.

Gwyn looked to the roof and growled, "ROBYN AB GODFELWE." He reached out his hand, and a howling vortex of snow twisted up around the imp, pulling him down to the street. Whittaker landed on his knees between Abby and Agent Six, his eyes bugging from his skull as the full implications of his actions came home to roost.

"ROBYN AB GODFELWE," the King repeated, "NO ONE SUMMONS ME."

"I know. I know," Whittaker babbled. "I-I wouldn't have done it—shouldn't have done it—but she was really pissing me off. Guess I kind of lost my cool."

"EXCUSES," Gwyn said. "YOU BOUGHT YOUR FREEDOM OF ME ONCE. DO NOT PRESUME THAT YOU CAN DO SO AGAIN." His eyes drifted to the white streak in Chris's hair. When he saw it, his stallion reared up with a terrible whinny and the howling snow coalesced into a silver scythe in his outstretched hand. "WHAT," he bellowed over the boom of the thunder, "IS THIS?"

Chris looked up, ashen-faced. He pointed a shaking finger at his chest in a gesture of mute confirmation. Gwyn bared his teeth.

"M-muh-my n-name—Christopher!" he spat out. "C-Christopher ab Robyn ab Godfelwe, O Great Gwyn. My m-mother's name is Melinda Mah. A—a—" He gulped and lowered his eyes. "A human."

Lightning flashed off the blade of the scythe. "YOU MOCK US," Gwyn growled at Whittaker. "YOU SUMMON US IN THE PRESENCE OF THESE… OBSCENITIES. GRAVE-WALKERS. HALF-BREEDS. THE *WÆRLOGA*. I SHOULD TAKE ALL YOUR HEADS THIS VERY HOUR."

"You do and you might as well cut your own throat!" Leanne rose to her feet, her fists balled and her cheeks flushed with anger. She pointed an accusing finger at the King and snapped, "That kind of talk is *exactly* how all this crap got started!"

A dozen faerie knights turned to look at her. Hands found hilts and the first inch of burnished steel cleared a dozen scabbards. Leanne was unfazed. "Do you know who stole your hound from Carcosa, O Great Gwyn?" She spat the name resentfully. "Sure, humans may have had a hand in it, but they had help from someone inside your own court!"

A dozen Dullahan swords flashed in the gloom as the knights drew their weapons fully and uttered a terrible war-cry. Gwyn stayed them with a single raised hand.

"EXPLAIN."

Leanne turned down the heat from a boil to a simmer. "Owain ab Gwylem was working against you from the start. He opened a way to Carcosa so that agents of the Golden Hand could abduct your hound and use it to exterminate changelings like Chris. The Golden Hand were loyal to nobody but their own twisted idea of purity, and they abused your father's name to justify themselves, O Gwyn, son of Nethe. But their ideas didn't come from nowhere." She cast a quick look back at Gareth. "And if you don't put that scythe away, you are just adding fuel to their fire. I implore you to show mercy as a king should, O Great Gwyn.

Revenge yourself on your enemies by being better than them."

For a moment, the world was still. Then Gwyn opened his hand, and the scythe broke apart into a thousand swirling snowflakes. The Dullahan lowered their swords.

"IT IS... ELOQUENTLY SAID. WHO ARE YOU, TO SPEAK SO BOLDLY TO A KING?"

Leanne raised her chin and adjusted her glasses. "My name is Leanne Millicent Waller, daughter of George and Elizabeth Waller. I'm the short, fat little gay girl who makes the tea." She touched the cross about her throat. "You may be *a* king, Your Majesty, but you are not *my* king."

"OWAIN AB GWYLEM..." Gwyn chewed on the name for a long moment. "I FELT HIS PASSING FROM THE WORLD. IF IT IS AS YOU SAY, THEN IT IS WELL THAT HE IS GONE."

Abby cleared her throat nervously. "If I may, O Great Gwyn?" The King motioned for her to stand. "I have walked in your lands, sire. You know this. And I have seen that everything Leanne says is the truth." She went to Jacquie and Gareth, babbling out many awkward apologies, and rummaged around in their pockets and under their shirts. At last, she came away with two small ivory discs. Then she ran to Six's Cadillac and opened the glove compartment.

"Look!" She held out the implements of Ms. Keane's mind-control. "Iris Keane used these to take control of innocent minds like the *Ci Annwn*'s. She forced them to kill for her. She was a *bean sí*, a wailing woman of the old world, who wished to do more than portend. A mortal named Ted Purdy assisted her and Owain ab Gwylem in the heist on Carcosa, and when he was of no more use, they got rid of him. I wish it were not so, but the rot was in your court, Majesty. It may still be. Leanne's right: the only way to stop something like this happening again is to cut it out. Cast it away on the wind."

Gwyn stretched out his hand. "AMEND..."

"But do not forget."

Ivory became cold snow in her hands before the wind snatched it away. Gwyn whistled to one of the *Cŵn Annwn,* who was still snuffling around the spot where it had got Ms. Keane in the death roll. It pawed at the pavement, not understanding where the toy had gone. At its master's call, it looked up, wagged its tail, and ran at Abby with a happy bark. Abby stumbled back into Leanne when the creature butted up against her legs. Then she dropped to her knees and gave the *Ci* an affectionate scratch beneath the chin.

"Hey, girl! Looks like those two did get you home safe! You glad to be back with Daddy?"

The *Ci* barked and licked her hand. Gwyn's lip curled upward. "I BELIEVE OLWEN IS TRYING TO THANK YOU."

"Is your name Olwen?" Abby cooed. "You look like an Olwen! Yes, you do!" Olwen circled around her, pawing the ground. She scratched the hound on the belly. "Olwen gots a fuzzy tum-tum, doesn't she? Yes, she does! Yes, she does gots a fuzzy tum-tum!"

The King's chuckle was deep and unexpectedly warm. "'CULT-BREAKER' I HAVE NAMED YOU, ABIGAIL HENDERSON. 'BEAST-MASTER,' I CALL YOU NOW."

"So, does this mean we're Even Steven?"

The King considered this. "YOU RETURNED MY *CI,* ACCORDING TO THE TERMS OF OUR AGREEMENT. BUT YOU FAILED TO BRING ME THE HEADS OF THOSE RESPONSIBLE. IT IS BY YOUR IMP'S... IMPETUOSITY THAT WE ARE CALLED. YOU STAND, AS BEFORE, ALONGSIDE THOSE WHO WOULD MOCK OUR VALUES. YET... PERHAPS... SOME VALUES ARE NOT WORTH PRESERVING." He looked skyward in thought for a moment, then back at her. "YOU HAVE HONOURED THE SPIRIT OF YOUR *ANOETH,* IF NOT PERHAPS THE LETTER. AND IF YOUR SUCCESS HAS COME WITH THE HELP OF YOUR FRIENDS, THEN IT IS MY FAILING FOR NOT *EXPRESSLY* FORBIDDING IT. YOUR PERFORMANCE IS..." He smiled, showing rows of sharp teeth. "ACCEPTABLE."

Her scarred palm began to burn, and she ripped off her fingerless gloves. The ice crystals in her flesh turned to flakes of snow and drifted away, leaving the skin pink and puffy and unmarked by Holly's everlasting ice. The tension flooded out of her, turning her whole body to jelly. She staggered back into Leanne's arms once more, breathing heavily and shaking from her toes to her head. She had no idea relief could be this overwhelming.

"Thank you," she gasped. "Thank you, O Great Gwyn. A thousand times I say it and a thousand again."

Gwyn raised his voice. "HEAR ME, HUNTERS OF HOLLY! WE HAVE NO QUARREL WITH THESE PEOPLE! THE BEAST-MASTER HAS SHOWN US HONOUR THIS DAY, AND WE WILL HONOUR HER IN TURN! WHEN WE RIDE TOGETHER ON *NOS GALAN GAEAF*, OUR WRATH SHALL NOT TOUCH THIS MIDDANGEARD! IT IS THE BEAST-MASTER'S WILL, AND SO IT IS YOUR KING'S WILL!"

The Dullahan sent up a great cheer. With a nod to Abby, the King brought his steed around for a running start. "WE SHALL SPEAK AGAIN, ABBY NORMAL." He cracked the reins and blew his hunting horn. With a great whinny, his stallion reared and rode into the sky. The Dullahan and the *Cŵn Annwn* followed in formation. As the hunters of Holly disappeared into the clouds, Abby saw Olwen look back at her one last time. She thought, but she couldn't be sure, that the *Ci* was wagging her tail.

Abby slipped an arm around Leanne's waist as they walked back toward the Letterbox. She could hear distant sirens: the first of the emergency services mobilizing to deal with the blackout. The others were rising to their feet now, the colour slowly creeping back into their faces. Mother Hyld touched Chris's face, eliciting grimaces and gasps from him as she examined his wound. "Come with me, young one. I shall mend this for you."

The Anointed Gate chugged as Abby's friends passed through it in pairs, with herself and Leanne bringing up the rear. Before they stepped into the Letterbox, Abby whispered in her partner's ear, "Hey, what do you think about getting a dog?"

CHAPTER 29

WEE FOLK, GOOD FOLK,

TROOPING ALL TOGETHER

WHITTAKER STRAIGHTENED his tie and checked himself out in the full-length mirror. He nodded approvingly at what he saw: navy blue suit with grey pinstripes, double-breasted waistcoat, dark green tie and matching pocket square. "Yeah. Yeah, this is more like it!" He turned on his heels with a flourish and flashed a grin that Chris remembered from his childhood. "What do you think? Be honest now."

Chris smiled and said nothing for a moment, content to simply marvel at his father in his element. The Letterbox's wardrobe was only slightly less impressive than its library, with fabrics, colours, and cuts of cloth that spanned six continents and a thousand years in the history of human textiles production. After he closed the book on Ms. Keane, the imp had spent three days eating something like his own body weight every eight hours in order to recover what he'd lost in the coma. The next five days after that, it seemed, were to be spent bathing, shaving, preening, and dressing. On the fourth day, Simon had at long last released the imp from any further obligation to him, leaving him free to spread his wings in the wide world. When he found Whittaker still hanging around the Letterbox two days later, he had gently reminded him of this newfound lack of obligation and encouraged him to go get his nightclub back. Whittaker pleaded in his own defence that he was still convalescing, that to send him out on his own before he was fully healed could be dangerous to his health, and besides he didn't have any decent clothes to wear.

Chris didn't mind waiting around for his dad to finish milking this thing. There were a few things that Whittaker still couldn't do alone in his weakened state, and the help Chris was able to give him in those moments of vulnerability seemed to be drawing them closer together.

Whittaker quirked an eyebrow as if to say, *Spit it out, kid.* "So? Yea or nay?"

"Definitely yea," Chris said. "Except... I dunno, I kind of liked the brown shoes."

"What, the spectators?" Whittaker shook his head. "Nah, nah, nah, those are garden party shoes. 'Sides, brown toes and a black belt? No dice. You gotta match your leathers, Chrissy. Black belt, black shoes. Remember that."

"Guess I have a lot to learn, huh?"

Whittaker's jaw tightened. "Yeah, well... it's not like I've been the world's best teacher, have I?"

"There's time."

Whittaker nodded and fell silent. He looked at his shoes, inspecting their polish. "Why'd you come looking for me? I told you what kind of guy I am years ago. I told you, it's not pretty what happens to people who run in my circles. You've seen that firsthand now."

Chris touched his cheek where Ms. Keane had cut him. The sutures still itched. He was putting the ointment on exactly as Mother Hyld directed him, but he had a feeling there would be a scar.

He looked at his own shoes. Pink and blue laces seemed terribly inadequate for a conversation about when to wear two-tone brogues. "When I started transitioning," he said, "Mom was... well, she didn't exactly understand it, but she told me she was cool with it. Then I went on the hormones, and I bought a couple binders and a bunch of new clothes, and the bills started piling up. Suddenly she wasn't so cool. She said it was something I was going to grow out of, or that I was getting confused by all the stuff I was seeing on TikTok or whatever. We fought about it for a while. It got pretty hairy a couple times, and I wound up sleeping on some friends' couches."

Whittaker made a noise in the back of his throat.

Chris looked up. "Then, one morning when she'd gone to work early, I went outside to get the mail. And there was this bag with ten gold coins in it, jut sitting in our mailbox. And these were big coins, I'm talking like…" He mimed the size with his thumb and forefinger. "There was an envelope in the mailbox too. Green wax seal, oak leaf design. All the note said was, 'For the kid.'"

Whittaker swallowed, a suspiciously wet sound.

"I don't think people really tell you who they are when they tell you who they are," Chris said, looking directly at his father. "I think they tell you who they are in how they behave when no one's around. I got those coins appraised, Dad. I had to know if someone was fucking with me. Twenty-five *hundred* dollars. Each."

Before Whittaker could move, Chris crossed the floor and hugged him, no so tight that he would aggravate any old wounds. "I once heard you say that you can't bullshit a bullshitter. Same goes for a bullshitter's son. Abby, Simon, and the others, they still don't trust you. Maybe they never will. That's fine. But I know who you are when no one's around. And I love you."

Whittaker coughed. Cleared his throat. Pushed away and checked his hair in the mirror. "I've been a dad before, Chris. Granddad, too. And I've buried all of 'em. It cuts you open the first time. By the fifth, you just want to leave the party before they do." He turned around and took Chris's hand. There was a tear upon his cheek. "I don't want to bury anybody else, but if you stick near me, that's what's going to happen. I'm of the fae, kid, and you're only half. If you're lucky, you'll wring an extra century or two out of life, but that life is still going to end. Mine won't."

"I'm not asking for forever, Dad. I'm just asking for you to share the time I have."

Whittaker sighed and squeezed Chris's hand. "I'll think about it." He looked at his shoes again. Looked back at his son. His stomach growled. "Hey, you remember that Cantonese place we used to eat at, out in Richmond? That still around?"

*****

An unfamiliar receptionist greeted Abby and Leanne when they arrived at T.G.W. She told them to sit and make themselves comfortable in a tone that suggested she wasn't enthusiastic about them doing either, then called Jacquie's office to let the boss know they'd arrived. Abby distinctly heard her use the phrase "those two you warned me about." Given that her face was still bruised and bandaged in about a million places, Abby didn't blame the girl.

The atmosphere of the office was far more subdued than Abby remembered; she could hardly hear any chatter down the corridor, and when Jacquie came to collect them, she noticed a number of empty workstations. As Jacquie explained, a full day's work had been lost in the six hours it took BC Hydro to repair the city's electrical grid. Some of T.G.W.'s systems still weren't fully online, and a number of employees had spent the last week working remotely or enjoying the much-appreciated extra vacation days the boss was now passing around like candy.

A worker in a custodial uniform was pulling a brass nameplate off one office door toward the end of the hallway. Abby saw Gareth's name on it. "So your brother's out of the picture," she said, as they entered Jacquie's office. The elf shut the door behind her and gave a sad smile.

"Officially, Gareth is taking an extended leave of absence from The Green World Initiative. But he and I have talked. Given what we now know about Iris Keane, and Gareth's own personal history with faerie nationalism, we've agreed that it wouldn't be appropriate for him to resume his role here any time in the foreseeable future. So, he's going to take some time to himself. He's talking about trying a new therapy regimen. Auberon willing, it will finally exorcise those last few demons in his head."

"That might be for the best," Leanne admitted.

"I should have asked him to withdraw sooner. It's only been a few days, but already people are telling me stories about him I never heard before. His viewpoints were making some people far more uncomfortable than I realized, and I failed to rein it in. In some small way, I fed the culture that spawned people like Iris Keane. I'll regret that for a long time."

"It could have gone worse," Abby reminded her. "A lot worse."

"We're still not sure how much damage she did from the inside," said Jacquie. "Was she bluffing about a data backup? Do the Golden Hand have more agents in this city? How secure is our pipeline right now?" She shrugged. "The only way to be safe is to wipe the slate. Rebuild the network from square one."

Abby and Leanne exchanged a look. Then a smile. "If it's a low-down, dirty, rat bastard smuggler you're looking for," Abby said, "we might actually know a guy."

"Believe it or not, his name did cross my mind." Jacquie smiled. "In a desperate moment of weakness, I hasten to add."

"All we're saying is that Whittaker *did* talk his way out of trouble with the King-Among-the-Holly," Leanne observed.

"And he convinced some dipshit Gospel to sell her soul to him," Abby added. "The man knows his business."

"I'll think about it," Jacquie said. Then she slapped her hands on the desk and stood. "Oh, but look at me! An elf of the green places forgetting host-obligation!" She bustled over to the credenza and started busying herself at the coffee station. "It's tea for you both, isn't it?"

"Have you got a good rooibos there?" Leanne asked. "I think I've had enough of silversprig to last me a lifetime."

While the water was boiling, Jacquie asked, "How's Chris doing, by the way? I know I shouldn't bother him on his vacation, but..." She shrugged. "I worry."

Abby reported that Chris was doing well and looking forward to getting back to the office in another few days. "I think some time with his dad has been good for him, but he definitely believes his purpose is here."

Leanne shook her head. "I still can't believe that's a string of words that makes sense: 'Robin Whittaker, Father of the Year.'"

"I would have given that boy a month of vacation if I could have," Jacquie said wistfully. "It's the least he deserves. But he definitely understands the logistics of our operation better than I do."

Abby jerked a thumb toward the door. "I hear there's a c-suite office just opened up a few doors down."

"One thing at a time," Jacquie said. "But I agree, he is wasted behind that reception desk." The kettle gave a merry electronic chime as it finished boiling. Jacquie fetched the mugs, the teapot, and the infuser, then started spooning out loose rooibos from the tin. Teabags might have been good enough for the punters who waited at reception, but not the big boss. With a look back at Leanne, she asked, "So what's this I'm hearing about an apprenticeship in the arcane?"

Leanne shrugged bashfully. "It's not much. Might not ever be much. But... I want to do more. Mother Hyld's said she'll teach me a few things—spells and charms, things like that. Simon's going to pitch in once he's better. Actually, it's a lot of reading right now, mostly, but..." By way of practical demonstration, she reached into the pocket of her fuzzy sweater and extracted a small, tarnished silver ring—a beginner's magical focus. She extended her right index finger, slipped on the ring, and whispered, *"Eagan heofena."* A faint, thready white light enveloped the ring, crawling slowly up to the tip of Leanne's finger. For a moment it held steady. Then it winked out with a faint pop. Jacquie applauded politely. Leanne just shrugged again.

Abby gave Leanne a gentle punch on the shoulder. "My girlfriend the enchantress."

"It's not much," Leanne insisted.

"It never is, to start," said Jacquie. She pointed at one of the pictures on the office wall: her and Jack Kang at an archery range, backs to the camera, arrows nocked, ready to give some poor hay bale hell. "First time Jack took me to the range, I couldn't hit the target even accidentally. Last year I took home a silver medal. He—you should have seen his face." She choked on the last syllable and blinked away a sudden tear as the memory hit her.

Leanne slipped her ring back into her pocket and stood. "Why don't you sit down, Jacquie? I think I know my way around a tea station." Jacquie sniffed and choked out something about host-obligation, but Leanne nudged her back to her seat. "Host-schmost," she countered. "You've been through a lot. Besides, this is the stuff I'm good at."

Jacquie sat. Abby took her hand. Jacquie squeezed it as she cried herself out. Then she sat back and whispered, "I'm sorry. I'm sorry."

"Don't be," said Abby.

Jacquie sniffed and wiped her eyes. "He should be here. He should... know."

"Know?" Abby asked.

Jacquie looked at her lap. "Faerie and human biology are more similar than a lot of people think," she murmured.

"That's what the Golden Hand don't appreciate. But that's why we can…" She shrugged. "You know. With you."

"What are you saying?"

"I'm saying we eat. We sleep. Our females have… cycles. Twice a year, usually." She looked up. Smiled. Her eyes were wet again. "And I'm late on mine."

At the tea station, Leanne went dead still. Abby's eyes bugged out of their sockets.

"It's a… longer gestation for us," Jacquie said, almost to herself. "Sometimes it's six months before you know it's happening."

Abby grinned. "Holy shit, Jacquie… are you saying…?"

Jacquie picked up the photo of her and Jack that sat on the corner of her desk. The one that showed her flashing the ring he'd given her. "We were so happy that day," she said with a laugh. "And all through that night. And it looks like he left me something to remember him by." Her other hand went to her stomach. She was crying again, but she was smiling. Abby shrieked and punched the air.

"How long have you known?" she asked.

"Only a couple days," Jacquie said. "Like I say, in a faerie body, it can be months before the, uh, the seed becomes a sprout." She laughed at her own expression. "That's part of the reason I called you two down here. I wanted you to be the first ones to know."

Leanne looked over her shoulder. "You mean Gareth doesn't yet?"

"He will, in time. But after everything that you all have done for T.G.W., I thought you should be in on the ground floor."

"A last promise kept," Abby said. "Well, ho-lee shit."

Jacquie reached down her collar and drew out the diamond ring on the end of its chain. Smiled at it. Kissed it. Let it hang there, in full view. "Jack never would have stood for it, if he'd been here to see what the Golden Hand were doing. Maybe that's why they—" She broke off. Wiped another tear from her eye.

Leanne brought the mugs over. Abby raised hers in honour of Jack Kang. After they drank a toast, Leanne said, "This was 'part of the reason' you called us down here. What's the rest?"

Jacquie took another sip and nodded. "Well spotted. I hope you both realize what an incredible thing you and your friends have done. For me, for T.G.W., for this city. Especially you, Abby. There are more children than you could count who are going to wake up safe, happy, and fed the morning after *Nos Galan Gaeaf* because of how you interceded with the King."

"It was nothing," Abby answered. The break in her voice suggested it was the exact opposite.

Jacquie continued: "I will be eternally in your debt for all that you did, Abby Normal. And it will be the honour of my life to repay that debt in whatever way I can, even if I never clear it."

"Jacquie, you don't have t—"

"I do. You know our ways, Abby. Equal pay for equal favours. Not only do I owe you, but you will dishonour me if you refuse my payment." She opened the top drawer of her desk and extracted an envelope sealed with green wax. Slid it across, then sat back as Abby broke the seal and unfolded the cheque inside. Abby's eyes bugged out when she counted the zeroes. Leanne gave a low whistle.

"Consider this a first instalment," said Jacquie. "Out of my own pocket, of course. For time, labour, and expenses, plus hardship bonus." She gestured to Abby's battered face.

"This—this isn't a cheque!" Abby stammered. "This is a mortgage!"

"A *good* mortgage," Leanne agreed.

"I—I—" Abby's brain still wasn't giving her mouth the time of day. "I can't—"

Jacquie smiled. "If it helps, you could also think of it as a birthday gift." At Abby's confused look, Jacquie nodded to Leanne. "She mentioned it when you were lost in the Elsewhere."

Abby turned to Leanne and received a kiss on the cheek. "It's the twenty-seventh today. Happy Birthday, Abby Normal."

Abby sat back, the cheque falling into her lap. October twenty-seventh. Exactly one year since Varr'rak the Shadow-walker had come to collect her for the Deacon. Since she'd started to learn the truth about Simon, Natalie, and herself. Since her mother had done the right thing, after so many years of doing the wrong.

She glanced at the cheque again. She'd never thought there could *be* that many zeroes in one person's bank account. "Well, fuck. Happy Birthday to me, I guess."

EPILOGUE: *NOS GALAN GAEAF*

WHAT ABOUT this one?" Abby said, scrolling to the next photo. She passed her phone to Leanne, who screwed up her face and made a skeptical noise.

"Kind of big, don't you think?"

"Says here she's an older dog." Abby scrolled down to the blurb below the photo. "Crate-trained, calm, and quiet. So that means no barking, and she probably won't need too many long walks."

"Abby, we live in a one-bedroom. This thing's a horse! She probably wouldn't be able to turn around without bumping into something."

"We could always—"

"For the last time, we are *not* keeping a dog at the Letterbox. You know Simon and Natalie aren't ready for that kind of responsibility."

Abby sighed and took back her phone. Scrolled to the next profile on the adoption website. "Fine."

Leanne put a hand on her shoulder. "I know. If you had your druthers, you'd clear out every shelter in the city."

Abby shrugged. "You know me. Heart's too big for my own good."

Leanne's hand moved to her cheek. "That's why I love you."

They lurched in their seats as the bus pulled to a stop. A gaggle of freakshows and movie monsters poured through the open door, chatting excitedly to one another and shaking out their umbrellas on the floor. Abby smiled to herself. Despite the heavy rain and high winds, this was looking like a Halloween for the books. She'd lost track of the number of Draculas, catgirls, wizards, and witches who'd come through MacReady's today. Leanne said she'd been dealing with the same thing at the Shoppe since opening.

As the revellers moved to the back of the bus, one grinned at Abby and raised a hand in greeting. "Hey! Work Stuff!"

She jumped. Then she recognized the sweater, the battered fedora, the cardboard blades taped to one work glove. "Elm Street!" She grinned back. "You on your way over to Fright Nights?"

"Neither rain nor sleet," said Discount Freddy. He looked out the window. The rainwater was like a second skin over the glass. "Actually, might skip the Coaster tonight," he admitted.

"I wouldn't blame you," Abby said. "It's cats and dogs out there." *And black hounds and pale horses and who knows what else,* she didn't add. "We were probably going to hunker down inside and watch a movie."

Discount Freddy nodded. "Good plan. Oh, hey! You ever get those deadlines figured out?"

Abby's smile was easy, relaxed. Come to think of it, it was probably easier and more relaxed than at any time in the last year. "It's all sorted. And I think the High Heid Yins were pretty happy with the project."

"Hey, glad to hear it." People were still trying to get on behind him, and as he was jostled along to the back, he gave Abby a nod and said, "You take care of yourself, Work Stuff."

"You too. And hey, it's only a little rain, right?"

"Yeah. Guess it could've been worse."

The crowd pushed him out of sight. Off Leanne's confused look, Abby shrugged and said, "You meet some interesting people in our line of work."

As soon as they got off at their stop, Abby's phone buzzed in her pocket. Instead of answering, she opened her umbrella, then took Leanne's purse while she struggled with hers. The phone kept buzzing. When Leanne conquered her umbrella, Abby gave her back her purse, took her by the hand, and started walking, hoping the caller would take the hint. They didn't.

The pair turned a corner and ducked into the first convenient doorway to get some shelter from the rain. Abby shook out her umbrella and then answered the phone. "Hello, Gil."

"Miss Henderson." Dr. Harkness sounded unbothered by the delay. "I'm surprised you're outside in this weather."

Abby looked up the street, then down. She didn't imagine she'd spot the tail Harkness had put on them, so she wasn't surprised when she didn't. "Yeah, well, Gwyn's big entrance fried the electrics in Leanne's car. Plus half the cars from here to Squamish, from what I hear. Repairs are going to take a few days."

"I'm not surprised. I'm still receiving reports of rolling blackouts across the Lower Mainland. Next time one of your associates attempts to summon a king of Faerie, might I suggest you do it somewhere more remote?"

"Thanks for the tip."

"I thought you might be interested to know that the stalwart Agent Six has found the link between Jack Kang and Ted Purdy." Abby's phone buzzed as a text message came in with an attachment. She opened it and saw a picture of two teenage boys in rugby uniforms, taking a knee on the pitch and smiling for the camera. Both had white streaks running through otherwise dark hair.

"It seems Mr. Purdy spent his troubled youth in the foster system," Dr. Harkness explained. "For one glorious summer when he was fifteen, he was placed under the care of Yuchen and Erica Kang. They had already adopted one boy out of foster care some years earlier, so a second would have been no problem. Unfortunately, Ted Purdy's behavioural problems proved quite insurmountable, and he was back in a group home by his sixteenth birthday."

So, there was the blackmail link. Foster brothers passing like ships in the night, sharing a secret that could get them both killed. That did get them killed, eventually. But for a little while, at least, it was also a secret that made Ted Purdy a tidy profit.

There was steel and venom in Dr. Harkness's next few words: "Adopting changelings out into safe human families. I suppose there will always be Jacqueline Swanns in the world."

Abby gritted her teeth and hissed down the phone, "What do you know?"

"As much as I need to, for the purpose of this conversation. I won't be tedious and list all the federal laws that The Green World Initiative have broken with their off-books activities, but suffice it to say I have enough information in front of me to make a lot of people's lives very uncomfortable."

Acid burned the back of her throat. "Unless..."

Dr. Harkness chuckled. "You are a very astute woman, Abigail, despite the façade you maintain."

"I told you already, I'm not working for you, shithead."

"I don't propose putting you in an off-the-rack suit and dark glasses, Miss Henderson. Pardon my saying so, but I'm afraid you are not quite Department material. I merely want your perspective on certain extraplanar phenomena. Your advice. Your occasional intervention, when and if another incursion presents itself. It is your prerogative to refuse, of course, but you will be the one explaining that decision to Jacqueline Swann."

She exhaled—a long, whistling, angry breath through her nostrils. "You and Ted Purdy should have met. You guys have a lot in common."

"Do I take it we have an agreement, then?"

"As long as you keep quiet about the T.G.W. pipeline. If one word gets out, that's it. I will burn the Ministry of Uncommon Knowledge to the fucking ground. Write that off as an empty threat if you like, but trust me, I will find a way."

She could practically hear the smile creeping onto Harkness's face. "So long as you play by our rules, I never even heard of Jacqueline Swann. Agent Six will contact you in the coming days with further details. For now, I suggest you and Miss Waller get inside and keep warm. Something tells me this will be a Hunt to remember." He hung up without so much as a *Happy Halloween*. Abby ground her teeth together and jammed her phone into her pocket. Leanne gently rubbed her forearm.

"That bad?"

"I should get business cards made," Abby grumbled. "Abby Normal: Paranormal Investigator, Flunky for the God of Winter, and Stool Pigeon to the Ministry of Uncommon Knowledge."

"Come on," Leanne said. "I'll make us some hot chocolate when we get home, and we can watch TV until November."

Abby half-smiled. "That's the best offer I've had all month."

ABBY NORMAL

WILL RETURN IN

BLOOD MOON

A NOTE FROM THE AUTHOR

In the modern world of digital publishing, word-of-mouth and person-to-person buzz can make or break an indie title. If you enjoyed this work, please consider leaving a review on Amazon or recommending it to your friends in person or on social media. Thanks for reading!

ABOUT THE AUTHOR

Samuel Thomas Fraser is an actor and author originally from the rainy mountains of Vancouver, BC, Canada, currently pursuing his PhD in English Literature at Queen's University in Kingston, Ontario. His creative and scholarly work has appeared or is forthcoming in numerous outlets, including *Cosmic Horror Monthly* and *Studies in the Fantastic,* while the novels of *The Abby Normal Series* are available from Amazon in both paperback and ebook format. You can find Sam on Facebook and Twitter as @STFupperlip, or @samuelthomasfraser on Instagram. To learn more about Sam and his work, visit samuelthomasfraser.com.

www.ingramcontent.com/pod-product-compliance
Lightning Source LLC
LaVergne TN
LVHW041103080826
845145LV00007B/1677

* 9 7 8 1 7 7 7 1 1 9 0 4 1 *